AN INDUCEMENT INTO MATRIMONY

SUSAN ADRIANI   JAN ASHTON   PAIGE BADGETT

KAY BEA   GAILIE RUTH CARESS   AMY D'ORAZIO

NAN HARRISON   MICHELLE RAY   MARY SMYTHE

Quills & Quartos
PUBLISHING

Copyright © 2022 by the author's individual contribution.

This is a work of fiction. Names, characters, businesses, places, events, locales, and incidents are either the products of the author's imagination or used in a fictitious manner. Any resemblance to actual persons, living or dead, or actual events is purely coincidental.

No part of this book may be reproduced in any form or by any electronic or mechanical means, including information storage and retrieval systems, without written permission from the author, except for the use of brief quotations in a book review.

Ebooks are for the personal use of the purchaser. You may not share or distribute this ebook in any way, to any other person. To do so is infringing on the copyright of the author, which is against the law.

Edited by Jan Ashton, Justine Rivard and Kristi Rawley

Cover by Carpe Librum Book Design

ISBN 978-1-956613-43-8 (ebook) and 978-1-956613-44-5 (paperback)

TABLE OF CONTENTS

SIXTEEN DAYS AT PEMBERLEY   1
Susan Adriani

THE PLEASURE OF UNDERSTANDING HER   35
Mary Smythe

THE HEART'S CONSENT   79
Paige Badgett

NO CHARM EQUAL   119
Jan Ashton

UNITED BY HAPPENSTANCE   167
Gailie Ruth Caress

THE FIRST MOMENT OF THEIR ACQUAINTANCE   213
Amy D'Orazio

SPEAKING THE TRUTH   271
Nan Harrison

A DUET IN DISPUTE   313
Michelle Ray

WHAT MIGHT HAVE BEEN   359
Kay Bea

Get a Free Ebook!   401

Sixteen Days at Pemberley

Susan Adriani

CHAPTER ONE

Longbourn, July 1812

My Dearest Lizzy,

How I miss you! Whenever you are from home, 'pleasure bent' as Papa likes to say, Longbourn is never the same; nor do I feel the same without you by my side. Fortunately, my young cousins are ripe with good humour and keep me laughing despite your absence. They are, all four of them, such a joy and provide a wonderful distraction from the succession of busy nothings that have dictated our days here since your departure. While each moment spent with them brings me sincere pleasure and a sense of fulfilment, no one's society, my dear sister, compares to your own.

I hope with all my heart you are enjoying this time with my aunt and uncle touring Derbyshire and visiting with such friends as my aunt Gardiner has known since girlhood. I can well imagine you seeing all the local sights, contentedly walking through miles of woodland, and scaling large, imposing boulders while my poor aunt and uncle call to you, reminding you to take care. Yes, I can see it all very clearly indeed—the expressions of wonder and delight on your countenance as the wind twists your skirts about your ankles and whips your curls into a frenzy while you stand at the edge of the world admiring the untamed beauty of the peaks!

As you can imagine, Papa feels your absence acutely. Daily, he laments the fact there have been few words of sense and no peace at Longbourn since you left us. Poor Lydia, having been denied permission to go to Brighton for the summer with Colonel and Mrs Forster, continues to sulk and complain of the injustice of remaining at home. I am afraid she tries my father's patience exceedingly, as does my mother by adding her voice to Lydia's. Even now, as rumours of Mr Wickham's unpaid debts circulate through Meryton, Mama refuses to believe such a handsome, gentlemanlike man is truly so unscrupulous and wicked as the shopkeepers in Meryton claim. Even my aunt Philips cannot make her see reason, and so she persists in her endeavour to persuade my father to send Lydia to her friends in Sussex.

Papa, of course, will not have it and has declared no daughter of his shall ever be known as the most determined flirt who made herself and her family ridiculous. Mama, of course, is indignant on Lydia's behalf. She sees only Lydia's popularity with the officers and the amusement being denied her so long as she remains at home. Needless to say, my father is more determined than ever to keep our sister out of the reach of Colonel Forster's officers, and Mr Wickham particularly.

Oh! What do we not owe to Mr Darcy for enlightening us as to Mr Wickham's reprehensible character, and for writing to our father of his own painful dealings with him? I suspect that his kindness has already spared us all substantial mortification, and our dear father much regret!

Since writing the above, dearest Lizzy, something unexpected has occurred; but be not alarmed. We are all well. What I have to relate pertains to my father and this business with Lydia. Oh, Lizzy, he has had a change of heart, or, more likely, I believe his patience has been tried to such an extent by my mother and Lydia that he has relented and declared that we are all to travel to the seaside and remain there for nearly a month! We are to leave by the end of the week!

My young cousins are delighted, of course, as are my sisters and my mother, but none more so than Lydia, who is under the impression we are to go to Brighton! Papa, however, has confided he has no intention of going into Sussex; he has secured a house for us in Kent instead. In Kent, he believes Kitty and Lydia will be in far less danger of causing mischief, as they will have no friends there to encourage their improper behaviour or tempt them into much worse.

Mama is beside herself with anticipation, although whether her present gaiety shall persist once we arrive at the rugged cliffs of Kent instead of the excess and pomp of Brighton I cannot say. Kitty and Lydia are preparing for our journey with much high spiritedness; but poor Mary has lost much of her initial exuber-

ance, as Mama has told her, in no uncertain terms, that she is permitted to bring only one book. With ten of us, I cannot imagine Papa will sanction undertaking such a long journey in a single carriage. Surely, he will hire a second conveyance to accommodate us all more comfortably, otherwise I fear the children shall have no choice but to perch upon our laps and we will be very snug indeed!

My only regret, my dearest sister, is that you are already from home and therefore unable to join us on our seaside adventure. If you were by my side, my happiness would be complete.

I must say adieu for now, as my cousins have been wanting me this half an hour, but I promise to write again once we are all settled in Kent. Until then, I remain your affectionate sister,

Jane

"OH, JANE," ELIZABETH MURMURED, STARING AT HER letter with a feeling of dismay in her breast. It was not Jane's sincerity she doubted, but the soundness of the scheme itself. Her dear father hated travelling anywhere beyond Hertfordshire; Elizabeth could not imagine him setting out on a hundred-mile journey with her mother, sisters, and young cousins of his own volition, regardless of whether there was one carriage or two. It seemed far more likely Mr Bennet would see to the arrangements for the trip, then simply send his family off on their own, thus sparing himself the inconvenience of spending two days in a confined space on a hot, dusty road with five enthusiastic ladies, four energetic children, and the constant hum of conversation. Mr Bennet valued peace and quiet above all things; without his family underfoot, he would enjoy several weeks' worth of it in the comfort of his own home. When faced with such an appealing prospect, Elizabeth doubted he would leave his book-room except to sleep! The only interruption to his reading would be the ringing of the dinner bell.

Uttering a sigh of frustration, she wondered what had possessed her father to form such a resolution. Although sending her mother and sisters on a seaside holiday would undoubtedly make them happy, it would defeat the purpose of denying Lydia permission to accompany her friends to Brighton in the first place. Britain was at war with the French; it was as likely there were large encampments of soldiers erected along the coast of Kent as there were along the coast of

Sussex. Should Mr Bennet remain at home in Hertfordshire, he would have no power to rein in his wife's zealous matchmaking nor Lydia's and Kitty's enthusiasm for handsome young men in red coats. Jane and Mary would be the only voices of reason and economy, and they would likely go unheard. Elizabeth shuddered to think of the outcome of such single-minded neglect.

In no mood to read her letter a second time, she set it aside and reminded herself that nothing was certain of yet. Her father would either accompany his family on their excursion to the seaside or he would not. There was nothing Elizabeth could do about it from Derbyshire except hope that all would turn out well as she awaited further news in another letter from Jane.

Tugging her shawl more closely about her shoulders, she abandoned her comfortable chair at the table and crossed the parlour to peer out of the window. Long fingers of sunlight greeted her, warming her through the glass. The day promised to be a fine one, with a deep blue sky overhead and barely a cloud in sight. Although the hour was early, it was not so early that Lambton was empty or still. Beyond the thick, whitewashed walls of the Red Lion, the village was alive with activity. Shopkeepers and solicitors and servants bustled along the high street, having already begun their day.

She watched the goings-on below for some time before spying her aunt and uncle Gardiner walking arm in arm at the top of the street, slowly making their way towards the inn. An hour earlier they had set out alone to visit the church while Elizabeth read her letter; now, they were accompanied by a gentleman whose figure Elizabeth knew well: Mr Darcy.

Elizabeth caught her bottom lip between her teeth as she watched him—his tall frame; his confident, unhurried gait; his regal bearing. He was presently speaking to her aunt. Nearly a full minute passed before he finished saying his piece, at which time a brilliant smile appeared on Mrs Gardiner's countenance as her lips formed words Elizabeth wished she could hear. With an inclination of his head, Mr Darcy returned her aunt's smile before he turned his attention to her uncle, who looked as well pleased as his wife.

In that moment, Elizabeth's own countenance flushed with unexpected warmth. For so long she had thought of him as the most arrogant, insufferable man of her acquaintance; more recently, she had begun to see him in a very different light. After meeting him unexpectedly as she toured his beautiful park with her relations, she was forced to admit the Mr Darcy she had known in Hertfordshire—so haughty and disagreeable and proud—had undergone a material change.

In Derbyshire, he was no longer arrogant but exacting.

He was no longer recalcitrant but reserved.

He was no longer exceedingly proud or unpleasant or severe, but perfectly amiable in every respect.

He was handsome as well.

Elizabeth had forgotten precisely *how* handsome and felt a sense of disquiet descend upon her, for Mr Darcy was even handsomer when he smiled. He had rarely smiled while they were in company together in Hertfordshire, and never in the presence of her family. Although he was slightly more animated in Kent among his own relations, Mr Darcy's aloofness had been as firmly fixed at Rosings Park as it was elsewhere.

Also firmly fixed were the long, penetrating looks that served to confound her and discompose her and annoy her no matter where she was or what she happened to be doing. Elizabeth had felt Mr Darcy's eyes upon her constantly. But for what purpose? Her beauty he had earlier withstood; surely, a man such as he, who appeared to consider himself above his company wherever he went, must only ever look at her to find fault.

How wrong she had been!

Although Mr Darcy *had* found much to criticise where her family was concerned, it did not follow that his censure of them extended to her, as was evident when he called upon her late one afternoon in Kent while her friends were dining at Rosings and Elizabeth was alone, nursing a headache. He enquired after her health, paced the length of the room, and then shocked her by announcing with more emotion than she had ever believed him capable that he ardently admired and loved her.

Instead of a litany of heartfelt sentiments that would have served him well as a professed lover, what followed was a recitation of every conceivable reason why Mr Darcy should, in actuality, feel nothing for

Elizabeth at all—certainly nothing that would inspire a man of his position and notoriety to ignore the expectations and wishes of his family and friends. And then, after begging her to relieve his suffering, he proposed.

Only after many months' reflection did Elizabeth conclude that Mr Darcy, who had long professed disguise of every sort to be his abhorrence, had likely viewed such a blunt, uncensored declaration as a perverse nod to her intelligence and discernment rather than as the insult it was in truth. In the end, however, it mattered not. The moment he had mentioned the inferiority of her connexions and her family's impropriety, Elizabeth had heard nothing, and therefore discerned nothing beyond the offensiveness of his words and his total disregard for her feelings by having uttered them.

Her refusal, and the language with which she had abused him the moment he had done, she would much rather forget—especially the part that pertained to the debauched Mr Wickham and the living he claimed Mr Darcy had denied him. Mortified and furious, Mr Darcy quit the house. Elizabeth, unable to support herself, sank onto a chair and wept. Other than one brief moment the next morning, when he handed her a letter—one she had read often—their paths had not crossed again until three days prior at Pemberley.

Elizabeth shook her head. The civility Mr Darcy had shown her as they had made their way along the picturesque, wooded paths of his ancestral home was as generous as it was surprising. Instead of treating her with contempt after the unjust accusations she had levelled at him in April, Mr Darcy had shown her nothing but kindness and respect, even going so far as to request her permission to introduce his sister to her during her stay in Lambton. As though he feared Elizabeth would change her mind or suddenly leave Derbyshire without a proper farewell, he had brought Miss Darcy to wait on her the very next morning.

The following day, Elizabeth and Mrs Gardiner returned the visit by calling upon Miss Darcy at Pemberley, where they talked of their recent travels, shared thoughts on music, and ate nectarines and peaches in a beautifully appointed parlour with a view of the lake.

Tonight, they would return as Miss Darcy's dinner guests along with Mr Bingley and his sisters, whom Elizabeth understood had visited Pemberley every summer for years.

Running her finger along the edge of the windowpane, Elizabeth endeavoured to ignore the quickening of her pulse as she watched Mr Darcy approach the inn and gesture for her aunt and uncle to precede him through the front entrance. Although she no longer disliked him as she had in Kent, neither was she ready to admit the opposite: that she had come to like him very well within the span of three impossibly short days. His metamorphosis from proud and unpleasant to amicable was unexpected, to say the least—as unexpected as his civility to her, his hospitality, and his smile. Constantly, did she ask herself, what had inspired such a transformation? Was it for her sake he was so altered? Surely, his improved manners were not the result of his having taken her reproofs to heart!

All too soon, she heard voices in the corridor—her uncle's jovial tenor and Mr Darcy's rich baritone. In the next instant, the door to the parlour was thrown open and Mr and Mrs Gardiner entered the room.

"Lizzy," said her uncle with a bright smile and a twinkle in his eye, "you will never guess with whom we had the pleasure of meeting this morning."

Her aunt looked pointedly at Elizabeth as Mr Darcy appeared behind her, removing his hat and ducking his head so as not to hit it on the heavy, oak beam above the door. His eyes found Elizabeth in an instant and settled there—on her face and her eyes and her mouth. The tips of his ears turned red, and a vivid slap of colour appeared high on his cheeks, but his steady, piercing gaze did not falter.

Elizabeth felt a heated blush bloom upon her own cheeks and endeavoured to appear composed, as composed as possible while he regarded her so intently, blushing like a schoolboy. Her curtsey was merely perfunctory, but her smile was welcoming and heartfelt. "Mr Darcy. This is indeed a pleasant surprise. I hope this morning finds you well?"

The corners of Mr Darcy's mouth lifted as he bowed. "I am very well, Miss Bennet. I confess I was surprised you did not accompany your aunt and uncle on their walk through the village. I know how fond you are of exercise, especially when the weather is fine. I hope you were not indisposed."

"Not at all, sir. I elected to remain behind to read a letter from my sister Jane. As I have not heard from her for some time, I was impatient for any bit of news I could glean from Longbourn."

"Of course," he replied. "I trust that your sister is in good health, and all of your sisters and your parents as well?"

"They are all in excellent health, sir." She glanced at her aunt and uncle and, with an arch look, informed them, "Jane writes that my father has decided to take everyone to the seaside."

"Has he!" cried Mrs Gardiner. "How wonderful, for the children especially. When are they set to leave, Lizzy? I ought to write to your mother directly."

"According to Jane, they were likely to have departed Longbourn yesterday."

"And where are they off to?" Mr Gardiner enquired, smoothing his hands along the lapels of his coat. "I understand Lydia was eager to go to Brighton with her friends, Colonel Forster and his wife, but your father decided against the scheme. Perhaps they are to join them after all?"

Elizabeth glanced at Mr Darcy, whose expression had become inscrutable as he watched her. "When last I spoke to my father, he was adamant that Brighton—and certain society there—was best avoided. His opinion has not altered. They are for Kent instead and shall reside there for several weeks. Where in Kent remains a mystery at present, as not even Jane is privy to that information as yet."

The Gardiners expressed their approval of Kent but shook their heads at what they perceived as a poor attempt by Mr Bennet to have a bit of fun at Lydia's expense. "How like your father to keep their destination a secret," said her aunt with more than a hint of disapprobation in her tone, "though I am very glad he saw fit to confide in Jane. Should their carriage become upset and fall into a ravine, we would have had no notion of their general direction."

"Now, now," said Mr Gardiner, patting his wife's hand with a reassuring smile. "Such morbidity, my dear, will never do. All will be well. Kent is a lovely county. I am sure everyone shall arrive in one piece to enjoy it."

"Kent," said Mr Darcy, looking fixedly at Elizabeth, "*is* very beautiful, as I am certain you recall from your stay with your friends in Hunsford. The southernmost coast is seventy miles or so to the south of it, and is home to many seaside resorts, most of which offer an impressive variety of attractions and comforts. I have no doubt your family will enjoy themselves, regardless of where they stay." His voice was warm, as warm as the look in his eyes. "I have been to Brighton as well, but found its amusements were not to my liking. I much prefer the subtle beauty of Kent to the ostentation of Brighton."

Elizabeth could tell at once Mr Darcy was not only pleased by what she had related of her family's destination, but relieved. He had taken the trouble of writing to her father, warning him of Mr Wickham's dissolution and depravity, and his warning had not gone unheeded. "I am certain you are right," she told him, endeavouring to keep her tone light as she returned his steadfast gaze. "I well recall the loveliness of Lady Catherine's park. If the rest of the county is as pleasant, my family may never wish to leave!"

Before anything more could be said of the seaside or Kent or Elizabeth's family, a serving girl arrived with their breakfast and her uncle extended an invitation to Mr Darcy to join them.

Mr Darcy glanced from Mr Gardiner to Elizabeth, then back to her uncle with something akin to regret. "I thank you for your hospitality, but I am afraid I must decline. I have business this morning with my steward and am expected back at Pemberley by half ten."

"I understand, sir. We will dine with you tonight in any case."

"Of course. I look forward to your coming, as does my sister. She was pleased beyond measure to have received Mrs Gardiner and Miss Bennet at Pemberley yesterday." He paused to clear his throat. "I sincerely hope you will give my proposal serious consideration. I cannot think of anything my sister, or I, would enjoy more."

"You are generous, sir," said Mr Gardiner.

A rueful smile appeared on Mr Darcy's countenance. "I am selfish. I desire to see those I love happy. Your society is most welcome at Pemberley." He bowed. "Good day, Mr Gardiner. Mrs Gardiner." He turned to Elizabeth and his voice took on a decidedly tender tone. "Good day, Miss Bennet."

Before Elizabeth could bid him a good day in turn—or utter a single word of sense for that matter—Mr Darcy bowed to her, turned on his heel, and quit the room.

"You are joking, of course," said Elizabeth to her uncle an hour later as they sat around the breakfast table, now nearly emptied of cold ham, seasonal fruit, and cakes. She reached for her water glass, diversion dancing in her eyes, and raised it to her lips.

Mr Gardiner chuckled as he speared a grape with his fork. "Indeed, I am in earnest. We are invited to stay at Pemberley as Mr and Miss Darcy's guests for however long we like."

Elizabeth stared at him, unable to credit what she had heard.

"Come now, Lizzy," said her aunt, giving Elizabeth a significant look. "Do not be missish. Mr Darcy extending such a generous invitation to us is clearly a compliment to you."

Elizabeth made no answer, and Mrs Gardiner sighed.

Mr Gardiner, likely sensing the ladies required privacy, set his napkin upon the table and rose from his chair. "I believe," he said to his wife, "I shall walk to the green and return in half an hour."

The door had barely shut behind him when Mrs Gardiner said, "Mr Darcy admires you, Elizabeth. A blind man could see his admiration. The question remains, do you return it?"

'*You must allow me to tell you how ardently I admire and love you…*'

Elizabeth averted her eyes to the window, where she could see the spire of the church in the distance. Not every word Mr Darcy had uttered to her at the parsonage that fateful afternoon had been ugly. "I cannot deny that I esteem him. Indeed, I *like* him. But you know it has not always been so. We have spent so much time over the course of our acquaintance misunderstanding one another and causing each other pain." She shook her head. "I was awful to him in Hertfordshire, and even worse in Kent. He would be well within his right never to speak to me let alone invite me into his home."

"And yet, Mr Darcy seems determined to do the opposite."

"Yes," Elizabeth allowed, forcing herself to meet her aunt's steady, encouraging gaze. "He has been beyond generous since we met at Pemberley the other day. Beyond civil in every respect."

Mrs Gardiner smiled gently. "It would be a brilliant match for you. A love match, if you could see your way to open your heart to him." She reached for Elizabeth's hand and gave it an affectionate squeeze. "I will not push you. I am not your mother. But I cannot in good conscience turn a blind eye to Mr Darcy's interest in you, not when he has singled you out the way he has—calling on you in Lambton not once but twice, and inviting us to stay at Pemberley as his guests. It would be ill-advised. The question remains: Would you like to be a guest at Pemberley while we are here?"

Elizabeth bit her lip. The idea of being in Mr Darcy's house—of *living* in Mr Darcy's house—unsettled her in ways she was ill-prepared to consider at the moment. Rather than give a reasonable answer, she resorted to humour. "The house is tolerable I suppose, and Mr Bingley appears to be as congenial as ever, but I am afraid the society of Miss Bingley and the Hursts leaves much to be desired."

"Lizzy," her aunt chided. "Do be serious."

"Very well," Elizabeth told her as a shadow of a smile appeared on her countenance. "If you insist upon my being serious, I shall tell you that I like Miss Darcy very much. She is a delightful young woman, if not a bit shy. I confess I should like to know her better."

"And what of Pemberley's master?"

Elizabeth laughed, but her levity soon took a more thoughtful turn. "I hardly know. Of late, Mr Darcy's behaviour has been beyond reproach. I can find nothing to criticise. But we have been in company together only three times in as many days." She toyed with a ribbon on the sleeve of her gown. "I suppose, if he continues as he is and does not revert back to the Mr Darcy of old, that knowing him better will give way to my liking him better. How much I shall like him remains to be seen."

Having had enough seriousness for one morning, she assumed an arch look. "In any case, I know that *you* should like to stay at Pemberley, Aunt. Since you and my uncle have been so kind as to bring me all the way to Derbyshire to see the peaks, the least I can do is ensure your comfort is of the finest quality while we are here. Yes. I will go to Pemberley."

"Oh, Lizzy! You will not be disappointed, mark my words. The woods are some of the most beautiful in the country."

Elizabeth grinned. "Will Mr Darcy show them to us himself, do you think, or will he arrange for one of the gamekeepers to give us a tour?"

Her aunt only laughed at her impertinent tone. "I have no doubt that Mr Darcy will be eager to show *you* all of Pemberley personally. The gamekeepers will be well occupied with their duties."

CHAPTER TWO

Four Days at Pemberley…

DARCY SMILED WARMLY AT ELIZABETH'S AUNT, WHO WAS seated beside him on a couch in the music room listening to Mrs Hurst perform a complicated piece by Haydn on Georgiana's Broadwood grand. Mrs Gardiner's elegant manners and intelligent conversation went a long way towards soothing the agitation he felt in the face of Miss Bingley's rudeness at his dinner table. He had known Miss Bingley for many years and had long considered her a friend, despite her penchant for sometimes treating those she considered beneath her with disdain. Bingley had once confided it was insecurity that made her do it; Darcy tended to believe it was jealousy. Whatever it was, her behaviour that evening was beyond the pale, and it was Elizabeth who had suffered the brunt of it.

Mrs Hurst's performance soon came to an end, and a smattering of polite applause filled the room. Across from him, Mr Hurst lay sprawled like a well-fed cat across a settee upholstered in pale yellow silk. Darcy pursed his lips disapprovingly. Bingley's relations had begun to grate on his nerves. He had invited the Gardiners to Pemberley because he genuinely enjoyed their society; the Hursts came part and parcel with Bingley, as did Miss Bingley and her platitudes and her pettiness and her lofty aspirations to never leave. Discouraging her interest in him had failed. Ignoring her had served him ill. Inviting Elizabeth into his home had made her jealousy flare from a spark to a conflagration.

Darcy felt a little thrill each time he thought of Elizabeth Bennet residing at Pemberley. She had been there for half a week. Presently, she was sitting beside his sister a short distance away, smiling and speaking quietly to her about music.

Suddenly, Georgiana's gaze, which had been trained on her lap, shifted to Elizabeth. "Oh no," she said, seemingly horrified. "I could not possibly…not in front of all of these people."

Elizabeth reached for her hand. "I absolutely insist," she said, giving Georgiana an encouraging smile. "Miss Bingley has sung your praises for so long I do not know how I can possibly continue spending another day in this house without hearing you myself. Come, else I shall enlist your brother to add his entreaties to mine. As you have already admitted you can deny him nothing, it seems a hopeless business. You had much better play."

Darcy had not expected his sister to give way, but after Elizabeth made another round of petitions, Georgiana emitted an incredulous little laugh and allowed herself to be tugged to her feet and led to the pianoforte. Once there, they examined sheet music together and Elizabeth did her best to make her new friend smile. Her efforts yielded success. After several minutes Georgiana appeared at ease.

Eventually, Elizabeth presented her with a piece of music that met with her approval, and Georgiana, after a slight hesitation, straightened her shoulders, seated herself at the instrument, and began to play Mozart's *Piano Sonata No. 9*.

Through the entire composition, Elizabeth remained by Georgiana's side, turning her pages and making her smile, diverting her attention from her rapt audience.

Darcy felt his heart swell with affection. He was proud of his sister, but his eyes were drawn to Elizabeth again and again. He had loved her for so long, but never so much as he did in that moment. Her inherent sweetness and her natural ability to put others at ease had been instrumental in coaxing Georgiana out of her shell, enough so to allow his shy sister to set aside her inhibitions and ignore her insecurities to play for their friends. Until tonight, Georgiana had declined doing so and professed a desire to hear her guests play instead, particularly Miss Bingley, who was ever eager to oblige.

"How ill-mannered Eliza Bennet is this evening."

Darcy was startled to hear Miss Bingley's voice, just behind him and to his left. He glanced at Mrs Gardiner, who was presently in conversation with Bingley on Darcy's right. Fortunately, she appeared not to have overheard the insult Miss Bingley had made about her niece.

Having elicited no reply, Miss Bingley continued in the same vein. "Why, she practically forced poor Miss Darcy to play! It was quite shocking to watch."

Darcy clenched his jaw in annoyance.

Behind him, he heard Mrs Hurst sigh. "Miss Darcy," she replied pleasantly, "plays so beautifully, especially for one so young. It is a shame her shyness hinders her playing for her friends."

"Oh, I quite agree," Miss Bingley allowed, "but that is hardly my point, Louisa. My point—"

"I know very well what your point is, Caroline," said Mrs Hurst, "and it is ill-advised to carry it. No one here wishes to hear your opinions. This…situation is beyond your reach. You must accept it."

Miss Bingley made an inarticulate sound, but before she could utter another word on the subject, Mrs Hurst said quietly but firmly, "Enough. Your chatter is distracting from my enjoyment of Miss Darcy's exquisite playing. You know how I adore Mozart."

Miss Bingley said nothing in response. Instead, Darcy watched as she marched across the room and out the door.

He was relieved to see her go and gratified to discover a possible ally in Mrs Hurst. Lord knows Bingley did nothing to silence his sister's tongue or discourage her interest. For the past four days the man had ignored her completely as he waxed poetic with Elizabeth about the handful of weeks that he had spent in Hertfordshire last autumn. He was full of recollections and recounted them all, especially those that pertained to Elizabeth and her sisters. His doing so only served to incite Miss Bingley's ire.

Darcy shifted his position on the couch as he directed his attention to Elizabeth. The fact that he had not had an opportunity to speak to her for any length of time since her arrival made him feel impatient and peevish. She was either spending time with Georgiana, indulging Bingley, or accompanying her aunt on calls to their friends in Lambton. He shifted again, wishing it was not so late so that he might invite her to take a turn in the garden or on the terrace just outside the music room.

He had not expected her to look at him then, but look at him she did as she lifted her eyes from the page that she had just turned for his sister. Even from such a distance, her eyes captivated him. Darcy thought of all the things he wanted to say to her, and one particular question he ached to ask.

He knew Elizabeth no longer disliked him as she once had, but to what extent her opinion of him had improved he had yet to ascertain. He supposed it had likely improved significantly; she was presently in his house and had agreed to be his guest until her aunt and uncle decided to return to London.

Darcy wanted so badly to go to her.

Would she welcome him if he did?

The Chippendale clock in the hall chimed eleven times, signalling the conclusion of their evening was fast approaching. The music ended, and a fresh smattering of applause filled the room. Georgiana smiled as she rose from her place at the Broadwood and clasped Elizabeth's hand.

Elizabeth praised her performance with a sincerity that warmed Darcy's heart and made Georgiana blush. Then she took a moment to admire the instrument, gently pressing the keys of the higher octaves with the hint of a smile playing upon her lips. "It is a wonderful instrument," she said. "You are fortunate to have such a generous elder brother. The pianoforte at Longbourn is sadly lacking compared to this one. I believe, Miss Darcy, that you and your brother have spoilt me!"

Georgiana reassured her she could play it any time she liked, then asked Elizabeth if she would consent to play. "One last song before we all retire. I know my brother would especially enjoy hearing you."

For the second time that night, Elizabeth met Darcy's eyes from across the room. The corners of her lips lifted and she smiled.

Darcy felt a flush of warmth, knowing her smile was meant for him and no one else. He returned it and watched her take a seat on the bench. Beside him, Mrs Gardiner was telling Bingley about Miss Jane Bennet's enjoyment of the seaside. Bingley appeared enthralled. Though he doubted either would notice his absence, Darcy excused himself in any case and crossed the room.

"Pray allow me the honour of begging a seat beside you, Miss Bennet, so that I may be of assistance to you."

Elizabeth smiled at him, and Darcy's heart skipped a beat. "You are welcome to sit beside me, Mr Darcy," she said blithely, "but as to your being of assistance, I cannot say." She turned towards Georgiana and addressed her. "Tell me, Miss Darcy, is your brother a proficient reader of music? Miss Bingley failed to mention page turning when she recited her very long list of Mr Darcy's accomplishments in Hertfordshire."

"My brother," said Georgiana with mock seriousness, "is an excellent page turner, so long as you inform him as to when he must turn each page."

"Oh dear," said Elizabeth, her eyes dancing with mirth. "That is hardly an endorsement, sir! You are likely to hinder far more than you will help. But I suppose we shall make do." She took a moment to rifle through some discarded sheets of music and soon made her selection. It was neither a sonata nor a concerto, but a lullaby. Glancing at Darcy, Elizabeth placed her fingers on the keys and began to play.

Darcy claimed his place beside her, but he spent far more time admiring her than he did looking at the sheet music. It did not matter. Elizabeth did not spare it so much as a single glance.

She knew the piece by heart.

Surely, she must know *his* heart...

CHAPTER THREE

Nine Days at Pemberley...

DARCY RUBBED HIS FOREHEAD WITH HIS HAND; HE SAT AT the desk in his study staring at a stack of correspondence that he knew he should answer but would much rather avoid. Resting his head on the back of his tufted leather chair, he gazed at his beautiful park through the massive bay window that encompassed most of one south-facing wall. Somewhere, beyond the lake and the fountain and the formal gardens and the maze, was Elizabeth. She had been at Pemberley for nine wonderful days, reading his books and walking his grounds and becoming fast friends with his sister. They had become such good friends that they now referred to each other by their Christian names.

The weather out of doors was very fine. The sky was a rich, cerulean hue that reminded him of the bluebirds that nested in the meadows every summer. Large cumulous clouds cast shadows over the land as they passed overhead like ships on the sea.

Darcy glanced at his correspondence and sighed. He did not want to remain indoors; he wanted to seek Elizabeth out, wherever she was, and spend the afternoon with her. He wanted to hear her play

Beethoven and watch her pick cornflowers and listen to her speak of everything under the sun.

Most of all, he wanted to know what she was thinking in her beautiful, impertinent mind.

Was she thinking of him?

There was nothing for it. He would not waste such a perfect day sitting inside wishing he was with Elizabeth and wasting precious time. His correspondence could wait.

Darcy quit the room, determined to seek her out and ask her to walk with him. The park, the ornamental garden, the meadow… Where they walked did not signify so long as she was amenable to spending time with him. She had yet to see the woods; Darcy had been surprised to hear it. Knowing how fond she was of walking the wooded paths of Hertfordshire, he had expected her to leap at the chance to explore Pemberley's.

She had not, and Darcy could not help but wonder why.

An hour later—after wandering aimlessly through the first floor of the house and narrowly avoiding Miss Bingley and the Hursts, inspecting the gardens, and walking the paved path that led to the woods—an under gardener directed him to the orchard.

That was where he found her—among long rows of cherry trees and apple trees and peach trees, sitting on a tartan rug spread upon the grass. Elizabeth was in the centre of it and his sister was beside her, a crayon in her hand and a smile on her face as Elizabeth tilted her face to the sky. Their bonnets were discarded upon the ground and their spencers as well, and what looked to be a letter. It was a lovely scene of domesticity —the kind of domesticity Darcy desperately hoped was within his grasp.

A gentle breeze ruffled the leaves on the trees, and Elizabeth shut her eyes.

She was beautiful.

She was guileless.

She was intelligent—far too intelligent not to know that he loved her.

Though he was reluctant to intrude upon their time together, he was not so reluctant that he was willing to forfeit such an opportunity to be a part of it. "I am very glad to see you have not been set upon by gypsies," he said, stepping forward until he stood before them. "Pemberley's woods are full of them."

Georgiana exchanged an amused look with Elizabeth.

"Gypsies," proclaimed Elizabeth, shielding her eyes from the sun with her hand as she looked up at him from her comfortable seat on the ground. "I was under the impression there were tigers in your woods, Mr Darcy. I confess it is a relief to hear that I may only be set upon and not eaten."

Darcy grinned. "I would not discount being eaten so readily, Miss Bennet. There are badgers, as well."

Elizabeth laughed. "I shall keep that in mind, sir."

Darcy offered her a belated bow. "Forgive me for intruding," he said as he returned her smile.

She shook her head. "You are hardly an intruder, Mr Darcy. This is, after all, your orchard."

Georgiana examined her crayons. "Do you intend to join us, Brother?"

"Only if you and Miss Bennet will consent to have me."

"What do you think, Lizzy?" Georgiana asked. "Perhaps we ought to turn him away…"

A familiar, teasing smile appeared on Elizabeth's lips. Her eyes sparkled with mirth. In the sunlight her eyes looked lighter, with tiny flecks of green and amber towards the centre. "I think we ought to take pity on him. Your poor brother has likely spent his entire morning answering letters of business and meeting with his steward. It must have been very tiresome."

"Very," said Darcy drily. He indicated the tartan rug with his hand. "May I?"

Elizabeth inclined her head, but her smile remained. "You may."

He took a seat beside her, as close as he dared, and nearly sat upon the discarded letter. He picked it up and saw Elizabeth's name written across the front in a neat, elegant hand. Beneath her name, the direction read: Pemberley, Bakewell, Derbyshire. Darcy ignored the little thrill he felt upon seeing it. "I believe this is yours," he said, handing it to her.

"Oh! Yes, it is a letter I received just this morning from Jane."

"I hope your sister is enjoying her visit to Kent. Did she happen to mention where your family is staying?"

Elizabeth glanced at Georgiana, who was presently absorbed in creating a masterpiece with her crayons. "They are near Margate. Jane says it is lovely and my mother is delighted with the town. My young cousins have gone sea bathing every day. I am happy to report that everyone is well pleased except for my youngest sisters, who were disappointed to find they were not, as they expected, going to Brighton."

"I can well imagine," Darcy remarked. "And your father? Was he able to join them?"

"He was. He has." She shook her head with a self-effacing smile. "Forgive me. I am so used to him being always at Longbourn. That he has developed a sudden interest in undertaking such a journey with my mother and sisters is owing to you, sir. Had you not written to him, I am convinced my father would have stayed at home and allowed Lydia to go to Brighton with her friends. Mrs Forster, who is barely three years older, would have made a poor chaperon. I shudder to think of the outcome of such an arrangement. I am more grateful to you than I can say."

Darcy bowed his head, profoundly uncomfortable with her gratitude. He had done what was right to be done. "You need say nothing, Miss Bennet. I should have spoken to your father long ago, when Mr... when I was first in Hertfordshire. I did not."

"It does not matter," she said softly, almost tenderly. "All is well."

Their eyes met, and the corners of Darcy's mouth lifted infinitesimally.

Yes, he thought. *Perhaps it will be.*

CHAPTER FOUR

Fourteen days at Pemberley...

THE BED ELIZABETH HAD BEEN GIVEN, AND THE ROOM IN which it sat, was a slice of heaven. The mattress was stuffed with soft feathers, the counterpane was a luxurious down, and the pale blue and silver paper on the walls made her feel as though she was in a scene from a fairy tale.

Fairy tales, however, rarely ended happily. They were morality tales, meant to teach lessons and deter disobedience. Truthfully, she had never liked them. Even as a young girl, she was not formed for melancholy; when misfortune struck, she put a smile on her face and endeavoured to find a silver lining. Why dwell on present miseries when happier circumstances would eventually present themselves and all would be well?

Exhaling a weary breath, Elizabeth smoothed her skirts and walked to the window. Rain lashed against the panes and a low rumble of thunder rose in the distance. The sound it made resembled a loaded wagon rumbling along a cobbled street. Despite the poor weather, her aunt and uncle had gone to Lambton to say their farewells to their friends. Georgiana was learning a new piece of music that arrived from

London that morning, and the Bingleys and the Hursts had left five days earlier.

Reminiscing about Hertfordshire and his acquaintances there had a profound effect upon Mr Bingley. One morning, when a footman had brought Elizabeth two letters from Jane on a gleaming silver salver, Mr Bingley had been suddenly seized by a powerful compulsion to return to Netherfield. He declared his resolution at breakfast and by midday his valet had packed his trunks, his driver had readied his carriage, and he was off. Apparently, it was precisely as Mr Darcy had once remarked in Hertfordshire: when Mr Bingley made up his mind, he acted upon it at once.

Miss Bingley had been beside herself with indignation, but she was allowed no say in the matter. Her brother was determined. She was given the choice to accompany him to Hertfordshire or to go with the Hursts to their aunt's home in Yorkshire. As she had received no invitation to extend her stay at Pemberley, to Yorkshire Miss Bingley went.

Elizabeth was glad to see her go. Her superior looks and snide little asides had tried Elizabeth's patience to its limits. The false flattery and repetitious platitudes she showered upon Darcy at every turn made Elizabeth feel irritable and ill. It never ceased to amaze her how, in the matter of weeks, her feelings for him had changed so completely as to render them the very opposite of what they once were. Gone was her abhorrence and dislike of him. Gone was her uncertainty. If anyone had told her in April that she would come to love Darcy in July, she would have laughed!

But nothing could be truer.

She *loved* him!

He had gone from being the last man in the world she would ever marry to being the only man she could imagine marrying. He was warm and generous and funny and sweet.

And thoughtful. When Elizabeth wanted to read, he had shown her his library. When she wanted companionship, he sat beside her. When she wanted conversation, he readily discussed any topic she introduced. He offered her sweets from his kitchens, long walks in his park, and flowers from a meadow whose bounty was painted in every imaginable colour of the rainbow. One day he had brought her a litter of kittens from the barn just to make her smile.

And they talked. Never alone, of course; her aunt and uncle had been ever conscious of propriety. Georgiana was their constant companion, but she was also quiet and easily absorbed in her music and her art. While she ignored them, Darcy had spoken to Elizabeth of countless things; yet he had not once spoken to her of his feelings.

She was certain he loved her. She could see it every time he looked at her, in his every gesture and expression. She could hear it in his voice. Why did he not declare himself? Surely, he could not mistake her feelings for him *now*, after two weeks of living in the same house together. Not only had Elizabeth taken every opportunity to speak to him, but she teased him. She walked with him. She smiled at him. She *welcomed* him.

Of course, she had done those things before, but in a very different context. In Hertfordshire, her conversation was meant to provoke him. In Kent, she teased him to amuse herself. When he joined her in the grove at Rosings Park, she had resented his company and secretly wished him away.

And Darcy had misread her intent *every* single time.

His declaration of love and his poorly worded proposal came to mind. Dismayed and disheartened, Elizabeth sat heavily upon the cushioned window seat before her and momentarily shut her eyes. To say she was embarrassed by her past behaviour was an understatement. She was mortified and ashamed. Darcy had since shown himself to be a good man—one of the best men of her acquaintance. She had hurt him deeply with her harsh rejection and her reprehensible accusations against his character—an honourable character she had since come to admire. Pain and disappointment such as he had likely suffered at her hands was no trifling matter. Such humiliation as she inflicted upon him—she, the woman he had loved and wanted to marry—did not fade with the rise of the sun.

It lingered.

It tormented.

It caused one to doubt.

Is it truly such a wonder he remains silent now?

CHAPTER FIVE

Sixteen days at Pemberley…

"How beautiful," said Elizabeth on a breath. She was standing on top of an enormous configuration of solid rock on the edge of Pemberley's woods. It had taken her nearly an hour to reach the top, but the view was well worth her effort.

She could see every aspect of the surrounding area for miles.

Darcy stood beside her, protective and close as the wind caused her gown to billow like a sail on a ship. "Lambton is over there," he said, pointing towards the village in the distance. The high street wound through the centre of it, from the line of neatly kept houses at the edge of the village to the ale house at the opposite end of it. "And that is Kympton." He indicated a second village approximately three miles to the south of it which was slightly larger in size. "My father would take me there often when I was a boy. During the summer months, my cousins, Colonel Fitzwilliam and his brother Viscount Emerson, would spend time at Pemberley. Emerson is eight years my senior and preferred to keep his own company, but Fitzwilliam and I were always together. We were forever thinking of ways in which to best the other. Our favourite pastime was that of racing one another to the village.

The pump in the church yard there has the coldest water I have ever tasted, and a wall of blackberries at least ten feet high."

Elizabeth smiled. She could easily imagine Darcy as a boy, running from Pemberley to Kympton, wanting nothing more than to best his cousin and closest friend. "And were you victorious?"

Darcy shook his head. "Not often, no, and never by much on the occasions I did happen to win. Fitzwilliam was older, and therefore taller and faster. But his advantages over me did not outlive boyhood, and so his days of victory were numbered."

"You cannot mean to imply you have raced each other to Kympton as men!"

"It was only once," he admitted, "right before I left for Cambridge. Fitzwilliam had just purchased his commission. It seemed a fitting way to mark the occasion."

"Did you win?"

"I did."

He looked so proud of himself that Elizabeth could not help but smile. "A long-awaited victory, then, and well earned."

"Indeed," said Darcy, and grinned.

A sharp gust of wind caught her skirts then, twisting them around her ankles, and Elizabeth was suddenly propelled forward towards the very edge.

Darcy caught her arms, holding fast to her, and pulled her back. "Elizabeth!" His grip was sure and strong, but the words he uttered beneath his breath were harsh and unintelligible.

Elizabeth's legs shook slightly as she endeavoured to calm her racing heart. Had she been alone, or with her aunt and uncle—who would not have accompanied her all the way to the top—she might have fallen to her death.

Darcy urged her to sit, lowering himself onto the bare rock and then guiding her to sit beside him. When she was settled, he released her with an exhalation.

Not yet ready to lose the reassurance of his touch, Elizabeth reached for his hand.

He surrendered it willingly, without hesitation, and squeezed.

Elizabeth relished his closeness; the feeling of his hand wrapped protectively around her own. There was a comforting weight to it, and a warmth that made her feel cared for and safe. A lump formed in her throat, and she swallowed thickly in an effort to dislodge it. If her aunt and uncle were not standing several hundred feet below them with Georgiana, patiently awaiting their return, she might consider remaining where she was indefinitely.

Instead, she tightened her grip on Darcy's hand.

"Will you show me the woods?" Elizabeth asked him later, once they were back at Pemberley and she had been told by her aunt Gardiner to rest. She had tried, but her head was too full, and her heart was too full, and she did not know what to do with herself.

Darcy set aside the letter he had been reading before she entered his study. He had risen to his feet immediately and bowed, but in his haste, he had not relinquished his letter. "Are you well, Miss Bennet?"

When he had clasped her arms and pulled her away from the edge, he had called her by her Christian name. At the time, Elizabeth had been distressed and had barely noticed. At the time, there were more pressing matters to consider. Now, after the fact, she recalled him doing it with startling clarity.

She longed for him to do it again.

Her lips lifted infinitesimally. "I am well enough to take a walk, sir."

Darcy regarded her with an inscrutable expression before inclining his head. Stepping away from his desk, he offered her his arm. "Shall I summon my sister?"

Elizabeth shook her head. "No," she told him quietly, and immediately felt her complexion become heated in the face of her boldness. "Not this time. I would prefer it to be only us."

They left the house through a door set before a garden ripe with summer blooms—hydrangeas, roses, and lilies of every variety and colour. An intimation of a smile appeared upon Elizabeth's lips as she beheld it, but she remained silent as they walked past the garden and continued towards the woods. Her aunt had called Pemberley's woods some of the finest in the country. When they reached them, and stepped from the paved, gravel path onto the soft, damp loam of the forest floor, Elizabeth had to admit Mrs Gardiner had not exaggerated in the least. Everywhere she looked she saw mature trees—sturdy oaks, sycamores, and elms. Interspersed among them were fragrant evergreens. Their canopies extended nearly a hundred feet into the air, a majestic tapestry of verdant leaves and needles that, despite its vastness, made Elizabeth feel insulated from everyone and everything as though she had entered another world.

"It is very beautiful here, and peaceful," she said to Darcy. "It would be a shame if a band of gypsies were to suddenly appear and demand recompense for our trespassing."

"That it would," he replied in a similar tone, "especially as I have left my purse at home."

Elizabeth laughed. "Perhaps the badgers will save us, then."

"Perhaps," said Darcy, with a slight, almost teasing smile of his own.

They came to a clearing where sunlight shone through the canopy, dappling the forest floor. Birds flitted from branch to branch, ruffling their feathers, their songs light and pleasing. A gentle breeze rustled the leaves on the trees. A few fluttered to the ground, lazy and meandering and slow.

At the far side of the clearing, there was an old stone bench, littered with seeds. Darcy led Elizabeth towards it, swept it clean with a brush of his hand, and gestured for her to sit. She hesitated when she saw there was an inscription carved into the top of it, ancient and worn, so much so she could not make it out. "Do you know what is written here?"

Darcy shook his head, leaned over the top of it, and ran his hand over the letters. "No. The inscription was as illegible when I was a boy as it is now. But according to my grandmother, who is long dead, it is a monument of sorts." He frowned. "I know nearly everything that there is to know of Pemberley and its history, but I do not know this. It has always grated on me."

"You like to know things."

"I do, but I believe that is a universal trait. Most people have an innate curiosity about the world in which they live and the people who share it. At least, that is my experience."

She looked at him then—at his handsome face, and his dark eyes, and his firm jaw. She could not see his neck, only a sliver of skin barely visible above his cravat. The sudden compulsion Elizabeth felt to trace her fingertip along that sliver of skin, to feel the softness of it, was immediate and compelling. Instead, she curled her fingers into fists so she would keep her hands where they belonged: to herself.

Darcy, however, had no such compunction. He reached for her hand and gently uncurled her fingers, first the left and then the right, before raising each one to his lips to press a lingering kiss to her palms.

The intimacy of such a gesture made Elizabeth's breath hitch. Neither of them wore gloves. She had not given a single thought to it before that moment; now, the impropriety of it was glaring. In the house, her only thought had been to get away, to be in a quiet place out of doors so she could clear her head and find the courage to ask Darcy why, when his every action spoke of loving her, did he persist in remaining silent about it. Of course, voicing such a question would be as impertinent as it would be inappropriate.

If he would not speak, and she *could* not speak, then what was left?

In cases such as these, perhaps it was better to let her heart speak for itself.

Before Elizabeth could change her mind, she boldly placed Darcy's left hand upon her sternum, directly over her heart.

His intake of breath was as sudden as it was sharp, but he made no attempt to retract his hand. After what seemed like a small eternity, he spoke. "Your heart..." he said roughly, but the words caught in his throat, and he paused for a long moment, struggling for composure. Once he obtained it, he murmured, "Your heart is beating like a hummingbird's wings, as though it will take flight."

"And what of yours?" Elizabeth whispered unsteadily.

"It is the same." Slowly, brazenly, his thumb caressed the supple flesh above the collar of her gown, making her shiver. Darcy exhaled heavily. "Surely, by now you know I love you. I have not stopped."

"I know," she said as her heart soared and her belly tightened, and her mind refused to be still. To say she was relieved by his declaration was an understatement. She was overjoyed and overwhelmed by a flood of emotions, and the tantalising pleasure of his touch. Wanting nothing more than to be closer to him—to touch him more intimately in turn—Elizabeth pressed her other hand to his coat, where she felt his heart was in fact beating every bit as violently as hers. "Your every action, your every look gave you away, but you remained silent."

Darcy shook his head. "I did not want to rush you. I knew your opinion of me had changed for the better. You welcomed my society with pleasure, yet I did not know whether that pleasure was afforded to your friend or your lover—No. Not to your lover. To your *husband*." He paused. "I have long known my own heart, Elizabeth, but I do not know yours."

Elizabeth's throat felt impossibly tight. "I believe you do."

"Do I?" he asked almost desperately. "You are too generous to trifle with me…"

His eyes were so full of emotion, so full of hope and love, all of it for her. How had she ever thought of him as cold? Elizabeth felt the hot pressure of tears in her eyes, and a lump form in her throat. Somehow, she managed to say, "You do. You do know it. It is yours, and you will always have it."

He stepped forward then, closing the distance between them to inches. The hand on Elizabeth's sternum slid upward, and the tip of Darcy's forefinger caressed her clavicle with a tenderness that was maddening. "And will you marry me?" he asked, with no little emotion.

Elizabeth's eyelids fluttered closed. "I will," she promised, urging him closer until she felt the solidness of his body against her own, and his warmth, and each exhalation of his breath on her face. "I love you," she said resolutely, with all her heart. "I love you dearly."

"As I love you." His right hand found purchase on her hip; his left caressed her cheek with unexampled gentleness. "Dearest, loveliest, Elizabeth," he whispered, and pressed a reverent kiss to her forehead, each eyelid, and the tip of her nose. "I love you, most ardently." His voice sounded endearingly uneven.

Elizabeth released a slow, tremulous breath and tilted her face towards the sky. Dappled sunlight shone behind her closed lids—warm, muted shapes of orange and yellow and red. She smiled.

It was then Darcy's lips descended upon her own, soft, definitive, and sure as he kissed her with all the tenderness and yearning, ardency and passion he had claimed to feel for her before, and which Elizabeth knew, beyond any doubt, that he always would.

The End

About the Author

Susan Adriani is a graphic artist turned storyteller. She cannot imagine a world without books, Google maps, copious amounts of tea, and Jane Austen.

Also by Susan Adriani

Call it Hope
Misunderstandings & Ardent Love
The Luxury of Silence
The Truth About Mr Darcy

The Pleasure of Understanding Her

Mary Smythe

CHAPTER ONE

IT IS A TRUTH UNIVERSALLY ACKNOWLEDGED THAT gentlemen imperfectly understand the minds of the fairer sex. However much a gentleman, particularly one of good fortune, must be in want of a wife, this truth is so difficult to overcome as to make the selection process excessively tedious. Fitzwilliam Darcy, for all his many blessings of nature and birth, was the same as any other man in this respect and so, at nearly eight and twenty, he remained a frustrated bachelor.

Opportunities to marry had certainly come Darcy's way since he had entered society, but none had tempted him away from his solitary status. He was beset by a plethora of pretty faces, many of whom he had been assured would make him an admirable wife, but physical beauty was hardly the only requirement in a bride. A finely crafted exterior was nothing to intelligence, integrity or sincerity, and these qualities had proved difficult to find amongst the denizens of the *haut ton*.

"How do you like the pheasant, Mr Darcy? I gave Cook a receipt for a marvellous sauce my sister's French chef uses in town, but I cannot say that she replicated it correctly. It is lacking a certain sophistication, in my opinion, although I suppose it is as good as one can hope for in this backwater little village."

Darcy attended Miss Bingley's haughty speech with only half an ear and his gaze affixed to his plate. He grunted a non-committal response when it seemed she had finished; the sauce tasted well enough to him, but to say so would only encourage Miss Bingley to say more in order to amend her previous complaints to align with his opinion. His head was already quite ill this evening—no doubt a result of prolonged exposure to the shrill tone of Miss Bingley's voice—and some quiet from that quarter would be welcomed.

Miss Bingley was a perfect example of the sort of lady he was supposed to marry, albeit he would choose one with grander connexions and a better-guarded tongue. She had been educated properly at a seminary, knew very well how to perform her duties as hostess, and was even somewhat clever—even if she abused her abilities to denigrate those around her. Miss Bingley would make some gentleman of lower status an elegant wife someday, assuming she could somehow learn to be more pleasant company, which Darcy and his aching head very much doubted.

"I think the sauce is delightful."

Darcy's eyes flicked up and away from his dinner to focus upon a less suitable bridal candidate at the far end of the long table. Miss Elizabeth Bennet was impertinent, countrified, indifferently educated, and lacked both a proper fortune and connexions. She was also the most intriguing lady he had ever met. She was nothing he should want, yet everything he did, a most vexing conundrum.

"Miss Eliza, you have not had the benefit of tasting it as it was meant to be prepared by a competent French chef," Miss Bingley replied with such condescension that it grated on his nerves. "Perhaps if you are ever in town, you shall be fortunate enough to do so."

Miss Elizabeth's lips turned up minutely at the corners as if she were more amused than offended by Miss Bingley's unsubtle set down. "I suppose you must be correct, however I think Mrs Thompson did an admirable job. I shall have to enquire after the receipt for our own cook at Longbourn."

Though the conversation lapsed at this point, Darcy continued to watch Miss Elizabeth for several minutes longer, enraptured by the graceful arch of her neck and the trio of curls which dangled down the back of it. They quivered with her every slight movement and looked so soft to the touch that he longed to unravel them with his own fingers and watch them spring back into position. To think, they had been wild and windblown only a few hours ago after her three-mile walk to Netherfield, a state which he found equally enticing, though in a different sort of way. He absently wondered whether it was similarly tousled when she woke in the morning, her eyes heavily lidded from sleep and her nightclothes in rumpled disarray.

When Miss Elizabeth glanced up and caught his gaze, Darcy hastily diverted it back to his plate, his ears disconcertingly warm. It was an excellent thing, indeed, that she could not read his thoughts or she would have been appalled at their inappropriate direction.

The remainder of the meal passed in superficial conversation which pretended to geniality. Only Bingley, who was pleased with all the world and everything in it, acted truly cheerful while the rest of the party seemed satisfied with their veneer of good manners. Miss Bingley alternated between pestering Darcy over his comfort and making snide remarks she expected everyone to agree with; Mrs Hurst nodded along with whatever her younger sister said and made the occasional comment in support; Hurst focused solely on his ragout; Miss Elizabeth was distracted and largely quiet unless spoken to directly. What a merry party they made.

At length the dishes were cleared away and Miss Elizabeth immediately excused herself to see to her sister's welfare. With a hasty curtsey to the party as a whole, she was gone. Darcy could not help but feel the loss of her presence as he observed his remaining companions. Save for Bingley, they made him wish that he, too, could disappear upstairs and nurse the eldest Miss Bennet. She, at least, was a tranquil sort of girl and would not aggravate his head with strident nothings. As for Miss Elizabeth, it was perhaps best not to dwell on how *she* tempted him.

"Well! That was abrupt," Mrs Hurst commented with a titter as soon as the door had closed behind their houseguest.

"Very badly done, indeed. But then, what else can you expect from country manners?" sneered Miss Bingley. "Miss Eliza, for all her pride and impertinence, is as uncouth as the rest of her family. She has no conversation, no style, no beauty to speak of."

Clearly Mrs Hurst thought the same, for she added, "She has nothing, in short, to recommend her but being an excellent walker. I shall never forget her appearance this morning. She really looked almost wild."

"She did, indeed, Louisa. I could hardly keep my countenance. Why must *she* be scampering about the country, because her sister has a cold? Her hair so untidy, so blowsy!"

With each successive jeer at Miss Elizabeth's expense, Miss Bingley's voice sharpened and became increasingly nasal. By the time she reached the end of her tirade, Darcy's head was throbbing in tune with each ugly word. Thankfully, Bingley was capable of championing Miss Elizabeth in his place because Darcy's headache was becoming so intense as to impede his ability to think.

The diversions for the evening soon moved to the playing of cards; Darcy hoped, rather than believed, that the game would prohibit the barbed witticisms that Bingley's sisters believed was genteel conversation. He was not proved wrong. Just as Darcy had determined to fold on his next hand and retire, the door to the drawing room opened to admit Miss Elizabeth. It seemed he would be required to remain a little longer, for the sake of politeness, though he strangely could not find it in himself to be resentful for it. Both his head and his heart throbbed at the prospect.

Bingley leapt up, asking, "How does your sister do? Better, I hope?"

Miss Elizabeth smiled at Bingley as she approached. "A little better, I think. She is resting, which can only improve her further."

"Do sit down and join us." Bingley waved at the card table. His sisters wrinkled their noses, none too discreetly in Darcy's opinion, before echoing his offer with what passed for pleasant expressions. Hurst merely studied his cards with disinterest.

Miss Elizabeth hesitated a moment, then declined, announcing, "As I have so little time to myself, I think I shall enjoy a book instead. Do not allow me to interrupt your game."

Hurst looked up at Miss Elizabeth, staring at her in astonishment. "Do you prefer reading to cards? That is rather singular."

Before she could speak for herself, Miss Bingley replied with simpering condescension, "Miss Eliza Bennet despises cards. She is a great reader and has no pleasure in anything else."

"I deserve neither such praise nor such censure," cried Miss Elizabeth, her brow delicately furrowed at the two smirking ladies. It seemed they had roused her ire at last, although Darcy could not understand her umbrage; to his mind, being a great reader was admirable. "I am *not* a great reader, and I have pleasure in many things."

"In nursing your sister, I am sure you have pleasure," said Bingley, glancing between the silently duelling ladies with some apprehension, "and I hope it will soon be increased by seeing her quite well."

Miss Elizabeth graciously leapt upon the change of subject and then wandered to the far side of the room to select her book. Darcy wished her much luck in finding something worthwhile; Bingley was decidedly *not* a great reader and his paltry collection showed as much. It was even probable that he had brought no reading material with him to Netherfield and depended upon whatever the owner of the house had left behind, should he ever feel an uncommon urge to read. For Darcy's part, he was glad he had brought a trunk full of books with him so as to have some source of entertainment when the weather was unaccommodating to outdoor pursuits. Or, more likely, when he needed an excuse to ignore Miss Bingley.

Darcy observed Miss Elizabeth out of the corner of his eye as she made her selection. She took her time about it, likely due to the dearth of acceptable choices, before finally settling on one. Darcy leant back slightly in an attempt to see the title, but it was obscured by her hand.

From there the conversation devolved into the sort of inanities in which Miss Bingley specialised: praising Pemberley and pestering her brother to somehow emulate it in his own, as-yet-unacquired, estate. In the midst of it, Bingley surreptitiously rolled his eyes at him and Darcy was forced to hide his amusement by looking elsewhere.

His attention was caught once more by Miss Elizabeth, who had abandoned her book—it must not have been terribly good, as Darcy had suspected; would it be too much of an intimacy to loan her something from his own collection?—to pull her chair up to their table. She stationed herself between Bingley and Mrs Hurst, her gaze darting between the assembled company with evident relish. Perhaps she was interested in Pemberley, as well? Darcy determined to be more cautious and say nothing of his own cache of books to her lest she believe him willing to offer her more.

The discussion transitioned from Pemberley to Georgiana in the sort of leap which only made sense to Miss Bingley. No doubt she hoped that praising his sister would garner her the approbation which admiring his home did not.

"It is amazing to me," said Bingley, "how young ladies can have patience to be so very accomplished, as they all are."

Bingley's simple comment, delivered with sincerity, raised an immediate objection from his sisters. They demanded he account for his opinion, which he did, but not very ably; Darcy could hardly applaud a young lady for being able to net a purse or cover a screen, as these were minimal achievements.

A glance at Miss Elizabeth, who continued to follow the conversation avidly, reminded him that Bingley was again in danger of giving away his heart and fortune to a potentially unsuitable lady. Miss Bennet *appeared* to be everything good and genteel, but she would not be the first young lady to craft herself an innocent disguise in order to draw in an unsuspecting man. Darcy did not know, as yet, whether her apparent interest in his friend was authentic. From what he had seen, Miss Bennet smiled far too much—could such an expression, bestowed so liberally, be genuine?—and did not seem to distinguish Bingley above any other gentleman while in company. Perhaps it was too soon to tell but Darcy did not expect a happy ending for Bingley here in Hertfordshire.

Darcy's eyes again found Miss Elizabeth and he could not but wonder whether *she* was everything she appeared. Could her flirtatious glances, her charming wit, merely be the bait she laid in her trap? Was she, like Miss Bingley, aspiring towards being mistress of Pemberley?

No, not her. She was so artless, so unaffected in all her interactions that Darcy could not believe it of her. What lady bent on impressing a gentleman would walk three miles through the mud when she must know that she would be before him? Further, Elizabeth seemed devoted to Miss Bennet's care; she had not lingered downstairs more than strictly necessary since she had arrived earlier in the day. Had she come with the purpose of enticing him, surely he would have seen her in the drawing room more often.

But it mattered not. Miss Elizabeth was as unsuitable as her elder sister was—more so, considering Darcy's requirements for his future wife versus Bingley's less bounded needs—and so he would think of her no more.

Intent on reordering Bingley's thinking, and perhaps give Miss Elizabeth a subtle warning, Darcy said, "Your list of the common extent of accomplishments has too much truth. The word is applied to many a woman who deserves it no otherwise than by netting a purse, or covering a screen. But I am very far from agreeing with you in your estimation of ladies in general. I cannot boast of knowing more than half a dozen, in the whole range of my acquaintance, that are really accomplished."

Miss Bingley agreed with alacrity and Darcy felt another stab of pain in his cranium. *Blast that woman's shrill tongue!*

"Then," observed Miss Elizabeth, "you must comprehend a great deal in your idea of an accomplished woman."

Darcy pivoted his head to look at her directly. She returned his gaze steadily, without hint of confusion or consciousness. "Yes, I do comprehend a great deal in it."

"Oh, certainly!" cried Miss Bingley, ever his faithful assistant. More than mere agreement, however, she carried on to list a great number of shallow, albeit necessary, accomplishments that ladies must possess in order to truly deserve the word. Darcy might have lived without his wife being able to draw or knowing all of the modern languages, although Miss Bingley made a fair point about comportment. His wife absolutely must conduct herself well in society else she prove an embarrassment to his name and status.

The longer Miss Bingley's list grew, the more unacceptable Miss Elizabeth seemed, which was very likely her aim. He knew that Elizabeth could boast some minor skill at the pianoforte—an enchanting skill, even if it were technically imperfect—but he had seen no sign of the rest. It was all quite vexing to Darcy because, had she been more of a paragon, perhaps he might have been able to present her to his family as at least being accomplished.

Darcy shook his head to dispel such thoughts for they would do him no good. Pain was his reward.

Still, he could not, in good conscience, allow Miss Bingley to denigrate such an exquisite woman who, through no true fault of her own, would not pass muster in his circle. Miss Elizabeth Bennet could have married well, might even have become a leading light in society had she been educated properly. As it was, she was practically perfect in *his* eyes even in the absence of it.

Education. Of course! "All this she must possess," added Darcy and felt a thrill race down his spine as Elizabeth's focus was drawn back to him, "and to all this she must yet add something more substantial, in the improvement of her mind by extensive reading."

With his attention fastened upon her, Darcy was able to see the slow progression of an impish smile spread across Miss Elizabeth's face. She must have recognised his hidden compliment, clever, clever girl. His heart pounded so hard that he could feel his pulse ricocheting inside his cranium.

"I am no longer surprised at your knowing only *six* accomplished women. I rather wonder at your knowing *any*." This statement was delivered with such sweet archness that Darcy could not be offended by it. To the contrary, he felt a warmth ascending the back of his neck, threatening to wash into his cheeks and embarrass him as their eyes remained locked across the table.

His dignity was spared, however, as Miss Bingley and Mrs Hurst objected to Miss Elizabeth's observation and declared that they knew many very accomplished young ladies amongst their acquaintance, contrary to what they had said only minutes ago. Darcy bowed his head to ostensibly reorder his cards, although play had ceased a while ago. *How she tempts me!*

When the debate finally drew to a close, Elizabeth rose from her chair and bid them all a goodnight. She gathered the book she had chosen earlier and turned towards the door.

Unwisely wishing to remain in her presence a little longer, and honestly in need of sleep himself, Darcy folded his hand and said, "I believe I shall retire, as well."

Miss Bingley protested, but Darcy bowed and walked away from the table. He caught up to Miss Elizabeth just before she reached the door and opened it for her, much to her apparent surprise. She preceded him through it and he followed.

As the pair of them ascended the staircase in silence, Darcy's head began to throb mercilessly. Perhaps he had stood too fast, or he had suffered from the change of room, but he felt himself nearly incapacitated as they reached the upper landing. He was developing a migraine, for certain.

Miss Elizabeth was slightly ahead of him and headed in the direction of the guest wing, where he presumed she and Miss Bennet were housed. Darcy had been placed in the family wing, no doubt a manoeuvre of Miss Bingley's to imply a stronger intimacy than actually existed, but he was determined to see Elizabeth to her door. He staggered along behind her until a sudden wave of agony overtook him and he swooned into the wall with a thud.

"Mr Darcy, are you well? Shall I fetch Mr Bingley?"

Darcy forced his eyes to open a sliver and found Miss Elizabeth's face close to his. At this range, he could see the fine strands of her lustrous lashes, count the freckles which formed a constellation across her nose and every minute fleck of gold in her extraordinary eyes. *So green.*

"Mr Darcy? Sir, can you hear me?"

The alarm in Miss Elizabeth's voice roused Darcy from his reverie and he struggled upright and away from the wall. He swayed a bit, but was otherwise steady on his feet. "I beg your pardon. I had not meant to frighten you. I am well."

Apparently determining he was not about to keel over again, Miss Elizabeth took a few steps back, although she remained tense as if prepared to spring forward and catch him should he require it. "Are you certain? Perhaps we should call for the apothecary."

"I am quite certain. 'Tis nothing but a headache, I assure you."

Miss Elizabeth's voice immediately lowered to a softer decibel, no doubt in deference to his affliction. Darcy greatly appreciated the gesture, as did his aching head. "It must be quite severe for you to stumble so."

A jab of pain behind his eyes agreed with her. "Indeed, but all I require is rest. I am occasionally prone to migraines and nothing is so effective a cure as sleep. I thank you for your concern."

Miss Elizabeth continued to stare at him another long moment, disbelief brimming in her fine eyes, before nodding. "Very well. Do you require assistance to your room? A footman might be called for the purpose."

"No, I am well enough now. 'Twas merely a spell of dizziness which has passed."

"If you are certain."

In spite of the miserable suffering he endured, Darcy could not help the soft smile which lifted his lips at Miss Elizabeth's evident concern for his welfare. It appeared genuine, for all he could tell in the semi-dark of the corridor, and touched him. Would she care for him the way she nursed her sister? *If only she were not so unsuitable!*

"I am quite certain. Goodnight, Miss Elizabeth."

She offered him a whispered goodnight in return and then disappeared into a chamber two doors down from where Darcy stood. He dawdled there, longingly observing the barrier between them, for several seconds longer. He then sighed, turned on his heel and proceeded back the way he came.

CHAPTER TWO

DARCY WOKE EARLIER THAN HE MEANT TO, ALTHOUGH FAR later than was his general wont. He had hoped, after at last dropping off to sleep sometime after three in the morning, that he could allow himself a lie in, but it seemed his brain could not stand repose past seven o'clock. His habit of waking at six to enjoy some exercise before beginning his work for the day thwarted any notion that he might roll over and return to sleep; once he was up for the day, there was nothing else for it.

Thus, Darcy reluctantly arose from his mattress and parted the curtains around his bed. Sunlight pierced the fog in his mind but, though he blinked at the suddenness of it, there was no resulting pain. Such relief! In the absence of his migraine, Darcy felt invigorated in spite of his lingering fatigue. He shook his head to clear away the last of the fog, stood and pulled the rope to summon Bailey. Excellent valet that he was, he had waited to be called this morning.

As Darcy was tightening the knot of his banyan, he heard the distinct shuffling of someone within his dressing room, presumably Bailey. There was another sound as well, indistinct and difficult to identify—muttering? Bailey did not mutter. Were he in the habit of it, Darcy would not have kept the man in his employ. But who else would be in his private dressing room, and at this hour? It was his valet's domain and other servants understood not to enter it unless summoned for a particular task.

Darcy watched the closed door warily; the shuffling had ceased, but the muttering continued. He caught snippets of it and thought it did, indeed, sound like Bailey.

Left it right here. Thought the master might require another dose. Ah, here it is!

The door opened abruptly and Bailey—only Bailey—stepped through it into the bedchamber. He bowed as formally and professionally as usual before standing at attention for Darcy's orders. In his hand, he held a triangular envelope which, presumably, contained headache powders. "Good morning, sir. I hope your head is improved this morning?"

Darcy stared at his valet for a moment, but detected nothing amiss. Perhaps Bailey occasionally muttered to himself and Darcy had simply never noted it. It might be something he did outside of Darcy's presence, in which case he would not have known.

What did it matter? So long as Bailey did not disrupt his master's peaceful quiet, it was hardly an issue. "Much. I shall not need more powders, though I feel that fresh air and exercise shall do me good. I would like to dress for riding."

"Would you like some coffee before you go out?"

"No, but I shall enjoy a cup when I return. See that it is ready."

"Very good, sir." Bailey bowed, turned and disappeared back into the dressing room.

Seems in a better mood today. He is rather insufferable when he's ill. Where are his riding boots?

Darcy grit his teeth together in vexation. As if the muttering itself were not bad enough, Bailey also felt it his place to comment upon his master's mood? This could not stand. "Bailey."

The valet responded immediately to his master's sharp command and returned to the room. "Yes, sir?"

"I can hear you muttering in there. If you value your position, you will cease it immediately."

Bailey's eyes widened incrementally, the only visible sign of surprise, and cleared his throat. "I beg your pardon, sir?"

What is he on about now? I have not said a word outside his presence. Perhaps he still suffers? Has he gone mad?

Darcy squeezed his own eyes shut and shook his head. He could have sworn that he had heard Bailey's insufferable muttering again, but the man stood before him and his lips had not moved. "On second thought, I believe I shall take another dose. There seems to be a slight buzzing in my head."

"Of course, sir."

Bailey appeared wary as he took himself off to the dressing room again to retrieve the powders and Darcy retreated to a chair on the far side of the room. Sitting seemed to help; the phantom muttering faded away as he reclined there, rubbing his temples. It returned in fits and starts as Bailey prepared him for riding, but Darcy had hopes that his ride coupled with the powders would resolve the infernal noise entirely.

Darcy enjoyed a long ride in the crisp November air. *It was just what I needed*, he decided as he approached the stables where the grooms and stable lads were hard at work tending the animals. He passed Bacchus on and made his way back to the house to make himself presentable for company.

He submitted himself once again to Bailey's ministrations, though they rushed through his ablutions quickly. Darcy heard nothing out of the ordinary, even if Bailey proved to be somewhat more talkative than usual, and he was relieved. No doubt the unaccountable muttering from earlier that morning was some lingering effect of his headache and too little sleep. As Darcy had suspected it might, a ride had put him back to rights.

As Darcy exited his chambers, refreshed and ready to face the household, he heard a number of chattering female voices up ahead and halted. *Am I truly going mad?*

Tentatively, Darcy crept along the corridor until he rounded the corner, whereupon he released a relieved breath. There, just about to descend the staircase, was Elizabeth, her mother, and two youngest sisters. The voices he had detected were not delusions, but rather the empty-headed prattle of ladies. He presumed that they had come to check on Miss Bennet.

Mrs Bennet confirmed this supposition without him having to enquire directly. "A few days of bed rest shall put her to rights and then she can visit with Mr Bingley! Do make sure she does not leave her room until her nose is the right colour."

"Aye, for she looks like Mr Hurst with it all swollen and red!" the youngest girl—Miss Lucy? Or was that one Kathy?—tittered to her next eldest sister.

Miss Elizabeth, he was pleased to witness, shushed the girl and scolded her for saying something so impolitic. "Mind your tongue, Lydia!"

Neither girl seemed to take her admonishment to heart, for they giggled behind their hands and held a whispered conversation between them which Darcy could not hear. *What silly, addle-pated children they are. Far too immature to be out in society.*

A slight shift of his weight caused the floorboard beneath his feet to creak and give away his position. Darcy winced at the sound and thought to retreat, but it was too late; Miss Elizabeth's eyes were now trained upon him. She nudged her mother and indicated his direction.

Stifling an exasperated sigh, Darcy moved fully out into the landing and bowed to the ladies. "Good morning. I hope you have found Miss Bennet in better health than you may have expected."

Mrs Bennet sighed theatrically. "My Jane suffers a great deal, but with the utmost patience. She will have to trespass a little longer on Mr Bingley's kindness, though she is thankfully in no danger."

"I am glad to hear it."

Insufferable, arrogant man! What is he about, skulking around listening to conversations he was not party to!

Darcy felt it particularly rude to admonish a person under one's breath, but he ground out an apology through his gritted teeth. "Forgive me for not announcing myself earlier, madam. I had not meant to overhear your conversation."

A few curious glances went around among the ladies. Mrs Bennet tossed her hair. "No one said you did! Come, girls, let us repair to the drawing room. The Bingleys are no doubt waiting for us." So saying,

THE PLEASURE OF UNDERSTANDING HER

she swivelled on her heel and began her descent, her two giggling daughters scurrying after her.

Miss Elizabeth, though she turned to follow her mother, did so with more sedate decorum than her relations. Darcy hurried forward to offer her his arm, which she took, lightly placing her hand upon his forearm. He experienced a pleasurable tingle where the weight of her fingers rested.

How abominably rude to listen in on other people's conversations! No doubt he intends to report back to Miss Bingley with all our silliness.

Darcy halted. "I beg your pardon?"

Miss Elizabeth looked to him, visibly confused. "Sir?"

"I already explained to your mother that I had not intended to overhear your conversation. I will thank you to not insinuate that I had nefarious purposes in doing so."

Straightening, Miss Elizabeth tartly replied, "Excuse me, but I have said nothing of the kind, sir. Your motives are your own and I dare not speculate on them."

Even when they are obvious.

Darcy blinked down at Miss Elizabeth, befuddled and more than a little alarmed that part of what she said did not appear to issue from her mouth. *What is this insanity?*

"Are you well, Mr Darcy?"

Miss Elizabeth's expression had softened appreciably into one of concern and—though Darcy took a moment to determine that she had, in fact, spoken to him—his initial distress lessened at her show of tenderness for him. He placed his hand atop hers and assured her, "I am. Forgive me for my words just now, I believe my migraine from last evening continues to affect me."

"Shall I send for someone? I do not believe Mr Jones has left yet."

"No, no, I am sure a cup of tea will do me a world of good."

Darcy moved to continue their descent, but stumbled slightly when he distinctly heard Miss Elizabeth mumble again.

I suppose migraine is as good a euphemism as any for being foxed out of one's mind.

He looked sharply down at her, ready to reprimand, but her face was placidly polite with no sign of either guilt or impishness to indicate she had spoken so inappropriately. And, really, it was not the kind of thing he expected from Miss Elizabeth; her younger sisters sometimes spoke out of turn, but even they were presumably wise enough to keep their counsel on a gentleman's proclivities within their hearing. How could he account for what he thought he heard?

I am for Bedlam, he thought.

As he and Miss Elizabeth approached the drawing room, a swell of noise greeted them and Darcy winced. So many voices at once! Miss Bingley and Mrs Hurst were bad enough by themselves, but the addition of the Bennet ladies made for such a deafening roar that his ears began to ring in protest against the onslaught. Darcy greatly wished to turn around and retreat back to his rooms, but with Miss Elizabeth on his arm he could not do so without seeming unforgivably rude. He cared nothing for what those inside the drawing room might think of him, but he would prefer not to offend *her* if he could help it.

And so inside they went, Darcy silently girding himself against the foolishness he was about to face.

Upon crossing the threshold, however, he was amazed to see that only one person within—Mrs Bennet, of course—was speaking while the rest listened to her with what looked like mixture of patient indulgence and thinly veiled annoyance, displayed in varying degrees depending upon the person.

"Indeed I have, sir!" Mrs Bennet was saying to Bingley, who nodded along encouragingly. "She is a great deal too ill to be moved."

And yet, Mrs Bennet's was not the only voice that he heard. Darcy could not account for it, but in spite of the evidence before his eyes he felt as though he were trapped in a room full of people all talking at once. But it could not be! The younger Bennet girls were whispering to one another rather than speaking over anyone. Miss Bingley was watching Mrs Bennet with contempt and trading peevish looks with her sister, who was presently sipping from her teacup. None of them could be the source of the disturbance. Bingley occasionally responded to something Mrs Bennet said, but nothing else, and Hurst was asleep on a chaise in the corner. *What in blazes is happening to me?*

THE PLEASURE OF UNDERSTANDING HER

"Mr Darcy?"

Darcy was, for the second time in not many minutes, pulled from his distraction by the sound of Miss Elizabeth's voice. He looked down at her warily, but found her awaiting some kind of response and so assumed she had actually said something.

"Are you certain you are well? You have gone very pale."

I hope he does not faint. I wonder if I can direct him to the sofa.

Darcy clenched his eyes shut a moment to gather himself before responding, "Forgive me again, Miss Elizabeth. I am not myself today."

If only that were true. Hateful man!

His eyes snapped open to fix upon Miss Elizabeth's lovely face, searching for some proof that she had actually spoken that searing comment, but she seemed merely concerned. Her fine eyes were shaded by the slightest furrow of her brow, as if she were pondering what she should do with him.

He truly does look ill.

"I think I should like to sit down," Darcy said.

"I think that a wise idea, sir." Miss Elizabeth tugged slightly upon the arm she still held and led him to the circle of visitors, directing him to a chair on the far side nearest the window where she left him to settle beside her mother. Darcy felt somewhat abandoned by this immediate removal, but in the next instant found himself set upon by Miss Bingley—offering him tea and every delicacy the house could offer—and understood Miss Elizabeth's desire to flee.

"I can send down to the kitchens for something more substantial, if you like. You were not at breakfast, so I am sure you have not eaten properly." Miss Bingley blinked with some rapidity, which Darcy assumed was a coquettish manoeuvre but rather made it seem as if she had something caught in her eye.

"No, thank you. I am perfectly satisfied with a cup of tea."

How utterly dull of you.

Darcy glanced up sharply from his beverage, certain he had heard Miss Bingley disparage him, only to find her accosting him with more of her cloying hospitality. "It is no trouble at all, I assure you, and you look as if you require something more nourishing than tea. I can see that you are a bit listless today."

Though how could anyone tell?

"I am sure a hearty meal would do you some good."

Darcy stared more openly than he usually dared at Miss Bingley, not a little unnerved that he could apparently hear her speaking words she did not actually say. "The tea will do."

As Miss Bingley wandered off to prepare his cup, he distinctly heard her muttering under her breath.

Tiresome, disagreeable man. I should not like you at all were it not for Pemberley

Another quiet, murmuring voice caught Darcy's attention and he ceased puzzling over Miss Bingley's unaccountable rudeness to listen.

Kitty, a fair but frozen maid; Kindled a flame I still deplore

Darcy pivoted in his chair to look behind him where Hurst was sprawled out upon a chaise, appalled that a gentleman would quote such an improper poem in mixed company, to find him snoring and apparently insensible to the goings on around him.

She kindles slow, but lasting fires; With care my appetite she feeds.

As he watched Hurst slumber—if, in fact, he truly slumbered at all—Darcy could clearly hear him reciting the final stanza of his poem, though his mouth was open in a snore. Hurst could not possibly be forming words, and yet Darcy could hear them in his head as surely he could his own thoughts. *Am I reading their minds? No, that is preposterous!*

"Lizzy!" Mrs Bennet's sharp tone recalled Darcy to the present and he turned back around to witness the matron giving her second eldest daughter a set down before company. Miss Elizabeth said nothing in her own defence, but her lowered head and pink cheeks told Darcy that she was mortified. "Remember where you are and do not run off in the wild manner that you are suffered to do at home."

"I did not know before," said Bingley into the awkward silence which followed, "that you were a studier of character. It must be an amusing study."

"Yes," replied Miss Elizabeth, casting Bingley a grateful look which he reciprocated with a soft smile of commiseration, "but intricate characters are the *most* amusing. They have at least that advantage."

"The country," said Darcy, desperately attempting to distract himself from the voices in his head which continued to press upon him with their brutally honest opinions and bawdy lyrics, "can in general supply but few subjects for such study. In a country neighbourhood you move in a very confining and unvarying society."

Conceited man, he probably thinks the only characters worth studying are contained within his own vaunted circle.

In spite of this cruel indictment of his character, Miss Elizabeth smiled in that playful way he found so enticing and said aloud, "But people themselves alter so much that there is something new to be observed in them forever."

"Yes, indeed," cried Mrs Bennet, apparently offended by Darcy's manner of mentioning a country neighbourhood. "I assure you there is quite as much of *that* going on in the country as in town."

Everyone in the room looked upon Mrs Bennet with the same sort of surprise that Darcy was feeling. He listened closely for any disembodied voices, curious as to what the rest of them thought of Mrs Bennet and her ongoing diatribe in favour of country over town.

To think she considers her own paltry society compares to what one can find in London.

Good God, what can I say to dispel the tension? A change of subject would be good, but what?

Graze on my lips, and if those hills be dry; Stray lower, where the pleasant fountains lie.

Oh, Mama! Not in company, not in company!

What a fine joke! Just look at Mr Darcy's countenance, one would think he had just swallowed something very disagreeable to his digestion.

"When I am in the country," Bingley burst out in response to Mrs Bennet, casting Darcy an apologetic grimace, "I never wish to leave it, and when I am in town it is pretty much the same. They have each their advantages, and I can be equally happy in either."

"Aye—that is because you have the right disposition. But that gentleman," Mrs Bennet sent Darcy such a scathing look that his spine straightened at the offence, "seemed to think the country was nothing at all."

It was Elizabeth's turn to interject, and she did so with perfect timing; her mother had just opened her mouth to elaborate further. "Indeed, Mama, you are mistaken. You quite mistook Mr Darcy. He only meant that there were not such a variety of people to be met with in the country as in town, which you must acknowledge to be true."

Oh, that I would have to defend that abominable man's opinion! But if it redirects Mama's conversation to a more proper subject…

With a fleeting, exasperated glance from Miss Elizabeth, Darcy had decidedly had more than enough. He set his tea aside, bowed to the assembled company and retreated from the room with alacrity. He knew he was being abrupt and unpardonably rude, but he could take no more of their secret remarks or Mrs Bennet's vulgar display. He required some time alone with his thoughts—and his thoughts *alone*.

CHAPTER THREE

Darcy thought to return to his chambers, but a glance about the entry hall reminded him that servants and their thoughts were everywhere. He seemed to be able to hear them through walls—Mrs Bennet was not the only one he could still detect behind the closed door of the drawing room—and could not abide the idea that he might be assaulted by phantom whispers as the servants went about their business. Neither did he wish to encounter anyone at the stables for fear of overhearing his groom's innermost concerns, and so Darcy walked briskly out a side door and into the garden with the intent to lose himself amidst nature. His horse had had nothing to say about his seat this morning, so he felt he must be safe amidst the lesser creatures of the land.

He gave the gardeners a wide berth as he left the cultivated shrubbery and emerged into the wilder landscape beyond Netherfield's park. It was damp and somewhat chilly outside, making Darcy wish he had endured interacting with at least one servant to retrieve his hat and greatcoat, but being away from the house was soothing to his troubled brain. The further away from the manor and its inhabitants he got, the calmer he was and the more rationally he was able to think.

Darcy climbed a subtle rise approximately two miles west of Netherfield, one which rested between his friend's leased estate and

Longbourn. The locals called it Oakham Mount due to the single large oak tree which had sprouted from its summit and the panoramic view of the countryside which was one's reward for reaching the top. There were more impressive prospects in the Peak District from which he hailed, but the familiarity of looking out upon a pastoral scene was enough to comfort Darcy's addled nerves.

He paced around the base of the oak tree, his ungloved fingers tunnelling into his hair as he considered his situation. *What in creation is happening to me? It seems utter madness, but I believe I can hear the thoughts of those around me! Have I lost my mind? Or could it possibly be real?*

Had anyone else come to him asking for advice on this very problem, Darcy would have suggested immediate consultation with a physician, perhaps even commitment to an asylum, but those places were like perdition and he had no inclination to remand himself into their care. Then there was his family name and Georgiana's prospects to consider; having the scion of the Darcy clan declared insane would benefit no one. Too many people depended upon him to provide for them and Darcy would rather suffer silently than let them down.

Further, there was no indication that his mental faculties were in any way affected by this new ability he had unexpectedly inherited. Aside from hearing voices, he felt as sane as ever and entirely capable of reasoning. Of course, those who suffered from madness often did not realise it themselves, but a quick check of his memory and general knowledge told him nothing was amiss in that quarter. He would have to be watchful for any impulsive thoughts or urges, but at present, Darcy did not consider himself irrational or dangerous.

And if it is real? Darcy halted in place as this idea skittered through his head. *What if I truly can read the minds of others? It seems impossible, but perhaps there are more things in heaven and earth than can be dreamt of in my philosophy. I would never have believed it had it not afflicted me, but if I am not running mad...*

Darcy was equally relieved and fearful that this might be the case: relieved, of course, because actually hearing the internal thoughts of others meant he was as lucid as ever; and fearful because he did not want the 'gift' of peering into the private inner workings of those around him. He had already heard many unflattering opinions of himself, all of which he would have been happier not knowing. He had

THE PLEASURE OF UNDERSTANDING HER

always suspected that Miss Bingley only favoured him for his fortune, but to know that she found him dull and disagreeable was something of a blow. He had assumed that at least some of her flirtation had been more than pretence; he was an intelligent, worldly man and worthy of her respect. Hurst's preference for bawdy verse was, if anything, worse than Miss Bingley's disdain, for how could Darcy sit in mixed company and pretend he could not 'hear' the man's lewd recitations? And Elizabeth?

A sigh escaped Darcy at the distressing recollection of her thoughts. If his ability were real—and Darcy was in a fair way of convincing himself that it was—that meant Elizabeth detested him. She found him arrogant, conceited, and rude. Darcy supposed that his reticence could have been misconstrued occasionally, but how could she dislike him so? Were her flirtations as empty as Miss Bingley's? Darcy did not wish to believe it so, but what else could he conclude by the tone of her inner monologue?

Perhaps Elizabeth was merely in an ill-humour due to her sister's poor health and her mother's visit? Yes, that must be it. Mrs Bennet would drive anyone to distraction, and Elizabeth was excessively attached to Miss Bennet. Of course she must be unusually fractious, though she hid it very well. Far better than did Miss Bingley.

With such an explanation at hand, and the arc of the sun above him marking the day as more than half gone, Darcy determined that he must return to Netherfield. It was nearly dinner time and he would be missed. Therefore, he turned his boots back in the direction of the house and descended the slope, forging a new determination.

I will use my new ability to determine Elizabeth's true feelings. If she genuinely despises me—which I doubt—I shall do what I can to improve her opinion of me. Carefully, carefully; I would not wish to excite her expectations, but I cannot bear knowing that she is alive in the world and thinking ill of me.

Darcy spent the time before dinner avoiding other people as much as he was able. Upon returning to the house, he had hurried up the stairs and hidden—there was no other word for it, much to Darcy's chagrin

—in his chambers, informing Bailey that he was resting and not to be disturbed.

The dinner itself was as unsettling a scene as the one which had taken place in the drawing room that morning, with the secret thoughts of the entire party plaguing his brain with unwanted and often disturbing information.

Miss Bingley, it transpired, not only found him dull, but considered him stupid. *This* Darcy could hardly account for since he had always considered his own mental acuity to be greater than hers, but the lady was apparently under the great misapprehension that she had fooled him with her arts and allurements and expected an offer for her hand any day.

Yes, dear Darcy, let Caroline take good care of you. Buffoon.

Seated next to her, Darcy had no choice but to overhear her panegyrics over the sorts of gowns she expected to soon order for her trousseau and the garish plans she had for redecorating his house in town. It seemed Lady Catherine was not the only person of his acquaintance enamoured of gold ormolu.

Across from him, Mrs Hurst was blessedly silent in her opinions, but proved to be as unwelcome in his head as the rest in playing the same tune over and over again without cessation. The song itself was unobjectionable, but it was one that never seemed to end and he wished desperately that he could tell her to desist. To do so would have been insanity, of course, and so he did not, but he was sorely tempted when she began replicating the rhythm with her fingers against her wineglass.

Hurst, to his other side, continued to spout the most ribald poetry Darcy had ever heard within the confines of his head. As those around them conversed—both aloud and otherwise—Hurst produced a steady stream of verse which only seemed to grow more disgusting with each successive glass of wine. It was taxing for Darcy to concentrate on the conversation of those around the table with such lewdness distracting him and made worse when Bingley and Elizabeth began to speak of poetry.

"Surely you cannot believe that! Have you never been wooed by a few pretty lines from an ardent swain?" Bingley cried out with a laugh.

THE PLEASURE OF UNDERSTANDING HER

"That singular honour fell to my sister. If Jane's experience is a common one, then I must say I was unimpressed."

"The young man was no Shakespeare, then?" Bingley asked

Elizabeth smiled. "I am convinced that their affection withered more quickly due to his paltry efforts. There has been many a one, I fancy, overcome in the same way. I wonder who first discovered the efficacy of poetry in driving away love!"

His pebbles they went thump, thump, Against my little wanton rump.

"I have been used to consider poetry as the *food* of love," said Darcy, eager to have his part in the conversation. If he spoke a mite too loudly to cover the vulgarity pouring silently from Hurst's mind into his own, no one seemed to notice it.

It was music, *sir, and after such strictures on improvement of one's mind by reading, I would think you embarrassed by such an error.*

Elizabeth bit her lip and paused a moment before her expression melted into snide amusement. Had Darcy not known better, he might have mistaken it as one of playfulness. How often had he misunderstood her looks?

"Of a fine, stout, healthy love it may," she conceded aloud, that maddeningly misleading smile still in place. "Everything nourishes what is strong already. But if it be only a slight, thin sort of inclination, I am convinced that one good sonnet will starve it entirely away."

Darcy only smiled, mortified that she found his conversation wanting. He did not dare attempt anything further.

"I enjoy poetry," Mrs Hurst commented to no one in particular. This statement, combined with the glance she traded with her husband across the table, implied something about the Hursts which did not bear thinking about. Darcy covered his shudder by shifting in his chair.

After the ladies left them, Bingley moved round the table to sit in Miss Bingley's vacated place, glass of port in one hand and a ready grin on his face. "Delightful evening, eh? It wants for the presence of Miss

Bennet, but her sister is nearly as charming and very amusing. We should be so lucky at every meal to have one of the Bennets with us."

Darcy could not agree, but was comforted by the echo of Bingley's declaration within his mind. So few, it seemed, said what they were really thinking, but Bingley was as genuine as he seemed from the outside. Darcy's esteem for his friend, which was already high, rose another notch. "Yes, Miss Elizabeth is a witty young lady."

"But you wonder at her disinclination for poetry?" Bingley jokingly suggested.

Darcy recalled a particularly obscene line he had heard from Hurst earlier and grimaced. "I believe I am coming round to Miss Elizabeth's opinion on the subject. The wrong sort of poetry could starve anything away."

They were quiet a moment before Bingley, staring into his glass, asked, "What do you think of Miss Bennet, Darcy?"

Do say that you like her! I have never met an angel more beautiful or sweet than Jane.

"Her connexions are not good and her fortune is almost non-existent. When Mr Bennet dies, I understand that the estate is to go to a distant cousin. You would be beholden to Mrs Bennet and any unmarried daughters in that event." *Although I would be tempted to take at least one of them off your hands... Stop it, Darcy!*

"Yes, yes, I know all that." Bingley waved his hand impatiently. "But what of Miss Bennet herself? Is she not all that is good, kind and beautiful?"

"She is a lovely young lady."

Bingley huffed an exasperated sigh and muttered within his mind about Darcy's deliberate obtuseness. "But do you think her interest in me is sincere? Do you think she could ever return my affection for her?"

Darcy was on the verge of cautioning his friend to guard his heart but stopped when a thought occurred to him. He need not *guess* at Miss Bennet's sentiments—he had only to wait for her to be well enough to be in his company. His new ability, as taxing as it was proving to be in most instances, could be of great service in plumbing the depths of Miss Bennet's serenity. Her connexions and fortune would never be what they ought for a man like Bingley who could marry higher, but at least Darcy could attest accurately to her true feelings. From there, it would be up to Bingley to determine his own future.

With this in mind, he replied, "I cannot say that I have been with her enough to have formed an opinion. However, I shall observe her at the next opportunity and tell you my thoughts then."

In the drawing room, Darcy had greatly hoped to distance himself from the company and enjoy a bit of private time with his thoughts—and his thoughts only—but it was not to be. Though he sat at the desk penning a letter to Georgiana, Miss Bingley followed him thither and began pestering him with the sort of nonsense which could only annoy her object. Asking him to add comments from her to his letter, offering to mend his perfectly good pen, complimenting the evenness of his lines. In between her spoken sentences, Darcy could hear her true opinions—Georgiana, apparently, was at least as dry as himself and only her fortune would ever attract her a husband—most of which set his teeth on edge. It would have been an unbearable experience had Elizabeth not been sitting on a sofa nearby where he could hear her humorous internal commentary on Miss Bingley's behaviour.

Oh, indeed, Mr Darcy's skill at writing long letters is most desirable in a potential husband. My, look at how precisely he forms each letter, so fascinating.

Darcy would occasionally look up at Elizabeth and trade smirks with her, once even rolling his eyes, and he perceived—both from her expression and her private monologue—that they were sharing a joke at Miss Bingley's expense.

Much against his will, the conversation in the room turned to Darcy's skill at letter writing, which Miss Bingley insisted was superb, and then somehow on to Bingley's malleability, a subject which had begun during Mrs Bennet's visit. Darcy had steadily attended his letter in spite of the distraction until Elizabeth entered the fray and he became too enthralled by her to continue. She defended Bingley's habits of ill-considered compliance with much energy and Darcy quite enjoyed parrying her every riposte in a likewise manner.

It was such an engaging experience to debate with Elizabeth thus—and she felt the same pleasure at a challenge to her intellect, Darcy could sense it—that he had, for the first time since receiving his strange new ability, forgotten there were other people in the room with them.

Until Bingley himself cried, "By all means, let us hear all the particulars, not forgetting their comparative height and size, for that will have more weight in the argument, Miss Elizabeth, than you may be aware of. I assure you that if Darcy were not such a great tall fellow, in comparison with myself, I should not pay him half so much deference. I declare I do not know a more awful object than Darcy, on particular occasions, and in particular places; at his own house especially, and of a Sunday evening when he has nothing to do."

The umbrage Darcy felt at Bingley's exclamation—one uttered, he very well knew, in a nervous attempt to halt what his friend perceived as an argument between himself and Elizabeth—was not to be expressed in mixed company. He forced a smile he hoped was congenial and settled back into his chair.

Goodness, I think Mr Darcy is rather offended. I cannot say that I blame him, even if I believe Mr Bingley only meant to tease us into harmony. I had better check my laugh.

This thought of Elizabeth's tickled Darcy's brain and he pivoted in her direction. Her ability to perceive his displeasure was oddly heartening and her restraint in not laughing at his pique said much for her consideration of others. Darcy was liking her more and more as they spent time together. Were it not for the inferiority of her connexions, he should be in some danger.

With the so-called dispute put to bed, Darcy returned to his letter and finished it quickly. Once he was done, he entreated Miss Bingley to play for them, if only to send her thoughts away from him and possibly drown out those of the rest of the party. He did not mind hearing Elizabeth's, but Hurst had yet to use up his reserve of ribald rhymes and his wife had begun jangling her bracelets in time to that horrid, endless tune.

Miss Bingley acquiesced easily enough—failing to hide her smugness as well as she thought—and sat down to play some Italian songs.

After a few of these, she varied the charm with a lively Scotch air which inspired him to boldness.

Darcy approached Elizabeth and, with his hand held out to her, asked, "Do you not feel a great inclination to seize such an opportunity of dancing a reel?"

She smiled but did not reply—not aloud in any case.

Am I now tolerable enough to dance with, sir? I had thought I was not handsome enough to tempt you.

Darcy felt the heat leach from his face. Her reference to his insult from that wretched assembly did not go unrecognised and indeed went a long way to explaining the animosity he sometimes sensed in her towards himself. *What an abominable first impression I made! She is quite right to despise me.*

He was initially inclined to withdraw his invitation and slink away in shame, but gentlemen did not compound their own misbehaviour with cowardice. A gentleman made amends for such slights, which Darcy intended to do, beginning with a dance to atone for the snub.

Darcy asked again, "Would you like to dance a reel with me, Miss Elizabeth?"

"I heard you before," she said, "but I could not immediately determine what to say in reply. You wanted me, I know, to say 'Yes', that you might have the pleasure of despising my taste, but I always delight in overthrowing those kind of schemes and cheating a person of their premeditated contempt. I have therefore made up my mind to tell you that I do not want to dance a reel at all—and now despise me if you dare."

"Indeed, I do not dare." He could never despise Elizabeth, even knowing her distaste for him. "However, I must plead my case and beg you to dance with me. I denied myself the pleasure at our first meeting and would like to rectify that."

The shock on Elizabeth's face matched the exclamation in her mind. She was at a loss for words for several long moments until, to his surprise and great relief, Elizabeth extended her hand and placed it within his. "If you insist."

To his satisfaction, and her bafflement, Darcy led her to the centre of the room where they engaged in spirited footwork which impeded their ability to speak. He could hear, from the depths of her mind, however, that she was reconsidering what she thought she knew of his disdain.

I can hardly suppose that I am an object of admiration to so great a man, yet that he stares at me so and shows me such attentions because he dislikes *me is still more strange. Is there something in me so reprehensible that he cannot look away? I know I am not as pretty as Jane, but I had not thought myself so disgusting as all that.*

This rumination was a punch to Darcy's gut. Not only did she dislike him, but she believed that *he* disliked *her*. If anything, Darcy's feelings tended too much the other way. Evidently she had not even considered his gaze as admiring until this moment, and even then she disputed it within herself. *Is this what my thoughtless comment has wrought?*

Darcy meant to put Elizabeth's misapprehension to rights. He could not have her thinking him so devoid of proper feeling as to stare at her as if she were some oddity on display in a menagerie, nor could he countenance her believing that he found her disgusting. It was an insult to his pride in every way. It was clear that Elizabeth had no expectations of him; thus, it could not hurt to amend his character in her eyes.

To start with, Darcy affixed Elizabeth with his most approving smile, one which was rendered more sincere by the bashful way she averted her eyes from it and thought him 'unfairly handsome'. It was a small beginning, but a promising one.

CHAPTER FOUR

AS THEY RAMBLED THROUGH THE GARDENS THE following morning, Darcy listened with impatience to Miss Bingley's teasing over his portended marriage to Elizabeth. Even could he not hear the bitter contradictions in her internal monologue, Darcy was certain he would have been able to guess at them; Miss Bingley was not subtle with her pointed 'advice' for his future felicity. He could not help himself in paying Elizabeth a few compliments, which Miss Bingley did not appreciate in the least.

If only I had been more circumspect in walking out! Nothing for it now.

The curious tickle of Elizabeth's mind invading his own caused Darcy to stop in the centre of the path. If he could hear her thoughts, she must be nearby. He turned and looked over his shoulder in time to see her walk round the corner of the house arm in arm with Mrs Hurst, her face the picture of friendly politeness as her companion rattled away about some nonsense or other. Alerted to his sudden lack of attention, Miss Bingley's eyes roved to the forms of Elizabeth and her sister and frowned.

Not her! Could Louisa not keep her away?

Aloud, Miss Bingley said, "I did not know you intended to walk." Only a slight flush in her cheeks, and the mortification echoing within her mind, informed Darcy that she was at all conscious of their previous conversation.

"You used us abominably ill," answered Mrs Hurst—*you foolish girl, provoking him where anyone could overhear*—"in running away without telling us that you were coming out."

Elizabeth glanced between the two sisters as Mrs Hurst disengaged herself and moved to take Darcy's free arm, her expression a study in suppressed amusement. The distracting way she bit her lip, as if holding in a chuckle, inspired in Darcy an inappropriate longing to lead her away to someplace more private.

And why should I not? Darcy thought as a new plan bloomed in his mind. *I have been searching for an opportunity to make my apologies, why not create one instead?*

"This walk is not wide enough for our party," he said, quickly evading Mrs Hurst's reach. "We had better go into the avenue."

An excellent opportunity to make my escape!

"No, no, stay where you are," Elizabeth entreated, her mouth tilting impishly. "You are charmingly grouped, and appear to uncommon advantage. The picturesque would be spoilt by admitting a fourth. Goodbye."

Before she could skip away, Darcy extended his crooked elbow to Elizabeth, silently insisting that she take it. "Nonsense. With all due respect to Mr Gilpin, there is admirable symmetry in pairs, even if a trio is to be preferred in certain instances. Come, allow me to show you a pretty little wilderness I discovered the other day on my ride. I think you will appreciate its natural splendour."

Elizabeth's cheeks flushed a bright pink and he felt a flash of mortification precede her amused chagrin.

It seems I have underestimated Mr Darcy yet again. I really should mind my rogue tongue.

"We have not the proper shoes for such an excursion," Miss Bingley protested, somewhat desperately. "Let us continue in the gardens, or better yet repair to the drawing room. I shall order tea."

A glance down at the hem of Elizabeth's gown confirmed the presence of sturdy walking boots. "Miss Elizabeth is prepared for a longer ramble. I shall show her the aspect and we can reconvene in the drawing room later. If that is amenable to you, Miss Elizabeth?"

Although her expression showed indecision, Darcy could hear Elizabeth contemplating his offer. Better to promenade with a man who had once insulted her, yet had improved upon further acquaintance, or submit herself to Miss Bingley and her jealous company? She struggled not long before replying, "I believe I would prefer to see the wilderness, if Mr Darcy truly does not mind showing me. I have been indoors so frequently of late that some fresh air and exercise must do me good."

Darcy smiled in satisfaction as Elizabeth, at last, took his arm and they bid their farewells to the Bingley sisters. They crossed onto the lawn and Darcy led her towards a slight rise along the far edge. It was a magnificent prospect from atop his horse and he knew Elizabeth, with her love of nature, would appreciate it.

Elizabeth's exclamations were enthusiastic and genuine, lending a glow to her countenance which bewitched him. How could he ever have considered her not handsome enough to tempt him? Even through the blaze of his headache, he should have noticed her uncommon beauty at a glance. He truly was the world's greatest clod for disparaging her so unfairly.

"I believe I owe you an apology."

Apparently startled, Elizabeth tore her gaze away from the brightly hued hillside below them and turned to him. "Sir?"

Darcy cleared his throat. "At the assembly I insulted you without cause and I am sorry for it."

Elizabeth's gaze averted and her cheeks flushed lightly pink. From anger, he realised upon reading her thoughts, not bashfulness; he had wounded her more deeply than he'd thought. "Think nothing of it, sir. You are not required to dance with perfect strangers against your inclination."

"Perhaps not but there is no excuse for my rudeness. You are one of the handsomest women of my acquaintance and so my sin is doubled for its untruthfulness."

Darcy sensed a rapid shift between various emotions—fury, affront, disbelief and, more tentatively than the others, some slight hope. She peeked up at him through the fine lashes he so admired, her mind in tumult. "Pray do not feel as if you need to counter your first impression for the sake of my feelings. You correctly identified my sister Jane as the most beautiful girl in the room and I cannot fault your good taste. False flattery is unnecessary."

"I am entirely in earnest: you are a lovely creature and only the blinding pain of a migraine can explain how I so foolishly overlooked it. As you know, I am prone to them, and that evening the noise, light and heat of being in so much company exacerbated my condition. I could barely stand to be there at all, much less dance and make merry. I could not even see you well through the squint of my eyes."

Elizabeth searched his countenance and he could hear her looking for signs of his insincerity. Darcy was careful to leave himself open to her perusal, knowing she required the reassurance of his honest admiration. Again, his heart thundered in his chest as he awaited the conclusion of the deliberation ongoing within her exquisite mind.

I hardly dare believe it, but he seems sincere. His migraines do appear terrible, if what he suffered the other day is any indication. How shameful that I thought him drunk! Moreover, he has gone to great lengths to improve my opinion. That dance…

"Very well, Mr Darcy. I forgive you."

That evening, the Netherfield party was unusually quiet. For once, Hurst was actually asleep and his wife, though she continued to play that same song incessantly in her head, was seated far enough away from Darcy that he could barely overhear it. Miss Bingley, for want of anything else to do, was prowling around the room. She occasionally drew near enough for him to discern her motives—she was conscious that her figure appeared to best advantage when walking and hoped to entice him, as futile as that exercise was—but otherwise left him to the company of Bingley and Miss Bennet by the fire.

As Miss Bennet was well enough to come down after dinner, Darcy had taken his opportunity to observe her while she spoke with Bingley. Her countenance revealed nothing, but her mind was alive with hope and tenderness for his friend. Miss Bennet's affections were still in their infancy, but they were honest. In observing his friend likewise, Darcy could sense that the pair of them were in a great way to be very much in love and it comforted him that there could be no question of Miss Bennet's sincerity. Bingley need not suffer a wife who secretly cared nothing for him.

Darcy's scrutiny transferred from the blushing couple to Elizabeth. In his own case, he was not certain he would be so lucky as his friend. He felt that Elizabeth's opinion of him was shifting for the better, and her attraction to him was undeniable—even if she took pains to hide it —but could it ever be more?

A quick peek up at him from that quarter, followed immediately by a pretty flush in her cheeks, inspired Darcy to excuse himself from Bingley and Miss Bennet's company—they hardly seemed to notice— and cross the room to sit nearer to Elizabeth. She did not look up from her book until he sat down, but he could sense her awareness of him thundering in her head like the tattoo of a rapid heartbeat.

I shall go distracted with him so close.

He felt a great deal of encouragement in that thought but asked only, "What are you reading?"

Elizabeth bit her lip, an endearing habit, and he sensed mischief afoot. "Poetry."

Darcy laughed out loud before checking himself. "Anything good?"

"Wordsworth, so yes. I thank you again for loaning it to me. I might not have had the opportunity to read this so soon had you not brought it with you to Netherfield."

"You are most welcome. A worthy poet and one of my favourites, both for his talent and his preference for my home county. May I?"

Elizabeth handed the slender tome to Darcy and he opened it, reading aloud from the first line.

Darcy's eyes darted back and forth between the verse and Elizabeth's face, watching her as the import of his recitation occurred to her. She became flustered, her cheeks filling with bashful warmth as his borrowed words washed over her and conveyed the depth of his admiration, an admiration he had fruitlessly struggled against since almost their first introduction.

He reads well and his voice is so smooth and melodious. Oh, 'tis too much! He could not, would never...stop it, Lizzy! Guard your heart!

Darcy thrilled at Elizabeth's internal monologue, which strongly hinted that his fears that she could not love him were groundless.

Perhaps, after this, she might reconsider the efficacy of poetry for nourishing an inclination.

"You read it so beautifully, sir," Elizabeth said in a whisper once he was finished.

She would not meet his eyes and so Darcy reached out to touch the back of her hand. She met his gaze as he thanked her for the compliment. Intending to say more, he inhaled deeply and began, "Miss Elizabeth, I—"

"Do let us have a little music," cried Miss Bingley, startling the both of them from their intimate tête-à-tête. Darcy heard the displeasure raging in her mind, though she smiled at him as if she had no notion that he had been wooing another lady in front of her. "Louisa, you will not mind my waking Mr Hurst."

Darcy cursed Miss Bingley and her interference, but supposed the drawing room was not the right place for him to express his sentiments to Elizabeth in any case. She and her sister were meant to leave Netherfield on Sunday after church services, so Darcy determined he must find a moment of privacy with her upon the morrow to say his piece.

CHAPTER FIVE

Though Darcy had feared that orchestrating a private rendezvous with Elizabeth would be difficult, an opportunity presented itself almost immediately after breakfast. It was a drizzly sort of morning, one which promised a day of unpleasant chill, and the kind of weather which often portended another headache. Such was the case presently; Darcy could feel one throbbing between his ears in spite of the powders Bailey had urged him to take. He was determined to ignore it and have his say with Elizabeth.

Elizabeth merely sighed at the view from the breakfast room window before declaring her intent to forego her daily constitutional. "I think I shall settle in with a book instead," she said to her sister, who continued well enough to be downstairs with the rest of the party.

When she stood to leave and make her way to the library, Darcy wiped his mouth quickly and did likewise, knowing this was his chance. "I believe I shall do the same. Excuse me." He bowed to Miss Bennet and Bingley, who were the only ones yet awake besides himself and Elizabeth, and indicated that she should precede him into the hall. Elizabeth blushed prettily and averted her face, but Darcy could clearly hear the thoughts gambolling around in her head.

I shall go distracted! No doubt I shall accidentally choose a treatise on animal husbandry with him so near.

Elizabeth entered the library ahead of him and went directly to the only shelves which actually held books, her attention seemingly fixed on making her selection. Internally, her awareness was all for Darcy and he revelled in knowing the effect he had on her equilibrium. It was much the same as she had on his; in growing affections, they were equal.

Darcy approached her slowly from behind, cognisant that she was presently inclined to be skittish around him, and halted mere inches from her back. His heart and mind pounded in synchronised rhythm, loud in his ears, yet he still heard the catch in Elizabeth's breath when she became aware of his proximity. Lightly, with just the barest touch of his fingertips, Darcy trailed a line down one of her arms.

Elizabeth jumped and whirled around, pressing her back against the bookcase. She looked flushed and winded, not unlike her state upon first coming to Netherfield to tend her sister, but there was an apprehension in her eyes he had not seen there before.

Pray do not tease me, sir, I could not bear it.

"Elizabeth, I…"

Darcy swallowed down his prepared speech about loving her in spite of her lamentable connexions and lack of fortune. His mouth was suddenly too dry to speak, his brain too muddled by the mixture of pain and longing to articulate his ardent feelings for her. All he could do was lean down and press his lips to hers and hope that she understood.

The sensation of kissing Elizabeth was as intense as it was heavenly. Her mouth was soft, if unmoving, and her breath on his cheek was a warm tingle. It was so incredible, almost too much to bear, but so blissfully perfect that he could never withdraw.

And then Elizabeth responded in kind and an entirely new wave of desire surged through Darcy with utmost force. When her trembling lips parted slightly and Darcy felt her timidly place her hand above his pounding heart, he became a tiny boat adrift in a stormy sea of torrential emotion. Longing. Desire. Ardent admiration and love. These potent feelings built to a crescendo in Darcy's mind and—

"Mr Darcy? Mr Darcy, do wake up!"

Darcy's eyelids fluttered erratically as he swam back to consciousness. He could not account for how it had slipped away from him in the first place, he only recalled the sensation of kissing...

Darcy's eyes shot open to the incomprehensible aspect of his dearest, loveliest Elizabeth hovering over him, her features twisted in a confusing mixture of panic and relief. She nibbled on her lip so forcefully that it was turning pink—or had that been a result of their kiss? He could not recall—and appeared to be blinking away tears. "Elizabeth?"

"Mr Darcy!" she cried with feeling, then covered her mouth as if overwhelmed by it. "Are you hurt?"

"Hurt?"

"You collapsed. I know not what happened; you were on the floor before I even realised anything was amiss. How is your head? Are you in pain?"

Darcy considered the state of his head, but found nothing amiss. There was a touch of persistent fuzziness at the edges of his thoughts, but the pain of his headache was gone and his mind cleared further with every passing moment.

Assured that he was well enough in spite of his apparent fainting spell—the humiliation of which he would dwell upon later when he was not charged with comforting Elizabeth in her obvious distress—he turned his attention to the perusal of hers. If he could read Elizabeth's thoughts, he could tailor his responses to better soothe her worries. But there was nothing.

Darcy made another attempt. Elizabeth's mind was rarely silent and worked nearly continuously on some clever thought or another, yet he could hear nothing. His ability, so recently given and often resented, had been taken from him. Raising himself upright, Darcy cradled his forehead in his palm and struggled to engage Elizabeth's mind as he had before, but his brain was empty save for his own thoughts. What one migraine granted him, another apparently revoked.

"Perhaps you should remain lying down, sir." Elizabeth's fretful admonition drew Darcy's gaze back to her. "Or perhaps remove to the sofa? If you cannot stand, I could call for help."

As Elizabeth scrambled to rise from her kneeling position,

hampered by her puddle of skirts, Darcy reached out and stilled her with a hand to her shoulder. She paused and looked to him, eager to help. Or so he assumed.

"I am well enough now, my migraine is gone."

"Another one?"

"Yes. I have been having them frequently of late."

"We should call for Mr Jones, or perhaps a physician. We have none here in Meryton, but Luton does, or we could send to London—"

Darcy stilled Elizabeth's lips with a tender caress from his own. She eased into the kiss, leaning her cheek into his palm when it rose to hold her to him, and much of her tension was released. He lingered there for several seconds, both giving and receiving comfort.

Pulling back the merest inch, Darcy whispered against Elizabeth's mouth, "Marry me."

For a long beat, Elizabeth was silent and Darcy cursed the sudden revocation of his mind reading abilities. Had he been able to hear her thoughts, the wait for her response might not have tortured him so, but instead he was forced to endure the ringing silence. It was untenable.

There was a deep inhale of breath, another bite of her lip, and then Elizabeth gave her answer.

"*Yes.*"

On Sunday morning, as the Netherfield party donned their coats and hats in preparation for church, Darcy was approached by Miss Bennet. Her hand was outstretched and her lovely face was glowing with obvious pleasure, and so he assumed Elizabeth had confided their new understanding to her sister. Darcy took it and they exchanged looks full of meaning and warmth. Even without being able to read her mind, he could sense that she was welcoming him as her new brother.

Miss Bennet's place was succeeded by her sister, who gazed up at him adoringly. *How could I have ever believed Elizabeth's former glances were filled with affection? There is no comparison to how she looks at me now.*

Much as Darcy wished to kiss Elizabeth then and there, it would hardly have been appropriate with so many other people about. He subdued the impulse with a clearing of his throat. "I intend to escort you and Miss Bennet home after services. I need to speak to your father."

"Oh?" Elizabeth tilted her head in a coy manner. "And what can you have to say to him, sir?"

Darcy chuckled and bowed his head nearer to her. "Minx. I hope he is less teasing than you when I ask his blessing to make you my wife."

Elizabeth opened her pert mouth for a new sally but was interrupted by a shriek of utmost outrage. "Your *wife?*"

Grimacing, Darcy looked over his shoulder to where Miss Bingley stood just behind him, apparently eavesdropping on their conversation. She was breathing very fast and her face had turned alarmingly blotchy. "Miss Bingley—"

"You have asked this—this upstart to marry you? Are you out of your senses? After all the attention I have paid you these past two years, currying your favour and that of your insipid sister, you choose to propose to *her*? You are stupider than I thought if you have been taken in by this adventuress's wiles!"

And on she went for several minutes whilst the rest of their party regarded Miss Bingley with horrified astonishment. At length, it apparently occurred to Mrs Hurst to usher her sister up the stairs and out of sight, aided by the firm grip of a footman. Darcy had known that the lady would not take the news of his engagement well, but he had never guessed at the madness lurking within her.

Once Miss Bingley's caterwauling had died down enough to allow someone else to speak, it was awkwardly agreed that the rest of them should continue on to church. After a few mumbled congratulations to the newly betrothed couple, they all exited the house, Elizabeth upon Darcy's arm.

As Bingley was assisting Miss Bennet into the carriage ahead of them, Elizabeth leant closer to Darcy and whispered, "I daresay others will agree with Miss Bingley's sentiments. Does that bother you?"

To which Darcy replied, "I care not for what any of *them* think, Elizabeth. The only opinion which matters to me is yours."

The End

About the Author

Mary Smythe is a homemaker living in South Carolina with a rather useless BA in English collecting dust in a closet somewhere. Mrs Smythe discovered the works of Jane Austen as a teenager and has since gone on to read everything written by Ms Austen at least once yearly, always wishing that there were more.

Also by Mary Smythe

A Faithful Narrative
Dare to Refuse Such a Man
Welcome Home
Pride Before a Fall

The Heart's Consent

Paige Badgett

CHAPTER ONE

THE HEART'S APPARITION

"Miss *Elizabeth* Bennet," Darcy repeated her name back to his butler—spat out like an oath.

"Yes, sir. She is awaiting Miss Darcy in the Lavender Parlour."

How could she? After her rejection of him in Kent last April, her sudden abandonment in Derbyshire in August, and her avoidance of his person at Bingley's wedding to her sister in September—he could not countenance what would bring Miss Bennet to Darcy House. And why request Georgiana to attend to her and not him? Did she have some plan to weave herself back into the fabric of his life? And through Georgiana, no less—the woman had no limits to the pain she was willing to bring to his door.

It did not matter that Darcy had licked his wounds of her rejection multiple times over the last year; time would never change how he felt —even if his love for her had transformed into bitterness and anger today. He had been a besotted fool for far longer.

Rumours of her being courted by a wealthy banker in town the previous autumn had sent him fleeing to Pemberley to avoid seeing her being wooed across London. He saw enough of Bingley to know that she was not betrothed, but he still kept a thoughtful and necessary distance from the woman. Seeing her only wrought disappointment.

"Shall I tell Miss Darcy of her guest?"

"No, Benson. I shall greet her myself."

Darcy marched into the parlour to find Miss Bennet perusing his sister's private collection of books. *No.* She could not just appear on his doorstep. He could not be put through this once again. His heart certainly could not sustain the agony of loving Elizabeth Bennet—not again. Not when he had spent so much time putting himself back in order.

Darcy entered the room in silence, hands behind his back, his eyes fixed on her. She looked up at him, just then, with a warmth he could not allow—even for all its falseness. She could only be there if she needed something, and he could not be the one to provide it to her.

"May I help you with something?" The words that left his mouth may have been all that was proper, but his tone was biting, and he could not find it in himself to stop it. "Perhaps you are lost. Can I find you a hack back to Bingley's?"

He refused to show her his hurt. He stood cold and still, a mirror of his marble flooring.

The shock and surprise at his greeting shone in her eyes—instantly, her beautiful expression withdrew to a place of wariness. She had not expected his cold greeting, but a recognition passed in her eyes, and she averted her gaze.

"Pardon me, Mr Darcy. I should have never come. I see that now."

"Just so." Mockery pervaded his tone.

She raised her eyes in surprise once again, narrowed in concern and then nodded. She looked sad. Was it possible her copper-coloured eyes were made even more beautiful when filled with sorrow?

"Please pass on my apologies to Miss Darcy. Her invitations to visit have been frequent, and I did not want to insult her generosity. I thought it would be worse to continue with excuses. I assure you, I meant you no harm."

That was a surprise. "Georgiana invited you here?"

"I told the butler I was here at the invitation of Miss Darcy. I provided my card."

"Of course. He did say you were here for Georgiana, but since your acquaintance was trifling and you have not seen her since last summer, I assumed—"

"You thought I used your sister's name to see you in private?"

"I was not certain why you were here."

Her wariness was dissipating, and the fire he was long acquainted with was igniting—he recognised it all too well. "I can assure you, sir, that I would not simply arrive uninvited to a gentleman's home."

There it was—that blasted passion that had drawn him to her in the first. He had to extract himself soon, or he would fall to his knees and beg her to reconsider his suit.

She stood more certain of herself now and raised her chin in defiance. "If your silence implies disbelief, let me assure you that I came to see your sister. We spoke only last night—at the opera."

Ah—it had not been since Pemberley since they saw one another.

It was not him she had come to see.

Though he was loath to admit it, her arrival had been as thrilling as it had been enraging. Of course, Georgiana would see her in public if Miss Bennet were staying with her sister in London. Certainly, Caroline Bingley still insinuated herself into Georgiana's life as often as possible. It would only follow that Georgiana and Miss Bennet would be in company.

And here she was, passion and derision emanating from her being, and he had treated her with contempt for merely calling on his sister.

"I shall see myself out, sir. Good day."

And all he could do was nod as Elizabeth Bennet walked out into the cold February air and out of his life once again—perhaps for the last time.

"Miss Bennet!" Mr Coble said as Elizabeth entered the Bingleys' morning room. She was immediately warmed by the room's roaring fire and the early afternoon sun that poured into the small space. The heat of it made her itch to remove her corset. It was stifling. "I thought you were merely to take some air in the garden. We were surprised to hear you took the carriage. Are you well?"

"Thank you for your concern, sir. I am well," Elizabeth responded. It was now or never. Mr Coble was going to ask again for a private conference, and she would not have the luxury of running or excusing herself for air more than once. He had already given her the winter holidays to consider his suit, and she had returned to London. She knew what was expected of her. No young lady could expect more than three marriage proposals. She would surely be put on the shelf, or so society would say. This was likely her last chance; although Jane had told her she was welcome to make her home with them in London, Elizabeth knew it was not fair to burden her new brother by marriage with supporting her.

Her fantastical imagination had led her to believe a tether existed between herself and Mr Darcy. But it had not been real. The gentleman had made that abundantly clear today, notwithstanding his general avoidance of her company. And she needed to face her future —a future that would make everyone happy, perhaps even herself. Mr Coble was a kind, unimposing man. He was not Mr Darcy. Mr Darcy made her blood boil and surge; he made her hot and cold, lost and found. Her world had tipped over on its edge when she finally saw him for who he was at Pemberley the previous summer. And yet, it was not to be. She would never know what his feelings had been then, as they were called home abruptly to support their family as they attempted to find her youngest sister—silly, unthinking Lydia, who had eloped with Mr Wickham from Brighton.

As their carriage had pulled away from Lambton, she had known in her heart that Mr Darcy would be lost to her from that day forward. She never looked at her aunt's note, written in haste to inform the Darcys that they had had to leave the area abruptly. It did not signify; the man she had finally realised was her match, in all the most important ways, was not to be hers. He would never lower himself to marry the sister of his worst enemy.

Their family's reputation was pieced back together by Mr Bingley's return to Hertfordshire last summer and his quick marriage to her eldest sister Jane. It was with the Bingleys that she now stayed in London.

Her uncle had introduced her to Mr Coble in October, putting him forward as a sensible match. Indeed, marrying Mr Coble would be a shrewd choice. Yet today, in the Bingleys' morning room, she had run —not to the park, not to the garden, but to Mr Darcy's house.

Elizabeth had not meant to use Miss Darcy ill, but the truth was, she had hoped to find the girl away from home. It was true that Mr Darcy's sister had invited her to call on numerous occasions; however, Elizabeth had lied about that being her only motive for calling at Darcy House. While she would have happily sat and conversed with Miss Darcy, she had in fact come for *him*. Desiring to be near him. To be in his home. To see what being in his realm would do to her heart. Could she marry Mr Coble knowing her heart still belonged to another?

"Miss Bennet, would you do me the honour of allowing me a private word?"

"Of course, Mr Coble," Elizabeth answered, forcing a smile that felt a violation to her spirit.

Jane smiled warmly in her direction and nodded her approval as she politely exited the room. Bingley had the audacity to wink at her with a wide, happy grin as he closed the doors.

Once they were alone, Mr Coble motioned that she should take a seat in the chair nearest the hearth, and he sat himself upon the chair opposite hers.

"Miss Bennet," he began. "As you know, I have long enjoyed your friendship and have only the deepest respect for you. Though I made my desires known to you in December, I am honoured to share them with you once again."

The nearby windows offered no draught to cool her from the suffocating heat of the fire and his words.

He cleared his throat and looked at her intently. "I wish to make you my wife. As you know, I am more than capable of caring for you and any future children we would be blessed with. And with my recent purchase of Graeton Manor, notwithstanding my house in town, I shall be more than able to keep you in the comfort you are accustomed to—even more so, I hope. You shall have more servants at your disposal in both homes than does your honoured mother at Longbourn."

Elizabeth nodded in a manner she hoped would convey a warmth she did not feel. "The choice of where you will spend your time shall be entirely yours to make. I will, of course, spend much time in town, where you can entertain your sister and friends as you wish. But I hope you will feel at ease to spend your time in the country if that is your wish. In fact, I shall need your guidance greatly to raise the place up from the dilapidated shamble of stone and mortar that stands today. The place needs a woman's touch—inside as much outside. The gardens are in such a sad state..." he trailed off.

"I hope I do not presume too much to think that perhaps you will accept my suit, as you have allowed me to ramble on... simply put, we shall suit one another, Miss Bennet. Our children shall be gently bred and our stations both raised in the world. Should I meet my demise, I have already drawn up a generous settlement to ensure you are always taken care of. I am also in a position to offer dowries for your unwed sisters and all of our daughters, should we be so blessed."

He smiled gently at her and took her nearest hand. "Miss Elizabeth Bennet, what say you? Will you agree to be my wife?"

He had not insulted her intelligence as Mr Collins had done when he proposed, nor had he insulted her family as Mr Darcy had. It appeared fate had intervened to provide her with the sort of marriage proposal she had imagined someday accepting. Yet it was missing something—something she could not name—that intangible knowledge of something feeling right. Instead, her stomach roiled silently deep within her, as if to scream, 'Something feels wrong'. It certainly was not the lack of love, for she had always known that was beyond what she was capable of feeling for Mr Coble.

Did she wish that he had spoken words of love? Even Mr Collins, in his delusion, had spoken of love. And she could not forget Mr Darcy's pronouncement of *ardent* love. This proposal was nothing but rational, sensible reasoning for a marriage partnership. It did not summon her anger, but neither did it engage her heart. The choice was perfectly sensible.

Marrying a gentleman's daughter would make it easier for Mr Coble as he leveraged his fortune to become a landowner in his own right. He was very proud of the small estate he had recently purchased. When she had returned to London a fortnight ago, he had been very pleased to show her a rendering of the manor drawn by a local artist. Mr Coble spoke of gardens and tenants and farming techniques he longed to impose.

He was an intelligent man, a shrewd gentleman whom she could trust to take care of her and their future family. He longed to leave his banking career behind him and join the landed gentry. Elizabeth admired him for his fortitude and hard work. He was a visionary and well respected in town. It would be an honour to be his wife. She could no longer ask the man to delay. He had given her time enough.

"Yes, Mr Coble. I shall be honoured to be your wife."

The moment the words left her lips, her heart rebelled, sending a wash of regret through her that nearly took her breath away.

And in the haze of celebratory words of joy expressed by the Bingleys, she could only think of Mr Darcy.

Regret was not a strong enough word to demonstrate how deeply Darcy felt the loss of Miss Bennet's company once she had departed his elegant townhouse. He stood stock still for nearly half an hour, staring out the window of his study, watching the street below as if he could conjure her up and start the day anew.

He had been cruel. Unfeeling. Blasted harsh. And it tore something within him to imagine that those could be the last words he would ever utter to her in privacy. He may see her in town yet, but there was no world in which he imagined Elizabeth Bennet allowing him a private audience with her ever again.

Damn propriety and honour and society. He wanted to march over to Bingley's house and give her an earful of the pain she had left at his feet. Her first refusal to marry him in Kent had been a tough blow, but even worse was the damnable *hope* he had felt at Pemberley—only to feel the same loss, even more painfully the second time.

But beneath all his anger and bitterness simply lay a man who loved a woman—a gentlewoman of good taste and lively spirits and sparkling wit. A lady whose cleverness had brought him to his knees and had seeped into his veins. And now he had gone and all but thrown her out of his home.

What kind of fool was he? To berate Elizabeth Bennet for showing his sister a kindness? Clearly, he was a madman. No man truly in love would do such a thing. She had once told him that he lacked gentlemanly behaviour, and he had only reinforced her initial impression of him.

He sincerely hoped she had come to call on Georgiana, because if she had indeed come for him, he had likely muddled any sliver of acquaintance that remained. Perhaps he had even now hurt his friendship with Bingley should she pass on word of his abominable behaviour.

It did not take long for Darcy to resolve that the answers were not going to come from pacing about on the thick carpet in his study; and furthermore, his curiosity about her visit was eating him alive.

It was the work of a moment to call for his carriage and depart. The act of leaving his home brought him neither comfort nor consolation. His welcome at Bingley's was uncertain; he had no idea how he would be received upon entering his friend's house after how he had behaved towards his wife's dearest sister.

His rap on the door was quickly answered.

"Thank you," murmured Darcy to Bingley's butler as he removed his hat. "Is the family in?"

"Yes sir, in the morning room." He gestured that Darcy should follow him up the stairs and down the hall.

The doors were opened, and the butler announced him to the room. Darcy's gaze flitted over a smiling Bingley walking towards him with an arm stretched out in front of him in welcome. A quick glance over his friend's shoulders showed a wide-eyed Miss Bennet, lips opening slightly in astonishment.

Darcy wanted to immediately reassure her that he was not the man she had encountered that morning. He was a man capable of affection and forgiveness and compassion. He was generous and gentlemanly, was he not? Despite her surprise to see him, he sent what he hoped would be perceived as a smile of warmth and kindness in her direction.

It did not do the trick, for, if possible, she seemed even more disturbed by his smile. Her mouth trembled, and her eyes glazed over in a nothingness that concerned him. He had much for which to atone.

"Darcy, my friend. You are just in time!" Bingley continued

towards him, while his wife rushed to Elizabeth's side and grabbed her by the elbow to steady her. "We are celebrating!"

Darcy drew his gaze away from Elizabeth's just as Bingley began pumping his arm in welcome.

"And what joyous news do you celebrate today?" Darcy responded in kind.

Movement caught his eye—an unknown gentleman and Miss Bingley moved from the front of the room to join the others nearer to the door as they greeted Darcy.

"My sister is betrothed!" Bingley clapped Darcy on the shoulder. "Come in, my friend."

Bingley pushed on his back and led him to the side table, handing him a fluted glass. "I know it is early in the day, but I daresay the occasion permits it, eh?"

"Thank you," Darcy nodded and tipped the glass in Bingley's direction. He turned to Miss Bingley and wished her joy, then nodded at the well-dressed gentleman to her side. He had no notion who the man was, but it did not signify. He was not there to see Caroline Bingley, nor her betrothed.

"'Tis not my betrothal we are toasting to," Miss Bingley cooed and placed her palm across her chest. She tittered and tutted as she crossed the room to join him and her brother. "It is Eliza to whom you should wish every joy."

The room stopped, and the air in his chest felt shallow. Surely his pull for air was audible.

It is not possible. His gaze went immediately to Elizabeth, watching her intently for a response. Darcy could do little to mask the shock and pain that certainly crossed his face.

As surely as the blood drained from his own face, he watched his beloved grow pale and her eyes seek his—holding strong to his gaze, with a question of her own. He nodded, trying to give an answer to the request in her eyes.

"I wish you joy," Darcy uttered into the void between them, and she fainted outright.

He was forced to grip the back of the chair sat in front of his path to ensure he allowed her betrothed and sister to attend her. It took all his energy to keep his feet rooted to their rightful place—across the room, watching in silence, as she was attended to by Mrs Bingley and the gentleman she had accepted.

He could not betray his true feelings—not now.

In the midst of the upheaval, and once Elizabeth again appeared well, the unknown man suggested that he leave to allow her time to recover and rest. He would depart for Hertfordshire at first light to secure Mr Bennet's approval. Elizabeth requested that he wait a moment so she might pen a note for him to carry to her father.

Darcy remained where he was, following her every move, and likewise, Elizabeth did not take her eyes off of Darcy. Not once.

She sat at an escritoire nearest to the window at the front of the house and wrote a quick note which she handed off to her betrothed with visibly shaking hands. Darcy had to peel his eyes away when the unknown gentleman wished her to rest and take care and kissed her hand.

Can the end of a great love kill a person?

Elizabeth was led out of the room by a worried Jane Bingley.

Darcy murmured wishes for her improved health and took his leave of her.

"I am Mr Coble, and you must be Mr Darcy," the unknown man acknowledged him with a nod. Understanding dawned on Darcy. *He is the banker. That explains his presumption. He is no gentleman. This is who she preferred?*

Mr Coble then took his leave, and Bingley apologised for all the mayhem, escorting Darcy to the door. "Was there something you came to discuss?" he asked absentmindedly while the butler handed Darcy his hat and greatcoat.

"No," Darcy murmured, and he felt some sympathy for his friend, whose concerned eyes followed the lady's voices as they ascended the stairs up to the bedchambers.

"We should have lunch at the club soon," Bingley offered.

To which Darcy could only answer, "Aye," as he nodded his farewells. He could not leave fast enough.

Elizabeth understood Mr Darcy's reaction. It was as if God had provided her a map to navigate his face and manner and tone of voice. He *had* come for her. And he was too late. His sombre countenance radiated through her—standing so severe, only his eyes betraying his hurt.

Had she only delayed her response by one day, perhaps now... No. No, she could not allow her thoughts to tend in that direction. There was no way to know what he thought and felt; her delusion was strong today. After his performance that morning, it was appalling that her heart would whisper anything other than the man's clear disdain for her.

But she felt it true. This was the truth. And then she had to go make such a damnable rash decision. No, not rash—she had made Mr Coble wait so long.

Why did he come now? Why not tell me earlier of his wishes? The look of shock on his face had nearly made her cry out!

What would her father think of her note?

"Lizzy, dear, please lie down," Jane instructed. "You gave us all such a fright!"

She begrudgingly took a seat on her bed. "I am sure I was only overwhelmed by the occasion. Or perhaps Rosie laced my corset too tightly this morning."

"Poor Mr Darcy," Jane said softly.

"Pardon?"

Jane looked at her sympathetically. "He did tell you he loved you once, did he not?"

"That he did."

"But that was ages ago," Jane said, waving the thought away with her hand.

Only eleven months. Less than a year. "Yes, ages ago," Elizabeth agreed half-heartedly.

"Where did you go this morning? I was concerned when you left the house without any notice."

"I only needed a moment to myself. I knew Mr Coble would propose today. He implied as much last night at the opera."

"And you felt it too cold for a walk?"

Jane was apparently disinterested in her vague replies.

"I simply took a turn about Mayfair."

"And are you happy, my dear? Are you well pleased with the outcome?"

Elizabeth nodded and squeezed her sister's hand. Jane desperately wanted everyone to be as happy as she was, and Elizabeth would never deny her sister's pleasure—only her own, as it happened.

CHAPTER TWO
THE HEART'S DISCONTENT

Darcy was too late. She had come to Darcy House for him. Not to insert herself into his life to make him miserable as he had first thought—she came for *him*. He was certain of it. The look of desperation in her eyes, before she fainted, had communicated all he needed to know. Elizabeth had come to his home, and he threw her out, and she left to accept another man. He pounded his fist on the soft velvet seat of his coach as he rode through Mayfair. He had made a complete muddle of everything.

Could he blame her? Had he finally decided to propose to another lady, would he have been able to make an offer before seeing Elizabeth's lovely face one more time? Without making one last attempt to secure her heart? Never. He completely understood. And now all hope was lost. All he could look forward to now were stolen glances of another man's wife.

His younger sister was alighting her carriage when his own conveyance arrived back at Darcy House. She gifted him with an encouraging smile he could not reciprocate no matter how hard he tried. An offer of tea was accepted, and he went through the motions, attempting to be gentle with *one* woman he loved that day.

Georgiana displayed such care and aplomb for navigating society that he could not reconcile that she was the same young lady who had nearly eloped two summers prior—returning to him broken hearted and lacking any confidence.

The lady now sitting across from him made him proud—her bearing regal and kind. He had, at first, begrudged her decision to have her first Season in town. His original plans for Bingley to wed his sister were dashed by the former Jane Bennet, and rightly so—they were a lovely couple and by all outward appearances, very happy. At least he had done one thing right by Elizabeth Bennet.

"Brother, what troubles you?"

"I am perfectly well, thank you." He lied through his teeth.

"What nonsense. You think I do not recognise the discomfort of my own brother?"

He relented. "How observant you are. Yes, well, I find myself rather discomfited in town. I would rather be in the country."

"This is my first Season!" she cried. "And we have only just arrived. We cannot escape to Pemberley so soon. Our aunt has spent so much time in her preparations for me. There would be talk. Perhaps you should take advantage of our time here? Come with me to the theatre or attend a ball."

He growled in response and threw his head back against the chair, closing his eyes to her encouragement.

"Come now. There are many lovely ladies who would be honoured to partner with you in a dance or promenade on your arm in the park."

She had the right of it. He should consider marrying now. "Perhaps I should consider meeting some young ladies."

Georgiana's eyes went wide with excitement, and she responded eagerly, "Of course! I shall be very happy to introduce you to some ladies of good standing and fortune. It is time you considered marriage."

"You sound like Lady Catherine."

"Well then," Georgiana replied playfully, "you could skip all this fanfare and simply offer for our cousin Anne."

"Never."

She laughed lightly and moved to sit nearer to him. "Of course not."

Almost a week later, absorbed in the crowd of yet another ball,

Darcy found himself listening to the tittering of an Irish heiress he had been introduced to—a Miss McGinnis, perhaps. Even so, his eyes only searched the crowd for Elizabeth. His heart felt void of any feelings for the ladies put before him. The *ton* had responded almost immediately to his efforts. After one ball where he danced every set and accepted all introductions, his sister had become overrun with morning callers. Mothers and brothers accompanied their marriageable sisters under the pretence of visiting their 'dear Miss Darcy', although the sheer number of new friends to his sister seemed to shout to the world that Mr Darcy was finally ready to take a wife.

And he did intend to, although his heart was not in it.

He excused himself from the young heiress—Miss McAdams, was it?—to find his sister.

"Georgiana, I appreciate your efforts," he whispered over her shoulder, "but some of these ladies are far too young for my taste. The last should be put back in the schoolroom, should she not? She could not be above sixteen."

"Miss Mackenzie is nearly three years my senior, brother. I believe she reaches her majority this year."

"Perhaps it is I who has become too old."

"You are too hard on yourself."

"And you are far too generous," he said, squeezing the hand Georgiana had rested on his arm. "But these ladies, they do feel young—far too inexperienced, surely, to imagine as the mistress of Pemberley."

Georgiana's light laughter could be felt more than heard in a room crowded with too many people. "These ladies are all of age, and you are perfectly situated to seek a wife among them."

Darcy suppressed his desire to roll his eyes.

"What did you think of Miss Hawkins? I thought she may be to your liking."

"Too quiet."

"And what of Miss Matthews?"

"Too tall."

Georgiana nudged him, "Lady Victoria has a light and pleasing figure. If I am not mistaken, she dances very beautifully."

"She had nothing of import to say. Rather dull if you ask me."

"What need do the aristocracy have for fervour, Brother?" Georgiana snickered. "I am of a mind to suggest that you have an incomparable lady against which all others are being judged. My question of you then is, does she breathe or does she exist in your mind alone?"

Darcy sighed and told his sister he was ready to depart.

"The night is young, and my dance card is yet full."

Darcy nodded solemnly and took himself off to the established card room.

Elizabeth entered the breakfast room, cautiously avoiding her sister's eye. Jane had been distraught since Bingley received a letter from Mr Coble informing him that Mr Bennet had not given his consent for the marriage. Mr Coble had gone on to his estate to establish a steward and promised to return to town in a few short weeks. He also sent assurances that he would wait for Elizabeth to reach her majority in March. The gentleman was without doubt that she would consent to the marriage with or without her father's blessing at that time.

Elizabeth had not the heart to tell her sister that her father's refusal did not surprise her in the least. Her note had begged him to withhold his consent. She was somewhat surprised she had not received a letter from him requesting more details about why she had proposed such a farce, but he was a self-acknowledged poor correspondent. Although Mr Bennet never was one to involve himself in the private matters of his daughters, it was likely he found it all amusing. Perhaps he, like Mr Collins, assumed she was increasing Mr Coble's love by suspense.

"My dear, you must eat," Jane remarked, shooing her like a mother hen to the nearest chair. "I am certain our father had reason for his refusal, though I cannot fathom it. Charles is of a mind to ride to Hertfordshire himself to ascertain the purpose of this delay."

Elizabeth nodded. She could not lie to Jane. She could not tell her dearest sister that she herself had sabotaged her own future. How could she explain that in the face of Mr Darcy's reaction to her betrothal, she had felt desperate to destroy all possibilities of marriage to another man—without any clear assurance that the gentleman she desired to devote herself to had any wish to make her his wife.

Elizabeth attempted to appear saddened, but she could not help but be relieved that Mr Coble had given her father the note.

"Let us find some way to amuse ourselves," Elizabeth said brightly to Jane. "Perhaps the theatre or a concert—what invitations do we have this week?"

"Lizzy!" Jane responded. "What if Mr Coble heard of our going out in society as if nothing is wrong? No. Charles and I feel we should wait for his return. We cannot give him anything negative to remark upon when he arrives in town. We cannot have him thinking you are out in society seeking another suitor."

Gone was her hope. Elizabeth felt her future was out of her control.

Darcy pulled at his gloves. The ball given by Lord and Lady Amtower was a complete crush. The ballroom was full of young ladies with cheeks aglow and gentlemen too fond of their own voices. All in all, it was the definition of misery. It was the fifth ball he had agreed to attend since Elizabeth's engagement to another, and he was nowhere closer to finding his own bride.

No sooner had he considered telling his aunt and Georgiana that he must excuse himself due to a headache than he saw Elizabeth's betrothed spin across the dance floor with a young lady he had been introduced to the week before—a Miss Evanston, he believed.

She had a maturity about her he could like. Her lightly freckled face, set off by her curly red hair, made her stand out in the crowd of stiff coiffures and milky pale faces that were accustomed to being hidden under a bonnet from the sun's rays. Her connexions and fortune were near to none, though she be a gentleman's daughter. Her position in society rather reminded Darcy of Elizabeth. By birthright, she was a gentlewoman, but she was not of his circle.

Darcy watched Mr Coble escort the young lady from the dance floor to the refreshment table. Miss Evanston was clearly flattered by his attentions. Perhaps the young miss was unaware of his recent engagement.

"Are you watching someone in particular?" Darcy nearly jumped to hear his sister speaking to him just over his shoulder.

"No, dear."

"Are you plotting an escape?" She laughed lightly.

He sighed. "I cannot see why you are required to attend so many of these events."

"It is less that I am required to attend and more that I enjoy the society, even if many of the events are a complete bore."

"I could have deferred your entrance into society, you know."

Georgiana's only response was a knowing smile. They had had this conversation many times, and each time she reassured him that she shared her aunt's wishes. She was ready to be out and enjoyed the greater society to be found in London.

Darcy had always thought her quite shy, but perhaps he had been wrong. Maybe it was he who always encouraged her appearance of reticence. Perhaps she had been emulating his own behaviour and felt stifled by their quiet life.

Whatever the reason, the choice to have her first Season had been right. His sister may not be ready to settle down in marriage, but she was making new friends and enjoyed the amusements of town.

Rarely in want of a partner, Georgiana wished him a lovely evening and left him to find her next.

Darcy warily scanned the room for the Bingleys. If *he* was in attendance, then surely, they were too.

Head pounding and lungs begging for fresh air, Darcy gathered his things and called for his carriage. He had no interest in seeing Miss Bennet with her betrothed and felt lucky to escape before the infernal awkwardness of seeing her on his arm.

After two weeks with no word from Mr Coble, Jane finally relented and agreed to visit the theatre. "He must be quite busy preparing the house for a new mistress," she said reassuringly to Elizabeth, while straightening her gloves. The queue of carriages must have wrapped around all of London for how long they waited to exit their conveyance.

Elizabeth felt awful for allowing her sister to worry for her. It felt all wrong to keep something of this magnitude from Jane.

After settling into the Bingleys' box, her eyes settled on the person she wished most to see in all of London—Mr Darcy. Even from so far away, his strong bearing and intelligent gaze calmed her. Surely Charles had told him about this business of her father refusing Mr Coble's suit? Perhaps tonight she would have the opportunity to show him she was not hurt by it—in fact, she was pleased. A soft smile settled across her own face, and she waited for him to look across the theatre so she might share her contentedness with him in a glance.

It was quite impossible, though, to gain his attention with so many visitors to his box. Elizabeth leant forward so she could get a better view of who was visiting the Darcys.

"Hm," Caroline murmured. Elizabeth did not care what had upset her, though she did mind when the feathers from the lady's headdress blocked her vision so thoroughly that she could no longer see Mr Darcy.

"And how am I to compete with that?" Elizabeth heard Caroline mutter.

"Pardon me?" she asked her quietly.

"All those baby-faced debutantes, Eliza," Caroline whispered and turned to face her. "The man is surrounded by heiresses, and they are not there for Georgiana's sake." She nodded knowingly and gestured across the theatre.

Elizabeth then took another look at the Darcy box, and devastation settled into her stomach. Caroline, much to Elizabeth's chagrin, was correct. The box was full of visitors, but the small crowd was predominantly London's newest ladies of marriageable age—all glistening jewels and pale silk gowns.

"I am sure you are wrong. They must be friends of Miss Darcy," she said, more for her own sake than for Caroline's.

"I highly doubt that," Caroline whispered and took to fanning herself. "Ah! Edwina is here! I do hope her handsome brother has escorted her." She quickly left to greet her friend before the performance began.

Elizabeth wished she could forget the hordes of ladies visiting Mr Darcy as quickly as Caroline had done. Of course, Caroline could be dismissive. She cared very little for the man and much more for what being *Mrs Darcy* could mean for her status. If she actually loved the gentleman, it would pain her as it did Elizabeth. Caroline would never have been so foolish as to refuse an offer of marriage from him.

Why ever did she put off Mr Coble! Mr Darcy was not going to renew his addresses! What man of his standing would? This impossible dream she had been chasing was becoming bleaker by the hour. He was certainly not seeking to check on her countenance from across the theatre. He was entirely unbothered by her continued unmarried status! He had too many visitors to care, to say nothing of Elizabeth's lack of pedigree, fortune, or connexions.

During the interval, Elizabeth claimed a need to refresh herself in order to escape the crush of theatregoers and dismiss her unrelenting nerves. She walked away from the crowd, towards the direction of an open window she spied at the end of an empty corridor.

A gentleman was immediately in her path, having stepped out from behind where a large potted plant had hidden him from her view. She had to stop short in her quick strides to avoid colliding with him.

Oh—the man was Mr Darcy.

"Pardon me," he stammered whilst grabbing her arm to stabilise himself and steady her in return. His eyes went wide with surprise when he saw that it was she. Elizabeth's senses were all alerted to the sensation of his hand on her arm and a jolt of desire and recognition poured through her. She wished that he always would be so near. Their eyes locked, she laughed gently at the scene.

"Were you hiding, Mr Darcy?"

He sighed. "You have found me out."

He blushed and smiled at her—a hint of embarrassment in his eyes. This only amused Elizabeth more, and she sympathised with his position.

"You must allow me to apologise for my abominable behaviour the morning you called on Georgiana," he said warmly.

His hand on her arm had been overlooked, surely, for it remained in its place, bringing her comfort and relieving her former apprehensions.

"It is forgotten. I assure you."

"Even so—" he protested.

"No, sir. Please do not concern yourself. I am well," she assured him. "Though I must wonder whether or not you are well, hiding as you are."

He smiled in return. Banter was the way to this man's heart, she believed.

"I am in a sad state, am I?" An informality she could only like laced his words.

"How disappointed the young ladies of London must be to find you missing!" she teased.

She had said the wrong thing. All amusement drained from his face, and he tugged at his cuffs, clearing his throat. He backed away from her. "Should you not be with Bingley or your betrothed? They cannot like you roaming about all alone." Gone was the warmth of mere moments before.

He thinks me betrothed. "I have accompanied Charles and my sisters."

"Of course," he responded. "I shall keep you no longer."

And then he was gone, all haughty and forbidding—but she knew better than to accept that those were his true feelings. She could only imagine how she would behave were the tables turned.

Miss Anna Hawkins answered most questions with a polite nod. Darcy's attempt at conversation made him appear loquacious in contrast to her blush-tinted cheeks and inability to look at his person as he guided her across the dance floor. She was lovely, but a man could not choose a wife who had never uttered more than a syllable in his direction.

Halfway through the set, Darcy gave up all efforts to engage the young lady in conversation. What was Georgiana thinking putting this young lady forward as a viable option for a life partner?

It roiled Darcy to imagine there were other men of his age examining his own young sister in the same manner. Georgiana was clear that she was not ready to wed, but of course marriage is why a young lady had a come out, was it not? She was considered marriageable by society regardless of her preferences. Fortunately, Lady Matlock was a keen chaperon who was of the same mind as Darcy, and he trusted her implicitly.

He separated from his partner in a figure that brought him up the line, passing the other gentlemen dancing the current set. Unfortunately, Mr Coble was one of the gentlemen in the set, which meant Elizabeth would not be far...she could, in fact, be dancing with the gentleman at this very moment. Darcy's eyes did a quick inventory of the ladies in the set and was relieved to see that she was not there. When Mr Coble and his partner took the same turn in the pattern, Darcy noticed it was once again the country beauty, Miss Evanston, who was Mr Coble's partner.

He could not like Mr Coble's manner with the young lady. He held her hand longer than the dance required and repeatedly leant in too close, causing the lady to blush.

Why would the man would show a preference for another impoverished landowner's daughter? Mr Coble's ties to trade and wealth, in parallel with his interest in women who were in no position to choose their husbands, was obvious to anyone who was paying the barest attention. It was a fine way to elevate oneself, to say nothing of it being necessary for a man like him. And yet, having one lady's agreement in marriage and then continuing to parade your preferences all over town? It was abominable.

Perhaps there was a familial tie that Darcy was unaware of. But still... it felt wrong. It felt like a breach of gentlemanly behaviour when one was betrothed—especially the possessive smile that the gentleman shared with the lady as he steered her off the dance floor.

At once, Darcy was brought back to the present and had his wits about him enough to politely thank Miss Hawkins for the dance and return her to her mother. He immediately made his excuses and set off to find Bingley.

It was odd. Mr Coble was seen all over town dancing with the same lady; yet he had not accompanied Elizabeth, er, Miss Bennet to the theatre. Darcy had not been able to take his eyes off of her that night, especially after their private interlude, and had been thankful Mr Coble was not there. But now he felt affronted, for *her* sake.

He approached a group of gentlemen and asked after Bingley. None had seen him in attendance. He checked the terrace, the card room, and the dining room. He never saw Bingley nor his wife or sisters. His next course of action was to seek out Mr Coble himself.

The man was easy enough to find. He was handing a glass of punch to Miss Evanston and excusing himself with an exaggerated bow.

Darcy nodded as he approached the shorter man. "Mr Coble," he began. "Where is our friend Bingley?" He hoped to glean some intelligence as to why the man was once again not accompanying his betrothed.

"Damned if I know," the man huffed. "I have not seen the family since the last I saw you."

"I beg your pardon?"

Mr Coble leant in Darcy's direction and quietly said, "Bennet refused my suit. From what I had heard of the man, I had not expected him to exert himself except to sign the settlement papers, if you take my meaning."

Darcy froze and had to remind himself to breathe. "You are not engaged."

It was not a question.

"For now. Bennet will have nothing to say in three short weeks when Elizabeth reaches her majority. The insult will be set to rights soon enough."

Darcy swallowed his emotions and provided no response—he could not—not after the man uttered her Christian name. Mr Coble took no notice of his reaction and added, "Bingley shan't worry for her reputation. My good fortune was not achieved by allowing men to manoeuvre me, and I do not intend that Bennet will be the first. I do not walk away from investments I have nurtured just when they are about to turn a profit from my influence, you see."

Darcy did see. And he did not like the way Coble spoke of Elizabeth, nor that he spoke to him in such a casual way after only one meeting. Surely, she did not desire to be this man's wife!

Darcy found his disregard for Elizabeth and her father an affront, but he could not lose himself in his anger—such intelligence was full of hope and possibilities.

Coble did not have consent to marry her, and Darcy would do what he could to ensure he never did—but only if that is what Elizabeth wanted as well. He too considered her a prize but did not feel he was owed anything from her that she did not wish to give.

CHAPTER THREE
THE HEART'S CONSTANCY

"Good morning, Mr Darcy. What a pleasant surprise," Jane said the next morning as she welcomed their unexpected guest into the breakfast room. He did not accept the offer to join them at the table, insisting that he had already eaten.

Elizabeth was taken aback by his manner—Mr Darcy was all smiles for her and Jane. Caroline would be furious when she came down later in the morning and found she had missed his visit. The thought brought a mischievous smile to Elizabeth's lips. So much for keeping fashionable hours.

Mr Darcy appeared impatient and could not seem to decide what to do with his hands. He straightened his cuffs, put his hands in his pockets, ran his fingers through his hair—the man seemed positively overwrought in his eagerness to see his friend. He would no doubt be pacing the room soon enough if Charles did not show himself quickly.

Elizabeth was amused by his peculiar cheerfulness and hid her grin behind her teacup. Something was amiss, and yet, when his eyes lingered on her person too long, she could not find it in herself to care. She held his gaze and smiled brightly back at him.

Concern shadowed Jane's expression. Mr Darcy's behaviour was not entertaining her in the least. "Please, sir, let me offer you some coffee or tea while you wait for Charles to join you."

He took a seat and acquiesced to Jane's offer for coffee. Elizabeth watched as he drummed his fingers on the tabletop, pretended not to stare at her, and then nearly leapt from his seat when Charles finally joined them in the breakfast room. Mr Darcy begged a private audience, and off they went to the study, leaving the ladies full of unanswered questions.

The next afternoon found Elizabeth still consumed with curiosity as she attempted to read a novel in the drawing room. To her knowledge, Charles had provided no intelligence about Mr Darcy's visit the day before.

Jane found occupation in the form of sewing, and Caroline was allowing audible sighs to escape her as she waited in vain for friends to return her calls. Elizabeth was about to retreat to the meagre library for a new book when the butler arrived to announce Miss Darcy to the room.

"We are so glad you are come, Georgiana! Take a seat over here by the fire with me," Caroline spoke enthusiastically to their guest.

Overzealous would be an apt description of Caroline's welcome to Bingley's townhouse. Expecting to see some fear and apprehension from Miss Darcy, Elizabeth was relieved to find only acceptance and goodwill. *My, how she has changed since last summer! London has been good for her.*

Jane serenely guided the conversation to include herself and Elizabeth after ordering refreshments for their guest.

Elizabeth could only be happy Caroline had finally surrendered to Jane presiding as hostess over her own home. Once the Netherfield lease had gone up, the newly married couple had taken a house in town, and Caroline had been eager to join them. Early on, she had been a challenge to Jane's authority, but that had since passed. She was welcome to live with the Hursts but had chosen to remain with the Bingleys when Mrs Hurst had 'inconveniently' found herself with child.

Elizabeth surmised Caroline ought to find herself a husband before Jane too brought a small, needy nuisance into the world. Jane would deny it, but Elizabeth suspected an announcement was soon all but certain.

Elizabeth interrupted a conversation about Caroline's new bonnet to ask, "Is your family all in good health, Miss Darcy?"

"Yes, Miss Bennet."

"Have you any exciting plans for amusements while you are in town?"

"Yes, there are many entertainments."

Elizabeth's presumption was unhindered by the brevity of Miss Darcy's replies. "Will you attend any upcoming balls?"

"I am excited about the Brownsbury Ball on Thursday."

"We have also received an invitation and have accepted."

Miss Darcy smiled and nodded.

"And will your brother be escorting you?"

"Elizabeth!" Caroline gasped and clutched her hand to her chest as if to fight off a fit of apoplexy. *Rather overdoing it,* Elizabeth thought.

"My, how direct you are today, Eliza." Caroline turned to Miss Darcy. "I must beg your pardon. My *sister's* sister displays her country manners unapologetically, does she not?"

Miss Darcy looked somewhat amused by the statement, a knowing smile on her lips. "There is no need to apologise. I, too, was raised in the country."

"But Longbourn is nothing to Pemberley!" Caroline protested.

"I am sure Miss Darcy can withstand my questions," Elizabeth said lightly.

Miss Darcy smiled warmly at Elizabeth. "My aunt is most often my chaperon. However, my brother has been keen to attend many events as of late."

After Miss Darcy's departure, Caroline forgot about her vexation at Elizabeth's impertinence; she was in raptures about the honour of the visit and the revelation that Mr Darcy indeed was seeking to be married.

"The rumours are true," Caroline tutted. "I assumed the scene at the theatre a strange happenstance, but he truly is seeking a wife! I heard he attended the Vanata Ball last week and danced every set. I told Edwina she exaggerated, but perhaps it was true!" Caroline looked both hopeful and defeated. And Elizabeth could only agree.

"I have no idea why *now*, but I shall speak to my brother at once," Caroline continued. "We cannot have his dearest friend trapped by some little upstart, can we? Some debutante seeking to raise herself in the world! They will take advantage of his trusting ways. I say, if it is society he wants, he should do so with his friends by his side."

Elizabeth's eye roll went undetected, by design. Caroline offering herself as chaperon to a man well-seasoned in society was the definition of absurd. Mr Darcy should fear Caroline's aspirations above all! Elizabeth herself certainly feared Caroline's ambitions—as she did those of all the other ladies thrust into Mr Darcy's notice.

Her mind whispered that it was her own actions that spurred him to seek a marriage. What absurdity! A man of his standing did not require Elizabeth Bennet to be off the marriage mart in order to finally seek his own partner. *No—what a ridiculous notion. That my choice would have any bearing on such a man!*

And yet…the voice inside whispered that perhaps there was still a chance.

"How was your visit with the Bingleys this afternoon?" Darcy asked Georgiana over dinner that night.

"Very fine." Georgiana seemed more attentive to her meal than the conversation.

"And is the family all in good health?"

"Yes, I believe so."

"Any news from that quarter?"

Georgiana stopped cutting her meat and set down her utensils quietly. "Nothing truly of note. We discussed a new milliner that Miss Bingley has discovered as well as upcoming events in town."

"Such as?"

Georgiana made a face of frustration. "The Brownsbury Ball."

"Ah," Darcy responded, trying not to appear too eager for information. "Will they all attend?"

Why this seemed to both annoy and amuse Georgiana was beyond him.

"Yes, I believe they plan to attend."

Georgiana then stood and excused herself, claiming a desire to retire early. Darcy could hardly be surprised at her fatigue; they had been out late in the evenings at various events thrice that week. He stood and bade her to sleep well.

Just as he was about to reclaim his seat, his sister poked her head back into the room to say, "Oh! When I told our friends that we expect to attend the ball, Miss Bennet asked particularly after you and enquired about your attendance." She raised her eyebrows in his direction—mischievous smile intact—and disappeared back into the hall.

Hope seized him. She is not engaged—even Bingley had confirmed that much. *And now she is asking after me.*

Surely, he had a chance. She was too good to trifle with him.

Darcy had warned Bingley about the fickle Mr Coble; his friend was surprised to hear that the man was returned to town. His constancy clearly was in question, and Bingley appeared at a loss for explanations.

Hoping not to encourage any drastic action, Darcy recommended that Bingley send a note around to Mr Coble to welcome him back to town; it was better to not upset the man, Darcy had advised.

His own motives were different. He wanted Mr Coble seen for who he was—a grasping interloper. But he did not want Bingley forcing him to make any promises to Elizabeth Bennet. Darcy hoped any concern for Mr Coble would soon be unnecessary.

"See here, Elizabeth—" Charles joined the ladies in the drawing room the next day. "I have a note here from Coble. Says he is in London and requests the honour of escorting you to the Brownsbury Ball."

Feigning joy at the request, Elizabeth responded appropriately, knowing the note brought them both pleasure. "Thank you, Charles. I shall be happy to have Mr Coble join our party."

"His dedication to you is commendable." Jane clearly was relieved that her sister's suitor had not been put off by being refused by their father.

Elizabeth still had not the heart to tell her the truth of it. She was embarrassed enough with the knowledge that her father's withheld blessing was her own doing. It was time to let go of girlish fantasies that Mr Darcy could read her mind. It was too late.

She deeply regretted her inaction during the previous opportunities she had to tell him of her altered wishes. She could have told him of her growing feelings at her sister's wedding. That would have been a better time. But she had been too ashamed of the financial support Bingley and her uncle had been forced to put forward to save Lydia's reputation after her elopement. She had been unable to even make eye contact with Mr Darcy at the church or the wedding breakfast. And now she was only full of regret.

Later that week, Elizabeth found herself on Mr Coble's arm entering the grand Brownsbury ballroom in Mayfair. It was suspected that the ball was to be one of the grandest of the Season. Many of fashion and of rank were rumoured to be attending. Proud to be in attendance, but none too happy with her current partner, Elizabeth tried to put on a happy face as they greeted their hosts and made their way into the throngs of people.

"What beautiful flowers," Elizabeth said to Mr Coble as they made their way through the crowd. He had said very little since arriving at Bingley's townhouse to escort her.

"Hm," he responded with a nod.

Elizabeth spoke again, "The room is quite grand, though I am doubtful it can hold so many people as we saw arriving. I believe half of London is in attendance."

They must have some conversation, should they not? Mr Coble seemed unusually short with her. The latest in her barrage of dull comments went unanswered.

"Ah," Elizabeth made one more friendly attempt. "I believe I spy Mr and Mrs Bates across the room. Shall we go greet them?"

"Do you not hear the band tuning for the first set?" Mr Coble replied. His words were soaked with irritation.

Perhaps silence was a better method.

"Elizabeth," Charles spoke over the loud voices in the room. "I should like to dance with you this evening. Is your first set available? Hurst has already secured Jane for the first, and I must have my share of the fun."

"Elizabeth shall dance the first with me," Mr Coble responded, before she had a chance to reply.

Based on his peculiar mood, Elizabeth was surprised to hear that he intended to dance with her at all. Perhaps he was well. She teased gently, "Shall I? I do not see any names on my dance card."

The gentleman did not look at her but continued to scan the crowd. "I did not imagine your card so full that it was necessary to claim my set formally."

Elizabeth could feel her skin heat with embarrassment.

Bingley, ever cheerful, broke into the awkwardness to write his name on her dance card with a calming smile and an encouraging nod. She could not have found a more exemplary brother should she have chosen him herself.

Everything about the evening seemed to annoy Mr Coble. She had never seen him so peevish!

She must write to her father and tell him to relieve Mr Coble of his worries and get on with their betrothal, for she could not countenance his petulant manner much longer. She had been entirely too childish. It was time she made right with the man who had much to offer her.

In his eagerness, Darcy had required much attention from his valet in his preparations for the ball. He smirked to recall the look on Johnson's face as he swapped waistcoats four different times. The effort had been worth it. As he joined Georgiana, she told him he looked well in his gold brocade waistcoat and blue jacket. He certainly had tried to put his best foot forward.

Georgiana looked resplendent in her soft cream gown with gold embroidery. They looked quite the pair, and Darcy thought his parents would have been well pleased with them.

Whether they would have been as pleased with his selection of a wife was another conversation entirely. Perhaps his father would have approved, but it was likely that his mother, Lady Anne, would have had higher expectations of his wife's ancestry.

The truth of the matter was that Darcy had the advantage of choice

—and he hoped Elizabeth would accept him this time. He had a mind to convince her that night but remained concerned that the result could be the same as the first. Still, he was cautiously optimistic.

Although they arrived after the dancing had begun, Darcy was immediately a hunted man—by the soft-spoken debutantes, the coy widows, and the insistent mothers. He had made his desire to find a wife apparent in the last month, and now he found it difficult to breathe amidst the incessant attentions. Once he finally succeeded in making his way through the throng of fervent ladies, he found the ballroom.

Georgiana was busy greeting friends and filling her dance card. Darcy scanned the room eagerly. His object was soon found, and his heart seized to see her dancing with Mr Coble.

Damn Bingley. He should not have spoken to his friend. The man likely orchestrated this reunion for Elizabeth.

The card room was overly smoky and the terrace full of partygoers seeking air, so Darcy sought a small alcove off the main corridor to catch his breath and form a plan.

His first proposal to Elizabeth had been a complete failure. He had rehearsed the words for days, but what good had that done him? Darcy knew he was better off speaking to her from the heart, but at his core, he was a man who preferred to be prepared. He had no desire to leave the outcome up to chance.

If he could secure a dance with Elizabeth, he would use that time to elaborate on all her fine characteristics, speak pretty words about her beauty, and, if necessary, grovel. She was a lady worthy of being pleased. He would leave her with no doubt of his devotion.

The music ended, and Darcy resolved that he was ready. As he moved to exit the small space, he ran directly into a young lady ducking into the alcove. *Elizabeth!* Like a siren, she drew him to her. Was it not so? They kept running into each other, quite literally, as if fate was forcibly telling them to get on with it!

"Mr Darcy!" Elizabeth gasped and put a hand to her heart.

"Pardon me, Miss Bennet."

"No apologies necessary, sir. I was moving too quickly for my own good."

He braced her shoulders to steady her. She seemed out of sorts.

"Are you well?"

"Do I seem unwell?" She smiled and laughed lightly. "Are you hiding once again?"

"Am I that obvious?"

In the dim light, she seemed to relax. "By some trick of fate, this is the second time I have found you thus!"

"'Tis true. I needed a moment to myself."

He had not removed his hands from her shoulders, and she had not moved away from him.

"I was just leaving to look for you," he offered.

"For me?"

"Might I secure a dance with you this evening?"

She seemed surprised by the request, as if she had been expecting him to say something else. "Oh! Of course. Would the supper set do?"

It would do perfectly. "Yes, I would be honoured."

He dropped his arms from her shoulders and took up her wrist so he might write his name onto her dance card. His thumb drew little circles onto the inside of her wrist, and he felt her pulse quicken. Once he had jotted his name down, he lifted her hand to his lips, leaving her with a long kiss on her gloved hand that he hoped would convey all the deep emotions left unsaid between them.

As if compulsively drawn to her, he reached out to brush her cheek and relieve her worries, for her concern and hope were written all over her face.

Over her shoulder, he made eye contact with Mr Coble as he stalked into the alcove with a gleam of anger in his eyes. Darcy dropped his hands, and Elizabeth followed his gaze to face Mr Coble.

"Elizabeth, I would speak to you now," Mr Coble fairly growled in her direction.

Darcy felt helpless as he watched her be dragged off by the elbow in a manner that summoned all his anger and resentment over his own position. She had accepted *that* man's request of marriage. Though it angered him, he had to acknowledge her choice until he had a chance to ascertain whether she would welcome his suit instead.

Mr Coble threaded Elizabeth's arm through the crook of his elbow and placed a possessive hand atop her own. He led her with haste through the crowded ballroom and out onto a darkened terrace. If she were not so relieved to find the crisp, cool air of early March, she might have been frightened by his severe countenance.

"Thank goodness for Miss Bingley sending me to your aid, for that man will only make a mockery of you! Dragging you into a private alcove and speaking to you in such a friendly manner when you are betrothed to another!"

Elizabeth was taken aback by his frankness and accusations, notwithstanding his irritability all evening. "You and I are *not* betrothed," she responded simply.

This seemed only to increase his ire. "You have accepted my proposal, and we shall wait the fortnight until you reach your majority so that we may properly announce our engagement. I have devoted myself to securing you for above four months. I did not become a successful man of business by mere luck! I have done my research, found the appropriate wife, and devoted the time into securing your hand. Your family requires the security I can provide, and I need a gentlewoman for a wife. I have put in the work. I beg you, do not tell me you have reconsidered. Not now."

"Perhaps I shall! My affection is not a loan you can call in, sir. I resent that you see me as a mere business transaction!"

"What is marriage but a transaction?"

Elizabeth's eyes turned back toward the ballroom.

"Do not tell me you suffer from some infatuation with Mr Darcy. You are far too astute."

"That is enough, sir." She spoke quietly, hoping to prevent him from making a scene.

"Is this why you asked me to give you time back in December?"

Elizabeth looked away, wishing he had not left the doors to the house wide open for anyone to overhear.

"Answer me, Elizabeth. Do you nurture a delusional hope that a gentleman of Mr Darcy's means might show some honourable interest in you? Do you suppose yourself to be grand enough to secure the likes of that man? He owns half of Derbyshire, for God's sake! Men like him only look at ladies like yourself for one reason and one alone—the type of arrangement I should not even speak of in the hearing of a gentlewoman!" He gripped her arm more tightly. "Elizabeth. Be sensible."

"You are wrong about him," she whispered through gritted teeth, never letting her gaze leave his.

"Unhand the lady, Coble. I have heard quite enough." Elizabeth turned to find Mr Darcy had joined them on the terrace and thankfully had closed the doors behind him.

"Mr Darcy," she uttered softly, ashamed that he had overheard Mr Coble berating her.

"Darcy, I understand how this may appear, but I have it all in hand. She is safe with me. We are to be married soon. Be off with you!" Mr Coble said irritably.

Mr Darcy's eyes remained on Elizabeth, never acknowledging Mr Coble or any word he had uttered.

"He *is* wrong about me, as you well know," Mr Darcy said gently to Elizabeth. "I would never offend you with an improper offer—I would offer you all I have to give if you would accept me. I love you, perhaps even more than the first time I confessed it. My affections and wishes have not changed, but one word from you will silence me forever. I wish you to be my wife. I love you, Elizabeth."

Elizabeth worried her bottom lip. In a breathless sigh of a response, she quietly said, "And I you."

"That is quite enough!" Mr Coble protested. He gritted his teeth, but his severe countenance was now trained on Mr Darcy.

Mr Darcy finally turned to the other gentleman on the terrace, responding with an equally menacing glare. "You heard the lady, sir. It is time you took your leave."

"I may not be a gentleman, but I know better than to seize another man's wife." Disgust suffused his tone.

Mr Darcy remained unmoved. "You yourself told me that you were not betrothed."

Mr Coble baulked at his response and opened his mouth to speak words that never came. Elizabeth was relieved he understood enough of his place in society to know that he should not challenge Mr Darcy. Eventually, he stalked away.

She watched as Mr Coble left them and was turning back to Mr

Darcy when she felt his hand softly on her arm. If not for his warm smile, she would find him quite forbidding. In the darkness, she could see the outline of his locked jaw, his furrowed brow, and his broad shoulders—taut beneath his expensive evening coat.

She knew better than to fear him, for she had learned to recognise passion in his eyes.

"I hope he did not hurt you," he said softly, pushing a curl off her forehead and cupping her face in his hand.

Elizabeth stepped more closely and accepted his open arms, welcoming her into his embrace. All of her anxieties and fears began to drain away. When she tipped her chin to look into his eyes, she was met with a warm kiss to her lips. The kiss seemed to seal their promise to one another—it was full of apologies for past hurts, hope for their shared future, and a precursor to all they could anticipate as man and wife.

The next morning found the Bingley house aflutter with confusion, joy, and resentment—from Charles, Jane, and Caroline, respectively.

Elizabeth and Darcy could not care—they were too immersed in their mutual happiness and contentment. Bingley agreed to travel to Hertfordshire with Darcy to ensure there was no confusion with Mr Bennet. Elizabeth was thankful for the gesture but sat at the same escritoire as she had one month prior to once again write a note to be carried to her father by her suitor.

My dearest father,

Are you sufficiently amused? I am certain you are. And yet still, I beg you to set aside your folly for one day. I implore you to accept Mr Darcy's suit and give us not only your consent but your fervent blessing, for this is the gentleman who owns my heart.

Yours affectionately,
   Lizzy

The End

About the Author

Paige Badgett lives in the Kansas City area with her husband and son. In her free time, she can be often found reading historical romance novels and stories inspired by Jane Austen—as many as she can get her hands on. Paige is a lifelong storyteller who credits her love of reading to her mother and her long-standing book club.

ALSO BY PAIGE BADGETT
Against Every Expectation

No Charm Equal

Jan Ashton

CHAPTER ONE

Church services had ended an hour ago, and, upon their conclusion, the two Miss Bennets had returned to Longbourn, where they were quickly acquainted with their visiting cousin. Whatever feelings the sisters may have had on their change of households paled to the disquiet that had settled on Netherfield. Its current master was adrift; much as Bingley rejoiced in Miss Jane Bennet's return to full health, he made little effort to conceal that he missed her presence in his home.

Darcy's attempt to divert him with a game of billiards had proved unsuccessful; he left his friend pacing in Netherfield's ill-tended conservatory and, in need of his own distraction, went in search of the Wordsworth he had seen Elizabeth Bennet paging through the previous evening. He had scarcely stepped through the doors of the drawing room before Miss Bingley renewed her invective against her unhappy situation.

"We have finally shed ourselves of company and are again happily at peace here. Charles is so eager to dance with Jane Bennet and make friends of these country folk, he has promised her sisters a ball. What shall we do, sir?"

Darcy, faced with a similar desire to dance with a different Bennet sister, shrugged. "There is little harm in holding a ball for his neighbours. If your brother is to live in one of the largest houses in the county, he shall be expected to host large gatherings." He picked up his book and paused, not quite certain whether he wished to read it or let his mind wander, as it often had these past few days as they resided under the same roof, to the wit and form of the most intriguing Miss Elizabeth Bennet.

Perhaps a ride. Bingley could use the exercise as well.

Miss Bingley's agitated voice broke into his thoughts. "Do you recall what Charles said to Eliza Bennet and her mother? That when he is in the country, he never wishes to leave it!"

"He also made clear he feels the same when he is in town," Darcy replied. "Your brother has a disposition ideal for wherever he finds himself."

Miss Bingley rolled her eyes and leant closer to him. "I cannot be happy in either when I do not have my friends. You are not lonely, are you, Mr Darcy?"

He feigned curiosity about a painting and moved a few steps away. She followed, obviously determined to offer ideas on how she could alleviate any confession of loneliness.

"I am well," Darcy replied, "and never alone when I have a book or a letter to read."

"Awful as it is that we are here in this isolated place, we are fortunate to have you here with us." She gave him a meaningful look. "At least much of the militia has left, but how are we to host a ball for country folks, and where none of the guests are more than slight acquaintances—"

"The Bennets are our friends," he said somewhat sternly. "We have dined or visited with a number of families, including the Lucases and the Mortons." His mind drifted briefly to the image of Elizabeth Bennet singing as she played a lively melody on the Lucases' instrument. Although untrained, her voice was warm and tuneful. Perhaps, he thought, it was because she had had no masters that she expressed the feeling of the music naturally, so joyfully. Had anyone at Netherfield thought to invite her to play whilst she and her sister were here? Of course not; *that* would have been too generous a gesture.

"I have a thought, if you could sit for a moment."

Darcy shook off his meditations and looked at Miss Bingley. She gave him a fond look and lowered her voice in what Darcy perceived as an attempt to be coy but instead made him squirm in revulsion. It was how he imagined a young Lady Catherine might have sounded when casting her charms at Sir Lewis.

He hid his sigh. With the Hursts seated only a few feet away—one asleep and the other idly paging through a fashion magazine as she listened in on their conversation—he was at least safe from overt flirtation. Against his better judgment, he sat in the nearest chair; Miss Bingley immediately took a seat across from him and spoke in a conspiratorial manner.

"Much as I despise exposing your friends in town to such country ways, it could help our cause to bring other men here to distract Charles from Jane Bennet."

Darcy had to credit Miss Bingley; her mind rarely rested once its course was set, and she clearly did not want her brother to further his fascination with Miss Bennet. He raised an eyebrow at her suggestion. "To host them for entertainments or involve them in a scheme of distraction?"

"Oh, so many entertainments. Shooting, fishing, card parties, and games!"

Hmm. Much as could be done with a local group of men. "Was a larger party not considered earlier?"

"Yes. My brother invited five of his friends here in addition to you—"

Five?

"—And all made their excuses. I cannot understand how all had previous plans." Miss Bingley gazed at him fondly. "Of course, *you* are the kind of man who does well by his friends."

Darcy refrained from opining that the dearth of unattached females at a house party, even one intended for sport and shooting, would discourage any man's attendance. As would the knowledge that Miss Bingley, who had made herself well known amongst her brother's friends, would be the hostess.

Still, he was disappointed by such a response. Bingley had said nothing to him about feeling slighted. Although preoccupied with his new angel, he must be unhappy with the absence of his 'friends'. Darcy felt some guilt himself over the situation. He had been in no mood for society in the months following his sister's debacle in Ramsgate and had taken a full day to decide whether he would accompany Bingley to the estate he had leased.

Yet even with Georgiana safely ensconced with a new and trusted companion, Darcy had not been out in society. He had assumed a small family party was all Bingley had planned. To learn that five other bachelors had declined invitations?

He chose not to ask after their excuses. No matter how agreeable Bingley was, his family's roots in trade—and an unmarried sister angling for a distinguished husband—would dampen enthusiasm for furthering the connexion. It was an unfortunate fact he had managed to overlook for the sake of such an agreeable and trustworthy friendship.

Miss Bingley's smile was, as always, far too familiar. "You have so many friends. I thought you could persuade a few of them to join us here. A little competition for Miss Bennet's favour and more company for my brother would certainly improve the situation we find ourselves entrapped in."

"You would have me go to town and fetch some fellows to join us here?"

"No, sir! You cannot leave us, but perhaps you could write a letter to one or two of them."

He sighed, unhappy at the prospect of importuning his friends in such a scheme. When Hurst snored loudly, causing Miss Bingley to jump, Darcy took the opportunity to excuse himself, but not before assuring the lady he would give her idea full consideration.

First, though, he wished to think about the sly smiles and fine eyes of Elizabeth Bennet.

Mr Darcy scowled. Often. If Elizabeth Bennet had made a game of it, counting the number of scowls Mr Darcy aimed at herself and others at Netherfield, she would be the winner; he scowled at no one so much as he did at her. Miss Bingley had captured a few, and Mr Hurst as well. Elizabeth was grateful her mother had escaped open censure;

Mr Darcy had simply turned his back to her. No, his dark looks and glares were most often meant for her.

As are his few smiles, she reminded herself. What did those imply, beyond further muddling her opinion of the man?

Elizabeth suspected, for reasons she could attribute only to his fixed stare and the odd sensation of irritation and amusement it stirred, that Mr Darcy took some interest in her conversation. She had felt it on every occasion in his presence, most acutely in her three days in his company at Netherfield. *Shall I take it as a compliment that he listens?* Despite his often fearsome expressions, Mr Darcy attended to her opinions and the replies she gave to Miss Bingley's jibes; he appeared to enjoy provoking both of them. *If I were a wealthy gentleman blessed with a handsome face and a fine education, I would be wary of encouraging ladies such as Caroline Bingley—but clearly Elizabeth Bennet is no threat.*

Still, she wondered why a man of such well-displayed discernment and disinterest—one who found her only 'tolerable'—paid so much attention to her conversation. He must truly be bored with the confined company at Netherfield. Or perhaps he despised it.

Or perhaps he is unhappy or unsettled. Certainly I am unsettled! Why am I thinking so much of Mr Darcy and his temperament?

Why indeed. His inscrutable stare stirred unfamiliar feelings in her. If at first it confused her to be regarded in such a way, the steadiness of Mr Darcy's gaze challenged her, bringing warmth to her cheeks and a thrumming in her veins. No one had ever looked at her as he did; whether it was a glower of disapproval over her impertinent remarks at Netherfield or his continued consideration of her tolerable looks, she could not say. What Elizabeth did know was that she had grown accustomed to his stare, and if he took it elsewhere, she would wish to know why.

She had tried to speak to Jane of her confusion, but her dear sister, fully recovered from her illness at Netherfield, was deeply under the spell of Mr Bingley. One could not speak sensibly to a lady in love about the animosity of her lover's friend. Although Jane concealed her feelings from the rest of the family, Elizabeth understood her sister too well to doubt the strength of her emotions. She had safeguarded Jane's secret when it was learnt the day after their return home that the Netherfield party would join them at their aunt

Philips's card party. Mrs Bennet was vocal in her joy at a renewed opportunity for Jane and Mr Bingley, and her youngest sisters—still distraught that much of the regiment had left before they had the chance to meet all the handsome young men in their fine red coats—were happy for any social gathering, no matter how familiar their neighbours might be. All of them were pleased to be away from Longbourn for an evening. Elizabeth hoped the joy of gossiping and winning lottery tickets would distract all of them from observing Jane and Mr Bingley.

Or seeing the severe looks given to me by Mr Darcy.

Tonight, in her aunt's drawing room, she once again felt Mr Darcy's eyes on her as she listened to Mr Hurst and Uncle Philips discussing the importance of a good pudding. She sensed his attention as she sipped punch and encouraged Mary to at least acknowledge that Henry Robinson had a fine voice. But Elizabeth felt his stare most keenly as she spoke to Charlotte Lucas and, realising Mr Darcy was drawing nearer, determined that he deserved his own share of provocation.

"What does Mr Darcy mean by listening to my conversation—"

"*Our* conversation? You shall have to ask him, Lizzy," said Charlotte in a dry teasing voice. "He is coming this way."

"How kind he is to offer me just such an opportunity to uncover his motivations. Mr Darcy has a very satirical eye and conceals his curiosity in a mysterious manner." Elizabeth was quite aware they had become a trio and turned in expectation of a raised eyebrow in an otherwise aloof mien. She was therefore surprised to find Mr Darcy smiling at her in a manner that softened his usually austere countenance.

"Miss Bennet, Miss Lucas, I hope you are enjoying your evening." His smile disappeared as he spoke, but a glimmer of mirth remained in his eyes. Elizabeth had not known Mr Darcy to be capable of displaying such feeling; while dwelling on the unexpected magnificence of it, she neglected to join her friend in greeting him.

"Thank you, sir. May I wish you good fortune in the games tonight?" Elizabeth heard Charlotte's voice as she returned his salutation graciously.

"I shall leave all the luck to those who will play," he replied.

She could not understand him. Was he not to play games? Did he disapprove of those who would?

"And you, Mr Darcy? You will not join the games?" Scarcely had Elizabeth finished speaking than she heard Lydia's loud gales of laughter from a card table behind her. Embarrassed, she steeled herself for Mr Darcy's look of censure. But he only looked at her curiously and shook his head.

"Then you may instead meet more of your neighbours," said Elizabeth brightly as she gestured at the room. "I regret that Mrs Sutton is ill and Mr Sutton, good husband that he is, could not attend. He greatly admired the fine design of the crest on your carriage."

"I am glad to hear it. I have a fine cartwright in town."

There was a pause, and Elizabeth wondered why he did not say more. *He accepts the compliment and no more! Can he not enquire as to Mrs Sutton's health or ask to be introduced to Mr Sutton at a future time?*

She gazed at him thoughtfully. "Do you find the roads tolerable in Meryton? I might think them a hazard to the wheels and axles of such a fine vehicle."

"I have no complaints."

Mr Darcy's reply dissatisfied Elizabeth; apparently she had not been firm enough in provoking him. "Truly? The rocks and grooves in our country roads do not affect your comfort?"

"Do I appear so delicate a creature?" he asked with another smile she found disconcerting. "The roads here are no worse than those I travel further north to Pemberley or east to Kent." He nodded in the direction of Mr Collins, across the room gesticulating wildly in a conversation with Mrs Philips and Mr Bingley. "I understand your cousin comes from Kent. My aunt is there as well and is quite discerning about the quality of her equipage and the roads she must travel. I am certain there are no errant rocks or ruts in the roads leading to her estate."

"From this I infer that my cousin is the authority whose opinion we should seek to determine the condition of these roads?" Elizabeth watched as mirth warred with alarm in his expression; his eyes lit up and his lips twitched in a manner newly familiar to her. She had seen it when he encountered her, muddied and dishevelled, on her way to Netherfield, and more than once during her stay there.

Mr Darcy's gaze moved to Charlotte, whose expression displayed her dismay over the conversation, and back to her. "I would not importune him for an opinion I am certain he would wish to defer to his patroness."

Smiling sweetly, she asked, "By which you imply he may profess opinions that are not his own?"

His lips twitched again and she knew he was recalling their conversation of only days ago. Good as her own memory often proved, and as recently as she had been in his close company, it surprised Elizabeth that he could remember nearly every word she had ever exchanged with him. Was it because some of their conversations had been contentious or because they had been anything but ordinary? And had his face betrayed so much diversion on those occasions?

"I find there is much to admire in one who can argue reasonably for his own opinion rather than show constant agreement with those they consider their superiors by birth or intellect."

With this pronouncement, Elizabeth was uncertain whether Mr Darcy was insulting Mr Collins or complimenting her. *Does he admire my ability to debate in our arguments?* She could scarcely think on it as she was equally bemused as to whether she should indicate her agreement with so forthright a statement. The opportunity was lost when Charlotte touched her arm and excused herself to speak to her mother. She watched her friend walk to Lady Lucas and saw Mr Bingley looking anxious, undoubtedly searching for an escape from Mr Collins. When he saw her with Mr Darcy, he smiled and made his way towards them.

"I beg your pardon if I have injured your cousin," said Mr Darcy in a low voice she might have called intimate. "I understand he is a guest at Longbourn."

"He is, and he is all that you say." She shrugged and gave him an arch look. "Houseguests can be so troublesome, can they not?"

Mr Darcy's eyes widened. "I am sorry for the circumstances that required your stay, but you must know that you and your sister were welcome and exemplary guests at Netherfield. Your company and conversation have been missed."

Astonished, Elizabeth found him gazing at her in something akin to warmth. "Thank you."

They turned to greet Mr Bingley, cheerful and clearly heartened to be away from her overly voluble cousin. He leant close and in a low voice, confided, "Miss Elizabeth, I have met Mr Collins, and feel quite overwhelmed. I thought Darcy to be the only man for fifty miles who prefers words of so many syllables." He smiled at his friend; when Elizabeth laughed, Mr Bingley quickly recalled himself. "It is quite admirable, of course, a parson of so much knowledge—"

"And so generous in sharing it."

Mr Bingley chuckled. "He is your father's heir, I understand?"

"Yes. Longbourn is entailed, and as you know, my parents were blessed—or cursed—with the births of five daughters." Her eyebrows rose, conveying the humour she preferred over the hopeless truth of their situation.

Mr Darcy remained silent, but her jest had rallied Mr Bingley, who cried, "Blessed indeed, Miss Elizabeth! You and all your sisters are wonderful ladies."

"We shall see if Mr Collins feels as you do when he decides which of us he will condescend to marry." She immediately regretted expressing her thoughts aloud. Their cousin as master of the Bennets' fate was a cruel joke, but to say such a thing to the man who showed signs of a growing affection for Jane!

Mr Bingley smiled, but his brow creased as he digested this new information. Elizabeth sensed Mr Darcy's revulsion; she had earned it. She was embarrassed for her own behaviour; her cousin was a ridiculous man, but it was neither helpful to her family nor polite to deride her own relation so publicly—certainly not when they were likely to depend upon his benevolence upon Mr Bennet's death.

Collecting herself, Elizabeth smiled at Mr Bingley and gestured to the far corner of the room where Jane stood. Looking somewhat relieved, his eyes lit up and he excused himself. Elizabeth, happy to see him so captivated by her most deserving sister, watched him weave his way through the room and past his own sisters, currently in company with Lady Lucas and Mrs Goulding. Miss Bingley wore an expression of utter displeasure. Had the lady had a mother like her own, Miss Bingley would have learnt that exhibiting petulance and disgust did no favours to one's complexion nor beauty. Mrs Bennet's admonitions for smiles and serene brows were followed by four of her daughters; Mary, who managed only squinting and seriousness, was indifferent to lectures on beauty but fortunately blessed with an enviable complexion.

Mr Darcy's voice interrupted her musings. "We should speak of more than roads, rocks, and relations."

"You astonish me, sir," she replied, laughing. "Has our conversation been so dull?"

"We are intelligent people," he said solemnly. "Both of us are well-read and interested in nature."

Elizabeth had no further interest in rocks or roads and chose to satisfy her own curiosity. "My relations have indeed been canvassed, and you have been frequently in company with them. Perhaps you can tell me of your own relations—your younger sister has much praise from Miss Bingley. Or is there a grumpy uncle or a devoted but ill-humoured aunt who never fails to remind you of some mischief you created when in leading strings?"

She was pleased to coax a surprised chuckle from him.

"You may prefer discussing geography or music to learning more of my 'ill-humoured aunt', so let me instead praise my sister. I have but one, but she is all that is good: kind-hearted if shy in company."

His expression softened as he replied, and Elizabeth asked her next question more gently. "She is much younger than you, I recall, and a gifted musician, according to Miss Bingley."

"Georgiana is but fifteen and takes great joy in playing the harp and the pianoforte. She would not wish to hear such praise, but Miss Bingley is correct: my sister's devotion to practising has seen her develop into a very talented musician."

She was pleased to hear such genuine feeling in his voice and her reply was equally earnest. "I have rarely had the opportunity to hear a truly excellent musician perform, one who is technically proficient but also displays an understanding and love for a composer's work."

When he did not answer, she wondered if he thought her to be angling for an invitation to hear Miss Darcy. Regardless, her curiosity demanded she ask the young lady's favourite composers.

Mr Darcy considered her question only briefly. "She is uncommonly fond of Mozart and Beethoven."

Elizabeth had no time to respond. A moment later, her own younger sister's voice pierced the hum of conversation in the room;

Lydia was shrieking in laughter at something poor Malcolm Bates had done. She excused herself, claiming some need to speak to her mother, and moved away more reluctantly than she could have anticipated; her mortification warred with irritation that Mr Darcy should be witness to yet another of the Bennets creating a spectacle.

CHAPTER TWO

DARCY WATCHED ELIZABETH MOVE SWIFTLY TO HER mother before his eyes were caught by Miss Bingley, entrapped in conversation with Lady Lucas; she, too, was watching Elizabeth, a vexed and—truth be told—rather ugly expression on her countenance. Darcy could easily imagine her thoughts, as she had voiced them often. When he returned his attention to Elizabeth, he hoped his own would not be so transparent. He had missed her company at Netherfield; it was her conversation, challenging and clever, that had enlivened the evenings. Much as he could admire her intelligence, he also felt resentment on her behalf—she was the sensible, responsible one who had to rein in her relations: her mother, her sister, her cousin. In this instance her efforts were in vain; Mrs Bennet appeared dismissive of whatever her daughter was saying to her, and soon Elizabeth had stepped away to speak to a young lady nearer her age.

He wished she would return to him and continue their conversation. He wished to know her thoughts on Georgiana's favourites. Elizabeth was not shy about disparaging her own talents as a reader or in cards or music, but he knew she was, if not merely modest, simply more amused by her deficiencies than by any need to boast of her talents. It took some effort not to reflect on another lady in the room who always desired flattery and attention and was equally pleased to bestow it—or mock those who could not earn her good opinion.

Darcy stepped to a side table and accepted a cup of coffee, then moved to stand against the wall and follow Elizabeth with his eyes. As she moved around the room, he was struck by how often her neighbours paused to greet her and how effortlessly she smiled and posed sincere queries as to their health and relations. In contrast to so many of his acquaintance, she spoke very little about herself. He heard her enquire after one elderly gentleman's prized cow and condole with Mrs Goulding on the ache in her knee; Elizabeth listened as if these were the most fascinating subjects in the world. It was only when he watched her in conversation with Mr Collins that she betrayed any impatience or discomfort, and even then, she made every effort to appear engaged and pleasant.

He had seen her use this same approach at Longbourn. In her efforts to allow Bingley and her sister time for private conversation, she would ask Miss Catherine about the bonnet she had decorated or compliment Miss Mary on mastering a difficult passage in whatever the poor girl was pounding out on the pianoforte. He had even heard her asking one of the maids about her ailing father. While she gave her opinion readily, she kept attention on the lives of other people.

She has done the same with me, with soft jests about uncles and aunts that hit too close to the mark, and with genuine interest in Georgiana.

She showed true care and curiosity rather than feigned concern; she did not affect interest to gain any claim of intimacy. Rarely had Darcy witnessed such behaviour from anyone in society, nor amongst his own family; not even his mother had shown such depth of concern in another's welfare—not even in *his*, he realised with some painful awareness. When he had fallen ill or suffered an accident or some melancholy, only his governess or Mrs Reynolds had come near to behaving as Elizabeth did, and both of those ladies were servants intent on pleasing their master or mistress. Georgiana, with no maternal example to learn from, was kind but lacked keen sensitivity; if comfort was requested, she would do all that she was capable of, but it was not her natural way. How much she could gain from knowing Elizabeth!

She is utterly charming.

As he caught sight of her smiling impishly with Miss Lucas, Darcy realised the dangerous direction of his thoughts. He closed his eyes briefly before becoming aware he was not alone in his contemplations. Bingley stood beside him, grinning.

"Your eyes are open, but you appear asleep on your feet, old man." Bingley chuckled. "You have yet to finish your coffee."

Feeling self-conscious, Darcy took a sip from his cup. The coffee had grown cold; he drank it nonetheless, hoping it would calm his unsettled thoughts.

"I say, Darcy, I realise you are not one for gatherings such as these, but are you well? You have been stalking the walls more than is your wont."

He glanced at Bingley, and seeing more levity than concern in his expression, assured him of his health. "I am merely wool-gathering. My thoughts are occupied with business."

Bingley sighed heavily. "You are not needed in town, are you?"

Darcy immediately seized on the suggestion. "Perhaps a day or two to attend to some matters." *And come to my senses.*

"I know better than to try and stand between you and your business affairs," Bingley said resignedly. "Do try to return before the shooting party young Mr Goulding has planned. Hurst has been rather verbose on the topic of your skill with a gun, and I believe there is some hope of a great performance. And the ball, of course," he exclaimed. "I have heard little tonight that did not express gratitude or excitement for the event. My dance card shall be full!"

Bingley clapped Darcy on the back before lowering his voice. "Promise me you will dance with Miss Bennet and her sisters. Mr Collins seeks a wife, and while I can protect Miss Bennet from his aspirations, a ball is a fine opportunity for him to make his choice."

Darcy turned and stared at him. "You are not serious."

"About Miss Bennet? I believe I am."

Darcy remained uncertain of the lady's attachment to Bingley, but already he recognised she was superior to most of her family. If not as sparkling and clever and handsome as Elizabeth, she was equally kind-hearted and decent.

"No, you fool," he growled. "About Collins. You *wish* him to choose a wife from among Miss Bennet's sisters?"

With a slightly affronted frown, Bingley replied, "It is not *my* wish, but rather that of her mother and Mr Collins. I would hope he has no interest in Miss Elizabeth. She is too clever for him, and I like her too much."

Dear God, no! She could not marry that man! Darcy nearly shouted aloud. Instead he simply nodded and said, "I had assumed Miss Mary to be the ideal wife for Mr Collins. He is ill-suited for a lady with the spirited intelligence and wit of Miss Elizabeth. She deserves a husband who can respect her clever mind."

He wondered whether he had given away too much, but Bingley only continued with his own thoughts.

"Caroline is unhappy enough with country life. Any connexion to Jane Bennet shall only displease her further. However, gaining a brother such as Collins might be enough to induce her to move to my aunt's house in Scarborough."

In spite of his own disquiet, Darcy nearly chuckled. His friend was far slyer than he usually allowed. "Indeed it might, yet can you bear such a brother?"

"I can bear any relation if I am wed to the lady I love, but I admit it would pain me to see any of Miss Bennet's sisters wed to a man they neither love nor respect."

"Well said." *I cannot imagine Elizabeth Bennet agreeing to such a marriage. She would wish for mutual felicity and understanding in a husband. Her keenness of mind demands it, yet how many men can match her? How many would allow her mind to flourish? The odds are against her meeting such generosity in a suitor.*

He felt a clap on his shoulder and saw Bingley once again staring at him, eyebrows raised. "I shall leave you to your wool-gathering, old fruit. Miss Bennet is now free of her conversation."

Darcy watched his friend saunter off before giving into temptation and again seeking out Elizabeth. He found her conversing with Miss Mary and a man likely younger than he appeared, what with his severe countenance and thinning hair. He pitied him; no man deserved to be balding before he had reached his majority. Whatever Elizabeth was saying softened her sister's expression and made the young man smile; both were blushing as Darcy, somewhat cognisant of propriety, managed to look away.

She is enchanting; the most interesting, nay, fascinating creature in this town. Kind and genuine to her company, sharing her warm laugh and playful demeanour. Who could not wish to be near her? What would it be to be loved by her?

An odd feeling, almost like drowning, swept over him. Darcy stepped quickly towards the open doors to the terrace; he leant over the side, taking deep breaths while summoning up disparaging thoughts as if they could ward off some inevitability.

Her father is indolent, her mother ill-mannered, her sisters wild. An uncle in trade, another a country lawyer…

Stop, he told himself. *Elizabeth humours their vanities and manages their faults.* None of their attitudes or behaviours had any bearing on the family's reputation. All the Bennets were well-liked by their neighbours and enjoyed the society of everyone in Meryton.

Can I say the same of my own family? He straightened and looked up at the darkened sky. *No. Does any neighbour have affection for Lady Catherine? My own uncle does not like her. She does not like him.* A small smile played at his lips as he stared at the bright stars dotting the unyielding ebony overhead. *My own family would disdain Elizabeth's connexions, yet she could outshine them in conversation while charming them enough to keep them from realising they had been bested.*

He had known her a few weeks, six at most. He was not an impetuous man given to reckless decisions. What was he thinking? He had pursued Elizabeth's company all evening, and he was considering pursuing her hand?

The enormity of the time he had spent thinking of Elizabeth Bennet and of the conversations they had had, or could have, or should like to have, came with the force of a blow. *I am in trouble.*

A day or two away from Meryton and the remarkable yet unsuitable lady who provoked his interest was a fine idea. Clearly the lack of stimulating conversation at Netherfield had led him to think too much on the one person who had provoked him, intrigued him, caused him to think about his responses. It was a male companion who should incite such intellectual raillery, not the daughter of a country gentleman too busy neglecting his entailed estate to ensure the conduct of and proper futures for his daughters.

Yes. He would go to town, go round his clubs, and collect a few men to come to Netherfield. His cousin always enjoyed a shooting party. Yes. He would achieve two goals by riding to town tomorrow.

If I cannot outrun this feeling, I shall have to give in to it. Marriage is not only about the heart, and this fascination must end.

After his decision was made, the evening passed dully. Darcy spoke to some neighbours, declined a game of cards, and contributed a thought or two to a discussion of the Corn Laws. Yes, this was as it should be.

Near the very end of the evening when he felt almost ill with boredom, he found he could no longer resist the one person whose company he most wished. He found her entrapped with three others at a card table with Mr Collins. She looked up and met his gaze and then, with a small smile, rolled her eyes. Himself trapped in a one-sided conversation with Sir William, Darcy managed not to laugh but to nod in common understanding. When Mr John Lucas announced he would perform a feat of magic with a handkerchief and Mrs Philips's finest porcelain sauce boat, the card tables emptied, and Sir William and Mr Collins joined the group gathered round the large table across the hall in the sitting room. Elizabeth stood watching the exodus; she glanced at him, an amused smile playing at her lips.

"Sir, are you not interested in tricks and illusions?"

He shrugged, thoughts of Wickham's petty cruelties flitting through his mind. "When I was a boy, perhaps. You?"

"As a child, I often served as Mr Lucas's assistant when he would practise his illusions. My face, he now advises me, is too expressive, and he requests I refrain from watching him perform and giving away his secrets." She grinned impishly. "Among my accomplishments, I am a despoiler of magic!"

Darcy's polite smile dissolved into laughter. "A heavy charge indeed, particularly as you must have endured many risks during his attempts to master tricks."

"I admit to a scorched bonnet and one or two stained gowns," she said, her words nearly lost as gasps and laughter erupted in the next room. "My mother and the maids were not happy with me, of course, but my father was pleased when Mr Lucas's many attempts to make me disappear failed."

Another wave of the heightened feeling that consumed him around Elizabeth Bennet shook Darcy. "As am I."

He had said it so quietly it was nearly a whisper. But Elizabeth, who missed nothing said or thought by anyone, had heard it; she looked at him, clearly surprised by his words and the serious manner in which he said them. Without thinking, Darcy stepped closer to her.

"Miss Elizabeth, would you reserve a dance for me at the ball?"

She stared at him, apparently considering his request. The voices of the crowd returning to the drawing room filled the silence between them. "Yes, I-I am engaged for the first three sets but—"

"The supper dance, then."

"Yes."

That was the last they spoke that evening; he had done what he fought not to do. The following morning, he left early; breakfast was still warm in his belly as his carriage drove past the entry lane to Longbourn. He should have ridden; it would be faster. But he knew himself too well; an hour's ride across the fields might help clear his mind, but to ride the road to London while distracted by his imagination was dangerous. He had always to think of Georgiana, and to keep himself safe for her sake. He could not be heedless, even while wrestling with…with whatever it was consuming his head and his heart.

CHAPTER THREE

THE BENNET LADIES COUNTED THEMSELVES FORTUNATE the following day when Mr Bennet gave in to his promise to escort Mr Collins around the Longbourn estate. Elizabeth watched as her father, employing what meagre eagerness he could muster, clicked the reins on the curricle and drove off with his garrulous cousin. She and her sisters enjoyed an hour to themselves, luxuriating in the silence; Lydia and Kitty took full advantage of the respite from Mr Collins's opinions and sermonising and exhibited more relaxed manners than she could recall. Then, with the exception of Mary, who was set on the idea of an empty house in which to practise on the pianoforte, the Bennet ladies set off on the path to Meryton. The Netherfield Ball was two days away, leading to much discussion of ribbons, laces, and shoe-roses and the usual argument over when each sister could expect assistance from Longbourn's sole lady's maid. Just as Mr Collins's endless and meaningless prattle stirred comparisons to Mr Darcy's quiet presence, her sisters' arguments and her mother's prattle reminded Elizabeth of her preference for solitary walks.

When they arrived in Meryton, Mrs Bennet was immediately caught up exchanging news with Lady Lucas and Mrs Philips. Elizabeth, torn between overseeing Kitty and Lydia's pleas for everything in the shops and assisting Jane with finding the perfect shade of ribbon to weave into her hair, could not help but listen in on her mother's conversation. Aunt Philips had assumed her customary role as elder sister to offer matchmaking advice to Mrs Bennet.

"I know you count on Mr Bingley for dear Jane," her aunt advised, "but I wonder that you never considered Mr Darcy for her. He is wealthier, his uncle is an earl, and he is at least two inches taller than his friend."

"Yes, Mr Darcy is all that, and he takes great pride in all of it," said Mrs Bennet. "Yet I do not think his hair is as fine as Mr Bingley's."

Mrs Philips laughed quietly while Lady Lucas sniffed, "Either gentlemen would do well for my Charlotte, would that she were a few years younger and had had a Season in town."

She sighed, and received a pat on her arm from Mrs Philips, who went on to offer reassurance that all of Meryton's ladies were safe from such considerations. "It is of no consequence. Mr Darcy removed himself this morning from Netherfield and left no word on his return."

"That was sudden," Elizabeth interjected, as much in disbelief as in curiosity. "Was his leaving planned or was he suddenly needed elsewhere?"

Mrs Philips appeared pleased at being the conduit of fresh information but could offer few details. "I do not know the particulars. My maid heard from her brother, who is a groom at Netherfield."

He has left? Astonished, Elizabeth turned back to Jane, who held up an ivory ribbon in her left hand to compare to the pale pink ribbon in her right hand. "Oh Lizzy, however shall I decide?"

Elizabeth picked up a maroon ribbon and thrust it at her sister. "Your gown is a soft rose with white trimmings. I say, be bold, Jane! For it is a ball at the home of a very handsome man who only proposed the event so that he could please you and your sisters and dance with you more than one time."

"Do you truly—?" Jane's hesitant voice turned more certain. "Yes, I shall be bold."

Bold. That is exactly what Elizabeth thought Mr Darcy had been, asking her to dance when so much of their acquaintance had been, if not unfriendly, at least rather contrary. She recognised she was not an innocent party; being called 'tolerable' by anyone, let alone by a man to whom one has yet to be introduced, was insulting to any woman, and made worse when he made little effort to apologise or redeem himself. She had not liked Mr Darcy; she had thought him proud and insufferable. But even when they had argued, she enjoyed his conversation; never had she felt quite so engaged in listening and thinking and forming replies, and never had she felt that her opinions were so considered and challenged. *Considered and challenged by a handsome, well-educated, wealthy gentleman. A single man of marriageable age. A man who softened last night in our conversation, sought my company, and asked to reserve a dance.*

Unless he had received sudden, dreadful news from London, he must have known he was leaving Meryton. She could not wish any misfortune on Mr Darcy or his family, nor could she believe he was playing a joke on her; he had spoken to her with such openness in his eyes, such sincerity in his rough voice.

Vexing, charming man!

As the group walked towards Longbourn carrying their purchases, Elizabeth spoke quietly to Jane. "Were you aware Mr Darcy was leaving?"

"I was not," confessed Jane. "He has not gone for good?"

Elizabeth shrugged as if the answer meant little to her. "It seems a mystery."

"Mr Bingley has often spoken of Mr Darcy's business interests and his concern that they consume too much of his time. But to abandon him at such a time?"

"Before the ball, you mean?"

Jane blushed. "Well, yes. I am certain Miss Bingley and Mrs Hurst are quite busy with their planning. Mr Bingley will be at wit's end."

"He has Mr Hurst to divert him."

Not long after their return to Longbourn, Mr Bingley, clearly in need of diversion—or, to Elizabeth's mind, desperate for pleasant and sentient company—called. The sun was bright and the November breeze warmer than usual; Elizabeth's restlessness lent itself quickly to a suggestion that they all walk out. Kitty and Lydia paused their squabbling to plead fatigue from their earlier walk to Meryton, while Mary braved their disdain to assert her wish to remain at home and greet her father and Mr Collins on their return. Elizabeth, pleased to escape the present and future company at Longbourn, followed Jane and Mr Bingley as they walked towards the garden path.

"Longbourn is such a happy, lively household," said Mr Bingley, paying an undeserved compliment to their family. "I am relieved to be away from Netherfield," he added with a sheepish grin. "It is in a bit of an uproar, what with Caroline and Louisa bustling about and ordering the servants here or there in their preparations for the ball. Caroline is quite exacting. 'Everything must be better than perfect!'"

Elizabeth bit back a grin at Mr Bingley's imitation of his sister. Jane was more polite, saying, "Then it shall be, as I am certain your sister is an ideal hostess."

"It is the first ball she has ever planned," he confided, "and she is intent on impressing her guests."

Intrigued as she was that Miss Bingley was less practised as a hostess and social arbiter than she had represented herself to be, Elizabeth's true interest lay elsewhere, although she adopted a casual tone to pursue it. "We understand Mr Darcy has left Netherfield," she said to Mr Bingley. "Will your sister be disappointed if he is not at the ball to dance with her? They made a fine pair at the assembly."

She hoped her eagerness for intelligence about the gentleman was not obvious; if Mr Darcy had not asked her to reserve a dance with him, Elizabeth assured herself that his presence—or the lack of it—would not matter to her.

Mr Bingley chuckled. "This time, he had better dance with more ladies, not simply my sisters."

Frustrated that Mr Bingley was showing a likeness to Mr Collins with his inability to answer a yes or no question, Elizabeth pressed him. "So Mr Darcy *is* returning for the ball?" She plucked some leaves from a chokeberry bush and ignored the curious look Jane gave her.

"Oh, of course! He has business of some sort, as he always does, but he assured me he will be here," said Mr Bingley. "You see, I am happy where I am, but Darcy is restless whenever he is not at Pemberley. I am certain he needed to attend to some matter with his steward or solicitor, and it could only be done in London." Mr Bingley smiled, then, squinting, pointed at something on the garden's far wall. "I say, that is the largest raven I have ever seen!"

Unwilling to inform the gentleman that he was looking at their gardener's hat, Elizabeth fell behind the couple. Although Mr Bingley tried to include Elizabeth in their conversation, once she had received her answer about Mr Darcy, she was content to fall farther behind and stroll in silence. Her mind was occupied. She had spent considerable time contemplating the Mr Darcy to whom she had spoken the previous evening and contrasting him with the man she had been acquainted with previously. He was nothing but arrogance at the Meryton Assembly; detached and disapproving of his neighbours at the Lucases'; cool politeness at Longbourn's dinner table; and somewhat more thawed in her three days in company at Netherfield.

Last night at her aunt's house, they had spoken, more in friendliness than in disagreement, but she had again felt—as she had in nearly every moment of their acquaintance—Mr Darcy's eyes, fixed on her in long, penetrating stares. Once she had thought these discomposing gazes to be of disgust, that any interest in her was borne of his own boredom and by her refusal to fit his assumptions about how a lady should look and act and speak. Last night was different. *He has gone from scowls to smiles, arrogance to amiability.*

Has he grown used to my impertinence?

Hearing her sister's light laughter mingle with Mr Bingley's chuckle, Elizabeth smiled. Now, *there* were two people who had not —*would not*—argue or misunderstand one another.

That evening, feeling herself a little exhausted of her mother's expectant effusions and Mr Collins's enthusiastic recounting of Longbourn's glories, Elizabeth excused herself to finish reading a book. She lay in her bed twisting her bookmark and unable to concentrate on the pages. Her attention shifted instead to the familiar tattered ribbon she used to mark her place. Suddenly she was overcome, realising with a start the reason she had been drawn to the bold maroon ribbon in the shop: it was the exact shade of the waistcoat Mr Darcy had worn the previous evening.

Must he dominate my every thought? I do not like him. Do I?

She sat up, remembering the half an hour she had sat with him in the library the previous Saturday at Netherfield, neither speaking nor, she suspected, reading. She had almost thought it a game: Who would be the first to surrender to laughter or a sigh and make eye contact? Or refer to the very inappropriateness of a single man and a single lady sitting in a room unchaperoned by anything but books? It had been warm in the library, a warmth she felt within her rather than from the small fire that burned in the hearth. After worrying briefly that she had caught Jane's cold, Elizabeth understood how this warmth differed from a fever.

Whether or not Mr Darcy had felt any similar sensation, he had adhered most conscientiously to his book, and would not even look at her—until he did, when she stood to excuse herself and felt the intensity of his gaze. While her eyes likely reflected her amusement, his were dark and held something akin to desperation. Was it not a game to him? Was he repressing himself from conversation?

She would ask him, challenge him as he challenged her, when—*and if*—she saw him again.

CHAPTER FOUR

DARCY SPENT A FEW HOURS IN HIS STUDY, ACCOMPLISHING nothing of worth as his mind drifted to a certain lady's words and to the particular shape of her ear, before he decided to visit his sister at their uncle's house. Unfortunately, his aunt and uncle were at home, and more than curious as to his recent doings. Georgiana sat next to him on the blue settee in Matlock House's excessively ornate sitting room; his aunt and uncle sat far away, regal in their tall gilt chairs, peering at him as if they had not seen him only a month earlier.

"Netherfield Park in Hertfordshire?"

Lady Matlock was bored with the current gossip in town and clearly wished for some interesting titbit to contemplate and turn into something interesting for her next dinner party. "I have never heard of it. No one of any distinction lives there."

"My friend Bingley is leasing an estate there, and with my advice, will determine if it is to his satisfaction. Meryton is a market town, and the people are—"

With a snort, Lord Matlock made his thoughts clear. "Bingley's father was a wool merchant. You are acting as his advisor, providing him with all that you learnt at the knee of your father and uncle about estate management?"

"No. Only my own son will be privileged to be taught all I have learnt, sir."

"A son requires a wife," murmured Lady Matlock. "Are there ladies present at this Netherfield?"

Darcy skirted a direct reply; while his aunt did not share Lady Catherine's opinion that he should wed Anne, she was at least as eager for him to marry. He never spoke of social engagements or ladies in her presence. "Truly, it is not a house party but an excursion to determine whether the estate is worth the having, and—"

"Bingley has sisters. One is unwed. She is there?"

"Of course. Bingley requires a hostess in order to become acquainted with the neighbourhood."

"Pray you are locking your chamber door at night," growled the earl.

Darcy glanced at his sister; she was looking out the window, and thankfully seemed unaware of her uncle's meaning.

"You have been exclusively in company with your friend and his family?" Lady Matlock peered at him. "No one else has joined you there?"

Darcy shifted in his chair as a vision arose of Elizabeth Bennet sitting across from him at Netherfield's dining table, playfully parrying Miss Bingley's invectives and enduring silence from the Hursts, and often from himself. She was unconcerned with her treatment, her only thoughts on her sister's welfare. Despite her own fatigue, her spirit and wit were undaunted.

He cleared his throat. "No one, although Bingley may have invited friends for the ball he has planned."

"A ball?" He had his aunt's full attention. "I have heard no one in town speak of traveling to Hertfordshire for a ball."

He raised his hands. "Please, I know very little. I have been immersed in assisting Bingley in learning the particulars of the estate. However," he said, smiling at his aunt, "I will write to you the day after the ball with every detail that I remember, from the names of those who attended to the story of the most outrageous event that occurs."

"I shall rely on you to do so, Nephew! There is always some ridiculous attempt at seduction, or a hideous gown paraded about by an ignorant girl, or some drunken fool who announces his love for a lady dancing with another man."

Darcy heard his sister's sharp intake of breath at their aunt's proclamation; however, Lady Matlock was clearly pleased by his promise, and when the earl rose, troubled by his gout, she followed him out of the room.

Relieved, Darcy could finally converse privately with Georgiana. After she gave him every assurance of her health and happiness and adherence to her studies, she had her own questions.

"Is Mr Bingley's house party not to your satisfaction?"

It was, in his mind, a polite way of asking whether Miss Bingley's attentions had driven him away. As much as Miss Bingley would boast of her admiration for and friendship with Georgiana, his sister had a subtle way of making plain her own unease with the lady.

He smiled. "I was as restless there as I often become in town, but in the main, I wished to come to see you."

She appeared pleased at his reply, so he continued. "I was asked which composers you especially admire, and I mentioned your partiality to Mozart and Beethoven."

"Oh? Who enquired of my preferences? Surely Miss Bingley has canvassed that topic many times."

He would have laughed had he not been somewhat alarmed that his first consideration was to talk about Elizabeth Bennet's thoughts on music. "Um, the sister of the lady admired by Mr Bingley."

"Ah, the lady with the muddied skirts and tanned complexion?"

Is this how I described Elizabeth in my letters? As a country vagabond?

Exhaling, Darcy gave his sister a stern look. "It was an unfair and incomplete description of the lady. Miss Elizabeth Bennet was indeed in disarray when she arrived at Netherfield to care for her sister, but she is far more than muddied and tanned. She is an elegant, clever lady who does much to enliven any room."

"I am sure I did not wish to insult her," Georgiana said earnestly. "She sounds lovely indeed. You and Miss Elizabeth are serving as chaperons to Mr Bingley and his lady?"

They had not been chaperons, not truly. But upon his return, he could very well be put in the position of escorting Elizabeth Bennet on his arm whilst following Bingley and Jane Bennet on walks or occupying a room and holding conversation with her as the other couple spoke quietly. Would he like to be in that role?

Of course I would.

They spoke quietly for another few minutes before his cousin Colonel Fitzwilliam strode in and agreed to accompany Darcy to his club for dinner. Half an hour later, they were seated at White's, where they were almost immediately hailed by two of Darcy's old classmates, Burvile and Stewart, who expressed surprise when they learned of his recent whereabouts.

"Bingley's 'estate'?" repeated Burvile. "You have been there?"

At Darcy's nod, the two men chuckled. Stewart explained that they, as well as a fellow called Weathersbee, had been invited to Netherfield but had declined upon learning Miss Bingley was to be the only eligible lady there.

"One lady does not constitute a true house party," said Burvile. "Bingley is a hale fellow, but my own sisters swear to despise me if I even look at Miss Bingley."

His own cousin laughed and joined his opinion to theirs. "She has grown rather desperate, what with Darcy showing no sign of surrendering to her charms."

Darcy sighed. He had offended others by frequently including Bingley, a man undistinguished in society, in gatherings. His friend's natural amiability won over whomever he met, and he would once again defend him. "Bingley is a good man, and his sister is no more desperate for a husband than many other ladies. She is simply more obvious in her attentions to her target."

"You," said three voices in boisterous unison.

Darcy lifted his glass. "Indeed. But it is of no consequence. Bingley is my friend, and he knows I have no interest in his sister."

"If he maintains a list of those who share your feelings, it must be quite long." Stewart smacked the table, pleased with his joke and unaware of the insult Darcy had taken from it.

"Miss Bingley is no more eager to marry well than any other young lady in society." Darcy spoke in a cool voice as he leant back in his chair. "Not every man must wed for fortune or connexions, but few ladies have the ability to choose a husband. Many in society are wed to those for whom they feel no affection or respect. Miss Bingley, like any lady, deserves a husband who enjoys her company."

Fitzwilliam, brother to an unhappily wed older brother and sister, nodded; Burvile and Stewart appeared surprised by such a long speech from a man known for his reticence. Darcy himself was rather abashed, and, concerned he may have put off Bingley's friends, quickly continued.

"The company at Netherfield may not be to your tastes, but the shooting is quite good, and Bingley has added some fine horseflesh to his stables. A few days in the country are beneficial for the clearing of a man's mind."

Burvile and Stewart exchanged glances. "And the neighbours? Are there ladies in Meryton there who would amuse us?"

"Does not every village and town in England claim the prettiest, most charming ladies in the country? Meryton is no different." It was no easy thing to keep his answer simple, when the most singular lady of his acquaintance was there, in Meryton. He refrained from mention of the ball and refused to consider the reason for it.

Fitzwilliam sighed loudly. "You pups sit in London, hoping the streets will dry of rain water so that you may escape your houses—your *fathers'* houses—to promenade or pay calls or go to your clubs or gaming hells. Get thee to the country."

Stewart and Burvile agreed to send notes to Bingley and went on their way to another engagement; Darcy and the colonel welcomed their dinners with alacrity. As he swallowed a bit of boiled beef, Fitzwilliam enquired whether Darcy was in fact uncomfortable as the only single male in a house with Miss Bingley.

He demurred, uneasy with the conversation once again centred on that lady—or any lady, for that matter, especially among company. "My true reason for discomfort is that I was unaware Bingley issued invitations to so many friends—all of whom declined—until Miss Bingley mentioned it. Bad form. Bingley is a good man and a fine friend to everyone."

"Not everyone can look past his family."

"They should," Darcy replied angrily. "The Bingley name is not disgraced, nor linked to any scandal. As if the *ton* is not full of scandals and secrets."

Fitzwilliam looked up at him from his plate. "You are spirited today, and I do not think all your efforts, sincere as they may be, to defend Bingley and his sister are meant only for them."

Darcy stared at him, waiting for the man he long thought of as his closest friend to deduce his secret.

"You are worried about Georgiana and the events earlier this year."

Ah, so his cousin could not see it nor sense it, this newfound and rather frightening sentiment in his heart. Would Elizabeth see it? Did she share it? Drawn as Darcy was to her eyes—*to her*—he felt a reticence in her enjoyment of his company. He was not the most charming of men, but charm mattered little to most women in society. Elizabeth, however, was charming and generous and would expect the same from any gentleman. *From me.*

"Or has Bingley met another angel?"

Darcy looked up at his cousin for a long, measured moment. "He has, and they appear to hold each other in mutual regard."

"You will not counsel him against it? A country girl?" Fitzwilliam returned his gaze sceptically.

"Miss Jane Bennet is the daughter of a gentleman and is kind-hearted and genteel. I have no reason to dislike such an alliance for him."

"Ah, but his sister will if she cannot raise their family's station."

The image of Elizabeth's eyes, flashing with anger or mirth, flitted through Darcy's mind. "Miss Bingley dislikes Miss Bennet's younger sister even more, for she has a wit and intelligence unmatched by any other lady of my acquaintance."

Fitzwilliam stared at him for a long moment. "Truly? That is high praise from the master of Pemberley. The lady sounds intriguing." His eyes lit up in merriment. "Perhaps I should join you at Netherfield. Did you not mention a ball? There are some who say I am your superior both in charm and in dancing."

"I will grant you the charm. You have an ease I envy." It would go unspoken that charm meant little for a man's future happiness and security in society if he did not also have a fortune. "I would prefer you did not. I do not need a rival."

His cousin's amusement faded as he assumed a concerned expression. "A rival? I hardly understand you, Darcy. You are smitten by a lady you have only just met—"

"Miss Elizabeth and I have been acquainted for a month."

"—who is neither an heiress nor connected to the *ton*."

"No."

"Well, then." Fitzwilliam sat back and took a long draught of his wine. "You have never been a fool about anything, let alone a woman. This Miss Elizabeth Bennet must be worthy of your regard."

"She is."

"Then I hope to make her acquaintance, and soon."

Darcy responded with a smile. "Perhaps you shall."

CHAPTER FIVE

THE CLUMSIEST MAN IN THE WORLD HAD CLAIMED HER first dance, and Elizabeth doubted her left foot would recover in time for her second.

Dancing with Mr Collins had been worse than she had anticipated; although confident in his abilities and clearly pleased to receive the attentions of the other ball-goers, he was terribly unschooled in the dances and seemed to have no sense of the musical pieces themselves. When Elizabeth went left, so did he. When she raised her right arm to twirl to the side, he did the same. Their hands collided, he bumped into the gentlemen beside him, and he trod on more than one lady's foot—mostly her own.

Her mortification matched her pain when she saw Mr Darcy standing at the edge of the ballroom. She was surprised he had eluded Miss Bingley, who likely hoped to open the ball with him; that lady's irritation was a small consolation to Elizabeth as she felt Mr Collins's damp hand take hers once again. It was bad enough that in her efforts to evade her cousin's smug gaze she could see the astonishment on the faces of her neighbours, and the amusement on her father's; what was worse was the expression of revulsion she saw on Mr Darcy's countenance.

Then his eyes met hers and his disgust turned instantly to what she could see only as sympathy. Elizabeth nearly gasped at the consternation in his expression; abhorrence, amusement, or pity were expected, but such marked concern?

If her cheeks were not already flushed from exertion and embarrassment, the blush she felt from his scrutiny—so different from the cool stares she was accustomed to—would have overwhelmed her.

He overwhelmed her.

Stumbling as she once again righted Mr Collins's position, Elizabeth felt Mr Darcy's penetrating gaze. When she glanced at him, he raised his eyebrows and looked at her searchingly, as if ensuring she was unharmed. Dipping her head, she managed a small smile to convey she would carry on; when he rolled his eyes, she nearly laughed aloud.

When Darcy had entered the ballroom, the swell of the crowd gave him pause; Netherfield's halls and corridors had been loud and bustling, but the ballroom was thronged with ladies in ballgowns and men in their finest jackets and silks. He had had it on the authority of Mrs Bennet that they dined with four and twenty families in Meryton. But this? Darcy could recognise only a few familiar faces—there were the younger Lucases, the Johnsons, the Robinsons, the Philipses and the Pratts. Had Bingley invited every man and woman in the entire county?

He moved through the crowd as rapidly as he was able, eager to see only one face. He returned nods of recognition; no one tried to stop him for conversation, and their expressions held more surprise than pleasure when they saw him. Darcy bit back his annoyance—had he ever been in a place so full of people casting judgment *on him*?—and tried to lighten his expression with a small smile. He fought not to widen it when he saw Elizabeth standing with Miss Lucas, smiling impishly.

Yellow is a fine colour to set off her dark hair and tanned skin.

Within moments, the improvement in his countenance had caught the attention of at least one man.

"Mr Darcy, you have returned to us." Mr Bennet wore a dark green jacket and his usual mocking half-smile as he looked Darcy up and down. "We thought you to have fled our small society for more stimulating associations in town."

"I was in London for a short time," Darcy admitted. "My intention was always to return to Netherfield in time for the ball."

"Business in London, and now returning to your obligations in Meryton. I do not envy you such an arduous life."

Much as Darcy understood Mr Bennet to be of a sarcastic bent, often unsocial and always mocking, he discerned there was more to his jibes. "When one cares for his friends, one is willing to do all that he can to defend them."

As Mr Bennet appeared to consider in which manner he could best, and most bitingly, reply, Sir William presented himself at Darcy's elbow, as jovial and effusive as ever.

"Mr Darcy, you are returned to us!" he cried. "The ladies will be glad to partner with you when the dancing commences."

"Oh, but Mr Darcy does not dance, as was made clear at the assembly last month. Lizzy was quite put out by it." Mr Bennet appeared to find sharing his daughter's condemnation diverting, and Darcy could only feel the shock of it.

"Was she?"

"Oh yes," Mr Bennet said drily, "there were far fewer men to partner with all the ladies, and you stood about and showed no interest in conversation, let alone dancing."

Darcy could defend himself—he was not comfortable in a roomful of strangers, especially those far beneath him. How rude that sounded, yet it was the only defence he could make without explaining the darkness of his mood that evening, defending Bingley while his own thoughts were mired in darkness—worried about his sister, furious at Wickham, and at a loss for what to do about either.

In spite of the riot of emotions roiling within him, he managed to reply calmly. "I regret the insult to Miss Elizabeth. I shall do my best to remedy the situation this evening."

"Make haste, Mr Darcy," came her father's smug counsel. "Lizzy is a popular one wherever she goes, and more gentlemen than you and Mr Collins are eager for her company."

"Oh, she is a jewel. Many prospects indeed," cried Sir William.

Darcy took a deep breath, debating whether to announce he had already reserved a dance. Clearly Elizabeth had not informed her father of it. He could not but wonder whether his behaviour at the assembly was the reason both for her hesitation to accept his request to dance and for her withholding mention of it to anyone.

Something, most likely his open-mouthed expression of dismay, must have piqued Mr Bennet's paternal feeling. He reached behind him, poured Darcy a glass of punch, and handed it to him. With no little embarrassment, he took a long drink of the cool liquid before thanking his benefactor. Mr Bennet nodded and leant his head closer; Darcy noticed for the first time that the older man was not quite Bingley's height and measured only up to the top of his ear. If Mr Bennet noticed his appraisal, Darcy was grateful he refrained from teasing him about it.

"You will find Lizzy here, somewhere, in a pretty yellow gown, her second choice for tonight. Lydia stepped on the hem of the ivory gown Lizzy wished to wear, and the tear could not be mended in time." Mr Bennet chuckled. "At least no shoe-roses were harmed, although her first dance with Mr Collins promises to alter their condition."

Mr Collins!

Heedless of what the father of the lady he sought might think of his intentions, Darcy thanked Mr Bennet and excused himself. The music began and couples took the floor, but he had no thought of rescuing an overlooked lady. As he moved about the room in search of Elizabeth and her odious partner, he heard voices murmuring as to the handsome picture made by Bingley and Miss Bennet. "What a fine pair they are," said a ruddy-faced man he recognised as Mr Long. "I have never seen such a smile on Jane Bennet's face," agreed the stout lady by his side.

Darcy glanced in the direction of their gazes and saw Bingley leading Jane Bennet around the dance floor; they were aglow in smiles. Across the floor, unseen by her brother, was Miss Bingley, the hard edge of her unhappy countenance softened by the elegance of her ballgown.

If Bingley be in heavenly love, his sister is in the furies of hell, he thought, unable to quell his own guilt for stepping aside in favour of Hurst's brother in opening the ball with Miss Bingley. Behind her, he saw a flash of yellow, and there was Elizabeth, dancing with her oafish cousin. There were smirks and giggles around him, and he read the triumphant glee in Miss Bingley's darting glances at the clumsy parson's missteps.

Elizabeth was smiling bravely and trying to persuade Mr Collins to use the correct steps while not incurring his pique. Could no one else see her kindness in directing him? Could they not see he was causing her pain and embarrassment? Much as she masked her misery behind a smile, no-one could assume any joy in that half an hour. How he ached at her mortification! Darcy took a position where he could watch her, and, intent on showing her the encouragement and sympathy she was owed, gazed at her with a gentle expression until the dance was finally ended.

Had her father been more disposed to shooting parties and fishing excursions, Elizabeth suspected she would have known sooner that Mr Darcy had returned as promised for young Mr Goulding's shooting party. Perhaps it was deliberately done, Mr Bennet withholding knowledge of his attendance; perhaps it was not. What *was* deliberate and cruel was her father's mocking gaze when he saw her limping off the dance floor. He was intelligent enough to know he must be careful about ridiculing publicly the man who would inherit Longbourn, but he could freely tease his daughters and neighbours. *Callously tease.*

Mr Collins's remarkable display of hubris and gracelessness continued when he followed her off the ballroom floor and began preening as he spoke on the importance of practising one's steps. She slipped away from him, eager to find fresh air and a seat to rest on before the second set was called. *At least my toes shall be safe with Mr Bingley!*

None of those men were truly in her thoughts, however. As she sank into a chair on the terrace, it was Mr Darcy and his tender gaze that filled her head. She could not say she was battling her feelings—she scarcely understood *his* thoughts as he gazed at her in a manner no man ever had—but she could not grasp the tumult of emotion as she thought of his worried, reassuring smile. *His handsome, tender smile.*

Elizabeth rubbed her toes gently through their satin coverings.

"Miss Elizabeth?"

She looked up to find Mr Bingley beaming at her. "The second dance is mine, yes?"

Surely a man as kind as Mr Bingley would not hurt her feet; she had seen his graceful steps with Jane. Sighing, she returned his smile and began to stand. Mr Darcy suddenly appeared, his brows furrowed, and strode across the terrace to come kneel by her. "Miss Elizabeth, are you well?"

Elizabeth sank back onto the bench, struck dumb by his open expression of concern. His gloved hand neared hers, and although they did not touch, she could feel his warm presence, smell his cologne, see the sharp edge of his whiskers.

"What has happened?" asked Mr Bingley.

"Mr Collins trod upon Miss Elizabeth's feet." Mr Darcy stood and turned to his friend. "Would you mind dancing with your sister in my stead, and allowing Miss Elizabeth to recover?" He glanced back at her. "If that would please you?"

She nodded.

"You are evading Caroline for another set?" Mr Bingley stood for a moment, shifting awkwardly between annoyance and laughter, before asking, "Shall I send your sister to you, Miss Elizabeth?"

His earnestness made Elizabeth smile. "She is engaged for this dance with our cousin. Perhaps you could ensure her wellbeing?"

Clearly alarmed, Mr Bingley strode away rapidly. Elizabeth bit her lip and glanced at Mr Darcy. "I thank you for gaining me a reprieve, but will you not regret losing your dance with Miss Bingley?"

His cheeks coloured and she was certain she had never seen anything so endearing.

CHAPTER SIX

OF COURSE SHE WOULD TEASE HIM. IF HER FEET ACHED and she was experiencing her own painful perdition, her countenance did not reflect it. Darcy glanced at the small group of older men, pipes in hand, leaning against the terrace wall. "Shall I hide in the event Miss Bingley refuses her brother and seeks me out?"

"Mr Darcy, are you in need of my protection? Possessed as I am of three younger sisters, I am well acquainted with the tossing of pillows and pulling of hair that may be required to fend off Miss Bingley."

The impish sparkle in her eye provoked him and despite the risk to propriety, he lowered himself to sit beside her. "I would not risk a hair on your head," he said quietly. "Perhaps one of our fellow stargazers would volunteer?"

With a warm smile, Elizabeth nodded at a rotund man whose wig and cravat were askew. "Mr Greyson was quite adept as a dancer when I was younger. He danced with me at my first assembly and never once stepped on my toes."

"And his were safe from your missteps as well, I am sure." At Elizabeth's delighted laugh, he continued, more seriously. "I did not intend to impose myself on you, if you did prefer to dance."

Her bemused expression made clear she thought him an idiot. "I have danced and dodged tonight and will be pleased to sit out this dance with you."

As she spoke, a most becoming blush spread above her bodice and on her cheeks; Darcy found it a relief to realise she too was unsettled. "I am glad."

His reply appeared to please her and she looked at him expectantly. "Your business in town was completed to your satisfaction?"

"I believe all was settled, and I will now set my attention on the pleasures of my visit here."

"I am glad," she said, looking away briefly before returning her gaze to his.

Darcy felt the awkwardness of wishing to speak of his feelings. But they were neither alone, nor could propriety allow him to speak more intimately.

After that, beyond his assurance that he would remain on at Netherfield, little of sense was said between them. They spoke not of books or rocks or roads, but shared small observations about the ball. Every word seemed awkward, shyly given. The chuckles and exhortations of the others on the terrace hummed like a chorus beneath their own conversation.

Finally, hearing the swell of music coming to its natural conclusion and anticipating the rush to the terrace for cool air, Darcy swallowed and in a low voice, said, "I do not wish to risk losing the pleasure of the time we will spend dancing and dining, but I must speak to you, now, before I go mad."

"Sir?"

He blurted out, "I admire you greatly. I wish to call on you, at Longbourn. Tomorrow and the next day and the next."

Her eyes widened; she remained silent, and he was overcome with anxiety. "I needed to say it, to state my intentions of wishing to know you better, but I fear the man you once held up as proud likely now appears to be little more than a prattling fool."

The heated crowd was nearing the doors by the time she gave him any relief. Darcy felt a slight pressure on his hand. Elizabeth's silk-gloved hand lay on his; he inhaled and looked up to find her eyes searching his.

"You are far from a prattling fool, Mr Darcy. I would be honoured by your calls, and anticipate more of our most remarkable conversations." She rose and gave him a most brilliant grin. "My third dance is promised. I shall see you for ours?"

She disappeared through the doors. Darcy sat immobile, finally standing to surrender his seat to some young ladies before following Elizabeth into the ballroom. He had come to this country town as a man of education and sophistication and had sounded like a green boy when he told the worthiest woman he had ever met that he esteemed her.

No matter. She welcomes my company. That is the material point.

Heedless of the astonished whispers created by his cheerful countenance, Darcy swallowed a cup of punch, nodded at a few neighbours, offered Miss Bingley an apologetic smile, and led Miss Bennet onto the ballroom floor. Much as his mind was elsewhere, he enjoyed their dance, if only to watch Miss Bennet's expressions when she would seek out and smile fondly at Bingley. *There is more there than a trifling attraction between them. She looks at Bingley to ensure his happiness.*

Content that his friend's heart was cared for, Darcy removed his gaze to where he most desired it and watched Elizabeth weaving through steps with Mr Lucas. She was laughing, her sore toes forgotten, when her eyes caught his and her cheerful smile shifted into something more intimate.

The next set dance would be his, and he could speak to her and learn more of her, and then escort her into supper as his company for the meal. He would not be a fool and trip over his tongue this time. If he could not control his heart, he could control his mouth.

His chance came half an hour later when the supper dance arrived, and he found Elizabeth and Miss Lucas emerging, deep in conversation, from the retiring rooms. When she caught sight of him, her expression transformed; she was radiant, as if seeing him, expecting his company, overfilled her with joy. Did he look as she did?

He stared dumbly as she approached and managed only a few words as he led her into the ballroom. Elizabeth looked at him shyly—had any other expression ever become her more?—and followed him to stand with the other couples. The feel of her small hand in his nearly overpowered the sensibilities he was so determined to control and seemed to completely tie his tongue.

"Thank you for accepting my hand for this dance," he said, once able to speak with some sense. "I have watched you dance tonight, and it is a pleasure to stand up with you."

If she were less self-conscious, Elizabeth would have laughed. The two of them, renowned for their debates and their conversations, were fumbling their words after having exposed themselves as vulnerable to the other. *One step at a time,* she told herself. *We have been drawn to each other since the first moment of our acquaintance; our understanding of one another is incomplete, but our desire to learn is…*

She could scarcely complete a thought let alone articulate a sentence, yet, frustrating as it was, she could not mind; not only was she dancing with the handsomest, most interesting man of her acquaintance, she would have supper with him, and he would call on her.

"Sense and vocabulary will return with the soup and vegetables."

"Excuse me?" came a deep voice.

"Oh!" Elizabeth's complexion turned a deeper shade as she realised she had spoken her thoughts aloud.

"I apologise for my own lack of sense." Mr Darcy turned slowly and stepped near to take her hands for the next spin. "I assure you, however, that I am well-prepared for a discussion of soup, whether we examine the topic while we eat it or before."

He grinned, she laughed, and a palpable expectation settled between them for the remainder of the dance.

Elizabeth was enjoying Mr Darcy's handsome smile when he offered his arm to escort her to dinner, but their expressions changed when Mr Lucas rose up on a chair in the entry and—after a glance to and a nod from an enthusiastic Mr Bingley—announced he would perform a feat of magic before supper. Hungry as the crowd was, they were all enthusiasm for a bit of entertainment before sating their appetites.

"I need a volunteer to assist me. Not you, Miss Elizabeth," laughed Mr Lucas. "You know my tricks, and I may ask you to look away rather than give away the secret." He winked at her. "Besides, this one is best suited to a tall gentleman with long arms."

Elizabeth stiffened, both at the familiarity of his wink and at the smug looks being exchanged by the men around Mr Lucas as he turned and gazed at Mr Darcy.

"Mr Darcy," he drawled, "would you mind? You were the finest shot in our party this morning, bagging four birds in less than a quarter hour. Two of them in one shot!"

The audience made known its admiration and cheered his name. "Ho! Mr Darcy!"

"Oh no," she murmured as she felt Mr Darcy's arm tense. She sensed his natural reluctance and understood it as no one else in the room could. If his wealth and name did in fact put him above their company, he had not endeared himself to her neighbours. What better than a public performance that promised the humiliation of a ruined cravat or soiled face to cut him down to size?

He stepped forward despite it.

"Yes, of course."

Darcy had seen the envious looks from the other men during the shoot. His gun was the finest, yes, but without his skilled aim and handling, the fine steel barrels, gold and silver lock, and polished walnut stock would have meant nothing. Patience and luck guided him; some petty feeling towards Lucas, who had spent much of his time in their company talking of his own long friendship with Elizabeth, had nothing to do with his desire to outshoot the man. *Surely.*

Lucas wished to exhibit himself with a card or coin trick? As if that would impress Elizabeth. Darcy patted her hand, still folded within his arm, and stepped forward, eager to get the trick over with and move on to his time with her.

"Yes, of course."

"Wonderful," cried Lucas. "Come stand here. Everyone else, gather round the hall table. Mr Darcy shall ensure our safety and catch the candelabras as I pull the tablecloth!"

When the shrieks quieted and the servants had doused the flames, Elizabeth stood alone with Mr Darcy in the vestibule, heedless of the rush towards the dining room and Miss Bingley's barely controlled animus at Mr Lucas. She could not restrain herself from reaching out, her hand flailing helplessly, to ensure his welfare.

"You were very brave, Mr Darcy. Unknowing of the danger ahead—fire, water, invisibility or a severed finger—you put yourself at risk to entertain Mr Bingley's neighbours."

"I had rather hoped for cards, but a little humility never hurt anyone," he said, brushing the remaining ashes from his lapel.

"Nor a near roasting? It was poorly done by Mr Lucas. He did not practise."

His eyes lit up and he broke into a silly grin. "My valet and barber will be unhappy, but of course my coat can be cleaned and my hair will grow back. I remain more concerned with you, and the state of your toes." His gaze fell to her wrinkled dancing slippers.

After glancing down at her feet, Elizabeth wriggled her toes. "All are in working order. I may even dance again tonight."

"I am glad." He took her arm and led her towards the dining room, near an open window where she could enjoy a cooling breeze and he could rid himself of the smell of ash. "I do hope for another dance with you, that is, if I have displayed adequate familiarity with the dance steps required to properly lead a lady."

Still blushing from his avowal of eagerness, Elizabeth laughed, hoping it might return her to some level of rationality. "Indeed sir, I am pleased, but not surprised, by your proficiency."

"No matter what some may say," he offered, "not every savage can dance."

"Nor can every savage execute an illusion properly." She brushed ash off his sleeve. "In every family there is at least one relation of little ability and even less understanding. My own family is not—"

"Perfect?" He shook his head. "Perhaps not, yet there is a happiness in company at Longbourn that I rarely see in large families. My own family is small, and in need of liveliness."

Oh.

"I have a wonderful aunt and uncle in London, but you have met my cousin. I cannot choose my relations—"

"But you can, when you marry."

She laughed. "Will we always argue?"

"We enjoy it, I think." He looked closely at her. "Is Mr Collins intent on proposing to you?"

"Listening to rumours and gossip, Mr Darcy?" She laughed at his astonished expression. "Whatever Mr Collins intends, I do not wish to dance with or marry him. He lacks all sense. Can you imagine anything more ridiculous?"

He shook his head gravely. "I can imagine nothing less appealing. It is a horrific notion. How greatly you would suffer."

Startled, she gazed at him. "It is only my toes, and my pride."

Mr Darcy's dark eyes remained intent on hers as he stepped towards her. Behind him, Elizabeth could see her family and neighbours settling down to the long tables. No one paid them mind; she and Mr Darcy were within their own small universe. "Perhaps in dancing, but in marrying, it is your heart that would be wounded. You deserve far better a man than your cousin."

How much she agreed, and how prideful to say so!

"I—"

Suddenly her hand was in his and he was speaking to her in a low, intimate voice.

"Elizabeth, I am a man of decided opinions, and one who has long prided myself on knowing my own mind; but then I came here and met you." With one gloved finger, he traced her hand. "I have never had to know my own heart and will admit, and only to you, that it has proved wiser and gained in happiness because it welcomed you."

The thrumming grew louder, stronger, nearly overtaking her breath. A rightness shuddered into place, and she inhaled deeply, before slowly releasing all her feeling into a gasp.

"Please tell me I have not frightened you," Darcy whispered. "I thought myself frightened until I realised the rightness of my feelings for you, and I hope, yours for me."

Elizabeth grasped his large, warm hand, and drew on its sturdy, solid strength. "Your words have returned, and with them your ability to challenge and unsettle me."

"Unsettle?"

"And flatter and warm me." The unease in his eyes disappeared and once again that dark intensity was focused on her. "You have never frightened me, Mr Darcy. Although we have spent little time together, I, too, have examined my own heart."

"What have you found there?" he asked earnestly. "What does your heart hold?"

"You," she said simply. "You, who are most unexpectedly charming, are well on your way to being my dearest friend."

"I wish to be more," he whispered.

Elizabeth leant her head against his chest. "You already are."

The End

About the Author

Jan Ashton didn't meet Jane Austen until she was in her late teens, but in a happy coincidence, she celebrates her birthday on the same day *Pride & Prejudice* was first published. A former journalist, she is a life member of the Jane Austen Society of North America, and co-founder of Quills & Quartos Publishing.

Also by Jan Ashton

A Famous Good Marrying Scheme
A Match Made at Matlock
A Searing Acquaintance
In the Spirit Intended
Mendacity & Mourning
One Minute More
Some Natural Importance
The Most Interesting Man in the World (*with Justine Rivard*)

United by Happenstance

GAILIE RUTH CARESS

CHAPTER ONE

STILL CAUGHT IN A MAELSTROM OF TURBULENT FEELING brought about by Mr Darcy's revelations in his letter, Elizabeth felt wholly unprepared to read yet another epistle as disastrous so soon. The very morning after receiving his letter, she unfolded a new note from her aunt in London in no trepidation of its contents; immediately she felt her spirits plunge as she read the report from Gracechurch Street that declared a shocking illness making its way through her younger relations there. Her aunt's distress over their need to cloister themselves until it passed was palpable in every line; her apologies to her niece and to the Collinses profound. But the firmness of the Gardiners' apothecary had made it clear: Elizabeth would need to prepare herself to stay on in Kent for at least three weeks until all the children had in their turn overcome this sickness.

Her hopes for her upcoming escape dashed themselves to pieces upon the page she held. Elizabeth released a quaking sigh as she folded the missive. Her longing for her removal could only increase when facing such a long delay of her reunion with Jane and more time to steep in her unhappy and unsettled spirits, away from the calm and kindness to be found with the Gardiners, in whose care she had hoped to understand herself again.

"Eliza, you sound troubled. You are still not yourself," Mrs Collins observed as she leant over the table to pour into her teacup.

Here at least, Elizabeth could give answer to some of her friend's concern, for her close guard of Mr Darcy's privacy had heretofore left her unable to divulge to Mrs Collins the contents of Mr Darcy's letter.

"My little cousins are ill. My aunt says the apothecary believes it is severe and catching. I cannot return to London as planned, perhaps for three or more weeks."

"Ah, such a blessing!" Mr Collins cried in delight, even as his wife tutted in kind dismay. "For now you and my dear sister Maria shall experience the fulfilment of her ladyship's benevolence! Lady Catherine's word is as good as her deed, and did she not express a wish to convey you to London herself if you completed the month at Hunsford?"

"Mr Collins, I could never impose—"

"Oh, but you must, Cousin Elizabeth! Once it is clear that you intend to remain, your refusal would cause her ladyship far greater disappointment than any inconvenience your acquiescence may create," Mr Collins replied stoutly. "And further, to refuse such generosity, and such an *honour* as her ladyship's own company in a barouche—"

"You are quite right, my dear," seconded Mrs Collins. "And how it would ease my heart to know that my little sister and my dearest friend will travel safely into town among her ladyship's retinue."

Elizabeth sighed. While she anticipated no reward for herself in indulging Lady Catherine, she was forced to see the practicality of accepting such an arrangement: a journey undertaken with every human comfort, attended and chaperoned at every turn. Such luxuries meant that she would not need to trouble her uncle Gardiner with arrangements for a manservant to meet the travel-weary girls at a coaching inn.

"Very well. If her ladyship wishes to make good her offer to bring us back to London, I must feel very obliged to her."

Mr Collins eagerly excused himself from the breakfast table and capered into the hall, his intent clear even before he declared it. "I shall go at once to inform her ladyship of this development, for her plans are perfected, wisely, quite far in advance. Let us hope such notice does not come too late, for it would not do to overset the arrangements of her ladyship's household."

His wife followed him into the hall calmly, offering him his hat. "Go on then, my dear, and give our regards to her ladyship."

Once the door had banged shut behind Mr Collins, Elizabeth took up her teacup and let out another sigh. So much of her energy in Kent had been devoted to keeping herself content despite her uncomfortable positions as houseguest and visitor in the territories of men whose offers she had refused. She now pondered how best to make herself equal to her homeward journey in the company of a woman whose very presence—and her connexion to Darcy especially—precluded her full escape from the burden of such recent history. For how could Elizabeth truly leave what transpired in Kent behind her if Lady Catherine must remind her of it at every turn in the road?

Every stage of Elizabeth's farewells to the place dragged on. There were days and days left to her in Hunsford. Mr and Mrs Collins felt they must fill them by bringing Elizabeth and Maria to visit nearly every parishioner to receive their well-wishes before leave-taking. Lady Catherine called at the parsonage several times, staying only long enough to pontificate on the plans already decided. Mr Collins contributed by fretting over every detail of the arrangements and giving unsolicited advice about the best ways to travel unobtrusively in her ladyship's company while giving every show of gratitude. Amidst all this, Elizabeth wisely sought the best possible means to achieve some equanimity, in the form of frequent walks to enjoy the blooms of Rosings Park and the lanes leading to the parsonage.

CHAPTER TWO

ON THE FINAL MORNING OF HER FAREWELL, ELIZABETH lingered in a grove in the dew of the morning for as long as she dared before she was summoned back to collect her reticule and neaten her appearance for the journey.

Lady Catherine's barouche had come at last. The shallow frame of the equipage was designed to be commodious, with room enough to seat all their company comfortably—but Elizabeth felt stifled nearly as soon as she had greeted Lady Catherine and sat down. Next to her, Maria Lucas quivered as her eyes took in the sumptuous fabric of their upholstered seat, the pounded brass trim around the doors, and the lovely clamshell of the folded top spread for shade overhead.

Her ladyship's maid had adjusted herself on the box seat when the driver called out to the team, and the barouche lurched rather inelegantly forward. Elizabeth suppressed a smile as her fellow occupants swayed in their seats. All elements considered, it was a beautiful day in the full swell of spring, they had an open-air carriage to enjoy, and Elizabeth was determined to find every possible reason to laugh at herself and her companions as they undertook the journey.

Maria Lucas squeezed her arm. "I daren't speak," she squeaked under her breath. "Whatever am I to say to her ladyship whilst we are trapped here for hours? Will you please try to speak to her, Elizabeth? I know you are not afraid of her."

"I despise whispering," declared Lady Catherine sternly from across the cabin where she sat in the forward-facing seat. "Whatever are you talking of?"

Elizabeth offered a smile that was as much determination as courtesy. "Of our journey, ma'am. I understand we are at your leisure until your driver is able to take us to Gracechurch Street." Elizabeth did not say what she had already presumed—that Lady Catherine's sense of rank would forbid her from ever entering the vicinity of Cheapside.

"Yes, I suppose you must be," nodded that elder lady. "And without my Anne here with us—for she is still far too delicate to come into London during such a wet spring!—I shall be more at leisure. We need not rush to House de Bourgh for its quiet, nor await her physician to send the draughts."

Elizabeth glanced at Maria, uncertain whether this portended well or ill for their adventure. She had hoped that Lady Catherine might grow weary enough of their company to have them sent to the Gardiners' home rather immediately. Lady Catherine instead seemed to be considering them with an almost patient air that spoke equally of sufferance as scrutiny.

"I am not unaware of your situations in life," said her ladyship at last. "Nor am I ignorant of mine, and the privileges I enjoy. There is a duty in my rank which I must claim in widening your acquaintance. You are dressed suitably for travel, perhaps, although too plainly for a call. However, the journey must be your excuse, if I am to introduce you to anyone of notice in town today."

Unable to resist the ironic notions provoked by such an offer, Elizabeth answered with arch humility, "I am not unaware that the inferiority of our families' connexions might prevent your acknowledging us among others, your ladyship. Some may say it would be wiser that we not seek to impose, nor presume to encroach, upon your sphere."

Lady Catherine seemed surprised at such conscious self-disdain. Her knotty brow crinkled further as she replied, "There may be wisdom in not reaching too high, nor beckoning the high-born to stoop. It is quite inappropriate in either case. However, there is no harm in having your station and situation generally made known."

The dowager once again took hold of her cane where it rested beside her, tapping it upon the carriage floor as she looked with directness at Elizabeth and added, "You might very well find yourself granted another kindness with an introduction to another clergyman, or to a second son of some lesser dependence. You may have lost your opportunity in securing Mr Collins, but it need not be the tragedy of your life, Miss Bennet. Indeed, I believe the example of Mrs Collins has taught you a valuable lesson: that a young woman of your birth and fortune is *induced* to marry; your security and complacency in life are bound up in this fact. You cannot afford to refuse any man, ever again."

Elizabeth felt a sting of mortification, and her mind immediately conjured scenarios of the scolding she might receive had Lady Catherine any knowledge of the *last* man Elizabeth had refused. Unwilling to betray anything of this secret while under her ladyship's remonstrating gaze, Elizabeth enfolded herself in silence and lowered her eyes.

Lady Catherine, apparently satisfied to sense that she had won her point, turned towards the scenery as the carriage rolled along. For several blessedly quiet miles, she commented only to note her approval of the roads, which had benefitted from four days without rainfall.

In the relative calm that settled over the breezy equipage, Elizabeth recovered from her embarrassment, only to find herself shifting uncomfortably in her seat and fiddling with her hat in a useless attempt to settle any lingering self-doubt resulting from Lady Catherine's last words.

Since reading, and then re-reading, Mr Darcy's letter, Elizabeth had experienced some of this phantom discomfort already. She had been forced to acknowledge that her judgment of his character had erred, especially her accusations of perfidy in regards to Mr Wickham. Her failure there seemed magnified as she reviewed the injustice of her subsequent prejudice against Mr Darcy, which she had allowed to grow unchecked by feeding it with anger at his interference with Jane and Mr Bingley. The harm that Mr Bingley's ensuing departure had caused her sister had been real enough, but it was humbling to discover from Mr Darcy's own defence of his part in it that the ill intent she had attributed to him had existed only in her own imagination.

It left her to now ponder: Had she known the real Mr Darcy at all?

She decided she had not. She had never sought to understand him before, and now she had severed any possible ties to him with her refusal. There was no way to call back her own words or undo what they had wrought. He had gone from Kent the very next day, and she knew immediately what he had meant by it—that she would never know more of him.

She could not decide what troubled her more: this abrupt severance and the enduring mystery surrounding Mr Darcy's real character, or her failure to understand him since the beginning of their acquaintance.

She was not to discover the answer now, for she was pulled most unexpectedly from her thoughts by Maria Lucas.

"Oh, look!" the girl called out, pointing most indecorously over the lip of the carriage. "There is an inn. Shall we stop, your ladyship?"

"I think not until we reach Bromley, Miss Lucas," Lady Catherine replied. "The horses are still fresh and the road is dry. With a fine day and no hurry to tire them, there is no need for a change so soon before London. That is, unless you require some refreshment."

"Oh, no," said Maria, looking abashed. "Your servants have packed a basket, and there is wine too. I do not think I will require—that is, I did not mean to imply that I lacked anything, ma'am."

The exchange made one tolerable addition to their conviviality in the carriage: it reminded them of the food available. With more practical grace than elegance, Elizabeth offered to pour some of the cold German wine thoughtfully packed for their refreshment on the warm day. Lady Catherine accepted a small amount. Maria reached deeper into the basket, discovering there a braided loaf and cut cheeses wrapped up in cloth, as well as a sampler of fruit.

They partook lightly of it all—more to keep busy than to slake hunger, as it was only then approaching calling hours when refreshments might be expected. Elizabeth finished her portion then sampled enough of the quiet to feel sufficient in her good humour to ask whether Lady Catherine was in the habit of travelling often.

"You might well wonder, with such comforts as this at my

command, that I do not travel more than I do. But then you might recall my Anne, who is often so delicate. There are some times in the early summer, or very early in the mildest part of autumn, when the weather holds and excursions may be possible. I have taken her only once to London, cesspool of sickness that the city is. When my daughter was younger and more hale, I more often ventured to take her all the way to Pemberley and to my brother's home at the Matlock estate."

Maria, who had just taken another sip of wine, said boldly, "The Earl of Matlock! Even I have heard of him and his holdings. But what or where is Pemberley?"

"Did you not know that Pemberley is the estate of my nephew, Mr Darcy?" Lady Catherine replied with superior amusement. "The land has long been in the keeping of his ancestors, and that great portion passed to him when his father died some five years ago. The house of Pemberley is situated in a very pretty spot in Derbyshire, and is surrounded by an immense property. One might think managing such an inheritance a challenge to a man so young, but my nephew is certainly a capable landlord. He even advises me in regards to my property at Rosings. I trust him most implicitly."

Elizabeth, still weary from her own rumination on the subject of Mr Darcy, did her best to turn the conversation away from admiration of the man. "I have never travelled to that part of the country. Is it located near the Peaks?"

"Yes, it encompasses some territory thereabouts. I never took Anne into the hills unless we were forced to traverse them on our way, but having been brought up in that part of the country, I am partial enough to that scenery."

This vein, once Lady Catherine entered it, suited her and Elizabeth, as chief listener, very well. Her ladyship went on describing some of the sights of the Peak District in a didactic style sometimes lightened by nostalgia.

Their own scenery in the farm lanes beyond the barouche, thus far rustic and lovely, flashing green and bright with the florid spring, slowly began to change. They approached the Bromley Inn at last and made the change of horses, and as they progressed once again a full half an hour later, their way became more congested with wagons and carriages. The struggle of villages and clusters of civilisation that heralded their approach to London were beginning to appear on the horizon. Lady Catherine took inspiration from the view and spoke with condescending admonition regarding the tradesmen taking advantage of the highway proximity, the creeping taint of their influence in society, and her suffering at the sight of the hovels that paved their path.

Elizabeth bit her lips again and again. Prudence told her that her breath would be wasted in giving instruction on the needs of the lower classes to a matron already so firmly set in her position and perspective. Their journey went on slowly as the horses led them inexorably onwards, off the highway roads and across the river, past the smoky throngs of workshops and shipyards and the clamour of street merchants, and towards quieter streets lesser changed by struggle and the shifts of time. There, gardens and gates and elegant houses stood aglow in the mid-afternoon sun like dignified monoliths to a nobler age.

"Ah," said Lady Catherine, "there is St George's. We are very near to my relations. I understood from Darcy that although he was to travel often this month on business, his sister might be at home receiving masters for her studies. Now *that* is a girl of taste and accomplishment. I daresay that you and Miss Lucas may benefit from exposure to such a specimen of breeding. She is much like her mother, my late sister, the Lady Anne," declared Lady Catherine, who then rapped sharply with her cane to alert her driver. He seemed to understand her wishes well enough without a single word. The carriage turned, and very shortly they drew up to a tall and elegant home with its own gated garden nestled beside it.

A groom scurried around the carriage to open their door, and Elizabeth felt herself turn breathless with the prospect of this unexpected call.

"As their nearest relation, I never pass by Darcy House when its knocker is up," said Lady Catherine, who withdrew her card from her beaded reticule and passed it to her groom. He rushed it up the steps to Darcy House, and they waited for a moment that seemed rather long to Elizabeth's beating heart. Presently, the door of the house above them was opened by a welcoming butler, and Lady Catherine sat taller and gathered up her cane to disembark the carriage steps. "Come, you will accompany me on this call."

CHAPTER THREE

MARIA LUCAS SPRANG UP FROM THE CARRIAGE SEAT WITH eagerness; Elizabeth followed at a pace that may have appeared sedate, but was instead weighed down by dread and disordered feelings. Her eyes darted here and there, gleaning bits of her own scattered senses from what she saw: well-kept steps and handsome cut stone, the fine cut of the butler's clothing and the pride in his bearing, the sheen of the long windows she passed, and the polished marble with its darker inset pattern on the floor as she drew inside. She raised her eyes enough to take in the graceful sweep of stairs and the gleam of gilded frames of portraits and landscapes. A tall potted palm sat upon the top landing, reaching still higher, gathering the light that came from some bright window set within the roof, placed to catch both sun and stars.

From upon that very stair, she heard a timid voice. "Lady Catherine! I mean, Aunt Catherine! How kind of you to call upon me so soon after my lessons."

Elizabeth turned her eyes upon the young lady and was immediately struck with the confusion of unrecognition. There was nothing here to resemble anything that had been described to her regarding Miss Darcy aside from her healthy height. Mr Wickham had called her *proud*—yet clearly, as she stammered and showed herself equally embarrassed and eager to extend welcome, she gave no hint of aloofness. Miss Bingley had declared her elegant, and while the girl's clothing was certainly fine and well-fitted, it was not a testament to fashion beyond comfort and usefulness, and somehow even seemed girlish in its trimming. The figure it covered was well-formed and womanly, yet the girl's soft-featured face showed her to be sixteen summers at most. In such a quandary of surprise and unmet expectations, Elizabeth found it was even difficult to trace in that countenance's good-humoured symmetry anything of the noble beauty of the girl's brother.

She felt her cheeks heat to think of Mr Darcy now—and as beautiful, no less. As she met Miss Darcy's astonished gaze, she saw the girl was blushing too.

It seemed that Lady Catherine had been speaking throughout this encounter. Elizabeth roused herself just in time to hear her ladyship say, "And this young lady is Miss Elizabeth Bennet, who I believe knew your brother when he came into her home county in Hertfordshire last autumn."

Miss Darcy dropped a hasty curtsey. "Miss Bennet, ah! And—Miss Lucas, it is a pleasure to meet you."

Elizabeth could not hold back an encouraging smile for her surprised young hostess. "You are very kind to receive us, Miss Darcy. And 'Miss Elizabeth' will do very well. My elder sister Jane is *the* Miss Bennet of all my sisters, you see."

"I take it, Miss Elizabeth," Miss Darcy replied with a smile, "that you must have at least one more sister, then?"

"I am the second of five sisters."

To Elizabeth's amusement, Miss Darcy's mouth made a circle of inelegant surprise in return. "I might envy you, for I have always wanted a sister," the girl replied. "But then, I have *such* a devoted brother that I never can complain of my situation."

"And he is equally devoted to your studies, as he properly should be," put in Lady Catherine. "You wrote in your last letter that he has gifted you a new harpsichord, I believe."

"A new *harp*, ma'am," said Miss Darcy, her soft tone seeming at odds with her pointed interest. "It is in the Welsh style. I have recently had a master sent up for it as well, for it is very different to the instruments I have thus far studied."

Lady Catherine shifted more weight onto her cane. "I do hope you have not neglected your pianoforte in your pursuit of this novelty. Where is your companion? She ought to direct you."

Miss Darcy shook her head stoutly. "I would never neglect my pianoforte. As for Mrs Annesley, she left only minutes ago, on an errand to her sister's here in town."

Lady Catherine nodded and continued, "Too many young ladies will not take the trouble if left to their own direction. I have often told Miss Bennet—" here the dowager turned to Elizabeth with some gravity, "—that she will never improve unless she *practises more*. I invited her to do so at Rosings, for I have provided Miss Jenkinson with an instrument, you know."

Elizabeth made no defence of her neglect. Miss Darcy, clearly embarrassed to see her aunt openly betray a deficiency in her guest, leapt in with fumbling kindness, "I did not know—at Rosings, I mean. I had heard once before, Miss Elizabeth, that you were fond of music and could play and sing."

This gave Elizabeth a moment's pause, for Miss Darcy could only have heard such a thing from her closest source. How much, she wondered, had the brother shared with the sister of his admiration, so invisible to Elizabeth until his surprising declaration just weeks ago?

"I confess that I enjoy the music itself far more than the practice it requires to perform it well, Miss Darcy," Elizabeth replied, laughing a little to put the girl and herself at ease. "And I admit to my curiosity about you and your skills, for I have heard now from many sources that you are quite accomplished at your instrument."

"Have you?" Miss Darcy asked anxiously. "Now you make me rather afraid to exhibit, should the performance not meet your expectations."

Maria, until now a portrait of quiet curiosity, exclaimed, "Oh, I do hope we might prevail upon you to play a little for us. We are not a fearsome audience. I can hardly play a note, and Elizabeth only keeps to her favourite pieces."

Miss Darcy would not promise to perform, but she invited all the ladies to come up with her to the music room. There, Elizabeth could only express admiration for the lovely room, clearly fitted up to please Miss Darcy with soft colours, dainty furnishings, and an entire wall of shelves and nooks to hold sheaves and sheaves of music. And the instruments! Elizabeth's wonder, and her wandering feet, took her to each one in its turn as Miss Darcy explained their provenance.

"This pianoforte was my mother's, and it still has a very lovely voice. The one I have at Pemberley was also one of hers from her girlhood at Matlock, and very delicate. My brother always has it tuned before I come home. And this pedal harp over there is the one I first learnt upon. It is something my brother gave me to bring me some joy after our father died five years ago. And—you see—his latest gift to me is this Welsh harp. It is very different to my pedal harp. Look how it is strung: there are three rows, and the outer two are octaves apart and may be played *in unisons*. And it must be balanced on my left shoulder instead of my right—rather backwards to my senses. But oh, the sound of it is so very sweet! I find myself quite enchanted with it already."

"So I see," Elizabeth said, and she watched Miss Darcy demonstrate briefly by plucking out a snatch of a merry folk song. The tone from the curved harp was gentle and bright, even somehow warm, like a sunlit garden of sound, and Elizabeth could feel immediately how its resonance could delight even the weariest of souls.

Miss Darcy invited her guests to touch it, to try plucking the octave strings together, and Maria made the young ladies all laugh when she found a semitone instead, flattening the pitch.

Having witnessed Miss Darcy's proficiency at the harp strings, the ladies soon prevailed upon their hostess to play the pianoforte that dominated the room. Miss Darcy consented readily, for she seemed somehow surer of her own powers in this domain of music. Indeed, Elizabeth felt certain that she now observed Miss Darcy in what was clearly her most comfortable situation—behind the keys of her long-beloved instrument.

Elizabeth had prepared herself to observe Miss Darcy's full technical prowess and all the markings of a well-tutored proficient. But what her ears detected ran far deeper as Miss Darcy poured forth the notes of a sonata. Here was more than practice and application; here was skill combined with rare passion, an almost hedonistic taste for and bold command of sound and the senses. Here was genius.

As Elizabeth listened in increasing delight, the enthralling power of the music overcame her. The heavy cares from many weeks, days, moments of discomfort and disordered doubts at last released their hold, and her suddenly weightless mind was freed only to be carried along by the river of sound whilst the tension in her body sank, coming to rest like a stone underneath its flow. As the last strains of the song eased, Elizabeth finally surfaced, taking a breath.

"That was capital!" declared Maria, as soon as the following hush allowed it. "I have never heard the like! Have you, Elizabeth?"

"No, never," she agreed.

Lady Catherine waved a hand in the air, as if conjuring her point. "And do you see now what you can achieve with great practice, Miss Bennet?"

Elizabeth smiled archly. "I have heard many young ladies who practise with constancy, but I have never heard another play *this* well. Not with the vigour, with the natural ease and flow, as your niece demonstrates." She turned to her young hostess. "It is clear to me, Miss Darcy, that you have something beyond even talent. Your love for music is plain to see."

Miss Darcy's ears turned red, but her voice was steady as she observed, "I think you must also be a lover of music to recognise such affinity in another."

Elizabeth laughed outright. "I am, I confess it. And I must thank you for feeding my fascination such a *feast*. I should not ask you to play again, but I am a very selfish creature!"

Miss Darcy smiled fondly. "You sound very like my brother. He is the most unselfish person I know, yet he will plead with me to play just a little more, a little longer, or to play his favourite again just to please him. Since he is so very good, I have never been able to say no to him. But then, I cannot imagine anybody would deny him anything he would ask."

Miss Darcy had not meant to cast shame on Elizabeth with such a sweet reflection, but suddenly, it was all that she could feel. Convinced now in the real power of Miss Darcy's affection for her brother, and surrounded by the evidence of Mr Darcy's own doting care for his sister, Elizabeth understood more of what she had rejected in April. She could see now what it was to be cherished by him—he, who had claimed to *ardently love* her.

She lowered her eyes to her hands, folded so tightly as to nearly cause pain. She heard a sudden rush of skirts as her hostess rose from the instrument, and Elizabeth feared that her discomposure had garnered Miss Darcy's attentive concern. However, when Elizabeth raised her gaze, she found Miss Darcy moving not nearer but farther away under the power of happy impulse, trotting to the doorway in a flurry of delight.

There, the very object of Elizabeth's thoughts stood leaning in the aperture as if her own regrets had summoned him.

CHAPTER FOUR

"Brother!" Miss Darcy took his hand and bussed his cheek. "I hope all went well on your excursion."

"Forgive me for my intrusion, Georgiana," Mr Darcy replied in low tones. "I did not wish to disturb your guests. I heard only that our aunt had called."

"And it is well you came up to see me, Darcy, for you left Rosings with hardly a proper leave," Lady Catherine scolded.

"Forgive me," Mr Darcy said, bowing. When he straightened, his eyes darted to find Maria Lucas's face—and then, with a widening expression of recognition, Elizabeth's.

Coldness washed over Elizabeth, then heat in her cheeks answered it. She was capable of meeting his eye only for as long a moment as she could withstand, until she felt she must direct her gaze downward again to her folded hands that were now wringing themselves in acute agitation. His eyes had looked dark and troubled, evincing as much surprised distress as she felt within herself.

He recovered first and bowed. "Miss Lucas, Miss Elizabeth. I hope your journey from Kent has been satisfactory."

A beat of tense silence followed as Elizabeth struggled to find her voice and respond. Maria, dazed as always in the presence of Mr Darcy, made no answer for her. Instead, it fell to Lady Catherine to reply, "But of course! They came into town with me in my own barouche."

"How very kind of you, Aunt," he replied mechanically.

"Yes, very kind," put in his sister boldly. "I am also grateful to Lady Catherine for forming my new acquaintance with these young ladies. We have had a lovely time today."

Here was one commonality certain to bring peace into the tempest of this most unexpected reunion. Elizabeth found composure enough to meet Mr Darcy's gaze and say sincerely, "Miss Darcy has been a charming hostess, sir. The praise for her talent has not been exaggerated. I feel privileged to have heard her exhibit for us."

Mr Darcy said nothing for a moment; then he managed to offer a brief nod.

"Thank you," said Miss Darcy, biting her lip and glancing uncertainly between them before she continued. "I find myself more easy and able to play my best when my audience is as encouraging as you have been. I never seem to play well for strangers."

The similarity of these words to some of the same spoken by Mr Darcy himself could hardly avoid notice; now, however, they struck Elizabeth wholly differently than before.

"I once believed that the sole responsibility for improvement in such cases must lie with the performer—that they must take the trouble of practising before strangers to cure themselves of this vulnerability," said Elizabeth slowly, daring to raise her eyes if only a little to Mr Darcy's face. "I have since learned that the receptivity of one's audience weighs greatly in a performer's success. If the audience is of a beneficent mind and gives charity to the performer without prejudice, the performance must always satisfy."

Here, she turned to Miss Darcy with a wan smile. "I have decided to practise such charity far more often, for I fear I have not always done so in the past. In your case, your gift with music presents its own merit and must inspire warm regard, regardless of your audience."

She kept her smile for Miss Darcy, for although Elizabeth had borrowed what familiar remarks she could from their conversation at Rosings in hopes of catching Mr Darcy's ear, she was still afraid to catch his eye. Eagerness to please Miss Darcy weighed in balance with her wish to avoid giving greater offence to Mr Darcy than she had at their previous interview. So she accepted Miss Darcy's warm smile, even as she shifted nervously in anticipation of what Mr Darcy, now so still and silent, might do or say next.

"Gracious," said Maria with a laugh, "how you do preach and teach! You sound like your sister Mary!"

Elizabeth turned to her in surprise. "Do I? I aimed to speak from self-censure. I assure you it was not my intention to school the room with such notions. I am poor enough of a student; I ought never position myself as a teacher."

"On the contrary," said Mr Darcy with a suddenness that nearly made her start, "I have always learnt a great deal from you."

Confusion immediately washed over Elizabeth at this inscrutable remark. Had he meant to compliment her? Or had he meant to rebuke her with a subtle judgment about his own lesson, hard earned, in so foolishly offering for her? He would not look at her. It was impossible to know.

Lady Catherine spoke staunchly into the silence. "Young women ought never put themselves forward as teachers, except to children. I am certain my nephew will hold to greater wisdom."

Mr Darcy kept silent. His sister—perhaps seeing him, as Elizabeth did, made rigid either by unbending restraint or paralysing uncertainty—bit her lip and offered to play again.

Maria immediately encouraged their hostess's return to the instrument, and the occupants of the room began to sort themselves once more. Mr Darcy took himself to the bookshelf behind his sister, ready to step in to turn her pages. Elizabeth moved back to her former place on a delicate chair beside the dowager, and Miss Darcy began to play.

Elizabeth had caught just enough of the theme of the song to begin to anticipate the movements of the piece, to follow and feel with it, when she felt Mr Darcy's eye upon her. She gave him the merest glance of timid curiosity, fully expecting to find something censorious in his returning look. Instead, she found it a mirror of her own. She held his gaze as long as she dared.

"I must have a word, Miss Bennet, if you will accompany me to the salon," murmured Lady Catherine suddenly, leaning towards Elizabeth over the tufted arm of her chair.

The request had been spoken softly, but there was so much sternness in her look that Elizabeth dared not refuse. She curtseyed and followed immediately, too hasty and unsettled to spare more than a backwards glance at Mr Darcy and his sister.

Lady Catherine led her on a little ways down the hall towards a room made cheerful with lavender paper and pale furnishings. Once Elizabeth had gained the room with her, Lady Catherine pulled the door closed and turned back towards Elizabeth in abrupt displeasure.

"Miss Bennet, you ought to know I am not to be trifled with! I have eyes as keen as any, and I have seen how *yours* seek out my nephew. I have never seen such artful provocation, and such low deceit—to stoop to baiting your snares with praise of his own sister! I now regret bringing you to pay this call."

Elizabeth's amazement gave way to greater feelings of offence. "Lady Catherine, if I sought Mr Darcy's attention, it was for reasons you cannot presume to understand at a glance. You have widely mistaken my character, ma'am, if you think me here to ensnare him."

"But of course, you should seek to deny it. I am ashamed of you! Such an appearance of innocence as you have may fool a lesser mind, but you will find me wise to your arts and allurements. I think it best that you and Miss Lucas are removed from the house immediately."

"You will not find me unwilling," replied Elizabeth, rising immediately to go.

"Not so hasty," hissed her ladyship. "I have by no means done. It is clear to me that by some contrivance or manipulation you have placed a considerable hold upon my nephew. I have never seen him less composed in the presence of any young woman. I intend to know *all* before it becomes a matter of gossip. Tell me, then, Miss Bennet—have you had an assignation with him?"

Elizabeth stood stock-still, white-lipped, until the molten outrage which had filled her spirit left her. "Your assumptions and your accusations, your ladyship, are as pernicious as they are ill-judged. You impugn my honour as much as *his* with such a question. What your nephew might say, had he heard you utter such an enquiry, I might only guess. You certainly have insulted me by every possible method. I must beg to take my leave of this house." She turned swiftly again to go.

Lady Catherine's arm shot out to bar her way, and she raised her voice to exclaim, "You will hear me out! It is for Darcy's own honour that I detain you. I care nothing for yours. So far there has been no scandal, and no falsehood has spread. So it must remain. Do I make myself clear on this matter?"

The door to the salon suddenly opened with a bang as it twisted back forcefully on its hinges, and Mr Darcy's voice immediately filled the shocked silence. "This is beyond bearing! How can you so slander Miss Bennet, and then dare to speak of *my* honour? Have you no sense to know when matters cease to concern you? This interview ends —now!"

Lady Catherine reared back and hissed, "*How dare I?* How dare *you!* For now I see it clearly. You have debased yourself, Nephew!"

Mr Darcy went white with anger, and Elizabeth flinched, both at her ladyship's insult and her anticipation of a volatile response from the gentleman. But when Mr Darcy spoke again, his voice rolled with the threat of a storm over a sea of calm. "You understand nothing. There is no debasement here but yours, and all from your *slanderous* tongue."

Lady Catherine gasped at his words, but, contrary to her nature, kept her silence.

Mr Darcy turned to Elizabeth and made her an irresistible offer. "You have suffered a grievous and unforgivable injustice. Please allow me to take you home."

CHAPTER FIVE

MR DARCY ACCOMPANIED HER SWIFTLY FROM THE ROOM, but once they were in the hall, he reached out suddenly, and very gently, took her elbow. She could feel that his hand was shaking—or perhaps it was herself who was so shaken.

"Miss Elizabeth—"

"Mr Darcy—"

"A moment, please. You seem unwell. Would you accompany me to the study, if only for a moment? I think it best that I return you to the company of my sister and Miss Lucas after we have both regained our composure."

Elizabeth nodded mutely and allowed him to conduct her past the door to the music room and down the stairs. Once they gained the quiet space of the study, he let go of her and gestured to a table glistening with crystal decanters. "Is there something I can get you for your present relief? I keep some sherry here, if brandy is not to your taste."

Elizabeth heard him asking her preference as if from a distance. She nodded at the sherry without much thought and made her way to a chair near the room's long window. She sank into the cushion and closed her eyes a moment with a sigh, and when she opened them again, she watched him busy himself pouring her a little glass. The mundane task seemed to steady his nerves a little, even as she felt hers unravelling at this act of kindness. After such distress just moments ago, the balm of his hospitality shook her once again.

He offered the glass to her, and she took a sip dutifully, her eyes still on him. She was absorbed by what she read in his expression as he equally read hers: the concern, the brightened emotion in his gaze, the rapid changes in his colour as his anger faded and passed into something simultaneously more and less composed. Far from the proud aloofness that she had always associated with him, in this moment he seemed so very open, so very near, like his own heart was racing as much as hers, and all his thinking and feeling in as much a tangle as she found knotted up within herself.

"Miss Elizabeth," he said at last, "there are no words to properly convey my apologies for what you have suffered just now. For Lady Catherine—my own aunt—to attack you with such unmerited ire in my own house!"

"There is nothing you must say to me," Elizabeth said gently. "The fault here belongs to Lady Catherine."

"Not entirely. She would not have attacked you thus without some cause. Forgive me. It is indelicate to speak of this—but I am certain when I first saw you today that my aunt perceived some change in me that raised her alarm. It was unconsciously done, but I undoubtedly betrayed my thoughts in that moment, and she presumed to judge you most ungenerously."

"It was nothing you have done," Elizabeth countered. "I do not think you heard—just now—when Lady Catherine disclosed that she saw something in *my* behaviour that exposed me to her worst suspicions. You cannot blame yourself."

He shook his head resolutely. "But I do. I blame myself for exposing you to her censure, and I have wronged you on one other point as well. For despite my influence with her, I have done nothing to check in her that sense of unscrupulous pride that sets her so at odds with others in the world. Indeed, I even mirrored it and was encouraging of that habit of thinking meanly of others. You know this —for did I not wound you myself, only a month ago? Did I not humble, demean, and pain you at the very moment when I should have raised you up as a woman worthy of my utmost regard?"

He groaned and covered his face with his hands as if the bitter irony were blinding him. He sank into the chair opposite her with a sort of boneless helplessness that Elizabeth found riveting. She watched him take a heavy breath, and just when her sympathies caused her to wonder whether she should say something to comfort him, her judgment convinced her of the justice of his painful epiphany. She would not interfere while he was still in its power. She sipped her sherry and waited for her senses and his to reunite into a semblance of calm.

Gradually, Mr Darcy gathered himself. His hands unveiled his face, and he regarded her with a sincerity that fixed her further into silence. "Please accept my profoundest apologies for speaking and thinking so, for paining you, for disparaging your own family when my own has treated you despicably. I am sorry, so terribly sorry. I find I am teaching myself at the price of your own pain, and I am humbled."

Elizabeth had ample evidence before her to know that he felt his own words keenly. Here was a man whose demeanour among others always showed the utmost self-control, yet he sat before her now entirely discomposed. A man whose pride had once given her a disgust of him, and who was now plainly disgusted by it himself. The transformation was remarkable, and Elizabeth hoped the great cost of his new humility gave it permanent value.

She set down her glass on the little table beside her, then rose. His eyes widened as she approached him, but this did not deter her courage. She placed her hand on his shoulder as she stood before him. "I believe that when a wrong is acknowledged, keeping hold of its memory is unpardonable," Elizabeth said softly. "I forgive you freely, sir."

A huff of air escaped him, like she had dealt him a blow rather than given him the succour he sought. His frame shook with it until he pulled in a breath and raised his face to her in wonder. His hand reached up for hers, pressing into it where it still sat upon his shoulder.

"You are too generous with me," he said softly. "Far too generous."

"*Generous*, am I? I do not think I merit the term. But then, I feel I hardly know myself. To own the truth, I have not properly known myself since I have known you," she admitted.

At his look of incredulity, she went on, "My own powers of understanding, which I once trusted, have been tested since our first meeting and have proved wholly deficient. It has been a painful lesson to acknowledge that I possess every weakness of vanity and mistaken judgment that can breed folly. Can you forgive me for exposing you to the worst of my nature, for thinking the very worst of you, almost from the beginning of our acquaintance?"

He regarded her intently for a moment, then he sat up a little taller. He did not remove his hand from over hers. Instead, he swept his thumb under her palm and took hold of her grasp properly. Elizabeth, caught suspended in her own surprise, did not recoil. He looked aside at their connexion for a moment and seemed to be steadying, gradually steadying in her grasp, gentled by it out of the intensity of his own discomposure. She squeezed his hand in silent understanding.

"Miss Elizabeth," he said, going very still at the sound of her name in his mouth. "You truly *are* too generous. Too generous to trifle with me, I think. You have taught me so much in just the span of a few weeks, a few moments. Dare I think that within all these lessons, you have taught me to *hope?*"

"To hope, sir?" Elizabeth repeated, even as she found the answer in the warm weight of his hand, still holding hers.

"To hope that your opinion of me is not as fixed as it once was—and to imagine that you are extending me such kindness from an impulse more liberal than charity. My own affections and wishes are unchanged, but I cannot fathom yours. If your feelings are still what they were in Kent, pray, tell me so at once."

Elizabeth tried to speak, swept back her breath, and tried again. His apology had been in keeping with his sense of honour, but she would never have presumed to expect from him this constancy of affection—not after the pain and bitterness his letter had revealed he carried from her rejection of his suit.

"I hardly know what to tell you," she said at last. "I find myself in the midst of more confusion than would allow for any confidence in my own feelings. In this moment, we have more to say to each other and more affinity to share than we could claim thus far in the whole of our acquaintance. And there is trust—there is certainly more trust between us, now, than ever before. We have both made great effort to deal with one another honestly, at the price of our pride. That represents something significant to me, although I cannot say *what* it signifies."

He nodded. It was clear by his cautiously approving gaze that this reflection did not answer all his hopes, although it did perhaps represent some improvements in the nature of their acquaintance. He released her hand.

Elizabeth withdrew enough to clasp her still-warm hand in the grasp of her other and regain her breath. Once she had gathered enough of her own composure, she was able to observe that his own hands now mirrored hers, and his face was a picture of contemplative gravity.

"I ought to find that answer enough to satisfy," he said at last. "I shall never forget how it was only weeks ago, when I witnessed that turn of your countenance as you spoke with such decided revulsion against my offer and my character. At least now, it seems you can bear my company tolerably."

Elizabeth nodded with enough vigour to concede the truth of what he said. Yes, her feelings had changed, although the depth of that change was still unknown. But the longer she stood in this quiet room with him as he spoke to her openly in this soft way, the more she felt she could like him. The thought cheered her enough to bring back her voice.

"Yes. You are tolerable, I suppose," she confirmed with a gentle smile, tilting her head as she waited for him to recognise this ironic recollection of his words from the Assembly Room where they had first met.

Clever as he was, he was quick to catch her meaning and her look, and he evinced his own understanding with a short, disbelieving chuckle. His laughter grew into something more as he covered his face again in an attempt to suppress the emotions that seemed to suddenly assail him.

As his shoulders shook, Elizabeth suddenly feared she had hurt him with her teasing. She had merely meant to make light of his slight by turning it into a compliment. She was just on the point of apologising for her thoughtlessness when he raised his head to look at her.

"No," he said haltingly. "Pray, do not apologise for using my own unjustifiable words most justly in my presence. It was well done, I assure you. You possess quite the talent for carrying your point."

He shook off his weighty mirth, took a bracing breath, and stood.

The effect was pronounced. No longer crowded into his chair and dishevelled by distress, he restored the length and breadth and grace of his usual form. Elizabeth was more familiar with this tall, elegant Mr Darcy that stood before her, certainly. Yet, she missed the Darcy she felt she had just started to come to know, the man who had been in the chair, sitting and thinking, talking and feeling with her. She had begun to fear she had lost that man until he approached her with an uncertain expression in his eyes that she now felt she understood and recognised, for she had seen Miss Darcy wear it: shyness.

He offered her his arm as if to lead her to a dance. "Miss Elizabeth," he said, "I ought to take you home."

Elizabeth agreed, although she felt no urgency either in herself or in him as she tucked her hand into the crook of his arm. He looked down on her with such a sweet expression of relief that she could not resist giving a little squeeze of reassurance.

He led her on amicably, parting only to overtake the stairs on their way towards the music room, where they met a shocking sight: poor Maria Lucas, crying into a handkerchief, and Miss Darcy settled beside her on the sofa in miserable commiseration.

Miss Darcy rose and approached them. "Miss Lucas had the misfortune of being a target for Lady Catherine's most terrible anger. She shouted at her and then she left. Oh, Brother, I do not know what to say to make this right! What are we to do?"

Elizabeth understood well enough that poor Maria had been scolded for the shame of her association. She went to sit beside the girl and put her arm around her as a sister might, and Maria responded as any child would by turning her face to sob wretchedly onto Elizabeth's shoulder.

Mr Darcy pulled out his own, dry handkerchief in offering to the girl. Elizabeth accepted it on her behalf.

"I can only offer my apologies to Miss Lucas, as I have to Miss Elizabeth, that such a thing has happened here at Darcy House. Lady Catherine has been the victim of her own misunderstanding, and yet she will persist in adhering to her folly," said Mr Darcy, before turning aside to his sister. "Obstinate, headstrong woman," he sighed. "I am ashamed of her, too, Georgiana. Do not let it distress you. Let us rectify matters with Miss Lucas and Miss Elizabeth by ensuring they are taken safely home."

Miss Darcy nodded, her expression a little shocked from hearing her brother so summarily denounce their aunt. Mr Darcy patted her hand and then moved to address the other young ladies.

"Are you bound for Hertfordshire, Eli—Miss Elizabeth?" he asked awkwardly, over the sound of Maria's hiccoughs and sobs.

"Not directly. I am for my aunt and uncle Gardiners' house in Gracechurch Street. They are expecting us."

He nodded. "I will be happy to convey you to any destination. You have only to say when you wish to go."

Elizabeth had just turned to Maria to assess her readiness to leave when the girl suddenly sat up in alarm.

"Oh, but my bandbox and my trunk—all that has gone away with Lady Catherine!" Maria exclaimed with renewed distress. "She has *everything*!"

"That is easily remedied," replied Mr Darcy. "She will have had no thought for your luggage in any case. I will not raise her notice by stopping for the trunks in my own carriage when a cart and some discreet servants will suffice."

Maria turned back to Elizabeth pleadingly. "Then I—I do wish to go now to the Gardiners' with you, Elizabeth."

"And I will go with you," volunteered Miss Darcy. "I shall also request that my maid accompany us—" and here she eyed Maria's reddened face with thoughtful compassion, "—after she has attended to you, Miss Lucas."

Maria nodded, and Miss Darcy prevailed upon her guests to accompany her to her own dressing room to tidy themselves. With a bow, Mr Darcy excused himself to dispatch a footman and his trusted valet to House de Bourgh for the ladies' purloined luggage.

CHAPTER SIX

THE LADIES WERE MADE COMFORTABLE ABOVE STAIRS, where they washed away their road dust, and Maria, her tears. Miss Darcy's maid finished rearranging their hair just in time for them to all be summoned below stairs. The maid followed them down in some confusion at these instructions until Miss Darcy gave her a few quiet words in an aside.

As they arranged their bonnets and pelisses in the vestibule, Elizabeth struggled with the awkwardness of this attempt at propriety, even as the maid's bemusement transformed into overtly curious glances.

For his part, Mr Darcy was the picture of proper decorum. He gave instructions to his driver, handed the ladies into his gleaming coach, and stepped into the cabin with great care for all their skirts.

Elizabeth saw Miss Darcy hide a smile as she took in her brother's reaction to their seating arrangements, and suddenly understood his surprise at how neatly Miss Darcy had managed to place herself in the seat between Maria and her lady's maid, leaving Mr Darcy to join Elizabeth where she sat, alone, on the facing seat.

Torn between consternation and admiration for her hostess's slyness, Elizabeth gave herself the gift of space and time by shifting unobtrusively towards the window. Mr Darcy's considerable frame settled onto the far end of their shared seat with similar care.

With a tap on the roof from Mr Darcy, the team surged forward. Maria, seemingly emboldened by the lavish comfort of the carriage, leant a little out the window to better take in the grand sights near Grosvenor Square and quizzed Miss Darcy on her knowledge of the families in residence along the edges of the green.

"I know that one well," said Miss Darcy, her dainty gloves pointing rather emphatically, if impolitely, at one of the grandest of the houses. "That one belongs to the Earl of Derby, built for his father, Sir Edward Stanley. My brother told me Sir Edward fought the Jacobites in the rebellion."

Elizabeth turned to look. "He sounds quite fearsome," she commented. "I imagine there are many great personages' homes here, each with stories representing valuable history."

"My father told me a great many stories," agreed Mr Darcy, his voice carrying with that tender, soft tone that made Elizabeth think fondly of the Darcy she had spoken to less than an hour ago in the study. "I have often wished for more Sunday drives with my sister so that I may tell her all the tales I know. I have been sadly neglectful."

"But you have already told me so many!" Miss Darcy protested warmly. "You must not fault yourself. I simply cannot remember them all."

As they made their way towards Charing Cross, the coach slowed. Miss Lucas sat forward to exclaim over the Mews, enjoining Miss Darcy to look out the window and admire the guards and the horses as they slowly drove through the busy streets. This was not a side of London that Elizabeth often saw, so she took in her view as well. They did not linger. The carriage jostled steadily along towards the Thames as their driver navigated through throngs of workmen and merchants towards the heart of the old City.

As the carriage rocked over the rutted streets, Elizabeth's attention, once so fixed outside the carriage by the sights and doings without, now withdrew into the cabin.

Mr Darcy had begun their journey situated rigidly on his own side of the seat. But now the solid weight of him had naturally pulled towards the centre as the road roughened, closer now to Elizabeth than before. Close enough that the air between them seemed suddenly a shared space, filtered through the straw of her bonnet into her own breath, tasting to her senses somehow redolent of him. She could feel the downward drag of the cushion whenever his body adjusted to some new obstacle under their wheels, could even feel the way her own figure jostled in time to the same. With all her senses bound to this narrow world of the carriage seat, she found ample opportunity for the reflection the day's events had made so necessary.

She had not entered his home that day expecting to see him again; she had even less expectation of his sudden defence of her in the face of his aunt's ire. Nor had she anticipated his apology, or such a fervency of feeling in response. Try as she might to remind herself of all the reasons she had once cherished to maintain her dislike of him, she found that in the face of his earnestness with her, they all seemed very feeble. And when her natural sense of justice asserted itself to demand she extend charity to him, those reasons lost all influence completely.

Once she gave herself leave to absolve him where she could, and to endeavour to understand him where she could not, she found it easy to grant herself further liberties: To appreciate his good qualities. To even admire him. As she turned her eyes beyond the rim of her bonnet to glance at him, only to find him regarding her in that same spirit of fascination, she realised her danger.

"You seem unsettled, Miss Elizabeth," he said cautiously, his tone guarded so as not to raise notice among the young ladies cheerfully chatting away in the seat facing them.

She could prevaricate, but such disguise seemed in every way abhorrent after the quarter-hour's honesty they had shared in his study. She was endeavouring to master her own feelings, and until they were ordered again and properly understood, she feared others detecting them, feared what they meant, feared whether they were untrustworthy. She did not yet know how to put them into words. But she realised that *he* at least, proved in his circumspection and loyal defence of her, was as trustworthy a confessor as any.

She turned towards him bodily, closing enough distance that when they were next jostled by the carriage as it rolled up from the dirt onto cobbled streets, her angled knees brushed his. She decided to confront the most pressing concern facing her arrival at Gracechurch Street.

"My aunt is a shrewd woman," Elizabeth said softly. "I wonder, what she will make of Maria and me coming back in a gentleman's carriage, with nothing but our hats to stand up in, with your servants coming after us with our trunks? She will undoubtedly begin to speculate."

"Are we to meet with yet another officious aunt? I had not imagined yours would be so fearsome as mine, or that you should be made afraid of any other creature today," he answered with amused concern.

"Oh, no! I must not have you think my aunt overbearing. Mrs Gardiner is the soul of discretion, and rather than an object of dread, she is one of my admiration and regard. I should hate to cause her disappointment or doubt. That is all I fear."

He nodded, and the tension left his face. He was relieved—relieved for *her* sake. "Let us hope then, that her own affection for you will protect her from her worst assumptions. If she is as shrewd as you say, then she knows well your character. She will come to the right conclusion, and your arrival will look exactly as it ought."

Elizabeth suppressed a smile. "I am glad to see your faith in aunts so restored, sir. But there is no way to represent today's events to her without relating too much of our history in the misunderstandings that have led us here. I am hesitant to divulge it all, for it is not entirely my story to tell."

This was a new consideration: she feared the loss of his own privacy as much as hers, evincing a value for him and his cares that she had not recognised in herself before, but perhaps, had held closely ever since receiving his letter in secret. He was looking at her with a keen interest, as if he recognised it too.

"Tell her what you feel you must. I see nothing to cast shame on you in any part, nor do I feel the need to conceal what has already earned your forgiveness. As for our present circumstance, it will all look as it ought, as I have said."

"As it 'ought'?" she repeated. "I do not know how that can be rightly represented."

"It will look as if you were protected on your journey home by a gentleman," he said plainly. "As if your safe return were important to me—important enough that I see you comfortably situated again. As if my attachment to you and your well-being weighed more in my consideration than any other appearance of decorum."

"Oh." She did not know where to look, but she felt him looking at her as openly as he had in the study, where such a gaze had worked on her heart to build trust between them both. Now, that look held more than just sincerity. It held a tenderness that was almost too much to bear. Feeling more shaken than she wished to reveal, she looked down at her left hand where her gloved fingers pressed fretfully into the seat cushion between them.

His hand came down over hers, covering her knuckles warmly, then threading between her digits softly, calming her. "It will look as though I loved you, Elizabeth. And that is the reality."

The first time he had claimed to admire and love her, such avowals had given her nothing but doubt and disgust. Now, as she sat next to him in silent surprise, she examined her feelings for any resemblance to that suspicion and distaste, or to anything of her former, ill-formed dislike.

She found nothing of the old remnants. But there were new feelings aplenty, rushing onto her, over her, gaining speed like her heart, rolling like the carriage wheels under the floorboards, like thunder before a storm, sweeping her heedlessly, helplessly along. Their progression came so quickly that she had no names to give such sensations, and could only submit to the fullness of the exhilaration they gave.

She turned her palm upward under his, latching on tightly, mindlessly seeking that stillness so particular to him as her anchor. She took a quick breath and exhaled as soon as she felt him respond, clasping her grip with warm encouragement.

It felt like coming inside out of the wind. And quite naturally following this sensation came a beckoning craving for closeness and warmth, as would draw a weary traveller to the fireplace. In her body as much as in her mind, this strange, acute longing grew, this need to be wrapped up in *him* for comfort, for relief.

Situated as they were in the company of the young girls and Miss Darcy's maid, there was no possible way to act upon this impulse. But as she let her fingers linger and twine with his, it grew ever more impossible to ignore.

She raised her gaze from their joined hands, no doubt giving him the wonder and wildness in her look. He read her expression at first with his own wide-eyed astonishment, then he smiled—*such* a smile—as if what he saw in her, as if she herself, were all his happiness.

"So soon?" he asked, in incredulous delight.

"It *is* sudden," she admitted in a small voice. "It is like all the decisions of my life were all wrapped into one moment. I did not trust myself to answer you at first—forgive me. Now I feel it so acutely—but—but we cannot speak of it here—"

It was painful, so painful to let go of his hand, but her doing so as a precaution against the awareness of their companions was almost immediately proved correct. The carriage slowed, and Maria turned to them with an enquiry as to their approach to their destination.

CHAPTER SEVEN

Elizabeth looked out the window, making a show of identifying landmarks to give her disordered sensibilities time to reunite into true sense. "Yes, Maria," she said at last. "We are very near Gracechurch Street now. See, there is the Friends' Meeting House. The Gardiners live not far from the edge of the court, set back from where the street meets it. I am certain my aunt will be awaiting our arrival."

They drew apace towards a brick house in the old city style, situated near a spreading elm and a garden gate enclosing the gap between itself and its neighbour. The porticoed door soon opened in observant welcome by the Gardiners' old housekeeper, Mrs Hatton, and Elizabeth was glad to see from the expectation in the dear woman's face that she had made the house ready to receive any visitors who were party to their arrival.

Mr Darcy was the first to disembark, and he handed Elizabeth out with a lingering hand, followed by the other ladies. As the women fussed over their skirts, Mr Darcy dismissed his driver to the nearby coaching inn. No sooner had he done so than Mrs Gardiner herself appeared at the door, tall and graceful. She eagerly drew down the steps where Elizabeth introduced her, and she then proceeded to invite all her guests inside.

"Gracious, my dear Lizzy," said her aunt quietly, making a pretence of helping Elizabeth unbutton her gloves while her elderly servant and Miss Darcy's maid tidily collected the bonnets off the other young ladies. "You have taken up with some new chaperonage, I see. Whatever happened to her ladyship? Was Lady Catherine unwell?"

"Oh, Aunt," Elizabeth whispered back, already resigned to being discovered. "There is so much I should tell you! It has been a day of misunderstandings. I am still attempting to assimilate it all. And where—and how—is Jane? And the children?"

"They are all well recovered, but the children were quite of out sorts while awaiting your return. Jane took them all down with Martha to sail their little boats by the water. They will return soon, certainly in time to dine. I did not wish for Hatton to lay the table until after you returned. You and Maria are both safe and well, I see, although I would feel better if your trunks had come with you. We shall see what I have for you girls to borrow in the meantime if you wish to wash and dress."

Elizabeth glanced away with a smile for the tall gentleman who now stood hatless, offering his arm to his sister to move into the sitting room. She turned back to her aunt, still grinning. "Our trunks are coming shortly, never fear. Mr Darcy has arranged it all."

The brightness in her tone drew her aunt up from her task with sharp alertness. "Lizzy, did—?"

"Oh, you have nearly worked it out already! But pray, be your perfect self and do not pry. Not yet. Mr Darcy and I have suffered our worst humiliations this afternoon, and he has been kindness itself. I would not subject him to further scrutiny today."

Mrs Gardiner nodded and went into the sitting room, where she was once again as gracious, unruffled and welcoming a hostess as she had been at the door, pouring tea and seeing to everyone's comfort.

With a slyness Elizabeth had considered yet never witnessed within the scope of her aunt's powers, Mrs Gardiner approached Miss Darcy and introduced the subject of Lambton, her girlhood village, which by happy coincidence was less than five miles from Pemberley and therefore a shared domain of memories for both ladies. As they chatted and Maria sank tiredly into a cushion, Elizabeth took up her aunt's teapot and approached Mr Darcy. His cup needed no refilling, but the pretence pleased them both the same.

She resettled the pot and then sat beside him, closer than she had dared to at first in the carriage, yet not so close as she would wish. Her own fatigue was battling with her excited spirits and the enchantment of their sudden, newfound understanding.

He turned towards her, moving his arm to rest along the back of the sofa, nearly close enough to touch her shoulder. The gesture oddly soothed her because of the way it carried an echo of her unspoken yearning.

"You have travelled nearly forty miles today," he said softly, his gaze assessing. "And you have suffered more than the usual trials of polite society. You must be very tired."

"I could never have believed only this morning that today would hold so many surprises," she mused in agreement, wishing as she nodded her head that she could lay the weight of it upon that sturdy arm he kept stretched so close to her shoulder.

"A thrilling day, truly," he amended. "When Lady Catherine made her attack, I would never have imagined it could end in anything but disaster—in the worst of mortification and the end of all association between us."

"Nor would I," she agreed, "but then, I had not expected you to leap into the fray with me. Nothing forges a necessary alliance quite like facing a common enemy."

"Indeed, and even enemies will touch toes under the table when they sup at the banquet of a common foe."

His implication was a little painful. She shook her head. "You were never my enemy, Mr Darcy."

"Of course not," he said with chagrin. "I was merely the *last man in the world* you could ever be prevailed upon to marry."

She frowned. "Ah, yes, I did say that. I also once told my sister Jane that nothing would induce me into matrimony but the deepest love." She looked up at him, her eyes a little wide. "I would regret such prognostications more deeply if I did not see their fulfilment now."

He smiled down at her in amusement. "Oh? Have you made yourself your own oracle?"

"Only in this matter. Your love for me somehow survived great disappointment, and mine for you grew from my own mortification today. Such a thing must have deep roots if it will persist amidst all those misfortunes. I suppose we must deduce, therefore, that with such a love between us, you are, in fact, the last and only man I *could* ever be induced to marry."

He laughed, loud enough in his surprise that the others in the room turned to look at them. He mastered himself under their curiosity, and quickly moved to stand. He bowed to their hostess and said, "It has been a delight to meet you today, Mrs Gardiner. But I am aware that it is passing five o'clock, and I would not waylay your plans to dine." He glanced at his sister, adding, "Would it be convenient if we were to return at another time to call?"

Mrs Gardiner agreed to this readily, and their company all stood to make their polite farewells.

After Darcy had bowed to his hostess and the ladies began to gather towards the door, he turned once more to Elizabeth. "I will return tomorrow whenever you wish. You have only to say."

Elizabeth handed him his hat, feeling oddly uneasy as she considered matters of discretion and decorum that he, being so well-bred, might wish to observe, and which she was increasingly willing to overthrow. "My aunt has already deduced some form of understanding between us. You will not be unwelcome, even if you come a little early for a call. The house is always busy with the children here, you understand—"

"So I imagine."

"—and Jane, Jane will be here, surely, as well. Perhaps my uncle also—"

"I shall be glad to make his acquaintance and see your sister again."

Elizabeth could not miss the amusement in his voice and look, and the pleasure of seeing him so diverted by her eager chatter chased away her embarrassment. "Then it is settled," she agreed.

"What is settled?" asked Miss Darcy curiously, coming to take her brother's arm for their departure.

"You will come again tomorrow whenever you wish," said Elizabeth. "And then you may meet my elder sister, Jane."

"I would be delighted to meet *another* sister," said Miss Darcy with an earnestness that added peculiar weight to her words. It was just heavy enough an implication to confirm Elizabeth's own suppositions about the girl's powers of observation. Elizabeth could only smile and press her hand as she extended it in graceful farewell.

The Darcys went away in their carriage only moments later. Elizabeth might have succumbed to the sudden pang of desolation she felt had Jane and Martha and the four Gardiner children not come hurrying home to meet her again with cheer and delight.

She had just kissed each young cousin and swung the littlest of them up in her arms when Jane, herself unburdened from carrying the child, wrapped both arms around Elizabeth.

"Oh, Lizzy! It has been such a long time," she said in relieved tones. "I am so glad you are come back to me."

Such familiar comfort wrapped around her in the figure of her sister was more than welcome. It soothed Elizabeth's tumultuous spirits like nothing else. "And I am glad to have you with me," she replied, her voice breaking with emotion.

Jane pulled back enough to look into her sister's face, her concern too evident.

"I am well! I am well!" Elizabeth insisted quickly, dashing at the strange, sudden tears. "There is nothing the matter with me, but I have so much to tell. So much has changed, and so quickly. My heart is reeling. I have never felt such a disarray of emotions. Indeed, the last few hours could scarcely hold them all."

"Come upstairs with me, my dearest," said Jane, reclaiming the child and passing him to back to Martha. Her tone was firm as she took Elizabeth's arm with gentle force. "There is time enough before we dine to unburden yourself, if only a little. Where is my stalwart sister? This is most unlike you."

Still dazed by her own force of feeling, Elizabeth allowed her sister to steer her past her aunt who was giving instructions to the nursemaid, past the door to the sitting room and up the stairs. They had barely gained the bedroom and shut the door when her sister's large, beseeching eyes begged her to speak. So Elizabeth did, at first haltingly, unburden herself of what had transpired in Kent, especially her rejection of Mr Darcy's surprising offer, then a little of what he had revealed in his letter regarding the untrustworthiness of Mr Wickham

—sparing the name of Miss Darcy—and his disclosure of his own involvement in discouraging Mr Bingley's suit, and why he had acted so officiously in the interest of friendship.

Jane was very quiet and stood listening. Elizabeth kept breathing and went on, talking of how the delay in her departure from Hunsford had led to the day's events with Lady Catherine, including the dowager's insulting insinuations, Mr Darcy's defence of her, and his sincere apologies.

It was harder to then explain how her own feelings had changed in the face of such humble honesty, how she had been persuaded to not only accept his apologies and his feelings but to return them. How even now, she wished for *his* return.

Even as she spoke, it sounded like the story of another young woman's confusing journey into love, as fantastical as a tale of a little girl getting lost in some mysterious wood and finding her own way.

"But this is incredible," said Jane, turning and pacing to the window and quite surprising Elizabeth, who had hoped her sister's faithful affection would ensure her ready acceptance of such a tale. "You quite disliked him, Lizzy. I remember it very well. Are you certain, quite certain, that what you feel, and what he feels, is not built on a moment's allegiance? I take it that Lady Catherine can be quite formidable, and—"

But Jane was interrupted with a knock, and then news of a delivery. The housekeeper herself was there, and, once assured the ladies within were arranged properly, let in a footman in Darcy livery bearing the old battered trunk that had followed Elizabeth on her journey.

Jane watched in silence while Elizabeth thanked the servants. The silence went on after they were gone, for Jane seemed unable to regain the words of caution and concern she had planned.

Elizabeth felt the burden of all her own sober reflections, her own vigilant considerations, remembering her own self-doubt even as her heart and his had opened to each other. In this moment, her sensibilities so little resembled those of her former self that she wondered whether she should take back all that weight of caution just to regain some sense of her own recognition. But something—perhaps the reassurance of her old trunk here as yet another talisman of Darcy's care—made her throw off that yoke easily. That bold welcome of change in itself seemed a symptom of the very audacity of love.

She hopped lightly from her perch on the bed and went over to her trunk, unlatching it and hoisting the lid.

She heard Jane gasp in surprise.

Lying on top of Elizabeth's folded articles was a tied nosegay of fragrant jasmine blossoms which had not been there before, white as any peace offering, and sweeter.

"Did Mr Darcy give you those?" asked Jane, as Elizabeth took up the bundle gently.

"Somehow, he must have," Elizabeth mused, wondering if Mr Darcy had intercepted her trunk himself on its way to Gracechurch Street only minutes ago, or if he had precipitously asked one of his discreet servants to place the blooms in her trunk even before Elizabeth herself had left his home in the carriage. In either case, the eagerness of the gesture spoke volumes.

Another knock, this one a light tap—which both girls knew to be their aunt's signal—sounded at the bedroom door. Jane, already on her feet, went to answer.

"Lizzy—" began Mrs Gardiner, who stopped immediately at the sight of the little bouquet in Elizabeth's hands. "Well, it is clear that much has changed since you went away to Kent."

"I have been explaining it all to Jane. I suppose I must start again. Or might I begin simply? There has been an exchange of honesty and forgiveness between Mr Darcy and myself on both sides today. And we have reached an understanding."

"Then it is settled? Is all really settled between you?" Mrs Gardiner asked. "You looked the picture of comfortable companionship in my sitting room, but when Jane brought you to this room only minutes ago, you were most discomposed."

Elizabeth shook her head. "It is not doubt. You must not think I doubt his sincerity or mine."

"I cannot claim to know enough of the gentleman to judge him," said Mrs Gardiner thoughtfully. "But you, my dear niece, I do know. And you so disliked him, so distrusted him before. I cannot account for that change so suddenly without good reason, and expect to feel easy."

"I have good reason, a very good number of reasons, to dispel that old dislike. I was very mistaken about the character of Mr Wickham—as I was telling Jane, his was the account that was untruthful, and I met another in Kent who could verify Mr Darcy's account. And as to Mr Darcy acting to separate Mr Bingley and Jane—"

Here she looked in distress to her sister, whose silence still unnerved her.

"I can accept his decision to intervene," said Jane slowly, pinching her eyes shut. "Mr Darcy loves his friend and could not perceive my true feelings. After all, Mr Darcy truly did not know me well. It is only painful, so inexpressibly painful, to realise that it is Mr Bingley who did not know or understand me at all, and that he did not endeavour to try."

Jane opened her eyes, only to look up at the ceiling in an attempt to combat tears. Elizabeth could not bear it. She dropped her bouquet in her haste to embrace her sister, and Jane readily welcomed the comfort, seeming to need it so much that even their aunt came round her back to hold her.

Jane took a deep breath. When next she spoke, her voice was muffled. "I could only wish he had courage like Mr Darcy's, that he might have had the boldness to defend my integrity against the speculation of family and friends—and, in the face of doubt, that he would ask me in all honesty about my own heart."

There was sufficient truth and grief in what she said to give Elizabeth and her aunt cause to hold Jane tighter. After sinking together for a moment, Jane steadied herself, then gently loosed herself from their embraces. Elizabeth stepped back to give her sister the liberty to restore her own composure, but was surprised when Jane moved away towards the trunk, then bent to retrieve the bouquet that had been left on the floorboards. She brought it to Elizabeth, placing it back in her hand. "Lizzy, he really does deserve you. You do deserve each other, I mean. You are both of you so brave."

Elizabeth smiled through the brightness of her own sudden tears. "Oh, but our bravery was born of need. We have Lady Catherine to thank, for had she not attacked me today, we might never have stood side by side in battle," she reflected with a laugh.

"She did what?" exclaimed Mrs Gardiner in surprised concern and borrowed offence.

Elizabeth barely had time before and after they dined to explain some of the day's upheavals, but it was enough to convince Mrs Gardiner, in the kindness of her generous heart, to contrive a way for Elizabeth and her beau to have a moment's privacy when he came to call again.

Before Mr Darcy called, quite alone, the next morning, Mrs Gardiner had time enough to set the children to their lessons with Jane. She was therefore well-positioned to facilitate the requisite introductions between Mr Darcy and her husband. As the two men entered with mutual enthusiasm into discussion about the merits of summer travel and sport in the Lake Country, it was clear to Elizabeth's amused notice that Mrs Gardiner shared her eagerness for the two unacknowledged lovers to have a moment alone. Mr Gardiner seemed to have prepared for this eventuality, however, when he suggested that Mr Darcy might like to reference a memoir written by a fine angler in his book room.

Elizabeth just as readily offered to show the way. And so it was neatly done, and they once again found quiet solace in a study.

"Your aunt is indeed a shrewd woman," said Darcy with something like fondness as he meandered over to peruse the shelves in a show of curiosity. "But your uncle is every bit as clever."

Elizabeth could only watch him and smile. "I am very grateful to my uncle, and to my aunt and yours."

He turned back to look at her. "Mine?"

She nodded, then came to stand before him on tiptoe, the better to wrap her arms around his neck with presumptuous affection. After the space of only a night since their sudden understanding, there was relief in the solidness of his body, and after a heartbeat of his surprise, the slow reciprocation of his own arms coming around her offered a tangible reassurance to the reality of their understanding. Emboldened by the bright happiness of his gaze trained down upon her, her own good humour only increased. "Yes, I must thank your aunt, for she gave me one very good piece of advice after she learned of my refusal of Mr Collins—that I ought not refuse another offer of marriage ever again."

He shifted his hands lower on her back to enhance their proximity, warming her. "And yet you did, initially," he observed.

"Ah, but that was before I heard her advice," said Elizabeth archly.

He laughed and drew her flush against him, tucking his face into the curls at her neck so he could smother his amusement. The sense of being wrapped up in him this way—so nearly as one body, breathing and laughing with him and sharing in the most delicious joy—overtook her so completely with such thrilling, filling comfort, such dizzying and heady delight, that before she knew what she was doing, she had taken hold of the collar of his coat with boldness enough to break him of his mirth, and kissed him.

The End

About the Author

Gailie Ruth Caress is a lifelong adaptive dabbler hailing from Indiana. Writing has always been her joy; crafting *Fearful Symmetry*, her first novel—in a genre of her own pleasure-reading—fulfilled a lifelong dream.

Also by Gailie Ruth Caress
Fearful Symmetry

The First Moment of Their Acquaintance

Amy D'Orazio

CHAPTER ONE

May 1812, London

From the very beginning, from the first moment I may almost say, of my acquaintance with you, your manners, impressing me with the fullest belief of your arrogance, your conceit, and your selfish disdain of the feelings of others, were such as to form that ground-work of disapprobation, on which succeeding events have built so immoveable a dislike; and I had not known you a month before I felt that you were the last man in the world whom I could ever be prevailed on to marry.

— PRIDE & PREJUDICE, CHAPTER 34

When will those blasted words stop echoing through my mind? Darcy rubbed his forehead as if to scrub the hated words away, then leant back against the plush squabs of his carriage. He desired nothing less than to dine at Matlock House…but it was required of him. It was not for Fitzwilliam Darcy to shirk his duty to his family, but how cold and hard that duty was compared to the sweet warmth of Elizabeth Bennet's smile.

It had been a miserable month since his failed proposal, a month during which bitterness and anger gave way to regret and despair. It was a month in which he learnt more of himself than ever he before knew and made resolutions to improve his character. He owed her that much, though it was unlikely she should ever know of them.

How clearly he could see now how gravely he had erred with her, right from the start! *'From the very beginning, from the first moment, I may almost say, of my acquaintance with you'*—it was no stroke of genius to discern her meaning there. She referred, of course, to his insult of her. How could he have been so rude to her, to any lady, in that way? And then to fail to apologise? Despicable.

'I had not known you a month'—the meaning here was understood as well. He met her in October; by mid-November, they had dined in company four times, and she had spent some days at Netherfield with their party. What had *not* happened in that first month? She had not yet met George Wickham. Thus was her meaning clear—she did not dislike him because of anything Wickham said. No, her disgust with him was all to his own credit. George Wickham had done no more than to second her already poor opinion of him.

Accursed assembly! If only he might do it over, to properly meet her and thus not set off on the course to his own destruction.

Lady Matlock had summoned him for dinner tonight, no doubt wishing for an explanation for his recent behaviour. Darcy had been avoiding parties as much as he could, and when he did attend, he generally arrived late and departed early. By no means did he dance. The ladies of the *ton* were of two sorts: those who reminded him of Elizabeth and those who did not. Either sort was undesirable as a dance partner, although for different reasons. In any case, Darcy was well prepared for the chastisement of his aunt and uncle, who had made it plain that they thought he—as well as his two bachelor cousins, Viscount Saye and Colonel Fitzwilliam—ought to marry.

He was poor company that night. He scarcely ate, though meals at Matlock House were always delicious, and for most subjects being canvassed, he remained silent. His mind and heart refused to dwell on anything but Elizabeth. He mourned her and the loss of his hopes; he relived the agony of being rejected, and he despaired of seeing her again even as he turned his mind in every which way to find a way to win her. There was nothing he could imagine proving even remotely successful, leading to an ever-increasing gloom as the evening wore on.

Lady Matlock did her best to provoke either argument or agreement from him on the subject of whether he needed to take a wife, but she was sorely disappointed. Her nephew did no more than nod meekly, push his food about his plate, and give the occasional disinterested sigh. When Lady Matlock withdrew after dinner, she cast a significant look at his lordship. "I have some letters I must answer in my study, and after that, I shall retire," she announced. "Darcy, I will bid you a good night."

Darcy dutifully kissed the proffered hand, and she left. As the door closed behind her, his uncle turned, studying him closely. Fitzwilliam, too seemed to be evaluating him in an uncommonly grave manner.

It was Saye who thought to dive directly into the heart of the matter. "Darcy, you are uncommonly dull these days, even for you. My brother says it is about a lady."

"A lady?" Lord Matlock perked up, suddenly interested in his nephew's malaise. "What lady? Who are her people?"

Darcy shot Fitzwilliam a vexed look. He had known it was a risk to confide in his cousin on their return from Kent, but he had been in such a state that he could not stop himself.

Fitzwilliam raised his hands in a gesture of surrender. "They dragged it out of me."

"Why should we not know?" Saye argued immediately. "I smell a story here and shall not rest until I know all."

Darcy shook his head. "Leave it, Saye. This is no laughing matter."

"Everything is a laughing matter if you tell it with spirit."

Darcy closed his eyes a moment. Prudence suggested he ought to leave before the whole of the affair was laid bare, and yet impulse compelled him to speak. "I met her last autumn in Hertfordshire," he began. "It did not begin well."

A quarter of an hour later, the tale was told. Saye found the entire thing funny to the point of hysteria. He wiped his eyes of the tears of laughter as he said, "You insulted her, argued with her, and encouraged Bingley to abandon her sister—"

"Bingley is in and out of love as frequently as most gentlemen change their shoes."

"And then, on the strength of a few walks, decided to propose?" Another burst of laughter came from Saye. "Did you suppose she would marry you for your money? Or was it your good looks you thought would prevail?"

"Clearly, I was not thinking at all," Darcy replied stiffly.

Lord Matlock opined gruffly, "It seems a most imprudent match. You should be glad she refused you as she did. You have been spared the degradation of your name." When none of the younger men spared him a moment's notice, he grew offended and thus rose and took his leave of them.

"You will be relieved to know that Miss Heathcote was asking after you at that dinner at the Scott's two nights ago," Fitzwilliam offered.

"I do not want Miss Heathcote," Darcy replied, his eyes fixed on the table cloth beneath his fingers.

"Taking up with a second lady is the easiest way to forget the first," Saye informed them. "Of course, at times, you must go on to the third, the fourth, sometimes even the fifth—and by then, you have forgotten them all."

"I cannot forget her," Darcy told them glumly. "Inasmuch as the remembrance pains me, it is what I have of her, and so will I hold fast to it. To meet another? It will not do. Never will another lady raise in me the feelings she so ably produced."

"Where you really erred was in interfering with Bingley's plans," Saye told him. "Otherwise, you could have gone back to Hertfordshire. True, you have erred quite grievously, it is true, but you are a fine figure of a man, and if your money and position do not tempt her, perhaps a bit of lust will."

Darcy's only reply to that was a disgusted look.

"Oh!" Saye snapped his fingers and sat up from his customary slouch. "I have it! We will have a house party and get her to stumble in on you while you are dressing. Then she will have to marry you."

A sudden thought struck him, and he gave Darcy a suspicious look. "You do not wear small clothes, do you?"

Both Fitzwilliam and Darcy gave him a look of incredulous censure.

"Then you think of a better idea," Saye retorted. "There are several things a man might use to tempt a woman into matrimony. Clearly,

THE FIRST MOMENT OF THEIR ACQUAINTANCE

she does not want his wealth or his position—I am merely cutting to what is left."

"I wish for her love," Darcy told Fitzwilliam, turning his head so as not to see his more vexatious cousin.

"Not many women could fall in love with a gentleman who had publicly humiliated her," said Saye, refusing to be ignored. "You should have offered her an apology the moment you believed she might have heard you."

"That is true," Darcy agreed, growing still more morose. "I ought not to have insulted her, and I should have apologised straightaway when I knew I had. I should have agreed to the introduction and danced with her. I should have been kinder to her when we were in company together. I should have opened my mouth and spoken to her. I should have—"

"There are many things you wish to have done differently," Fitzwilliam concluded. "Perhaps if you could persuade her to give you a second chance—"

"She has no inducement to do that, and even if she did, it might make her tolerate me, possibly even like me, but it would surely not make her fall in love with me."

Saye rose, going towards the fireplace next to which hung a small decorative gilt mirror. Catching sight of himself, he struck a little smiling sort of pose and then grew sombre. "Ah! Here it is: you must somehow adopt a disguise, and present yourself to her as another, someone who is not yet known to her."

When neither his brother nor his cousin replied, he repeated it. "Is that not a splendid idea?"

"A disguise?" Darcy asked. "I have no idea what you mean."

"Pose as another, another man, one who has not insulted her. Then you may court her as the other man and, once she is in love with you, show her it was you all along."

Fitzwilliam immediately groaned as Darcy said, "You cannot be serious."

"I am entirely in earnest," Saye replied. "Might do her well to see your waggish side."

"I do not have a waggish side," Darcy replied. "I am a gentleman of honour. Disguise of every sort is my abhorrence."

"We shall have to hope it is your honour which will warm your bed at night then," Saye replied. "You must loosen up a bit, sir, if we are to extricate you from your plight. Put aside all these vain scruples so we can help you."

Darcy turned to Fitzwilliam, intending to exchange a roll of the eyes or something of the like in response to Saye's absurdity. To his shock, Fitzwilliam appeared to be considering it. "Fitzwilliam? Surely you see how stupid—"

"The scheme does have some merit," Fitzwilliam began slowly.

"I am not about to perpetrate a hoax on a lady, hoping to earn her affection!"

Darcy's protest went unheeded. Turning to his brother, Fitzwilliam asked, "How could we possibly disguise him sufficiently to fool her? She is clever, and their acquaintance is of many months' duration."

Saye strolled to where Darcy sat, peering down at his cousin critically. "What about his hair? A moustache or a beard, perhaps? We must cover his face as much as we can."

"No, I will not grow a beard," Darcy snapped. "I am not going to pull a prank on her!"

Fitzwilliam had also risen and moved to stand over Darcy and peer at his face. "Your only alternative is to let it lie, and that I believe is a most unhappy choice. What have you to lose?"

"Assuming you have related the tale faithfully," Saye added, "it seems she despises you rather passionately. When a woman loathes you so ardently, you can hardly sink further."

"I shall not do it," Darcy said, but his voice had begun to lose conviction.

"What if it were by correspondence?" Saye said to Fitzwilliam. "He might pose as Georgiana and establish a friendship using letters through which she might gain a more favourable opinion of him."

"They are not acquainted," Darcy informed him, but this went unheard as the two brothers continued to conspire.

Fitzwilliam shook his head. "I do not think that would work, not quickly in any case. We must make him a man she will not recognise, one whom she will know with a new mind."

"He is too tall," Saye remarked casually, turning his attention from the study of Darcy to again study himself in the mirror. He adopted an

THE FIRST MOMENT OF THEIR ACQUAINTANCE

attitude of pensiveness, watching himself as he stroked his chin in deep thought. "It is difficult to disguise such tallness."

"I am not so enormous," Darcy protested mildly. "Among my family members, my height is common enough."

"There we have it!" Fitzwilliam exclaimed. "You must be a different Darcy. A cousin perhaps? Surely she has not met any of your Darcy cousins?"

"She has not," Darcy replied, "...because there are none."

"Does she know that?"

Darcy considered a moment. "I do not think she knows anything of my family besides the fact that my parents are deceased and I have one younger sister."

"Splendid," Saye replied, changing his attitude from pensiveness to enthusiasm and delight. "What shall we name him? Something funny to be sure. What about Pego or Lobcock?"

"I am not doing this." Darcy rose, going to the mirror and removing it, carefully placing it face down on a nearby table. Saye scowled at him. "This is not a novel or some sort of fantastical theatrics. I am not going to wilfully deceive the woman I love. That would be selfish and cruel, and would wholly support her poor opinion of me."

"Are you not doing it on her behalf as well as yours?" Fitzwilliam asked. "You know, yours is the second proposal she has turned down, and while I should not have liked to see her as Mrs Collins, he is an eligible match for her. If she goes about ignoring prudence, she might find herself required to find employment."

"Collins believed he could have her?" Darcy barely suppressed a shudder thinking of it. "Distasteful as it might be, I cannot behave in such an ungentlemanlike manner."

"So what you are saying is that your behaviour to Miss Bennet thus far has been, *unfailingly*, that of a gentleman?" Saye raised one eyebrow, skewering Darcy with what he no doubt believed was a severe look. "You have behaved in an ungentlemanly fashion in her presence on a multitude of occasions—what is once more, particularly if it carries with it a chance to win her?"

"A gentleman, having realised his past mistakes, would not seek to further compound his poor behaviour," Darcy retorted, returning to his previous seat.

"She might find it amusing, this little farce," Fitzwilliam conjectured. "She has a lovely sense of folly."

Darcy huffed with annoyance. "I recall once saying to her that it has been the study of my life to avoid those weaknesses which often expose a strong understanding to ridicule. Now to play a trick like this? What will she think of me?"

"It is perfect! It will show her that you considered her rebukes!" Saye cried cheerfully.

Fitzwilliam came close again, leaning in and studying Darcy's face minutely. With a quick motion to his brother, he said, "I think a beard should do nicely."

Saye joined Fitzwilliam in peering at Darcy's face. "He might cut his hair a bit, too. The sides are not so very long now, but along with a beard, I fear he might resemble some sort of wild animal."

"I beg your pardon!" Darcy was ignored as Fitzwilliam reached over, tugging back some of Darcy's hair to make it appear shorter.

"Shorter here and brushed up a bit there…" Fitzwilliam considered a moment. "Perhaps in a suit that was less fine, even a bit outmoded…the dress of a gentleman of lesser means."

"To be sure!" Saye exclaimed. "For a cousin would be of lesser means, undoubtedly. George Darcy's younger brother perhaps? A man who has studied the law?"

Darcy rose and went to the window to escape his cousins and their poking and prodding. Obviously none of this would happen. It was far too ridiculous to even imagine.

Behind him, his cousins continued to scheme. "Let us not name him anything too outrageous," Fitzwilliam said. "If someone were to call him Cornelius and he did not respond, it could be telling."

"Who would be calling him by his given name?" Saye asked. "No one should call him anything but Darcy."

"But he still requires a given name," Fitzwilliam replied. "Trust me —the key to any clandestine mission demands that these sorts of details be considered."

"My name is, and shall remain, Fitzwilliam," Darcy said firmly. It was time he took the situation in hand, and made his cousins aware that he would not participate in their farce. "I have never been one for theatricals and I do not intend to begin now."

"What about William?" Saye said to his brother.

"Of course!" Fitzwilliam agreed. "Like enough to Fitzwilliam that it would seem natural to him to answer to it, should anyone say it or refer to it. Now, Darcy…"

Fitzwilliam turned to him. "You spend most of your time at Pemberley and are very little in town. You live…on the estate somewhere and you take care of its legal needs. You also serve as magistrate."

"No, no, no." Darcy shook his head emphatically. "There is no means of success here! Imagine this bit of puffery works, and Elizabeth falls in love with my cousin—my cousin who is actually *me*. Then what? Then I reveal myself and say, 'Ha ha, what a fine joke this is?' Then I will know what it is to earn her love and to lose it just as quickly."

"You will need to take care," Saye cautioned him, "that she does not just fall in love with you, but you must make her feel she cannot live without you. Make her desperate for you. Then, when she is angry at you for deceiving her, you do all you can to make amends and earn her forgiveness. Love conquers all, and you are free to enjoy a happy ending."

"No," Darcy replied firmly. "The risk is too great."

"With great risk comes the potential for great reward," Saye rejoined.

"Again I ask, what have you to lose?" Fitzwilliam entreated.

"My dignity," Darcy replied. "Forgive me, but this is unthinkable. Now if you will excuse me, I must return home to retire."

CHAPTER TWO

Two days later, Saye and Colonel Fitzwilliam were at their club, playing a game of cards, when Darcy entered. He took a seat at another table, selecting one of the broadsheets and reading for some time while they finished.

Fitzwilliam arrived first at his table, taking a seat and motioning to the server for a drink. Saye soon followed. Both brothers regarded Darcy carefully, no doubt seeing the evidence of sleepless nights and a headache brought on by too much brandy and too little food. They also might have observed that his man had not shaved him very well, if at all. A faint shadow of a beard extended over the lower part of his face.

Darcy, for some moments, regarded them in return. At last he said, "So this cousin of mine, must he be bearded?"

Within the hour the three gentlemen were at Darcy's tailor, offering the man a commission which puzzled him exceedingly.

"You want two suits of *in*ferior quality, made in the fashion of two or three years past?" Mr Bridgewater enquired, his bemusement plain.

"Yes," Saye replied impatiently. "And take care you do not fit him quite perfectly. In fact, my brother here will stand in his stead at the fittings."

Darcy, who was already regretting the scheme, said, "This is foolish. Let us leave and tax this poor man no more."

"I beg your pardon, Mr Darcy!" Bridgewater mistook Darcy's aggravation as being aimed at himself. "I assure you it will be my honour to fashion these suits for you. I was only unsure of your wishes but now I understand completely."

Fitzwilliam decided to speak up. "It is for a caper...of sorts. Some old university mates, a lark, so to speak." He gave the man a conciliatory smile. "Darcy is always so well turned out, of course...to wear an outmoded, unfashionable suit..."

"Something more in the way of a country style," Saye mentioned.

"To wear a country-styled, outmoded, less elegant sort of fashion will be exceedingly amusing to us all."

"Yes indeed," the tailor agreed enthusiastically. "And you would like two such suits?"

"Two," Fitzwilliam confirmed, while Saye, who had been studying the samples of the less expensive materials, pointed to two he thought would serve well.

Darcy, watching it all, shook his head, wondering if it was merely an exercise in futility, or if it would prove to be the thing that made Miss Elizabeth Bennet despise him forever.

"Darcy, I will be first to admit, I find this notion exceedingly puzzling."

Bingley had come to Darcy's house in response to his friend's summons. Once there, Darcy had made a clean breast of his errors with regards to Jane Bennet's true attachment to his friend, and had explained the forthcoming scheme to him. Bingley appeared delighted by the former and utterly bewildered by the latter.

He was agreeable to the idea of returning to Netherfield but the particulars of the scheme seemed to elude him. "Would I be required to have a beard as well? For I must say, I do not care for them and it is not so easy for me to grow one."

"No, no, only I shall wear a beard." Darcy explained.

"It still does not come in anywhere close to here." Bingley gestured at his cheeks. "I thought surely by the age of three and twenty I should not have the downy cheeks of a callow youth but—"

"You do not need to have a beard, Bingley. Only I require a change in appearance."

"I could probably be shaved on alternate days and still have the smooth cheeks of—"

"You do not need a beard, so it does not signify."

"…a youth. My man did say, however, that many times—"

"Bingley!"

Bingley finally stopped ruminating on his difficulties in growing facial hair and looked up at his friend.

"I need a beard because I wish to convince Elizabeth that I am—" Darcy swallowed hard "—my cousin. You will still be Charles Bingley. Your only part in my little farce is to remember that my name is Mr William Darcy, and I am a barrister."

"How is it that we are friends? From university?"

"Um…yes. Yes, from university. Mr William Darcy is…he is younger than Fitzwilliam Darcy by…by two years. Or shall he be older? Or the same?"

"The same seems less likely," Bingley observed reasonably. "And if he were older, I might not have known him at university."

"You might have met him at Pemberley. He resides there, in one of the houses."

"To be sure," Bingley replied. "Although…"

"What?" Darcy asked.

"What about Wickham? It is one thing to perpetrate such a story on those with whom your acquaintance has been limited, but Wickham knows perfectly well you have no cousin named William Darcy, a barrister who lives at Pemberley."

"What irony it would be to have my lies shattered by Wickham," Darcy grumbled. "However, I am assured by Fitzwilliam that in a fortnight the regiment shall remove to Brighton for the summer. Mr William Darcy cannot appear at Netherfield until then."

Darcy leant forward. "I must put aside my little scheme for a moment and beg your forgiveness for interfering with Miss Bennet. I should have encouraged you to seek the truth of the matter for yourself."

"The fault is wholly my own." Bingley cast his friend a rueful grin. "You have always given me excellent advice but I must learn to use my own sense as well."

He chuckled. "For example, in this, your second attempt at love, I shall not follow your example. Though I am commonly the fool in love, in this instance, we shall let that be you."

CHAPTER THREE

June 1812, Hertfordshire

How I do wish Mama would permit me to remain home. Elizabeth looked wistfully at the new book on her bed. It was not to be; Mrs Bennet was determined to marry off both of her eldest daughters by the autumn. Since Elizabeth's return from her visit to Kent, her mother had been relentless in finding opportunities to put her in front of eligible gentlemen.

Elizabeth watched her reflection for a moment as she toyed with the comb in her hair; then she rose, going to the drawer in which she had hidden his letter. She extracted it, but did not unfold it. She hardly needed to open it by now; its contents had been nearly committed to memory.

She did not regret her refusal, although the weeks since Mr Darcy's astonishing proposal had at least taught her there was much more to him than she had ever suspected. She did regret having never truly known him, and she would readily own there were likely many ways in which they were well-suited.

However, no matter what, she knew she could never marry a man so serious. If nothing else, she wished for a husband with whom she

THE FIRST MOMENT OF THEIR ACQUAINTANCE

could laugh and indulge herself in teasing and mirth. She had no doubt that life with Mr Darcy would be filled with things noble and solemn and grand, but which held precious little in the way of levity or merriment. She might have misjudged many things about him, but in this was she sure. For someone who loved to laugh as she did, a man like Mr Darcy would never do.

In any case, it did not signify. She was unlikely to ever see Mr Darcy again, and if she did, he would no doubt stay as far away from her as he could. He certainly must loathe her after her refusal; likely his greatest regret was that he ever said he loved her.

A knock came at her door; it was Jane. "Our sisters have promised they will leave us if we are not soon prepared to go, Lizzy."

"Would that they should!" Elizabeth exclaimed. "I would much rather stay home and read a book."

The two sisters departed Elizabeth's bedchamber, after Elizabeth slyly tucked his letter back into its hiding place. As they descended the stairs to the carriage, Jane mentioned, "Mama is not to be our chaperon tonight. Her head is exceedingly ill, and our aunt encouraged her to keep to her bedchamber."

"Who will attend us then?" Elizabeth asked.

"Aunt and Uncle Gardiner," Jane replied. "They are eager for the diversion."

I despise beards. Darcy gave his cheeks a vicious scratching. *These clothes are an abomination as well.*

He looked down at his breeches. They were not well cut and pinched him right in the place a man least liked to be pinched. The material was not fine either, not the worst he had ever seen but dear God, how did gentlemen of lesser means survive? He privately vowed that—should he ever be forced to retrench—he would choose to have one pair of well-made breeches of a fine material than to have several pairs of poor quality.

With a loud huff, he settled back into the seat of the carriage. *This* entire scheme is a fool's errand. Miss Elizabeth shall never believe such fat-witted nonsense.

"Um, Darcy?" Bingley leant forwards, his face barely illuminated by the lanterns that swung outside of the carriage.

"Yes?"

"You will recall that you said I should tell you if you appeared disagreeable."

Darcy sighed. "Yes?"

"You do remember that request, do you not?" Bingley sounded anxious.

Darcy replied in a resigned tone. "I remember."

Bingley hesitated, clearly uncomfortable in his new role as Darcy's instructor in the fine art of appearing amiable. "You do appear just the slightest degree disagreeable right now. Not too frightening, not by far! Just vexed, shall we say? Yes, vexed and perhaps a bit…hot."

"Thank you, Bingley," Darcy said from between gritted teeth.

"It is not the worst I have ever seen you, but perhaps you could smile a little?"

"This blasted beard!" Darcy could restrain himself no more. "It itches and it is hot! How am I to make Elizabeth fall in love with me when all I can think of is how damned itchy and hot I am!"

Bingley chuckled. "You must try not to think of it then."

"Easy enough for you to say," Darcy growled. "You had a shave just before we departed."

"I did, it is true," Bingley said soothingly. "But see there?" Bingley showed him a small mark near his neck. "My razor was dull, I fear, and I got a cut. At least you do not need to worry that you are bleeding onto your cravat."

"This cravat is tied so stupidly, bleeding onto it could only improve it." Darcy scoffed but immediately regretted it. This was just the sort of ill-humour that led to him insulting Elizabeth last autumn.

Hearing the sound of music, he looked out the window to see they had arrived at the assembly hall. His heart gave a quick series of thuds; looking across the carriage at his friend, he thought Bingley appeared to have gone slightly pale.

Bingley smiled grimly. "I have only one goal for this night and it is to re-establish my acquaintance and determine whether she despises me, or if there is a chance she might yet like me. Low expectations make for surer success, or so I hope."

Darcy placed his hat on his head and gave his beard one last violent tug. "Into the breach, shall we?"

The hall was crowded, the music was loud, and the heat of summer made the air feel far too close. Darcy resisted the urge to scowl as Sir William Lucas was immediately upon them. It was only then that Darcy realised a problem he had not considered previously; he would need to deceive not only Elizabeth but the rest of Meryton as well.

"Mr Bingley! Mr Darcy! I heard that you were returned to our fair county and I—"

"Um, forgive me, Sir William," Bingley interrupted with a hurried glance towards Darcy. "You have called him by the correct name, but I fear this is a Mr Darcy who is unknown to you."

Sir William's brow wrinkled almost comically but his simple understanding was soon satisfied. For such a man as he, to know one Mr Darcy was pleasure enough; to know two was utterly joyous. His greeting was hearty and sincere, and Darcy was glad of it.

As they finished speaking with Sir William and began to move about the room, various members of the neighbourhood presented themselves to Bingley to extend their greetings. The word of the 'second' Mr Darcy went through the little place like wildfire. It mortified him to be the principal actor of such a deceit, but he supposed he was too far in it now to grow faint-hearted.

Remembering that his object was to prove himself agreeable and kind, he consented to introduction after introduction, all to persons he already knew. Many offered their comments on the similarity in appearance he shared with his supposed 'cousin'.

"Of course, Mr Darcy is a good bit taller than you are," Mr Goulding pronounced. "Several inches I do believe."

"Darker hair," Lady Lucas decided. "And curlier. But other than that, you are much of a pair!"

"You are taller than he, but thinner," determined Mr Philips. "Your cousin must have a heartier appetite."

My 'cousin' is not a heartbroken man for whom food has lost all appeal. Darcy only smiled and said it had always been so since their youth.

"In any case," Mr Philips continued. "It is good to have another man of the legal study here tonight. We have a case of some delicacy here in town, and I hope you would grant me the honour of your opinion on it."

"Oh!" Darcy stammered. This was a complication he had not imagined. "Well, you see…that is to say…Hertfordshire is different—"

"Nonsense!" Mr Philips declared. With no further preamble, he launched into a rather detailed account of a nearby estate belatedly discovered to be under an entail. The former master, recently deceased, had for nearly a decade been somewhat out of his wits, and his son-in-law had the run of the place. The son-in-law, having no idea of the entail, had laboured diligently, providing a rather substantive increase in the coffers, and now was petitioning for something of the increase.

Darcy hoped he made the appropriate noises and interjections, particularly when Mr Philips exclaimed, "Of course you must have known of a similar case in Derbyshire! Highcroft near Bakewell… has it been five years since that matter was settled?"

Fortunately Bingley came to his rescue before he was required to reveal his ignorance. "I have seen Miss Bennet," Bingley hissed while drawing him away. "As beautiful as ever she was—nay! More so! One hundred times more so! How ever shall I face her? Come, you must go with me. I will ask her for a dance."

Darcy's heart began to beat wildly as they crossed the crowded room, intent on going where Miss Bennet stood with a small, fashionably dressed lady of about thirty or five and thirty who was engaged in conversation with Mrs Goulding. Still Darcy did not see Elizabeth, and thus was his anticipation mixed with disappointment. In a brief moment of dismay he worried what he might do if she chose to absent herself this night.

He had almost persuaded himself that his efforts for the night were to be in vain when in an instant, they all converged. Himself, Bingley,

Miss Bennet, the fashionable lady…and Elizabeth. All at once and without warning, he was upon her. He schooled himself to appear calm.

Elizabeth was shocked to see him; her eyes flew wide, and her hand went to her chest. "Mr Darcy!"

CHAPTER FOUR

THOUGH HE FELT IMMEDIATELY THAT HE HAD BEEN exposed, Darcy schooled himself to be calm. *Calm and amiable*, he warned himself while he offered a bow. "Forgive me, Madam, but you have me at a disadvantage."

"Do I?"

"You appear to be acquainted with me, while I do not recall meeting you." He smiled, doing his best to be charming. "I surely would remember an acquaintance with someone so lovely."

Darcy turned to Bingley who had already become lost in his admiration of Miss Bennet. "Bingley, perhaps you will do me the honour of an introduction, should the lady agree to it?"

Bingley's colour was high and his eyes could not be moved from Miss Bennet. With a vague sort of bowing gesture, he said, "Miss Bennet, Miss Elizabeth, allow me to present Mr William Darcy."

"Mr William Darcy?" Elizabeth echoed, with clear bemusement.

Miss Bennet appeared enthralled by Bingley, and the elder lady was engaged in another conversation; thus was Elizabeth left to do nothing but converse with Darcy, which suited him very well.

"Mr Fitzwilliam Darcy is my cousin," he told her.

Her eyes slowly roamed across his countenance. "Your cousin?" She looked dubious. "You are very much alike, sir."

THE FIRST MOMENT OF THEIR ACQUAINTANCE

"We have heard it all of our lives," he said with a genial smile.

Her eyes swept over him again; she at last gave him an uncertain smile and a curtsey. "It is my pleasure to meet you."

"The pleasure is wholly mine." His smile broadened, his cheeks aching with the effort of it.

From the corner of his eye, he noticed Bingley escorting Miss Bennet towards the set of dancers just forming. How good it was to see Bingley happy, and to imagine the pleasure Elizabeth might find in it.

He turned back to her. "Will you do me the honour of dancing the next with me?"

Her eyes went wide again, and a spark of mischief came into her countenance. "You are fond of dancing, Mr Darcy?"

Darcy did not falter. "Given an agreeable partner, I am."

Her lips pursed and he thrilled in delighted anticipation of being teased. "Are you certain I will be an agreeable partner? After all, we have only just been introduced. What if you come to find me exceedingly disagreeable?"

He chuckled. "I daresay I must take my chances, Miss Elizabeth. After all, nothing ventured, nothing gained, or so I have always believed. Shall we, then?" He gestured towards the lines of dancers. She nodded, taking his arm as they made their way towards the set.

The first part of their set was spent in relating to Miss Elizabeth the story that had been agreed upon. She appeared to think it true, responding to him agreeably and even a bit warmly at times. When at last he had depleted his pre-arranged topics of conversation, they were silent for a moment. It was then that Elizabeth posed the first question of her own.

"Sir, I wonder if I might be so bold as to ask a question of you?"

Darcy smiled, noticing that the action was becoming less forced and more habitual. "Anything you like. I am well-pleased to answer."

"Are you in your cousin's confidence?"

"His confidence?"

She smiled, seeming a bit apologetic. "Do you know the particulars of my acquaintance with your cousin?"

Darcy was not sure how he should answer, and thus prevaricated awkwardly. "Oh, ah, yes, he told me you were a fine lady and excellent company, and that I should seek you out at my earliest opportunity."

"Did he?" Elizabeth asked. After a moment's silence, she asked, "Was it recently that he said so?"

"Recently?"

"Since his return from Kent."

"Oh, ahh, yes. Yes it was."

Blast! He had thought long on safe topics of conversation and nevertheless, and within minutes she had him knotted up in tangles! He did not wish for this cousin of his to put the real him in any sort of jeopardy. Did she think William Darcy was mocking her in some way? Offending her?

There were a few moments to gather his thoughts as they moved through a pattern and then, on an impulse, he said, "My cousin told me he considers you one of the handsomest women of his acquaintance."

She glanced up at him. "Did he?"

Darcy nodded, rather too emphatically, but he felt himself on thin ice and wished to seek firmer ground. "Yes, but also he said he admired your wit to much the same extent as your beauty."

Elizabeth looked at him rather doubtfully so he added, "He has always admired any lady who does not fear the improvement of her mind by extensive reading."

Elizabeth tilted her head up towards him to reply to his comment. In so doing, her eyes held a momentary look of interest and warmth that was intoxicating. Her neck was exposed to him, the skin creamy and soft-looking and he noted, for not the first time, how particularly dainty and well formed her ears were. He was distracted for a moment, envisioning himself placing a kiss onto the delicate skin where her jaw, her neck, and her ear were united.

He spoke without thinking. "I know you do not like to discuss books in a ballroom, but perhaps you will tell me of some of your favourites."

She stared at him and he realised, a moment too late, his mistake. He had made reference to their conversation during their dance at Netherfield—a conversation of which William Darcy would have no knowledge.

THE FIRST MOMENT OF THEIR ACQUAINTANCE

Frantically, Darcy began speaking, in an effort to overcome his error. "That is to say, I believe most ladies would not like to speak of books in a ballroom. Is that not true? After all, are not ladies' heads generally filled with other things in a ballroom?"

"Such as what?" Elizabeth raised one eyebrow at him. "What is it you think my head is filled with, Mr Darcy? As we have only just met, I am interested to know what it is you would imagine I think of."

He stammered like a fool, thoroughly unnerved. "I...I am sure I do not...the size of the room or the number of couples. There are many couples I see—" He glanced around him quickly to confirm it was true, noting thankfully that it was so "—but the room is by no means insufficient for it. That is to say, it is a fine room and the couples are... well, Hertfordshire has many handsome couples indeed and... and dancing is a charming amusement for young people. Do you like this dance?"

Elizabeth stared at him another long moment before lowering her eyes. Then, peeking at him through her lashes, she remarked, "So... you talk by rule then when you are dancing?"

The conversation was too familiar to him. Had it been said before? Did she recall it? His heart began to pound while he sought to determine whether he had revealed himself. He began to stammer another response but she saved him.

"I agree. I think it would be exceedingly odd to stand up together for half an hour without saying anything. I cannot abide someone who will not trouble himself to speak to his partner."

"I agree," he said, his heart still hammering madly. Then he considered what she said. There was a reproof in it—was there not? An intimation of his past arrogance. He decided to rectify it immediately.

"At times, it is not the trouble which keeps a man from speaking during a dance. There are some times when a gentleman simply cannot speak."

"Why is that?"

What did she know? It was impossible to tell. She appeared teasing... She was not angry and yet it was a chance to improve her opinion of him. He took a breath, hoping to avoid an additional misstep.

"Often times the lady with whom you most wish to dance is the self-same lady who is able to render you stupid and tongue-tied in her presence. So you are silent, not because you do not want to talk but because you cannot."

"You must be accustomed to dancing with exceedingly formidable ladies." She laughed. "What do these fearsome creatures do that is so intimidating?"

"Dreadful things," Darcy replied with feeling.

"I cannot imagine a sensible, educated gentleman such as yourself to be so squeamish."

Little did she know that she was doing it right now! He felt as though he were eighteen years old again, stuttering through his first conversation in a ballroom. "They tease," he replied, speaking in a tone of mock reproof. "Their eyes sparkle and their cheeks blush so prettily, all the while moving through a dance which seems designed to show them to advantage. It renders a man near insensible."

"It sounds dreadful," Elizabeth said. "Quite heartless."

"Just so," he agreed. "And yet..."

Their dance ended just then and he released her hand with great reluctance.

"And yet what, Mr Darcy?" She awaited his words.

He leaned close to her. "And yet, in the society of the right lady, we would not forgo it for the world. 'Tis a most exquisite form of torture."

He bowed to her, then offered his arm to provide escort to where her sister and Bingley were walking. When they had arrived at the little group, their chaperon, the elder lady, was there again, once more in conversation with another matron.

They did not interrupt her conversation but stood, speaking among themselves for a moment. Bingley's dance had presumably been a success, Darcy noted. He was as enraptured by Miss Bennet as he had ever been. It was with pleasure that Darcy noted Miss Bennet's like admiration of Bingley. She stood a step too close to him, he noted, and gave small, surreptitious glances at him frequently.

"Mr Darcy, I do hope your cousin is well," Miss Bennet said. "Do you anticipate his joining you during your stay at Netherfield?"

"No," said Darcy.

THE FIRST MOMENT OF THEIR ACQUAINTANCE

"Perhaps," said Bingley at the same time. The two men shot one another a look that sent Bingley wide-eyed and worried. "That is to say, one never knows with Darcy! Fitzwilliam Darcy, I mean. Not the Mr Darcy you see before you, but rather his cousin. He blows hither and yon! I would very much like it if he joined us but now that I think of it, I suppose it is impossible for him. Yes, upon further reflection, it is most decidedly out of the question. He is exceedingly busy in town."

"Mr Darcy blows hither and yon?" Elizabeth asked. "I had never ascribed caprice to him."

Blast it, Bingley! Darcy thought. *Stop talking!*

"Mr Bingley," Elizabeth continued, speaking in a light tone although Darcy could see keen interest in her eyes. "I had understood it was you who was able to be off at a moment's notice. Now you tell me it is Mr Darcy who has that peculiar talent?"

Bingley looked very much like a hound caught in the kitchen. "I would not say a moment but—"

"No, no," Darcy hastened to interrupt him. "I assure you, Mr Darcy is most decidedly not inconstant. Once he is fixed on something," he tried to look at her intently, wishing her to apprehend his meaning, "…he is firmly fixed. He does not waver, at least not on matters of true importance."

"Ah, yes," Elizabeth said, her gaze steady on Darcy's. "I do recall once he said his good opinion once lost was lost forever."

Darcy opened his mouth, wishing to explain himself but at the last, recalling he must speak for his cousin, not himself. "I am loath to speak for him, for I cannot know the particulars of the conversation to which you refer. However, my cousin was very lately betrayed by someone who was once a dear friend to him—to us both. I would imagine it was that situation in particular which was recalled to his mind when he said that."

Elizabeth looked down, seeming chagrined. Softly, she said, "Oh yes."

Bingley's head had swivelled back and forth between them during the exchange. He clearly knew he had erred and so leapt in at the first opportunity to remedy his mistake. "I only meant to say that when Darcy is in London he is always longing for the country. One never knows when he might make an escape from the obligations of the social season."

There was a brief pause until Miss Bennet spoke, a look of sweet bafflement on her features. "I thought when we danced, you had mentioned Mr Darcy was much occupied at Pemberley."

Bingley shot Darcy a panicked look.

How could I have ever imagined Bingley equal to this? Darcy recovered the slip smoothly. "He was until recently, but then he came to town."

"I see," Miss Bennet murmured.

Was it his imagination, or did she dart a glance at Elizabeth? Darcy had the increasing sense that they were exposing his ruse and began to cast about his mind desperately for another topic of conversation. Everything he could imagine was fraught with the possibility for error and he stood, in a rather stupid fashion, until Bingley hit on the answer.

"We are leaving our partners to thirst, Darcy!" He turned and bowed to the ladies. "Miss Bennet, Miss Elizabeth—may I interest you in a cup of punch?"

Both ladies agreed, and with much relief, the gentlemen were off to recover their senses and procure some punch.

CHAPTER FIVE

"Did you enjoy dancing with Mr Darcy?"

"I did indeed," Elizabeth replied to her sister, watching as Mr Darcy strolled around the room, greeting people with ease and friendliness. "He is all that is amiable."

"Do you suppose he knows of Mr Darcy's proposal?" Jane asked. "I should think it quite odd if he did, and yet showed you such preference."

"Did you think he showed me preference?"

Jane nodded emphatically. "You are fortunate our mother is not here; she would be calling for the banns to be read."

Elizabeth rolled her eyes. "Let us assume he does know of Mr Darcy's proposal—and I think surely he must—then yes, his preference would be peculiar. Unless…"

"Unless what?"

Elizabeth did not remove her eyes from Mr Darcy. "I do not recall mention of a cousin in any of my conversations with Mr Darcy."

"Likely there is much you do not know of him."

"Yes," Elizabeth agreed. "However I would imagine that a cousin who lived on the same estate as he did must earn some mention, do you not? Do consider that I do not speak only of our time in Hertfordshire, but of the weeks in Kent as well. Mr William Darcy was not discussed, not by Mr Fitzwilliam Darcy, nor by any of those who must be mutually acquainted with him."

"That is true," Jane said. "But what can it mean?"

"In fact," Elizabeth said, with greater vigour. "Lady Catherine scolded him for being unable to come to her more often. He always claimed the duties of his estate drew him away. Would you not think that with Pemberley in the hands of a trusted cousin, he might go where he pleases for as long as he wishes to be there?"

"He likely did not wish to be in Kent and used his obligations at Pemberley to exempt himself," Jane said in a reasonable tone. "You have said yourself, he appeared quite disgusted to be there."

"Your answers have far too much logic for me, Sister," Elizabeth said, at last removing her eyes from Mr William Darcy. "I fear your sense shall overcome my fancies."

"And what are your fancies?" Jane asked.

"Something is afoot here," Elizabeth pronounced. "And I intend to find out just what it is."

She turned, addressing Mrs Gardiner, who had recently finished her conversation with Mrs Jones, the wife of the apothecary. "Our dance partners have gone to retrieve some refreshments for us. I do hope you will meet them when they return."

Mrs Gardiner gave Jane a little look. "I am exceedingly curious to meet Mr Bingley, of whom I have heard so much. And Lizzy? Was Mr Darcy your partner?"

Elizabeth smiled. "How did you guess?"

"He is very the image of his father," said Mrs Gardiner. "I cannot claim intimacy with that family, but such distinguished personages are always known to those in the towns, even if they themselves do not recognise the townsfolk."

A thrum of excitement coursed through her. Of course! Here beside her was the greatest proof of all. Surely a cousin would be known to Mrs Gardiner?

The gentlemen were approaching again, and Elizabeth made haste to speak to her aunt. "It may surprise you to know that it is not Mr Fitzwilliam Darcy who you see but Mr William Darcy. A nephew; I believe he is the son of Mr George Darcy's younger brother."

"I beg your pardon?" Mrs Gardiner looked confused. "But I did not think that—"

The gentlemen were then upon them and Mr Darcy was first to speak, nodding respectfully to Mrs Gardiner before saying, "Miss Elizabeth, pray introduce me to your friend."

Elizabeth gave him a wide smile and if it was a bit like the smile a cat would give to its mouse, she did not intend it to be so. "It would be my pleasure, sir."

She made the introduction, pleased with the amiability of Mr Darcy and Mr Bingley towards her beloved aunt. Before they could introduce any subject for conversation, however, she interceded further. "Mr Darcy, my aunt spent her youth in Derbyshire."

Her eyes were intent upon Mr Darcy's countenance when she pronounced it, and thus she did not miss the slight widening of his eyes or the fleeting distress that marked his looks. "A town called Lambton," she added.

"That is but five miles from Pemberley," Bingley cried out jovially. A moment later, he grasped the implication of this news and sobered.

Mrs Gardiner stepped forward, her features showing her intelligence and kindness. "I could not claim an intimacy with your family, sir," she said. "But we did attend the parish church at Kympton and saw them all when they were in Derbyshire."

Mrs Gardiner tilted her head at Darcy, seeming as though she studied him closely, though politely. "My nieces tell me you are the cousin of the present Master of Pemberley."

Elizabeth nearly laughed aloud. Mr Darcy stared at Mrs Gardiner in horror but did not speak. One could almost hear his mind spinning.

"I must own I find it exceedingly surprising. I can remember once, when I was only a girl, you... your cousin fell ill and the town was so very fearful he would not last it. Oh, how much everyone hoped and prayed! Of course, no one wished to see a child perish but I had understood it was also because there were no near male relations to inherit Pemberley."

Mr Darcy glanced quickly at Elizabeth and she dropped her eyes quickly, not wanting him to see what she felt. She was nearly positive he was pretending to be his own cousin, but why? She could not imagine.

Mr Darcy shifted on his feet, seeming to be at a loss for words. Elizabeth waited, wondering what explanation he could, or would, give them. The silence seemed to stretch long.

Just when she began to think he would remain mute forever, Mr Bingley gave a strangled cry. He then lurched forward and his glass of punch—a glass that had been largely untouched—poured directly onto Mr Darcy. The drink, a deep claret colour, splashed liberally over Mr Darcy's waistcoat, dribbling onto his breeches as well as colouring a small portion of his cravat and shirt.

Mr Darcy leapt backwards, his action too late to be of any help. "Bingley!"

"Oh my!" Bingley exclaimed. "What a dreadful clumsy oaf I am! Someone must have bumped me!"

Mr Darcy removed his handkerchief and began to dab uselessly at his clothes. He gave his friend a strained smile, which more resembled the baring of his teeth, but he did not get angry. "It is nothing, just a spot."

"I do hope your suit is not ruined!" Mr Bingley exclaimed. "Come, let us find someone to help!"

Mrs Gardiner stepped forward. "May I be of use? I might—"

"No, no!" Mr Bingley took hold of his friend's arms and began to push him towards the side of the room, ignoring Mrs Gardiner. "I could not importune you, ma'am. Come with me, Darcy."

Darcy permitted Bingley to direct him towards a small room to the side of the dance floor, looking back only once to see Elizabeth standing with her sister and aunt, staring after them in astonishment.

Bingley immediately sent two servants to retrieve some water. Sir William arrived to see whether he could assist. Darcy opened his mouth, a curt refusal on the tip of his tongue, but Bingley hissed, "Amiable!" under his breath, so Darcy forced a smile.

"Nothing at all, Sir William. A minor spill. I am certain to be back among the dancers by the time the next is called."

Sir William clapped his hands, made a few silly and absent-minded remarks about not being denied the pleasure of watching them dance, and then was gone.

As soon as the door closed behind Sir William, Bingley heaved a sigh, then removed his own handkerchief and mopped his brow. "You are most welcome, sir," he said to Darcy.

"Welcome?" Darcy was incredulous. "I am welcome? You suppose I should thank you? Have you gone witless?"

Bingley reached over to dab uselessly at Darcy's waistcoat with his sweat-laden handkerchief. "I aided you in escaping just in time! What singular misfortune to come across someone who knows your family when otherwise you might have passed very creditably."

Bingley began to pace as they awaited the servant with the water. "What if you say there was a breach in the family…some time past, perhaps some blackguard of a great-uncle of sorts?"

Darcy sagged against the wall, closing his eyes for a moment. "The game is up," Darcy told him tiredly. "Elizabeth is far too quick-witted to believe—"

Bingley shook his head, fully resolute. "We can think of some explanation. A brother who was believed dead, but after your father died, appeared suddenly—"

"I cannot lie any more! An uncle brought back from the dead? It is too much!"

Bingley crossed his arms over his chest. "Very well then. You reveal yourself. Then what?"

Darcy sighed. "Then we…I am sure I cannot say."

"Then she is angry. She will be angry because she will not yet comprehend what is good in this little farce."

"What good is there in this farce?"

"That you have shown yourself willing to do anything to be with her," said Bingley. "That you would even be another man if it would meet with her approval."

Darcy considered that moment, then slowly nodded. It made sense, and it held promise.

"So you need only show her that you are an agreeable fellow. Then when you reveal William and Fitzwilliam are one and the same gentleman, she will realise there was more to you than she knew and that she is in love with the William part of you."

"She may already suspect William is me in disguise."

"Then I return to my previous point—she is behaving rather warmly to you. So whether she thinks you are William or Fitzwilliam, you have much to gain by continuing. You could win her heart either way, but in either case, it is far too early to give up."

Though Darcy hated to admit it, Bingley was correct. Elizabeth had been alternately warm and teasing, sometimes curious, sometimes dubious, but never with indifference or spite. Bingley noted it, and yet Bingley knew nothing of his letter. Had his letter, the letter he had given her after his botched proposal, made her think differently of him?

He supposed it all must depend upon whether or not she knew he was Fitzwilliam—which was very hopeful—or whether she truly believed he was Cousin William—much less hopeful.

He could not give up until he knew, for certain, whether her teasing smiles and sparkling fine eyes were for him or for William. Who better than William Darcy to lead the discovery?

CHAPTER SIX

When the gentlemen had disappeared into one of the back rooms, Elizabeth stood contemplating the mystery she believed had been laid before her.

Upon her first view of the gentleman calling himself Mr William Darcy, she had believed, wholly, that he was in fact Mr Fitzwilliam Darcy. However, his marked amiability, the ease and friendliness in his manner—all had caused her to doubt. When he flirted with her, her doubts were relieved; the man was, in no way, Fitzwilliam Darcy. He must be William, as he said he was.

Had not Mr Fitzwilliam Darcy made very plain the upright sobriety of his nature?

'Follies and nonsense, whims and inconsistencies, they do divert me, I own, and I laugh at them whenever I can'—she had said those very words to him the previous autumn, adding a challenge afterwards —'But these, I suppose, are precisely what you are without'.

Mr Darcy had replied, 'Perhaps that is not possible for any one. But it has been the study of my life to avoid those weaknesses which expose a strong understanding to ridicule.'

Thus this Mr Darcy could decidedly not be Mr Fitzwilliam Darcy. Mr *Fitzwilliam* Darcy would do no such silly thing as this.

There was but one thing that gave her pause.

Surely a gentleman would know he should not flirt and make love to the lady who had so recently rejected his cousin? He claimed to be in Mr Fitzwilliam Darcy's confidence. This would surely make him more cautious in his dealings with her, would it not? She would have expected 'William' Darcy to avoid her as assiduously as his 'cousin' might have.

There were other things as well; that certain something in his manner. The attitude in which he stood, the movement of his hands when he spoke, even his speech; surely a cousin who spent most of his time in Derbyshire would have the accent of Derbyshire, would he not? And yet Mr William Darcy spoke as one who spent a considerable amount of his time in London.

A beard and an ill-fitting suit were not sufficient disguise for the nobility of Mr Fitzwilliam Darcy's appearance. Mr Darcy was—she would admit this now—a very handsome man. It took a great deal more than whiskers to disguise that.

Why would he do such a thing as this? What did he hope to achieve? Surely to make her laugh at him could not be his object. Was it a sort of revenge on her?

She could not deny this: he had surprised and intrigued her. She wished to know more of him and understand what it was that compelled him to do as he did.

She would not expose him, she decided. Indeed, she wished to study him further, to see what he was about. She thought she had surely misjudged his character before and now it seemed, in thinking him too serious and staid, she misunderstood him again. Mr Darcy was proving far more intriguing than ever she had imagined.

It was entirely fascinating to see just how far he would take this nonsense of his.

She turned to her sister and her aunt. "I require your forbearance."

Both ladies agreed and stood looking at her expectantly.

"The gentleman who just left us, accompanied by Mr Bingley is, I believe, Mr *Fitz*william Darcy. He has chosen to don a disguise tonight, although to what end I cannot say."

Mrs Gardiner protested this conclusion. "Who would attempt to deceive an entire assembly of people?"

"There are too many similarities in their appearance, but not only that. There is a certain something in his air, the way he walks; it is too like the manners of Mr Fitzwilliam Darcy."

Jane said, "Cousins will often share these sorts of things, similarities in not only looks but also gestures. It is not so very uncommon."

"Yes, but..." Elizabeth stopped herself. What she had nearly said—but would not, could not ever say—was a secret she held deep in her heart.

It had been not the first moment of their acquaintance but rather the first moment that she had seen him, eight months prior, at the assembly much like this one. She had observed him enter and felt... something. A tug, so to speak, ill-defined but exceedingly pleasing. She recalled fancying it as a recognition of souls, although she discarded the notion at once, realising he was far too high for her and she must not harbour hopes for such a man.

Then of course, he slighted her and so it went from there. However, had he not slighted her, she did not know what might have become of them. Her injured pride made her determined to dislike him.

But now she felt it again. This man, in his shabby-looking whiskers and an unfashionable, cheaply made suit, produced another tug, still more powerful than the first.

"But what, Lizzy?" Jane interrupted her sister's musings.

"They are returning," Mrs Gardiner cautioned them in a hushed voice.

The gentleman tarried a moment by the window; a breeze blew and no doubt Mr Darcy hoped to dry his breeches. As the gentlemen stood there, the ladies lowered their eyes, using their particular talents to observe the gentlemen through their eyelashes whilst looking as though they saw nothing.

Mr Darcy's breeches were bothersome to him it would seem.

"See there," Elizabeth murmured. "You see how Mr Darcy has just adjusted his breeches?"

"All gentlemen do that," Mrs Gardiner said under her breath while nodding at a passing acquaintance.

"Not Mr Darcy," Elizabeth replied, opening her fan in front of her face. "I never before saw such an action, not in his weeks in Hertfordshire, and not in Kent. Yet tonight, I have seen him troubling himself several times tonight. Perhaps as many as ten times."

Jane was not persuaded. "Mr Bingley has 'troubled himself', as you say it, ten times in the five minutes they have been standing there. I think perhaps you merely did not notice it before."

"No, no," Elizabeth insisted. "What I mean to say is that I am certain such movements can only suggest that Mr Darcy is wearing attire that is not his own."

Mrs Gardiner had opened her fan also and spoke behind it. "Lizzy, you might not be aware of this but the male anatomy…well, it can be rather inconvenient at times—most particularly during warmer weather, such as we are having."

"How do you mean, Aunt?" Jane asked.

Mrs Gardiner glanced around. "The heat causes sweat and the sweat can lead to…discomfort."

"Discomfort?" Mr Gardiner had arrived, his approach unseen by any of them. His voice seemed extraordinarily loud, very nearly booming. The ladies jumped and shushed him.

"What?" he asked in a theatrical whisper. "Oh! Is it—" He glanced around anxiously. "Is it a lady's particular discomfort?"

Mrs Gardiner laughed. "Quite the opposite in fact."

Mr Gardiner appeared bemused but before he could speak again, Elizabeth spoke. "Whether Mr William Darcy is who he says he is or whether, as I believe, he is Mr Fitzwilliam Darcy, let us go along with it."

The other three agreed and if Mr Gardiner was wont to question further, a quickly hissed word from his wife forestalled his questions.

The gentlemen abandoned their post at the window and were approaching their little group. The two Gardiners and two Bennet ladies straightened themselves. As Mr Darcy made his way past a group of gentlemen—including the rather corpulent Mr Hatchings whom he no doubt believed obscured him from view—he again adjusted his breeches; Elizabeth noted it and gave Jane a significant look. Jane hissed, "Mr Bingley has adjusted his breeches three times in the walk over Lizzy; it means nothing!"

"Mr Darcy, you are well recovered from Mr Bingley's mishap," said Elizabeth as soon as the gentlemen drew near. It was not entirely true;

his waistcoat still bore evidence of the spill but it was to Mr Darcy's good fortune that the dark colour of the garment hid most of the stain.

He bowed. "We have done our best, have we not, Bingley?"

Mrs Gardiner spoke. "Mr Darcy, pray forgive me. I believe I spoke wrongly before, confusing your family with another I knew in Derbyshire."

"Oh." Mr Darcy looked uncertain for a moment. "It was no matter."

"I forget sometimes that it has been nearly twenty years since I last called that county my home." Mrs Gardiner smiled warmly. "I hold Derbyshire in great esteem."

With that they were able to put aside the subject of the Darcy family for a time, as Mr Darcy compared his recollections of youth in Derbyshire to those of Mrs Gardiner. The subject was ended when Mr Bingley asked Elizabeth to dance the next with him.

CHAPTER SEVEN

A PLAN HAD FORMED IN ELIZABETH'S MIND, AND THUS DID she consent with alacrity to dance with Mr Bingley. She was pleased to see Mr Darcy asked Jane for the same favour, although she could not imagine Jane would be of any help in eliciting information from the gentleman.

The dance began and to Elizabeth's delight, it was not one of the faster ones. Indeed, it was one that allowed for a great deal of talking in the pattern. When all the polite little nothings were dispensed with, Elizabeth sallied forth into her true subject of interest.

"Mr Bingley, I must own I am rather disappointed Mr Fitzwilliam Darcy did not accompany you to Netherfield."

"Are you?" Mr Bingley's eyes were alit with eager interest almost immediately.

"But you have said he is excessively busy and I do not doubt it. I am sure there are a great many amusements to occupy him in town."

"Yes," said Mr Bingley. "But then again, no. I do not doubt that he would much prefer to be here." He gave Elizabeth a wide-eyed look that no doubt he believed was subtle; it was not.

"Here?"

"Indeed!" he replied warmly.

THE FIRST MOMENT OF THEIR ACQUAINTANCE

"Why?"

"Why?"

"Yes, why are you so certain he would prefer to be here?" She asked with as much innocence as she could muster. "After all, would he not be here if he wished it?"

"Oh...I..."

"Perhaps you did not want him here. How silly of me to assume you had invited him!" She smiled broadly.

"No, no I did invite him but—"

"But he did not wish to attend you. I understand completely. I do not think he was fond of Hertfordshire when last he was here."

"He thinks Hertfordshire is second only to Derbyshire," Mr Bingley protested.

"So you invited him and he wished to be here, and yet he is not. Why would that be, sir?"

Bingley looked panicked. He darted a glance over towards Mr Darcy.

"Oh, I see. He dislikes his cousin—is that it? Family does not always make friends, and familiarity does breed contempt, does it not?" She gave an exaggeratedly understanding nod to Mr Bingley.

"Um." Mr Bingley looked back over at Mr Darcy and Jane who appeared to be engaged in quiet conversation. "I...I cannot say."

Elizabeth permitted Mr Bingley ample time to gather his wits about him. He appeared to regret asking her to dance, and she did not wish to be an unpleasant partner. Thus did they spend more time speaking of subjects of little consequence.

When the dance had nearly ended, she began again. "You see, I was hoping especially to see Mr Fitzwilliam Darcy soon that I might tell him... But no, on this subject it is best to be silent." She stopped speaking, careful to put a look of distress on her countenance.

She had piqued his interest. "What subject is that, Miss Elizabeth?"

She opened her mouth as if to speak and then stopped, shaking her head. "No, no. I must not."

"I assure you, whatever you would say I will hold in the strictest confidence."

"It is only that I wish…I wish I might…perhaps you could tell him for me." She stopped, wanting to seem as though the words were being slowly dragged from her.

Mr Bingley's eyes were alight with anticipation. "Upon my honour, whatever you wish me to tell him shall be told, with all due haste."

She waved him off. "No, and in any case, what can it signify?"

"It can signify a great deal," Mr Bingley proclaimed. "I would not force your confidence. However, I implore you to tell me. I assure you, he wishes to hear it."

She wrinkled her brow. "How do you know?"

Mr Bingley spoke in a hushed voice. "I just do."

"You cannot."

"I assure you, I do. Just tell me."

Time to blush, Elizabeth told herself. She purposely made herself think of the most humiliating spectacle her mother had ever raised in her presence; it worked very well, staining her cheeks a heated red. To keep the appearance of maidenly discretion, she looked to the side while she blushed.

"It is too much a secret, sir," she said. "I should not speak of it. Pray, forgive me."

Mr Bingley protested, extolling his discretion and keen ability to advise, but she scarcely heard him.

The dance had brought her around so she caught Mr Darcy's eye. He danced with Jane and he spoke to Jane, but his gaze was only for her. Their eyes met; familiar and intent, it was for her alone.

It is him, she thought in amazement. *I could not mistake the feel of those eyes upon me.* She smiled, a small smile, and his gaze seemed to grow warmer.

Mr Bingley rattled on while she continued to gaze at Mr Darcy, and he continued to gaze at her until at last she could bear no more. She dropped her eyes, suppressing the urge to giggle or skip; her entire being felt girlish and light. She turned a dazzling smile on Mr Bingley, who appeared taken aback by it.

He was so very different, so altered; if it was indeed Fitzwilliam Darcy, he had changed considerably. For me? she wondered. *Have my reproofs wrought such an alteration?*

She considered what he had said earlier: 'The lady with whom you most wish to dance is the self-same lady who is able to render you stupid and tongue-tied in her presence.'

Had he spoken those words in earnest? Could he be so affected by her? Could such a man be in her power? It softened her to think of it.

She assumed that since handing her his letter that morning in the grove, he had likely expended significant effort in forgetting her. She presumed to know his mind, and had painted him alternately despising and disregarding her as the weeks passed since his proposal.

Evidently inasmuch as she had misjudged him the first time, so had she continued. He had written her his letter to exonerate himself, but evidently his suffering had not ended there. It was nearly two months since that fateful night in the parsonage. What had been wrought within him in that time? Could he truly still love her despite all that had gone between them?

She had been determined to tease him, perhaps even force him to admit to his little piece of mischief, but she now found that she dared not. With her improved understanding of him, it was not possible. He was in her power and she...

I daresay that I must admit that I, likewise, am in his.

Nevertheless, she was not yet ready to give up the game. She would not tease the truth out of him, cruelly playing with his sensibilities. Instead, she would try another tactic.

The dance ended and Mr Bingley bowed, offering his arm and escorting her from the floor. She thanked him when they arrived at Mrs Gardiner's side, but as he turned to depart, she stopped him.

"Pray, sir, do this for me."

"Anything at all Miss Elizabeth."

"If you should happen to write to Mr Darcy...Mr Fitzwilliam Darcy that is, could you tell him something for me?" She smiled sweetly at Mr Bingley, who really looked almost wild, he was beaming so broadly.

"Yes?"

"Tell him that if, from the first moment of our acquaintance, I had known what I know now, I would have behaved quite differently."

Mr Bingley's smile dimmed. He looked like he did not know what to make of such a statement as that.

Elizabeth, feeling quite bold, retained hold of her courage sufficient to add, "And I do hope I shall see him here soon. Very soon."

CHAPTER EIGHT

"She said what?" Darcy stared at his friend, disbelieving the words just related to him.

"That had she known what she knows...or if you knew what she knows...no, no, if she knew what you knew she knows... Blast!" Bingley gave a helpless little shrug.

Darcy ran his hand over his face, summoning his patience. "You spoke of William? Or of Fitzwilliam?"

"Both," Bingley replied. "She asked why I had not invited you—I mean why I had not asked Fitzwilliam Darcy—to come to Netherfield."

"I *am* Fitzwilliam Darcy," said Darcy drily. "And you said...?"

Bingley looked at the ceiling as he struggled to remember it. "Then she said something about a secret."

"A secret!" Darcy exclaimed. "That is very good!" He thought for a moment. "Or perhaps not. Perhaps it is disastrous. A good secret? Or a bad secret?"

Bingley wrinkled his brow. "In truth, I cannot say."

Darcy let out a frustrated growl. "Bingley! You are no help!"

Primly, Bingley informed him, "You look disagreeable again."

"I do not care!" Darcy roared at him. "Now think on this, man!

Think hard, like you have never thought before. What did she want you to tell me?"

Bingley pressed his lips together, and knit his brow exerting great effort into remembering precisely what Miss Elizabeth had said. Darcy watched him anxiously, his heart leaping with excitement when his friend's lips at last parted to relay the treasured message to him.

"Forgive me, Darcy, but I truly cannot recall it."

Darcy's heart sank, but he refrained from lashing out in anger. "Never mind then. I will continue on as I have been, and we shall see where it will take us."

He turned to depart the small alcove where they had escaped to talk. Elizabeth was engaged to dance with some other young man, but Darcy was determined the next set would be his.

"There was one thing I do remember quite clearly though," Bingley called after him.

He turned back. "What was that?"

"She said she hoped to see Fitzwilliam Darcy here in Hertfordshire very soon. That portion I recall precisely. *Very soon*—her exact words."

A burgeoning sense of hope took root in Darcy's chest as he thanked his friend and hurried off to find Elizabeth, his steps quickened by his joy.

Still, the problem of when to reveal his true identity plagued him. Now? Was it done? Could he have her? Or should he wait, show her more of the changed man he was?

Elizabeth watched as Mr Darcy came towards her, a strange expression on his countenance. Delight? She knew not what might have delighted him. "Mr Darcy."

"Miss Elizabeth Bennet," he replied. "You are much sought after as a dance partner this evening."

With a sheepish grin, she admitted, "I will own I would much prefer to sit out for the rest of the night. I am exceedingly fatigued."

"Oh." Delight faded and he appeared pensive for a moment.

With a gentle smile, she prodded, "It is quite warm in the room, do you not think so?"

"I do," he said absently. "What about—"

"Some air, sir, would be a relief."

"I believe all the windows are opened," he said. "Alas, the breeze is only to the advantage of those standing near them." He looked over, and Elizabeth followed his gaze seeing that Mr Bingley had taken Jane near the windows to enjoy the very breeze they spoke of. Still, he did not take her hints and she decided she must be direct.

"Mr Darcy?"

"Yes?"

"Would you escort me onto the terrace for some air?"

For a moment he looked surprised, then abashed. With a chuckle, he said, "I am rendered insensible in your presence, Miss Elizabeth. I could not take your meaning."

An odd sort of smile came over her lips as she took his arm. As they walked to the terrace, Darcy formed a resolution to speak in a forthright manner and see where it led. "Miss Elizabeth, I wonder if you would think me impertinent if I asked you a question."

"Not at all, sir," said she. "Although we have only just met, I feel as though our acquaintance has been of many months duration."

"As do I," he said warmly. "Well then. You will recall, of course, that you asked if I was in my cousin's confidence."

She nodded.

"I am. In fact, he tells me everything. Everything of importance to him, he discusses with me." Darcy swallowed. "He told me of his failed proposal in Kent."

She appeared undisturbed by this news.

"Forgive me, but you do not seem surprised."

She tilted her head, regarding him coolly. "I am not."

"No?"

She shook her head.

He studied her. Did she know? Or did she not?

"In fact," she said, "I have wondered if he sent you here."

"Sent me?"

"Perhaps Mr Darcy wished to learn something of my heart in this matter. I cannot know where his thoughts might tend at present, nor can he know mine. A cousin, a new friend who will insinuate himself into my good graces, might be ideal."

"I beg your pardon if my advances have appeared anything less than genuine, Miss Elizabeth. I assure you, I have no ill will or malice towards you. In fact, I am rather charmed."

"Mr Darcy, being that you are in your cousin's confidence and thus fully aware of his intentions towards me, do you not think it rather bold to flirt with me? I cannot think Mr Darcy would approve."

"Pardon me," he said quickly. "It is not my intention to romance you. You are entirely correct. It would be inappropriate, knowing my cousin's heart as I do."

"What is your intention then?"

"My intention?" Darcy stammered a bit. "I...I do not know that I had any intention." He swallowed as a breeze tickled the curls at her neck.

"You did not wish to know my mind and my heart?"

"If you wish to tell me," he said with a grin, "I would love to hear it."

She laughed lightly. "No, I fear it is best kept between Mr Darcy and myself, should I ever see him again."

"You will see him," Darcy said, taking a step closer. "I believe he will come just as soon as he knows he is welcome."

"I believe he can guess what his welcome will be."

"He cannot," Darcy replied. "The time since Kent has taught him that he understood very little about himself."

"That is regrettable indeed," said Elizabeth. "And a feeling I apprehend all too well—I, too, wish I had understood more of Mr Darcy."

"You do?"

Her voice low, she added, "I have sought to know more of myself since my time in Kent. As I said to Mr Bingley, had I known, at the first moment of our acquaintance, what I know now, I would have behaved very differently."

It was maddening, the urge he had to take her in his arms. They

THE FIRST MOMENT OF THEIR ACQUAINTANCE

stood close, but not improperly so, facing one another. He indulged in taking one step nearer to her. "I believe if my cousin knew of your feelings, and understood whether they were matched to his hopes and wishes, there might be a second chance at this for you both. A second 'first moment of your acquaintance' so to speak, and a chance to begin on the right path."

"What are your cousin's hopes and wishes?" To his delight, she stepped a bit closer.

"To call on you," he whispered, moving his feet several inches in her direction.

Her eyes went wide and she stepped back, her fine eyes betraying some confusion. "To *call* on me?"

"Um, yes."

She considered that a moment, her eyes turned towards the moonlight. "Previously he asked for my hand in marriage, but now he wishes only to call on me?"

"The offer of his hand was rejected, as you well know. Now he seeks only to aim for that which he might reasonably attain."

"I see." Elizabeth had a faint smile dancing upon her lips. "I do believe I might agree to having him call on me—but with one stipulation."

Darcy leant in. "Anything. I mean, I know he will agree to anything. What is it?"

Using a crooked finger, she beckoned him a little closer. Leaning towards him, she whispered into his ear.

CHAPTER NINE

THOUGH HE LONGED TO HEAR THE WORDS PASSING FROM her lips, for a moment, he could scarcely attend her. She had beckoned him closer and then risen up on her toes to whisper in his ear. The warmth of her body so near to his own, the sweet whisper of her breath and her scent conspired to elate and enchant him even before he heard her speak.

"It is a truth universally acknowledged that a lady cannot help but to love a gentleman who makes her laugh...Fitzwilliam."

He was unmasked. There was nothing for it but to laugh, rather helplessly as they stood there, she joining with him in it. When at last he was recovered, he said, "I recall you once said that follies and nonsense divert you."

"And I recall you once said that the study of your life was to avoid those weaknesses which often expose a strong understanding to ridicule."

"Perhaps I did," he acknowledged. "That, however, was before I learnt that the pleasure of earning your smile was well worth some silliness and loss of dignity on my part."

She laughed, a light little laugh, and dropped her eyes, but he had not yet said all there was to say.

"Last autumn I was pleased to boast of pride, and quick enough to make mention of my temper. I declaimed any inclination towards being an object of ridicule. However, now I have shown you how much I have changed in the latter so that you might know how I have tended to your reproofs with regard to the former."

"I cannot hold you up to any ridicule," she said.

"You cannot? But why?" He made a little face at her. "Do you not see me here in whiskers and these ill-fitted clothes which Bingley has seen fit to douse with punch? Does it not divert you that I have behaved in such a stupid manner?"

"It is diverting, that much I will own," Elizabeth continued with—dare he hope?—a fond look at him.. "But as I have told you once, I cannot ridicule that which is wise and good."

She laid her hand on his arm. He covered it at once with his hand. "You, sir, are far too much of both to be an object of ridicule, no matter what you are wearing. I may laugh with you, but never will I laugh at you."

"Elizabeth." He breathed her name in reverence and in love. "Dearest, loveliest Elizabeth."

"But I have not told you my stipulation."

"Anything at all," Darcy vowed. "Say the word and it shall be given to you."

"Now that I have learnt of your capacity for diverting me and making me laugh," she said. "I will insist you keep to it. Jane and Mr Bingley may have their smiles. You and I however—we will laugh."

"Each and every day," Darcy said firmly. "I assure you of that. You shall never want for laughter."

"Of course, one stipulation does beget another—would you grant me a second?"

He kissed her hand. "I am yours to command."

"Excellent," said she. "Then do make haste to get those whiskers off your face."

"You do not like them?" He forced an innocence to his tone. "I had thought to set the new mode in London."

"Truly?"

"Yes," he said, reaching up to stroke his lower face with his hand. "I am exceedingly fond of my beard in truth."

"I see," she said. "Well. That settles that then."

He smiled, pleased with his newfound talent for teasing. He would torment her a bit and then appear at Longbourn on the morrow, newly shaven and dressed in appropriate garb.

"It is a shame, that is all."

Her tone raised suspicion in him. He looked over to see her looking rather dispirited. "You surely do not dislike it so much?"

"It is not that," she assured him. "My uncle Gardiner had a beard for some time, and I shall admit that I thought it rather distinguished."

"Then what?"

"No, do not make me say it."

"You must."

"I cannot."

"I insist. As your future husband, I insist you tell me at once."

"Future husband? I thought you only wished to call on me?"

"Having had such success in obtaining your agreement to that much..." He swallowed, feeling their levity flee. "I confess my previous hopes have been rekindled."

She said nothing for a moment.

"My wishes are unchanged, Elizabeth. They have been thus for many months now but one word from you will silence me on this subject forever."

For a moment her breath caught, and she was required to inhale deeply before saying, "My word is yes."

It was his turn now to catch his breath and he reached for her hands, pulling them to his chest, and rested his forehead on hers. They stood a moment in silent exultation with one another.

"This brings me to my second request," she whispered.

"Anything, I will give you anything at all," he said. "You have truly made me the happiest of men."

"Just that I had thought it would be nice to...well, I would not like my first kiss to be given through scratchy whiskers."

No more needed said. Darcy bowed hastily, excusing himself from her company to find the man who had so ably assisted him in the matter of his punch-stained attire earlier.

THE FIRST MOMENT OF THEIR ACQUAINTANCE

Darcy was gone nearly half an hour. Elizabeth occupied herself in speaking to her aunt of the astonishing events which had transpired, both for herself and for her sister.

When she had finished speaking to Mrs Gardiner, she set about telling all who had gathered the truth of Mr Darcy's little farce. It was interesting to Elizabeth—particularly given her enjoyment of the study of character—to observe how the majority of those gathered pretended to have known of Mr Darcy's true identity from the first.

"Of course, I did not believe it." Mr Goulding said. "A man of such fine tall bearing is difficult to disguise."

"I might have believed a brother," Lady Lucas decided. "But a cousin? No, it was not to be believed. No two could be that similar."

"Mr Darcy has lost a bit of weight," said Mr Philips. "But perhaps it was the effect of the cut of his coat. In any case, it confused me only momentarily."

"Theatricals!" exclaimed Sir William, bouncing on his toes as was his habit. "How exceedingly diverting! Such a fine amusement for young people. He must consider a bit of Shakespeare for his next! He cannot deny me the pleasure of seeing him perform Shakespeare!"

Elizabeth had just completed her task when Mr Darcy re-entered the assembly. Her breath caught when she saw him.

He was the Mr Darcy she had known from the first, and yet not. He was every inch the gentleman, with a fine, tall person draped in well-fitted and expensive clothes, as well as handsome features, and a noble mien. Elizabeth looked at him with great admiration, admiration which swelled, knowing as she did, that his manners were so very different now than they were then.

Darcy moved through the hall with one thought in his mind: to get to Elizabeth, hie her back to the terrace, and kiss her. Alas, it would seem that every person in Meryton must come to him and speak of his little farce. He had scarcely moved an inch before another approached him, exclaiming over his jest and the fact that they themselves had known the truth from the first. It might have amused him had his senses not been filled with the imagined feel of his betrothed being held within his arms.

Bingley stopped him just as he drew near to where Elizabeth stood with her aunt and uncle. The last dance was nearly through and he felt the prodding of elapsing time. "I had a very enjoyable dance with Miss Bennet."

"Excellent. Pray excuse me I—"

"Does she still hold me in regard? Does she not? It is impossible to know!"

"Her sister says she does, so she must," Darcy said briskly. "Perhaps you ought to speak to her directly."

"I cannot, not right now," Bingley replied glumly. "She dances with Hartleigh."

"Tomorrow then. You and I shall call at Longbourn as early as may be." Darcy edged away from his friend as they spoke. Bingley moved with him.

"Tell me, what is your opinion on next day calls?"

"My opinion on what?" Darcy stretched his head in an attempt to see Elizabeth.

"Next day calls. Saye once told me that a gentleman must never call on a lady before two days have elapsed from the time of a dance."

Darcy looked at Bingley with some confusion. "A next-day call is perfectly proper and even expected."

"'Tis his own rule, I suppose." Bingley shrugged. "He said himself he prefers three days, but I think that is excessive. He also said something on the order of 'men before hens'—I had no notion what to make of that. He said he will write it all down in a book for us."

"Saye is an idiot," Darcy said impatiently. "Whatever book he writes will be best used as kindling."

"But if you call on her too soon," Bingley mused aloud, "is there not the danger of vexing her? A day or so of reflection might lead her to recall you in a more favourable light."

Elizabeth had caught his eye, and Darcy gave her a private look. She blushed, sending a thrill directly through him. "I need to leave you now," he said to Bingley. He turned and began to close the distance between Elizabeth and himself.

Bingley remained close to him, muttering about Saye and how long he ought to wait between dances and calls. Darcy ignored him, for soon they had converged on Elizabeth's group, which was her uncle, her aunt, and her sisters, as well as Sir William Lucas and Mrs Goulding.

Darcy hoped the size of the group would make it easier for him to steal her away, but it was not to be so. On the contrary, they seemed to close ranks around her, making it impossible to even speak to her privately in what he soon realised were the last moments of the assembly. They stood in pointless, annoying conversation until, at last, all hope had to be removed from him.

"Well, young ladies," Mr Gardiner announced before too much time had elapsed. "The evening has passed with great pleasure, but I, for one, think longingly of my bed!" He began to move his party from the hall.

Elizabeth sent Darcy a wistful glance which encouraged him. He moved close, touching her arm to halt her. "Can you not linger?"

"My uncle is not one to tarry."

"Perhaps if he knows of our changed understanding?"

"If he knew of our changed understanding, he would surely not tarry," she said with a little laugh. Then, clearing her throat just a bit, she said, "I find I often have difficulty sleeping after such an assembly as this."

He grinned. "As do I."

CHAPTER TEN

Ninety minutes later...

Where is he? Elizabeth wondered.

She sat on the bench beneath her window, her legs curled under her. She remained fully dressed, believing he had understood her invitation—her bold, perhaps wanton invitation. Maybe not, she fretted. Or maybe he understood and was disgusted by it.

Or perhaps he is injured, she worried. *Lying on the road somewhere, tossed by his horse. No, more likely, he is disgusted and wondering how he ever could have professed love to such a wanton creature.*

She had nearly given up on him when she, at last, heard the approach of a horse, a horse which stopped a considerable distance from the house. Believing it could only be him, she nearly ran down the back stair, wrapping a shawl around herself as she hurried into the dark night.

He was tying his horse to a nearby tree when she arrived, and she gave him a fright. He straightened hurriedly, exclaiming, "Elizabeth! Is it you?"

"It is," she said, suddenly feeling a bit shy. "I am sorry for startling you."

"Never mind that," he said. His voice was so warm and low; he sounded pleased, and all of her fears from before fled in the face of it. "I did not think I would see you."

She drew nearer to him. "Then what are you doing here, sir? Has another of my sisters engaged you for a kiss this evening?"

He chuckled, stepping away from his horse to close the remaining distance between them. "No. I meant to say, I had supposed I would find you in the yard, not out in the lane."

"I could not wait to meet you."

She could barely see him in the dark night though they were no more than a foot apart. Clouds had drifted over the moon, and the night was a milk-laced black. He reached for her hand, pulling her closer to him. "Neither could I."

Her heart thudded within her chest as he bent his head toward her. The first kiss was no more than a glancing touch of his lips on her cheek. Her body was scarcely touching his, and each of her hands remained clasped within each of his as his kiss alit upon her cheeks, a few on the left and then a few on the right. His lips were soft, much softer than she had expected, and she found herself turning her face, encouraging him to move them from her cheek to her mouth.

"This feels like a dream," he whispered a few moments later, his mouth breaking contact with hers only long enough to utter the words. "I have yearned for you for so very long."

She pressed herself against him, her hands linking around his neck. "How long?"

"From the first," he said. "The first moment of our acquaintance."

"Need I remind you how easily you then withstood my charms?"

"The first night I had been acquainted with you, I dreamt of you, of loving you, and holding you, and forever keeping you near me. It terrified me then just as much as it thrills me now, particularly as I know my dream shall become a reality."

There was something in the obscured moonlight and the ease of his own confession which prompted her own. "I, too, recall feeling something the first moment of our acquaintance, something I scarce could comprehend. A sense that there would be something to us, that something had just begun." She smiled. "And so it did, even if our beginning was...uncommon."

"Because you despised me?" His tone remained easy, but she perceived the uncertainty beneath the light words.

"Because I did not know you," she said, drawing close again and surprising him with a kiss of her own. She was quick to learn, and in the art of kissing, there was no exception. She pulled his head down with her hands, pressing a short but ardent kiss upon him. "And how grateful I am to have this opportunity to begin anew."

"As am I." He said, keeping her close and continuing to press his lips to her. "A second beginning, for us to be friends, lovers, and husband and wife. Perhaps not the first moment of our acquaintance but the first moment of our life and our love."

"Wonderfully perfect," she agreed, and they celebrated then, a newfound understanding, as lovers do for nearly all the night long.

The End

About the Author

Amy D'Orazio is a longtime devotee of Jane Austen and fiction related to her characters. She currently lives in Myrtle Beach with her husband and daughters, as well as three Jack Russell terriers who often make appearances (in a human form) in her books.

Also by Amy D'Orazio

A Fine Joke
A Lady's Reputation
A Match Made at Matlock
A Short Period of Exquisite Felicity
A Wilful Misunderstanding
Heart Enough
Of a Sunday Evening
So Material a Change
The Best Part of Love
The Happiest Couple in the World
The Mysteries of Pemberley

Speaking the Truth

Nan Harrison

CHAPTER ONE

Fitzwilliam Darcy sat in stony silence, revolted by the scene before him. Bone-weary, he wanted nothing but to rest but could not leave his hosts to deal with the spectacle alone.

They should have been asleep in their beds, recovering from the ball Bingley had insisted upon holding. The ball had ended, or should have ended, more than an hour ago when the Robinsons and Lucases had departed. One family had had other ideas. Someone—presumably Mrs Bennet—had arranged for their carriage to be the last to leave. Their wraps had been brought out, but not only had the carriage not arrived to carry them back to Longbourn, word had come from the grooms that a wheel had mysteriously broken en route.

Thus Darcy, as well as Miss Bingley and Mrs Hurst, was captive to the vulgar, noisy mayhem of the Bennet family while the wheel was repaired. Hurst, after dozing off on a settee, had been awakened abruptly by a particularly loud shriek of delight from Mrs Bennet; he had subsequently stalked off to his rooms without a word to anyone. Bingley was too entranced with Miss Jane Bennet to notice Mrs Bennet prattling shrilly of gowns and flowers; Mr Collins noisily asleep, drooling in an armchair; or even Mr Bennet, who not only failed to control his plainly intoxicated youngest daughters but seemed wholly entertained by the proceedings.

The eldest Miss Bennet was as oblivious as her host to the din around them. Bingley wore an expression of rapturous joy, his eyes alight. Darcy had never seen his friend so openly in love. Miss Bennet on the other hand, while engrossed in Bingley's words, seemed as calm as ever.

The Bennet whom he could not tear his eyes from was standing by the parlour window, far apart from the others, her posture straight and her head held high. Miss Elizabeth Bennet was, after a long and extremely trying evening, still dignified, and so very beautiful. Anyone who had not spent many, many hours observing her closely would never have guessed that she was suffering deeply. Darcy could see the tension in her shoulders and neck, the white-knuckled clasp of her hands, the distress and humiliation in her eyes. She had spoken to her father almost an hour before. He could not know what she said in his ear, but the man had merely raised his eyebrows at her, laughed, and shaken his head. Elizabeth, her head bowed, had silently retreated to her place by the window.

Miss Bingley rose from her seat near Mrs Bennet and moved to sit next to Darcy; her gaze was fixed, staring daggers at the older woman. Leaning towards Darcy, she hissed, "If we do not stop Charles, he will find himself engaged to Miss Bennet! We must end this infatuation now and sever any connexion to that family! After Charles goes to town tomorrow, we must leave Netherfield and never return!"

Darcy agreed. Bingley's feelings were so obvious, some might have thought him honour-bound already. If Miss Bennet returned his affection, it might be another consideration; however, to Darcy's eyes, the lady wore the same expression of smiling reserve that she wore for everyone else in the neighbourhood, child or adult, male or female alike.

His frown deepening, Darcy glanced at Miss Bingley, showing his agreement with a slight, sharp nod of his head. That lady's bosom swelled, and she preened, encouraged by their mutual understanding.

At once, he felt an invisible weight, almost as if something had physically touched him. He looked up into the magnificent eyes of Miss Elizabeth Bennet. They were fixed on him, large, dark, and deep. Darcy realised immediately that she had observed his communication with Miss Bingley, and knew exactly what had been said, or in his case, unsaid. Her countenance was inscrutable, but she seemed to be reading him right to the very depths of his soul. He caught his breath, discomfited, feeling like an insect pinned to a collector's board.

While he watched, she moved to Mr Bennet's side once more. She leant up to her father's ear, spoke, and turned to leave the room. The older man called a few words after her, but through the noise Darcy could not say for certain what they were. He might have heard the word 'missish' or something about 'enjoy the show', but what he did understand clearly was the misery in her eyes as she turned away from her father.

Darcy waited for Miss Elizabeth to return; the minutes seemed to crawl by. His uneasiness gave way to concern, then worry. Miss Bingley was still sitting next to him, simpering, taking his acquiescence to her schemes as the tacit acknowledgment of a familiarity he did not return. He pulled his watch from his pocket to check the hour. It had been something more than twenty minutes since Miss Elizabeth had left. Where did she go? Had she retreated to a quiet room? The library perhaps?

Yielding to impulse, he rose and bowed slightly to his hostess. "I am going to retire, Miss Bingley." He did not wait for a response and made for the door.

Spying a footman at his post in the wide corridor, Darcy asked whether he had seen Miss Elizabeth. The young man pointed down the grand curved stairs towards a side corridor on the ground floor. "Miss Elizabeth decided not to wait for the carriage, sir. She thought the moon was bright enough that she could walk home."

Darcy gaped at the footman in disbelief. "She walked? At night? In the cold?"

"Aye, sir. She knows the path to Longbourn."

But the footman was speaking to Darcy's back, for he was already hastening down the hall.

As Darcy entered his chambers, Talbot, his valet, rose sleepily to ready him for bed. Instead, his master issued a rapid-fire series of orders, and within minutes was changed from his evening clothes into a sturdy ensemble he wore on tours of the estate with Bingley. Talbot hurried into the dressing room and returned with warm shearling gloves, a beaver hat, a heavy coat, and a fur-lined cloak. Darcy snatched them from his hands and left the room. Taking a side staircase, he found the door and hurried out into the predawn darkness.

Elizabeth walked quickly to a small side door. Glancing down at her silk dancing slippers, she wished she had her sturdy half-boots with her, but they would have to do. Donning her pelisse, she slipped outside.

She knew she had made a mistake before she reached the kitchen gardens. It was far colder than she had expected. Reaching the bridle path, she turned around to gaze at the elegant manor house, still brightly lit. She sighed shakily, the cloud of her breath visible in the light. She simply could not return with her tail between her legs, to be the object of her father's mockingly raised brow. She drew her pelisse more tightly around her shoulders and hurried down the path to Longbourn, looking forward to the warmth of a fire in her chambers and the comfort of her bed.

After days of steady cold rain leading up to the evening of the ball, the temperature had plummeted overnight. It was a mercy, Elizabeth reasoned, as she hurried along the path. The ground had hardened and the rainclouds had moved on, leaving the sky clear enough to show the signs of encroaching dawn. Although the stars were fading, the three-quarter moon was still bright enough to illuminate the path, causing it to sparkle like diamonds under thick hoarfrost. Her eyes on the eastern sky, Elizabeth studied the narrow, faint glow and reckoned that there was still an hour or so before the sun cleared the horizon. The intricate web of bridle paths twisted and braided themselves through woods, meadows, and fields, but she knew the way as well as she knew her own hand. She also knew that the way to stay warm was to keep moving. Checking the fastenings on her pelisse, she gathered her skirts in her hands and began to run.

She could not deny what she had seen pass between Mr Darcy and Miss Bingley. That lady had furiously whispered in his ear. Their subsequent glares at Jane and Mr Bingley; that exchanged glance; and Mr Darcy's grimace and quick, tight little nod made obvious their thoughts. At that moment, Elizabeth believed with absolute certainty that Mr Darcy and Miss Bingley planned to separate the couple. The evidence was plain: their disapproval of her family had been barely concealed, Miss Bingley greatly wished to rise in society, and had Mr Darcy not declared himself to be of a resentful nature? Was not his ill-treatment of poor Mr Wickham proof of that resentful nature? Mr Darcy would not hesitate to interfere.

Mr Bingley had mentioned his need to go to London and Elizabeth did not doubt that his sister and friend would contrive to keep him there. Perhaps they would spirit him all the way to Derbyshire! Mr Darcy had great influence over his younger friend. It would be easy to direct Mr Bingley's attention elsewhere... And Jane would suffer. Poor, poor Jane.

Hot tears rolled down her cheeks, and her nose began to run. Elizabeth increased her speed, although she could not escape the pain and mortification attendant upon the performance her family had staged all evening. It had gone far, far beyond humiliating. Of course, Mr Darcy would never let his friend marry into *that*; no one would. It did not matter that Jane was wholly unlike her mother and younger sisters.

Jane might never have another chance to marry for love. Or marry at all.

Then there was Mr Collins. By order of his esteemed patroness, he believed he had the duty—nay, the *right*—to choose a bride from among her sisters. The evening he arrived he had ogled Jane in the same way that he had stared at the roast duck served at dinner. Mrs Bennet had warned him away from Jane, leading him to impose his company upon Elizabeth at intervals throughout the ball. Elizabeth suspected her mother had directed Mr Collins's attentions to her, but she had been confident, should he importune her with any sort of proposal, that Mr Bennet would intervene.

That confidence had begun to erode with a remark her father made earlier in the evening, after she and Mr Collins had danced. "Surely being mistress of Longbourn would go a long way in compensation for the occasional ruined slippers, eh, Lizzy?"

Was it a teasing remark, or a warning? Had Mr Bennet decided that marrying her off to her cousin would absolve him of all future responsibility to his estate? Or, if Mr Bingley disappeared, would Mr Collins resume his attentions to Jane? Would he insist upon having his choice? Dear, lovely Jane, who would strive not to disappoint her parents, would likely agree to it. Elizabeth could never let that happen —in this she was determined.

She had gone almost three quarters of a mile when her feet, especially her toes, began to itch and prickle from the chill. By the time she reached a split in the path marked by a fencepost, they felt as if they were on fire. She stopped briefly and, leaning against the post, took off her shoes one at a time, chafing each foot as hard as she could until the burning sensations receded. She hoped the slight relief would last until she reached Longbourn. She started again, although not at the rapid pace she had set before.

Elizabeth was tired, so very tired, having been awake for almost twenty-four hours. Her exhausted mind played and replayed the images of Jane and Mr Bingley. Her heart ached for the young gentleman as well; he was so obviously in love. Did not one of his family care that Jane made him happy?

To distract herself from her despair, she tried to plan for the worst: Mr Bingley would depart, and Jane would be left to Mr Collins and her mother's lamentations.

Or she could marry Mr Collins herself.

The cold was seeping through her pelisse. *Why are ladies' wraps so useless?* Her father had worn a thick woollen coat over his evening attire, and would be riding home in a carriage with heated bricks at his feet. She shivered; her feet were starting to hurt again.

She passed the branch in the path that led to Meryton, relieved to know that she was more than halfway to Longbourn. Her steps had become lagging and clumsy, her feet hurt, and her toes and fingers were numb. *Just keep going, Lizzy! Almost there.* She tried to increase her speed, but the next thing she knew, she was on the ground, flat on her back, staring wide-eyed at the pearlescent grey sky.

Elizabeth lay in shock for a few moments, recognising she had slipped on the frost. Once she had recovered her wits, she sat up, gingerly moving her arms and legs. Although she ached from head to toe, nothing seemed to be broken. She rose and, looking down at herself, groaned at the state of her gown and her hair.

She had begun the evening with such anticipation, hoping to attract the attentions of the charming Mr Wickham. She had laboured over her gown during the long rainy days, carefully adding new trim at the neck, the sleeves, and just under the bodice. Kitty had helped arrange her hair into a fashionable style. She had fussed over every detail and believed she had never looked so well. Even her mother had noticed.

It had been all for naught.

Of necessity, she concentrated on making her way home. Shivering, Elizabeth gathered up the remnants of her energies and fortitude and hobbled slowly, stubbornly along the path until at last she saw the stile marking the beginning of her father's land. She was trembling uncontrollably, and could not feel her fingers.

But now, so close, she knew she could make it.

CHAPTER TWO

DARCY QUIETLY CLOSED THE SIDE DOOR BEHIND HIM AND took a moment to orient himself in the darkness. He had ridden many of the bridle paths and country lanes in the neighbourhood during his stay and remembered that the path emerged under the great spreading elm at the bottom of the kitchen gardens. He was confident that he would catch up to Miss Elizabeth quickly. He hurried across the lawn to the ancient tree; its bare, crooked limbs were bleakly silhouetted against the dim glow near the horizon. Next to it, he could see the open path.

The lack of light was more disorienting than he thought it would be. He walked on as quickly as he could, not sure enough of his way to run. Landmarks were difficult to make out. When he saw the first split in the path, he stopped. It branched off to the right, as did the way to Longbourn. He had not expected it so soon. Was this the turn? Darcy followed it for about a quarter of a mile when it made a sharp angle to the west, and he knew it was the wrong way.

Retracing his steps, he continued in his original direction and after an interval, stopped at another turning. The sky was gradually lightening and he was able to see footprints in the muddied ground. *Miss Elizabeth's?* With renewed confidence, he hurried along the path, his surprise turning to astonishment at how far she had gone so quickly. He had expected to catch up to her much sooner.

As he walked, his mind returned to how she had observed him responding to Miss Bingley. His actions clearly had upset her, although she had already appeared agitated. She had run off, putting herself in harm's way, because of something *he* had done.

Why would that distress her? Did she wish her sister to succeed in trapping Bingley? Miss Elizabeth did not seem the type to support such artifice although she also loved her sister dearly and would want the best for her.

As his mind whirled, Darcy continued to follow the small footprints. The path left the woods and continued across a field, a little bridge, and then a wide meadow. Without the shadows cast by the trees, his vision was much improved. He was beginning to feel the cold himself, in spite of his thick coat and gloves, when he came upon a larger patch where the fallen leaves that covered the path had been disturbed. Had something happened here? Had she fallen or been attacked by a wild animal?

Pull yourself together, man! This is Hertfordshire, not the wilds of Scotland! He ran his hands over his face, took a steadying breath, and searched the area. He found a crumpled handkerchief and some hairpins. A small pink shoe-rose, its torn threads dangling, lay next to the path. Darcy knew it was hers; he had watched Elizabeth dance all evening, his reward being the occasional glimpse of a well-turned ankle. He continued walking, his sense of urgency rising.

"Eliz…Miss Bennet!" He was greatly relieved to see her at last. She was limping, and even from a distance he could see her shivering—but she did not seem to hear him

He hurried forward and put his gloved hand around her arm to stop her. She turned with a little cry, eyes wide in dazed confusion.

Darcy himself began to shake with anger, relief, and other emotions he could not even begin to identify as he took off his own coat. It was heated from his body and his exertions, and it would warm her faster. He hastily set it on Elizabeth's shoulders then wrapped the fur-lined cloak around her, pulling the hood over her head. His coat swamped her with a few inches of fabric pooling at her feet, the sleeves ending almost at her knees. The cloak was even bigger, adding to the effect.

Darcy picked her up as if she were nothing and sat her on the stile. Sitting down next to her, he removed his gloves and took her feet in his bare hands. They were like blocks of ice. Pulling off her ruined slippers, he set them aside and rubbed her stockinged feet to bring some feeling back into them.

Elizabeth cried out in pain as she regained sensation in her feet. She threw back the hood of the cloak and tried to wrench her feet from his grip.

"Mr Darcy, what do you mean by this? You must let me go!"

"What on earth were you thinking, Miss Bennet! Why would you do such a foolish thing as run off into the night?"

The coat and cloak were heavy and smelled wonderful—like wool and leather and soap—and Elizabeth was tempted to close her eyes and quietly drift off to sleep in their blessed warmth. She could not do so. She took a deep shaky breath to calm herself. "I left because I saw you. I saw you, and I know—"

She broke off, and took another breath. "I saw your exchange with Miss Bingley and did not misunderstand the meaning of it. You intend to remove your friend from Netherfield entirely. Mr Bingley might stand up to his sisters but he will not stand up to you, which is why Miss Bingley enlisted your aid. My sister will be bereft."

She could see Darcy manage, barely, not to scoff. "I did not see evidence of any particular regard in either her countenance or comportment. Miss Bennet looks upon my friend as she looks upon all others. Perhaps she is merely securing a rich, kind, and generous husband for herself."

Elizabeth gasped, and with some effort, bit back an angry retort. Instead, raising a brow, she asked sweetly, "Oh? How exactly, if I might ask, would you have her behave to demonstrate her regard for your friend? Should she stroll about the room to show her figure to advantage? Should she fawn rapturously over his handwriting and beg to mend his pen?" She made her eyes very round, puffed out her lips in a pouting moue, and fluttered her lashes furiously in razor-edged mimicry of a certain Miss Bingley.

She could only suppose he was offended, as Mr Darcy choked and made a valiant attempt to turn it into a cough.

Elizabeth's chin rose, her eyes reproachful. "Jane would never act so brazenly, sir. She is reticent by nature and does not display her feelings for all to see. I do not suppose a gentleman would ever understand how carefully a lady must regulate her behaviour in public, if she wishes to find genuine friendship and regard, without provoking gossip. And if she does not wish to further excite an excitable mother."

Her voice faded away; her shoulders slumped, and she almost wished the cloak would swallow her up completely. She looked down, then raised her eyes to his and spoke softly. "Do you think I do not know, sir?"

Her direct question seemed to surprise Mr Darcy and he looked at her in confusion. "What is it you think you know?"

Elizabeth huffed impatiently, rolling her eyes. She repeated her question slowly, as if speaking to a small child. "Do you think I do not understand how dreadful is my family's behaviour? My parents, my younger sisters? Since I was old enough to interpret the curled lips and disdainfully raised eyebrows of others, I have understood it. This evening was very difficult, perhaps even more so than most.

"Even at the conclusion of the evening, when we first learned that our carriage wheel was broken, I begged my father to request the use of Mr Bingley's carriage so we might take our leave. He declined. His sense of humour can be hurtful at times."

She paused, considering her next words. Mr Darcy's expression showed him to be listening closely, so she pressed on.

"I suppose you have been raised to the consider the idea of marriage for love to be irresponsible. For you and your family, the institution of marriage is for strengthening political alliances, increasing property through financial settlements, or gaining powerful connexions. Indeed, Mr Collins says that you and your cousin are betrothed, and your marriage was planned in order to join two great estates. I wish you joy, or perhaps I should more accurately say, I wish you every material success in your marriage."

Mr Darcy's countenance remained enigmatic, but his eyes were upon her, seemingly arrested.

"Only consider, sir, perhaps what is best for you is not best for your friend. Do you not think that Mr Bingley needs a marriage of respect, even affection? How would he fare in a marriage of cold convenience determined not by regard but by whatever connexions can be traded for his fortune? What is best for your friend? Not his family or his status, but for *him*?"

Mr Darcy had stopped rubbing her feet, though he still held them loosely in his hands. Elizabeth, her emotions spent, recalled herself to the situation at hand and quickly pulled her feet away. She put her slippers on again and stood.

Reflexively, Darcy also stood. He watched as Elizabeth removed first his cloak, then his coat, and laid them on the stile. "I do indeed thank you, sir. It was kind of you to take an interest in my safety. I know you will believe whatever is to your advantage to believe, and you will justify any interference in your friend's affairs by claiming you do so in his best interests. You and your party will remove to town, Mr Bingley will end his lease, Jane will grieve, and I will be forced to accept Mr Collins. I bid you goodbye and a safe journey."

She curtseyed and turned away from him, in the direction of Longbourn.

"What? What did you say?"

She turned to face him.

"Would you please repeat what you just said?" he rasped. "About Mr Collins."

"Mr Collins is, as I daresay you have heard, my father's heir presumptive. His noble patroness, Lady Catherine de Bourgh, has encouraged him to take his choice from amongst my sisters for his bride. He initially fixed his attention on Jane of course, but my mother informed him that Jane's affections were engaged elsewhere. From the events of the evening, it seems his next choice will be me."

Darcy could only stare at her, wide-eyed, shaking his head helplessly. "No. No. You must not."

"I must, sir. I suppose I could argue. You know me capable of that," she said with a twisted little smile. "But I have not reached my majority and must do as I am bid by my parents. In the end, I am at their mercy."

Darcy stepped back, horrified. Miss Elizabeth at the mercy of that fool, having to listen to his blathering pretensions, having to obey his foolish whims, and endure his marital attentions. His stomach lurched, and the fine wine and expensive delicacies he had consumed at the ball threatened to make another appearance. If she married Collins, it meant that every time he visited Rosings, he would have to witness her suffering and degradation at the hands of a man who was not worthy of cleaning her boots! It was not to be borne! But what could he do? Darcy rubbed his hands over his face.

But what did she mean when she said her sister would be bereft and that her affections were fixed elsewhere? Did Miss Elizabeth believe her sister to be in love with Bingley? If so, there might be some truth in it.

With another brief thanks to him for his aid, Miss Elizabeth turned and ran swiftly along the path in the direction of Longbourn house. In the distance, he could hear the rumble of carriage wheels. She would return just in time.

Darcy donned his coat and picked up his gloves. He marvelled at how delicate her feet had felt in his hands—yet they could dance all night at a ball and walk three miles at dawn. Gathering up his hat and cloak, he turned to retrace his steps to Netherfield, his mind fully awake, replaying the extraordinary conversation he had just had—how they had sat together side by side, how they had talked, what she had said.

What a sight she had been! Freezing, bedraggled, and agitated beyond anything he had before seen in her. But even in her dishevelment, more beautiful than ever. She had looked like a forest sprite, nay, a rebellious little dryad, with her hair wildly unbound and decorated with leaves. She could have stepped right out of an oak tree. The sun had cleared the horizon behind her as they sat together on the stile, limning her flushed cheeks and long dark lashes in gold. Curling strands of her hair had gleamed; how had he not seen before all the colours contained therein? Copper, auburn, chestnut, mahogany, and dark chocolate, all swirling riotously together. Her bewitching eyes had been as eloquent as her words, in turns indignant, wistful, stubborn, mocking, and sad.

They had sat together, just the two of them, with no interference. No Miss Bingley, no noisy matrons, no voluble neighbours, just themselves. She had given him a piece of her mind, and more. One moment she was tearfully defending her sister, in the next she was ridiculing Miss Bingley and making him laugh; and *then* she was speaking to him as if he were an obstinate child. Had she *rolled her eyes* at him? Darcy sighed. It appeared that Miss Jane Bennet was in love with Bingley, or at least, Elizabeth believed she was. This was a complication he had not foreseen. He had thought the lady's heart was not likely to be easily touched but then again, how well did he know her?

If there was one thing he had learned since entering society, it was the importance of carefully regulating his countenance, his behaviour, his conversation. Ambitious ladies would leap on any attention, even a mere courtesy, taking it as a sign of regard. A little flame of gossip, a little fire of a rumour would spark and then grow, its flames fuelled by scheming ladies and fanned by matchmaking parents until it blazed out of control.

It had never occurred to him that a young lady might also object to attention and need to disguise her feelings. But then, why could not beautiful women be reticent and unsure of themselves? Georgiana certainly was, though she was still a girl.

Bingley was expected to improve the connexions of his family through marriage and Miss Bennet, although the daughter of a gentleman, was not connected with any family of note. Most gentlemen of the first circles sought to make alliances that improved their connexions.

Darcy's own parents had had an arranged marriage approved by their families. The Darcys had wealth if not a title, and the Fitzwilliams had status but a lesser fortune. In the end, his parents had seemed content and were unfailingly congenial to one another, although his mother had been most often in town with her family and his father most often at Pemberley. It had been an exemplary alliance, and both families had benefitted from it. Surely Bingley could likewise find satisfaction in a convenient marriage knowing that he had honoured his father's wishes? Would he be happy with an alliance that did not improve his standing, if he had the love of a woman like Jane Bennet?

'*If wealth and connexions are the primary object, why do you not marry Anne?*' Darcy could almost hear his aunt's haranguing diatribes and the earl's insistent lectures. Why did he not marry his cousin? Why did he resent the idea?

Because I shall not give away the power over my marital felicity.

Everyone, even Darcy's closest relations, wanted something from him, giving nothing in return. For as long as he could remember, he had marched to the steady drumbeat of duty, duty, duty. Among his peers he was courted for his money, his connexions, his ancient name. Everybody expected something from him.

Except Bingley. Bingley never asked anything of him.

He had come to Bingley's rescue when they were in school because he could not stand to see the younger boy bullied so maliciously. Then he had discovered that he enjoyed his company, particularly as they grew from boys to men. Bingley was intelligent and expressed his feelings freely. There was no artifice in him. He could laugh at himself and had an unabashed enthusiasm for life. Darcy would hate to imagine that, in urging Bingley to marry for status, it would contribute to his friend's unhappiness.

The sun was gaining strength, and the frost was melting, even in the shade. It was going to be a beautiful day. Darcy quickened his stride; his body yearned for sleep. He shifted the bulky cloak to one arm and reached for his gloves, only to discover the handkerchief, hairpins, and shoe rose in his coat pocket. He stroked the pink satin lightly with his thumb and put it in his breast pocket. He must remember to have them sent to Longbourn before his departure.

CHAPTER THREE

THE GREAT ELM, ITS BARE BRANCHES MOVING SLIGHTLY IN the breeze, welcomed him back to Netherfield. Now, at last, he could go to bed. He would have Talbot wake him when Bingley was making ready to go to London, and they would discuss his intentions for Miss Jane Bennet.

Darcy decided he would not deliberately deter Bingley from his heart's desire. He would merely point out his concerns as a friend should, but he would not interfere.

He rounded the kitchen gardens and turned toward the side door when, as if summoned by his thoughts, there was Bingley, still in evening dress, rapidly pacing back and forth in the garden. His face was flushed, his hands were clenched into fists, and he was muttering to himself. Something was amiss.

"Bingley, I am surprised to see you still awake! Should you not sleep before you ride to London?"

Bingley startled out of his temper and stared at Darcy. "Good heavens! You are up early! Surely you were not planning to ride the estate today?"

It had slipped Darcy's mind that he was still dressed in his working clothes, but Bingley had already forgotten him, beginning to pace once more in an agitated manner. Darcy had never seen him in such a state. "What has upset you?"

"Caroline. No sooner had the door closed behind the Bennets when she had a fit of rage the likes of which I have never seen before."

"About what?"

"How Miss Bennet's family was a vulgar disgrace, and that they were all fortune hunters. That I was stupid not to see that I was being taken in! She said that any association with the Bennets would be an embarrassment, that she could never hold up her head again if I continued the connexion! Louisa supported her assertions, reminding me her own marriage to Hurst was planned to raise our family's status, and that it is imperative that I find a wife amongst the first circles. She said that to do otherwise would be traitorous to my father's memory."

Darcy sighed. Miss Bingley, known for her short temper, had apparently been driven into such a paroxysm of fury by the Bennets, that she had tipped her hand, resulting in a determined resolution unusual for Bingley.

"I am of course ever mindful of my father's wishes." Bingley shook his head. "Father was ambitious. It was not enough that our family built a great fortune. Nothing would do for him but that the Bingleys would rise to the highest ranks of society. He believed that if we had wealth, it could be done in one generation. After my first day at Harrow, I knew that was not so, but I never had the heart to tell him. You were the only reason I survived school. No one dared bully me once it was known we were friends."

"You never told me all this."

"Of course not! And suffer the reputation of a talebearer along with my low origins? I still experience this treatment occasionally." Bingley pulled his coat more tightly around him, and Darcy was reminded that, even with the bright morning sun, the air was still very cold.

"I wish to hear more, if you would tell me, but first let us go in. You are not dressed to be outdoors. Shall we meet in my rooms?"

Bingley agreed and they entered the house. Half an hour later they were in the sitting room attached to Darcy's chamber, dressed in banyans, shirts and breeches; trays with coffee and a small breakfast were set on the low table between them.

"Will your sister be looking for you anytime soon?" Darcy asked, as he poured out two cups of coffee.

Bingley snorted. "I expect she is in bed, with her hair in curling papers and her face slathered in creams. We should be safe for now."

Darcy shuddered at the picture that conjured in his mind. He needed a big swallow of coffee and a rasher of bacon to distract him. Both gentlemen ate a bit, and Bingley continued his story.

"I have many friends, and feel accepted for the most part. But among the older and established families, it is assumed I will be suitably grateful for any attention shown to me. For example, in the last year, I have received propositions for marriage from two families. The first was from Lord Havering."

Darcy, buttering a piece of toast, turned a surprised face to his friend. "Havering! That would be a most excellent connexion for you."

"On the surface perhaps. Havering had the interests of his eldest daughter in mind; she is eight years older than I, with the personality of a dragon, besides. She has had several seasons and garnered no interest from their peers. It also turns out that his heir has gambled away much of the family assets and they are in dire need of my tainted fortune. Not to mention of course, that I would have no say in how it was spent once I was married."

Darcy groaned sympathetically.

"A few months later, I was contacted by Sir Raymond Harwood."

Darcy interjected, "The Harwoods are well-connected, and he has some influence in society."

"Apparently not enough influence. His daughter had a liaison with some very high-ranking personage who refused to marry her when she conceived his child, so they thought I would jump at the opportunity to raise an aristocrat's by-blow. If the child were male, I would have had to accept him as my heir! Sir Raymond was shocked when I turned him down! I may be an agreeable man, but I do have some pride."

Darcy was indignant at how Bingley had been treated, but guiltily recalled the first horrible days after he had discovered Georgiana with Wickham, and how the villain had insinuated that he had already taken her virtue. He had thought then to marry her off to Bingley if she had been with child. Thankfully, after some gentle questioning from Mrs Reynolds, it became apparent that Wickham's claims were lies.

He felt a heavy weight of remorse and shame settle on him. He was supposed to be Bingley's friend, yet he was just as bad as the others—assuming the man had no pride or desires of his own and would be grateful to be of use to his betters.

Bingley had not finished. "Your own cousin, the viscount, barely returns my bow, and if a handshake is offered, extends only two fingers. His wife does not acknowledge me. Colonel Fitzwilliam, of course, I can count as a friend, but none of your other relations."

He paused to sip his coffee and pile some ham on his plate. "My own sister wishes me married to someone whose prestige will benefit her. I need not tell you whom she has chosen for me."

"You do need to tell me, as I have no idea."

"Your sister."

"Georgiana is still a child!"

So Wickham is not the only one who has thought to use Georgiana for their own purposes. How many others in the ton *are thinking like this?* Darcy recalled himself, his friend was still speaking.

"As I am aware. She is like a sweet, bashful little sister to me, not a prospective bride. No, Caroline believes that one wedding between our families will beget another."

Darcy fought not to grind his teeth. *As if I could consider a lady who would use Georgiana for her own gain! The woman is delusional.*

"Miss Jane Bennet has not had the advantages that my sisters have had, but she is gentleness personified, a lady by both birth and temperament," Bingley continued. "My sisters have mocked her mother and called her a fortune hunter but if she is, I must say she is not very good at it. *You* are the big fish, Darcy, yet she practically ignores you."

Darcy cleared his throat uncomfortably and shifted in his seat. "I am sure Miss Bennet is an estimable young lady. But have you considered her family? Their lack of decorum, their low connexions? Perhaps your sisters wish you to take some time and consider your options carefully. Think of the promise you made to your father. Think of what your decision to pursue Miss Bennet will mean to those it affects the most, your family."

Bingley looked at him sharply. "You are in agreement with my sisters?"

Darcy suddenly took a great interest in the bottom of his coffee cup. *Bingley is not a child. Tell him the truth.* "I did, at one point, agree with your sister. I have since come into some information that has changed my opinion."

"What information? And from whom?"

"Miss Elizabeth Bennet saw me observing her family, and apparently read my mind."

"Is that what you were discussing when you danced? I wondered what you and Miss Elizabeth could be speaking of with such spirit."

Darcy decided to let Bingley believe what he would, not willing to describe his sunrise tête-à-tête with Elizabeth. It reminded him that he should have taken up the subject of Wickham with her, but now it was too late. Perhaps he would write to her father after he left.

"Bingley, you seem to have a deep regard for Miss Bennet, but the lady herself is more reserved. I initially believed her heart was untouched, but Miss Elizabeth has told me otherwise."

Bingley's face lit up. "I hoped that she had, but to have it confirmed by her sister!" He shook his head in wonder, then turned to Darcy and laughed. "You are a fine one to complain about reserve. Where do you think I learned to read an inscrutable countenance? Miss Bennet's feelings are not on her face, but in her eyes! You must look in her eyes!"

Darcy made one more point. "An alliance with the Bennet family could also be expensive for you. Mr Bennet has not handled his affairs well, and his daughters have no dowries. If he were to die, you would have to support the entire family."

Bingley nodded. "I have already considered that. Yes, that would be an expense. I have several investments that are doing very well, and I will increase those and keep setting aside more. I hope Mr Bennet lives a long life and that the ladies might all marry well. I must confess that the idea of helping the Bennet ladies pleases me. What fun it would be to have Miss Elizabeth in London for the Season! I daresay Colonel Fitzwilliam would adore her!"

Darcy frowned, not wishing to imagine Miss Elizabeth with his cousin. "Surely you would not send Mrs Bennet into society with her?"

Bingley chuckled and shook his head. "Mrs Bennet is rather appalling, is she not? But Darcy, you never met my mother. Mrs Bennet reminds me of my mother in some small ways. She was raised to a level of society that made her anxious, and the ostentatious manner in which she dressed herself and furnished our home in Scarborough were trying to fit that. When they disparage Mrs Bennet, my sisters choose to forget their own mother, a woman who also ascended to a higher society by her marriage and by her husband's hard work." He smiled wistfully. "My parents loved their children and made great sacrifices for us, but if my sisters met our parents on the street today, they would likely cut them."

Bingley sipped his coffee, sat back in his chair, and sighed happily, no doubt with thoughts of Jane Bennet in his head. His face split into a wide grin, which quickly turned into an even wider yawn. "I am for bed. I will take my carriage instead of riding to London, and I will stop at Longbourn on the way."

Darcy stared at him. "You are not thinking of making Miss Bennet an offer today?"

Bingley, rising from the chair, looked askance at his friend. "I am going to do what I should have done weeks ago. I will ask to formally pay my addresses to Miss Bennet. I will indeed make her an offer, but I wish to first demonstrate that I am worthy and constant in my affections."

"Perhaps I will accompany you," said Darcy, surprising even himself. "To lend you my support."

Bingley raised a sceptical brow. "If you wish. I shall leave at one o'clock so I can visit Longbourn and still have daylight enough to make London. Meet me in my rooms."

"Your sisters plan to return to London tomorrow to speak to you further on the subject. If you wish to avoid them, you may stay at my home." Darcy rose and went to a highboy, pulling open a small drawer and withdrawing a key. "Here is a key to the kitchen door at Darcy House. I will give you a note for the housekeeper and join you there tomorrow."

Bingley took the key and went to his bedchamber. Talbot appeared and soon Darcy was in bed. He lay there tired, warm, and pleasantly full, waiting for sleep to come. His mind kept circling back to how wretched Elizabeth had looked when he caught up to her on the path. It had shaken him. She had always seemed so confident and indomitable. She obviously did not like that he had seen her brought so low and had rallied enough to show him a good fight, to hide any sign of weakness.

But he had seen how vulnerable she was, how her fate hung by a thread—just like that little pink shoe-rose. She had a clear-eyed understanding of her circumstances. The thought of her with Collins! It would be a disaster, a tragedy for her, and it would break his heart. He groaned, realising he had passed the point of danger with her.

Since he had first spoken to Elizabeth and especially since she had stayed at Netherfield, Darcy had occasionally permitted himself to imagine some situation between them such that they would be forced to marry. Besides the more intimate nocturnal yearnings he felt, he had envisioned scenes of tender domesticity: reading together, walking, holding her hand in the darkness of his box at the theatre, sitting with her on his lap, feeding her bites of cake. He had imagined her eyes meeting his, sweetly mischievous as she reached up to untie his cravat. Little vignettes from a life he could never have.

He must leave, the sooner the better. He would help Bingley dodge his sisters and return to Hertfordshire, and he himself would go to Pemberley for Christmastide, and spend the winter avoiding his relations and steeling himself for another Season. He determined to find someone like her: warm, witty and intelligent, but with an acceptable position in society.

CHAPTER FOUR

IT WAS JUST AFTER MIDDAY, AND LONGBOURN WAS QUIET. This in itself was unusual, but it had been an unusual day. Or night? It was all so confusing. As was their custom after a late evening, their mother and sisters kept to their rooms, as did their houseguest. Elizabeth and Jane were the only ones stirring, though Mr Bennet had risen just before noon and disappeared into his book-room.

They were sitting together in the small parlour, sewing for the parish. Elizabeth needed the quiet repetitive task to calm herself. She had slept fitfully a few hours, just enough to relieve the worst of her exhaustion. The sisters spoke little and concentrated on their work. Elizabeth watched Jane with foreboding in her heart; she was smiling softly and humming a little under her breath, occasionally raising her beautiful face to gaze dreamily at nothing.

If it had not been for Jane's impending disappointment, Elizabeth would be glad that they had seen the last of the Netherfield party. She cringed at the memory of the scene she had enacted for Mr Darcy. What a disordered disaster she had been! She had not understood just how dreadful she appeared until after she had scurried up the back stairs to her room and caught sight of herself in the cheval glass. Her cheeks and nose had been red, chapped, smudged, and tearstained.

Her pelisse was dirty, especially the back where she had fallen. The hem of the gown she had laboured over was filthy and ragged, her slippers and gloves were beyond repair. Her hair had been tangled with dead leaves and tiny twigs. She had tried to brush it out then, and again when she awoke, but some knots were too snarled; she had given up and concealed them as best she could, intending to try again later.

She had sat there, swathed in his coat, scolding Mr Darcy as he held her feet in his hands! Merciful Heaven! If word of the incident got out... She shuddered. *Calm yourself, Lizzy! You will never see him again.* She prayed they would both soon forget the encounter, as well as each other.

Mrs Hill entered the parlour. "Mr Bingley and Mr Darcy, Miss Bennet."

Jane rose to her feet, her sewing falling forgotten to the floor as the two gentlemen stepped through the door. A wide, delighted smile lit her face for a moment, then her mask of composure slipped back into place. But her eyes! Jane's blue eyes glowed, even as she welcomed them and invited them to sit and have refreshments.

Mr Bingley did not even try to hide his pleasure, but he offered an apology. "Miss Bennet, I wish we could sit with you and Miss Elizabeth for a while, but I must be for London before much more of the day has gone. Would it be possible to take a short walk in the garden before I take my leave?"

Elizabeth remained seated, her needle suspended in mid-air over her sewing; her cheeks were scarlet, eyes wide in surprise, as she stared at Mr Darcy. That gentleman met her eyes gravely and bowed slightly, a slight smile on one corner of his lips.

"Lizzy?"

She blinked. "Jane? Did you say something?"

Her sister looked at her curiously. "Mr Bingley and Mr Darcy have invited us to walk with them."

Elizabeth rose from her seat, a little breathless. "I... Yes, I shall fetch my pelisse and meet you by the door." She moved quickly to exit the room, which suddenly seemed much too small, when she remembered that her pelisse was dirty. She took Mary's cloak from the peg by the back door while Jane informed their father and had a word with Mrs Hill.

All too quickly they were in the garden, walking in pairs. Mr Bingley had immediately offered his arm to Jane, and they were already several yards ahead. Elizabeth set her fingertips tentatively on Mr Darcy's proffered arm, but he was setting a maddeningly slow pace. Elizabeth could not meet his eye and was experiencing a rare loss for words when he spoke.

"Are you well, Miss Elizabeth?"

"As well as could be expected." She was wondering how to apologise for her behaviour when he interrupted her thoughts.

"Are you surprised to see Mr Bingley?"

"A little." She glanced up at him. "I feared his reliance on the judgment of others."

"Miss Bingley had already quarrelled with him about it, and as a result his mind was made up. He is at this moment asking your sister whether she will allow him to pay his addresses to her when he returns."

Elizabeth stopped and looked up at him, eyes wide with delight, her hand tightening slightly on his arm. "He is? Oh, how happy Jane will be!"

Darcy nodded. "Yes, I could see her regard for him as soon as we walked into your parlour."

Her smile widened and one winged brow arched. "I am happy you were able to see for yourself." In a lowered voice, she said, "And I thank you, sir, for listening to me. Now Jane will be happy and I—" Her voice caught.

Mr Darcy frowned. "Yes, about Mr Collins. I have been thinking about your predicament. Would Miss Mary wish to be considered by your cousin? She seems to have the most in common with him."

Elizabeth wondered why a man such as Mr Darcy would spend time thinking about her 'predicament'.

"Mary has always said that she prefers to remain unattached. I asked her again a few days ago, and she answered that while she would consider marriage with a clergyman, she finds Mr Collins's interpretations of Scripture to be self-serving and designed solely to please his patroness. Even if that were not true, the man seems to look no further than appearance, not considering character or inclination. He is…I beg your pardon once more, Mr Darcy. I have already been speaking too freely."

"Allow me then to say it for you. Mr Collins is a stupid, ill-favoured man who, because of the entail, has been given a chance to acquire a pretty wife far above his reach."

Elizabeth stopped and looked up at him in surprise. "Yes, that is it. I thank you for thinking of my plight, but Mr Collins has not yet made an appearance today. I doubt you will see him. Soon Mr Bingley will be on his way, and you will return to Netherfield to prepare for your own departure. I do not believe there is anything any of us can do."

He returned her gaze, then cocked his head to one side and very gently pulled a small leaf from behind her ear. "You missed one, Miss Elizabeth," he said softly, and carefully put it in his pocket.

His gesture made her blush, and Elizabeth looked away to see Jane and Mr Bingley had stopped walking and were staring at them. When the couple turned back towards the house, Elizabeth and Mr Darcy had no choice but to follow and soon all four were returned to the parlour. After some hushed words with Jane in the hall, Elizabeth watched as Mr Bingley knocked on her father's book-room door and was invited in. The interview was short, and within half an hour that beaming gentleman was handing Jane a few folded notes, accepting a jug of hot tea and a basket of sandwiches from Mrs Hill, and boarding his carriage.

Mr Darcy took his leave of the ladies, assuring them that it was no trouble for him to find the stable boy who was walking his horse. Elizabeth watched him walk away, confusion furrowing her brow. 'A pretty wife?' When he had earlier dismissed her appearance so rudely? And did he think he could just touch her person when he pleased? *Vexing man! I am glad he has taken no interest in me nor I in him!*

Darcy was about to mount his horse when he was hailed from behind. He turned to see Mr Collins hastily stumbling after him, wheezing noisily and struggling with his neckcloth. It was evident that he had dressed in a hurry. The man halted before him and bowed so low he nearly tipped forward.

"Mr Darcy! Sir! You honour me with your condescension! And so soon after we spoke at Netherfield! Had I foreknowledge of your kind visit, I should have risen early and had a letter prepared for Lady Catherine de Bourgh!"

Darcy stared at him for a minute before he understood. Collins believed he had come to Longbourn to carry correspondence to Lady Catherine for him? This bizarre turn of events could be useful, however.

"A word if you please, Mr Collins."

Darcy retired early that night, the combined effects of the last day and night having caught up with him. The next day would be trying, with long hours to spend in the company of Miss Bingley and the Hursts, but then he would be back in his own house—safe from any temptations, no matter how delightful.

He let his head rest on the soft pillow, closed his eyes, and savoured the memory of his last look at her. He would keep the image with him always, along with the little shoe-rose and the leaf. He need not worry about Elizabeth's future. Collins had been deterred, and Bingley would care for the Bennet ladies in their hour of need.

Surprising her had been more gratifying than Darcy cared to admit; in truth he was feeling rather smug. It was no easy thing to steal a march on Miss Elizabeth Bennet, and he had done it. He could picture her as a tiny girl, all big eyes and unruly curls, outsmarting older children and adults, all with a winsome, mischievous grin. Perhaps, after he was safely married, he would hear about her from time to time.

He floated into slumber, lulled by the careful, rational plans his brain was making, and did not hear the tiny part of his heart wishing that someone would look at him the way Miss Bennet had looked at Bingley.

"Have a care with that!" Caroline Bingley shrieked at a footman struggling to lift an overstuffed trunk. Mrs Hurst was already being handed into Darcy's carriage.

Miss Bingley had announced plans to leave at the crack of dawn, which for her apparently started when the sun was halfway across the sky. Darcy had been ready to leave for several hours. He had not shared his change of heart over Bingley's plans with the man's sisters. Other than inviting Charles to stay in his home while in town, he was determined to stay out of the Bingley family squabbles.

Even had any doubts remained about Bingley's choice to propose to Miss Bennet, the joy on Miss Elizabeth's face, the teasing sparkle in her eyes, and her slight squeeze of his arm had made it all worth it. He would warm his heart with those memories in years to come.

"Mr Darcy! Mr Darcy! Sir!" A boy was running towards him with a note clutched in his hand. He handed it to Darcy who scanned the contents quickly and approached his own carriage.

"Miss Bingley, Mr and Mrs Hurst, I have just been given an urgent message from your brother's steward. I must stay behind to see what has happened, and once it is sorted out, I will follow you to London."

Several hours later Darcy wanted nothing more than a long gallop. It had been a frustrating afternoon, finding the steward, riding all over Netherfield estate listening to the man drone on about problems that, as someone who had not purchased the estate, were not Bingley's to solve. The man might have handled matters himself. Darcy questioned his competence as Netherfield's steward.

Equally maddening, it was too late to reach London before night fell. He found himself riding the same bridle path he had walked at dawn a day earlier. He turned abruptly; he needed to clear his mind, not go to Longbourn. Darcy took the turning that would lead him farther from the village and let his horse have its head. They raced through fallow fields and took a hedge with a great leap, followed by a few fences, before they slowed to a canter. He stopped to water the animal in a brook and looked up to see a flash of blue, a small form high up on Oakham Mount.

Like iron to a lodestone, he was compelled to follow.

CHAPTER FIVE

LONGBOURN WAS IN AN UPROAR, EVEN BY BENNET standards. Mr Collins had made an acrimonious departure, after informing Mrs Bennet that her daughters' behaviour would never meet the lofty standards of Lady Catherine de Bourgh.

Adding insult to injury, Lady Lucas was triumphant. Not only had Mr Collins proposed to *her* daughter, but he had done so while impugning the comportment of the Bennet ladies. Within hours, all of Meryton would know that the heir to Longbourn had rejected his fair cousins in favour of Miss Charlotte Lucas.

Elizabeth had fled the house to escape her mother's temper. After walking for some time, she sat on a fallen log and heaved a great sigh. *What else can possibly happen today?*

"Miss Bennet?"

She startled and turned to see the man she had not expected to meet again until Jane and Mr Bingley married.

"Mr Darcy!" she exclaimed. "Did your party decide to remain?"

"Netherfield's steward required my assistance. Miss Bingley and the Hursts departed." He stepped forward. "Are you well? You have not suffered any consequences of your chill?"

What a polite way to describe it. "Yes, thank you, I am well. Perhaps I should demand that you fetch me your warm cloak again?" She patted the log, and he accepted her invitation, keeping a decorous distance between them.

"I am at your service, madam. And your family?"

"We are well, though not all of us. Mr Collins has proposed to and been accepted by my friend Miss Charlotte Lucas and is on his way back to Kent. My mother is not best pleased."

Mr Darcy raised his eyebrows. "I did not expect him to act so precipitously."

Elizabeth caught her breath and narrowed her eyes in his direction. "You did not expect... Sir! What have you done to Mr Collins?"

He blushed, a sly little smile turning up one corner of his lips "He followed me when I was leaving Longbourn yesterday. I merely informed him of my aunt's preferences for her rector's bride and mentioned that she does not appreciate females who speak their minds or have opinions. I might have said, also, that your younger sisters would most certainly not meet her approval. I am sorry to say that I cast some aspersions on your family. Do you mind very much?"

She barked a laugh and waved a dismissive hand. "Not at all! What did you say that was not true?" She looked at him directly, searching his face, then said, tentatively, "You did this for me?"

"I could not bear the thought that you would have no choice in your future life. Although I regret Mr Collins is now under the impression that we are boon companions."

Elizabeth laughed, a full belly laugh, her head tipping back, her hand rising to her chest. She described the scene at Longbourn and then they were both laughing heartily.

"Even my father has been roused to action, once he understood that his younger daughters were held in such disapprobation by the neighbourhood. Kitty and Lydia are no longer out, and he will be seeing to the improvement of their minds himself."

The mention of her younger sisters seemed to bring some other concern to Mr Darcy's mind. Growing more sober, he related his tangled history with Mr Wickham, even to the point of rescuing his own sister from the man.

Elizabeth's smile faded as he spoke, slowly replaced by a sombre, dawning comprehension. She could not take her eyes from his. "Mr Wickham lied about you."

"He often does. Does that disappoint you?"

Elizabeth's hands rose to her flushed cheeks. "Only in myself. Oh! I have been so stupid! I have judged you based solely on my own vanity and prejudice! I was an all-too-willing audience for his treachery."

She raised her eyes to his. "And now, once I troubled myself to look, I see that you are among the best of men."

He smiled at her. "And once I troubled myself to listen to you, I found a true friend." He raised his eyes to the sky. "We will lose our daylight soon. Shall I walk you home?"

Arm in arm, they followed the path to Longbourn. When they parted, he took her hand and kissed it, mounted his horse, and rode away. Elizabeth stood as if paralysed, watching him until he disappeared around a bend. Suddenly her heart sank, and she wanted to weep. She had wished him gone for weeks, and now that he was leaving, she already regretted him. He had called her his friend, but she wished for more. Every man she would ever meet would compare unfavourably to him. How could she not mourn for missed chances? But there had never truly been a chance for her, had there?

Her sigh turned into a small sob, and she turned to walk home as the light faded.

Darcy made his way back to Netherfield in fading twilight, lost in thought. He rode slowly, the reins slack, his horse at a walking pace. He finally understood; he had been fooling himself that there had been any other decision to make. He would marry Miss Elizabeth Bennet.

He had seen regret, even sadness in her eyes as they parted. It both thrilled and pained him.

He had never told anyone about Ramsgate, other than Richard. Not Bingley, not even his uncle and aunts. He had few close friends, most of them only acquaintances, and even fewer confidantes—again other than his cousin, who was often stationed far away.

Before he met Elizabeth Bennet, this had suited him. He had been content with polite conversation but now he wanted more than civilities. Darcy wanted a true friend and intimate, a kindred spirit with whom he could share everything, every day; to live and love and bare his soul. Bare. Naked, in both the literal and figurative sense. He groaned. *Now I will never sleep.*

The next morning, Darcy woke to a steady, driving rain. After a morning of restless pacing, interrupted by attempts to read or to write letters, he decided to ride out—rain be damned.

He would ride into Meryton. If he did not see Elizabeth, he could at least patronise the book shop. He was disappointed in the former but well-satisfied in the latter, and purchased several volumes. He was turning to leave just as Miss Bennet entered the shop.

"Mr Darcy!" she exclaimed. "You remain at Netherfield?"

"I decided to wait for Mr Bingley's return. He is expected tomorrow. Is your family well?" he asked, his eyes searching behind her.

Miss Jane Bennet suppressed a smile. "I thank you, they are, although I am a little concerned for Lizzy."

"Is Miss Elizabeth ill?"

"No, I would say rather that she is out of sorts. Even the prospect of taking the carriage to the bookseller did not please her."

His heart leapt. For me? Does she miss me?

But Miss Bennet was still speaking. "Perhaps, sir, you and Mr Bingley would join us for dinner tomorrow evening?"

Darcy smiled broadly. "We would be honoured, madam. I feel very certain that I can accept on behalf of my friend. You may depend upon us."

Darcy was working at the desk in Bingley's study when the man himself walked in late the next morning. "You must have departed at dawn," he said by way of greeting him.

"In fact, I did and have already stopped at Longbourn. I understand we are to dine with the Bennets this evening. Perhaps it will be something of a trial for you, but remember that for all her faults, Mrs Bennet keeps an excellent table."

Bingley flung himself into a chair opposite the desk. "I must thank you for your hospitality in town. I was able to conclude my business quickly and privately with no interruptions. Now, put down that pen. It has been days since I have had an opportunity to thrash you at billiards!"

Shortly thereafter, Darcy was bent over the green baize table, lining up his shot, and Bingley was filling a plate from the tray of cold meats, cheeses, and bread that had been brought in. His friend had been rhapsodising over Miss Bennet for more than an hour when he surprised Darcy with a question. "One thing I do not understand is why Miss Elizabeth would confide in you about Jane's feelings for me. I did not think she liked you at all! How on earth did that conversation come about?"

Darcy's shot went awry, and the cue ball flew off the table. He stood and stared at Bingley. "She disliked me?" he asked in shocked disbelief.

"Well, obviously she has forgiven you, but you must remember how she argued with you, and refused your invitation to dance!"

Baffled, Darcy muttered, "But surely she was…I thought she was flirting… Why would she dislike me?"

Bingley shook his head in disbelief. "You insulted her, you great ox! The first time we entered local society. You looked her straight in the eye and said she was not pretty enough to dance with!"

Darcy reeled. So many of Miss Elizabeth's little asides were suddenly placed into perfectly understood, dreadful sense. He dropped his cue on the table and sat, his head in his hands. "Not only was it unpardonable to speak the words, I put the incident out of my mind as unimportant."

How many careless insults had he tossed off in his life? How many innocent people had he hurt with words or deeds? He had never even considered the consequences. In this, he was no better than Wickham.

"Darcy?" His friend recalled his attention.

"To answer your question, Miss Elizabeth saw me glaring at you, somehow knew exactly what I was thinking, and gave me a dressing down I will not soon forget. Your words later that morning confirmed what she said, and I realised that it would be wrong to interfere with your attachment to Miss Bennet."

His young friend laughed. "Darcy, I have never been so grateful to anyone in my life. And I tried to return the favour to you. I saw how you and Miss Elizabeth seemed companionable before I left for London. How did you and my steward get on with your investigation of farm drainage?"

Darcy gasped. "That was you?"

Bingley was smug. "It worked, did it not?"

"Yes. Yes, it did." Darcy's smile was rueful. "I think she has forgiven me. I hope she might even like me a little. I will know this evening when I ask whether I might call on her."

CHAPTER SIX

"Mr Bingley and Mr Darcy."

Mrs Hill announced their dinner guests. Elizabeth rose slowly, her eyes moving past Mr Bingley to the tall man behind him. Her smile was tentative, but widened as he returned it with his own.

When Jane had reported Mr Darcy's acceptance of her invitation the day before, Elizabeth had stared at her, blinking. *He stayed! He was still at Netherfield! Why is he still here? For me?*

Now, as they all settled themselves in Longbourn's drawing room, she felt that it might be so. He sat next to her. Slightly breathless, strangely shy, she had a hard time meeting his gaze, so dark and intent.

"Are you well, Miss Elizabeth?"

She had to wonder at herself. What had happened to her? She was not a reticent, tongue-tied girl! Twice now, Mr Darcy had had to initiate their conversation!

"I am, sir. Did you find some books to your liking?"

"Yes, the bookshop in Meryton is well-stocked." They sat quietly for a few moments as Mrs Bennet's raptures over Mr Bingley rang out from the other side of the room.

Elizabeth closed her eyes in frustration, unable to bear such polite nothings. She and Mr Darcy did better when they spoke their minds.

"You chose not to return to London."

"I did."

"Why, if I may ask?"

He tilted his head to one side, seemingly choosing his words. "Before I even understood what I was searching for, it seems that I found it here, and I no longer wish to leave."

"Oh," she said, her eyes widening. She blushed, looking down at her hands. "You have found it in Meryton?"

"I have found it at Longbourn."

She raised her eyes to his. They gazed at each other for a long moment. Simultaneously, they opened their mouths to speak, but Mrs Hill was already announcing dinner.

The entire party moved to the dining room and found their seats, Elizabeth's next to Mr Darcy. He seemed pleased as he held her chair, then sat down next to her. She leant toward him, whispering. "Do not congratulate yourself on this arrangement, sir. We have been placed together because Mama is punishing me for failing to secure Mr Collins."

He chuckled and murmured, "I am grateful to her for it. By the by, your handkerchief and hairpins are in my pocket."

She made a face at him. "You might have told me! I spent hours searching for them on Wednesday!"

Elizabeth was relieved with the progress of the evening; the dinner party gave her no cause for embarrassment. The courses were varied and delectable, the wines excellent. Mrs Bennet's euphoric conversation was directed at Mr Bingley and Jane; Mr Bennet seemed to get enjoyment from watching them, and even Mary seemed more animated. The silliness of her youngest sisters was not missed; Kitty and Lydia were required to take their dinner in the old schoolroom. She and Mr Darcy conversed almost unnoticed throughout, and when the ladies rose, the gentlemen chose to join them.

She was searching her mind for a way to speak to Mr Darcy privately, when Mr Bingley exclaimed, "What a remarkable backgammon set! I say, Darcy! You like to play, do you not?"

"Perhaps you would enjoy a game, sir?" Elizabeth asked. At his assent, they settled themselves and the intricately inlaid rosewood game board near the fire and apart from the group. She set out the game pieces as they spoke quietly.

Mr Darcy gestured with his head towards Mr Bingley and Jane. "They will do well together."

"I am happy to hear you say so. Far be it from me to say 'I told you so'."

Mr Darcy chuckled softly but then his expression transformed into something deeper, more private. She saw it then. All of it. The quiet intensity, the wry humour, the deep intelligence...the ardent love. It was in his eyes!

"Miss Elizabeth, I wish to apologise to you for something I said at the assembly where we met. I think you know to what I refer. It was wrong of me, for two reasons. First, it was wrong to insult a lady. Second, it was simply incorrect. For some time now I have considered you the handsomest woman of my acquaintance. You are handsome enough to tempt me—to dance with, to walk with, to argue with, to play backgammon with...to marry..."

She gasped. "I... But you are to marry your cousin."

A look of pure panic crossed his face and he spoke to her with some urgency. "No, that is a fiction my aunt holds onto, a wish she made when her daughter and I were in our cradles. My cousin and I will never marry. It is you I wish to marry.

"Or perhaps you need to know me better. Could I...may I call on you?"

Elizabeth had never known such happiness, nor such disbelief. She stared at him. "Yes, yes to both... to everything. But are you sure? You have seen me in all my untidy glory. I bring nothing to a marriage, no wealth, no connexions—only my forthright nature, my penchant for misjudging others, and my heart as well, if you care to have it."

Under the table, his hand crept to take hers. "I am sure. Perhaps I need a little untidiness in my life. Some muddy hems, a smudge here and there. A few leaves in my hair. I admire and love you. You make me a better man and that is a treasure, a gift beyond price."

She reached out then to entwine her fingers with his. "We shall quarrel. We are wilful creatures, you and I."

"Let us quarrel, and then we will make up."

"I shall always be thankful to you for my rescue on the bridle path," she said.

Darcy gently squeezed her fingers. "You did not need rescuing; you were almost home. I was the one in need of rescue." He leant closer over the table. "Shall I speak to your father?"

Elizabeth glanced towards her father. Mr Bennet was not even looking their way, which pleased her. She squeezed his hand, still under the table. "Would you mind terribly if we kept this to ourselves for a little while? I am not ready to share my treasure just yet."

Having been subject to unwelcome attention for most of his life, Darcy was only too happy for their joy to remain unnoticed. After several days, however, his sense of honour required that they go before her father, who, caught by surprise, gave his permission immediately. Mr Bingley and Jane soon followed with their own request for his blessing.

As she exhibited often over the next month, Mrs Bennet was thrilled with the news, not only for a chance to plan a grand wedding beyond what she had ever thought possible, but because her elder daughters' betrothals quite restored any claims to social distinction she had lost in the Collins debacle.

The Bingleys, both so amiable and obliging, would be happy. The Darcys would also be happy, but they were cut from more complicated cloth. With their marriage vows, they resolved to trust and depend upon each other: to build their lives, to live their joy, to love and honour deeply, and to respectfully and honestly speak their truth for the rest of their lives.

The End

About the Author

Nan Harrison is a happily retired librarian with degrees in

anthropology and library/information science. She still thinks like an anthropologist and believes that libraries are the last bastion of civilization. She is an excellent walker

ALSO BY NAN HARRISON
Any Fair Interference

Duet in Dispute

MICHELLE RAY

CHAPTER ONE

I HAD REFUSED MR DARCY.

No one in my family would speak to me. Not even Jane.

Now I was alone in every way. I could not think at Longbourn, for all would push me into a marriage I did not desire. No, I did desire it, but not this way. I would have to escape.

Mrs Hill had concerns but assisted my packing efforts nevertheless. "You need not run away, Miss Lizzy. You know your parents will get past this."

"I do not wish to witness their disappointment. And I do not wish to surrender."

Later that day, as I sat in the coach on the way to London, I thought how it had all begun months earlier sitting in the room I shared with Jane, my younger sister flitting about as Jane readied herself for an assembly that I dreaded attending.

"But you love dancing, Lizzy!" whined Kitty, resting her head on my shoulder.

"I know, but today, I want—" I realised I could not speak the truth, which was that I had had inspiration for a piece I was composing, and I wished to remain home to finish it. I lied. "I feel…not quite myself. Unwell. A headache coming on."

"If you do not go, Jane will not, and then how can she ever meet someone and marry and leave the house so I can have a room of my own?"

Jane, who was at the dressing table, spun around and gasped with mock outrage.

I tapped Kitty's nose. "Kitten, *I* would have a room of my own if Jane left us, not you." Her brow furrowed as she tried to sort that out, and I wished she had more of Father's intellect. Jane removed her brooch, clearly preparing to stay home. That would not do. It was not that I needed a room of my own, for sharing with dear Jane was my greatest pleasure; but she was in want of a husband and who was I to prevent such a happy event?

"Very well. I shall attend the assembly."

Kitty leapt off the bed and twirled. "I long to come out so I can enjoy such festivities. I would never consider staying at home." Hurrying to the doorway, she paused and turned back. "In one year. One year! I shall dance every dance and be the talk of the assembly."

"So I fear," I muttered as she scampered from the room.

A snicker caught my attention. Jane was at the mirror tying a ribbon to the end of her braid.

"You knew I would agree."

"Of course, Lizzy. You always do when the younger ones beg. You have never been able to deny any of your sisters."

I sighed and flopped back onto my mattress, studying the familiar crack in the paint overhead. "They are too spoilt."

"True." Jane crossed the room and sat on the edge of the mattress. "You do not have a headache."

She knew me too well. I stood, avoiding an answer, and went to collect my dancing shoes.

"If you go tonight, you might forget about the piece as you sometimes do when you enjoy yourself enough."

At that moment, the notes rose and fell in my head. It was impossible to quiet them at times, a most aggravating, yet often thrilling, conundrum. I slumped into the chair at the dressing table. "My enthusiasm has waned for these assemblies, Jane. It is always the same people, doing the same things, at the same times."

She approached and took me by the shoulders, studying our reflections in the mirror. "You have been out for only two years. I have been attending such gatherings for four years complete, and I do not complain of it."

"You complain of nothing, dearest. You are a saint. I, alas, am not."

Jane pursed her lips, her reaction to any compliment. "It might be exciting. One never knows who might suddenly happen upon our little town."

"You are too optimistic." Despite my reluctance, I continued to ready myself.

At that evening's assembly, Jane had met Mr Bingley, which set the rest into motion. After calling on her the next day, he had invited us to a house party at which his friends and sisters would be present. Mama had us nearly packed that night, though the date was set three weeks hence. Inwardly, I was reluctant to attend, but gave no hint of it lest Jane take it as an opportunity to decline, given her natural tendency towards shyness. Not all social interactions fatigued me. I did enjoy gatherings when I was not plagued by musical notes running through my mind. I enjoyed walks and hunts and games and conversation, if the person was interesting. The one activity I loathed was cards; unfortunately for my inclinations, in the first afternoon at Netherfield, whist was on the agenda. I resigned myself to my place on a sofa in the parlour.

"Miss Elizabeth?"

The woman I had been speaking to—heavens, what was her name? —had been telling a tale of her children, whom she had left in town. I recall she had not been concerned about them, as it would only be for four days. But what else had she said?

When I merely blinked at her, she cocked her head and asked, "Have you any brothers or sisters other than Jane?" From her tone, I suspected she was repeating the question she had already asked, as the hint of irritation I detected matched that of my family when I drifted from them.

I was poor company at times, and endeavoured to amend myself. After describing my sisters and Longbourn, I attentively listened to her explanation of her gardening ventures. It was compelling enough that I thought to obtain some cuttings and see if I, too, could grow the variety of roses described at Longbourn. The lady went away satisfied with me.

After a half an hour more, the card games concluded and, with guests milling about, I took the opportunity to slip away and find the music room. As I entered, I gasped, for in addition to the presence of a flute, two harps, three violins, a lute, and a pianoforte, the room was festooned with shimmering curtains that accentuated the height of the room and its many windows. Its carved columns and cornices were tastefully accented with gold, which somehow highlighted the lightness of the room. The pianoforte I found within was magnificent. The instrument we had at Longbourn was lovely, but this one was decorated with interesting inlay, and the sound was perfection.

I warmed up with Haydn, and once my fingers felt nimble enough, paused and played a piece of my own I had recently begun to compose. Looking out the window at the view of birds flitting about, I changed the notes to rise and trill and quickly fall only to rise again. The sound made me smile as it matched the birds almost perfectly.

At the clearing of a throat my head snapped around. A handsome, tall man with dark brown hair and proud posture stood in the doorway. "Forgive me. I did not mean to startle you."

I pushed the bench back and glided out from behind it. "I have already recovered from my fright, so all is forgiven."

He took a step forward. "The first that you played I recognised. Haydn, was it not?"

I offered a smile of acknowledgement. "Indeed, sir. Are you a great lover of music?"

"I appreciate certain composers more than others."

"Who is your favourite?"

"Beethoven."

I raised my eyebrows. "You prefer the serious?"

He shrugged. "I enjoy Rossini, as well."

I nodded my approval, and he stepped closer. "You?"

"Bach is always a joy to play. The intricacies and changes of mood thrill me. *Prelude and Fugue No 21* is a current favourite, though I admit that if you asked me a month ago or should you ask a month hence, my answer might be different."

"Are you fickle?"

"Not in my friendships, but in music I would say I am changeable, as different compositions and challenges attract my attention. There is too much to love in the works of the greats."

A hint of a smile crept into the corners of his lips. "So which 'great' were you playing after Haydn?"

"Myself," I said before I realised my error. "That is not to say I consider myself one of the greats, but the music, to clarify, was a composition of my own."

His eyes narrowed. "Yours?" I nodded and he stared a moment. "*Your* composition?" I nodded again and he shook his head. "That cannot be."

"I assure you it is, sir. It is a piece I began creating last week but have not yet finished."

His eyes lit up, making him even more handsome. "Extraordinary."

"Do you play?"

He shook his head. "John Locke said, 'Music wastes so much of a young man's time'."

"Yet it is acceptable for ladies to waste their time with it?" When he did not answer, I added, "I suppose most pursuits of ladies are about wasting—or is it passing?—time."

He studied me as if measuring the seriousness of my words. I was in earnest and at the same time teasing. We ladies were merely passing our time until becoming wives and mothers. And then what? Wasting more time. But what did gentlemen do if they did not have a profession? Pass time. But I would not scandalise this stranger with more of my observations. Instead, I decided to continue the quote debate.

"Sir, did not Shakespeare write, 'If music be the food of love, play on'? Would it not be helpful for more men to know music then?"

"Do you use music to search for love, Miss...?"

"Miss Elizabeth Bennet. And no. I use music to waste—or is it pass?—the time." I smiled wryly and he returned a smile. "In actuality, sir, it is neither a waste nor a passage. It is a passion I cannot shake."

"Would you wish to?"

I sighed. "It consumes too much of my mind, but I cannot stop it. It is a blessing and a curse, I daresay. Shakespeare's line goes in its entirety, 'If music be the food of love play on, that surfeiting the appetite may sicken and so die.' This suggests one can kill love with too much music."

"One must be in love first to kill it with music. Are you in love, Miss Bennet?"

I raised my eyebrows. "I am not, Mr...?"

"Darcy."

His eyes sparkled and made my stomach flip. But I had no time for flirtation. Not when the composition was swirling in my brain. I needed to get back to it. *No. No!* The music would be there later. Or it would leave, which might improve my life. Especially if my future might include one such as Mr Darcy.

I asked, "You have never learnt to play? Not even dabbled?"

After a brief pause, he nodded the slightest bit.

I clapped. "Show me, Mr Darcy, how you have wasted your time!"

He crossed to the piano, but rather than sitting, he reached over the bench for the keys and began to play a tune I knew from my childhood. *"Oranges and Lemons!"* I said with cheer, and he nodded, continuing to play, occasionally hitting a wrong note, but who could mind? The song reminded me of one Christmas morning at our old square piano—we had traded up for a pianoforte after one particularly good harvest year—many years ago. Kitty and Lydia's heads were hardly higher than the seat, and while our mother plucked out the tune, Jane, Mary and I took the little one's hands and danced in a circle singing loudly, inhaling the scents of meat and sweet spices of our Christmas breakfast, which was about to be served.

Full of nostalgia and joy, I set my fingers upon the higher keys and Mr Darcy and I played together. I sang:

Oranges and lemons
Say the bells of St Clement's

He smiled broadly, then sang in his low, commanding voice:

> *You owe me five farthings*
> *Say the bells of St Martin's*
> *When will you pay me?*
> *Say the bells of Old Bailey.*
> *When I grow rich*
> *Say the bells of Shoreditch*

We went on line by line until the end, when we sang the ominous bit together, changing our voices to deep, scary tones:

> *Here comes a candle*
> *To light you to bed*
> *And here comes a chopper*
> *To chop off your head*

We dissolved into laughter.

A noise behind brought us up short. A young woman stood in the doorway, her eyes narrow and her bearing regal yet somehow suggesting disapproval with the slope of her delicate shoulders. "Mr Darcy, we were wondering where you had gone to."

Now sober, Mr Darcy bowed. "I beg your pardon, Miss Bingley." He turned to me, his jaw set. "You two have met? Miss Bingley, Miss Elizabeth Bennet."

"Yes." The lady drew out the word like a blade slicing a side of beef. "Mr Darcy, my brother desires your company." Mr Darcy turned to me, but before he could speak, she said, "We are going for a walk." Her eyes flicked to me, and though there was nothing inviting in her look, she said, "All of us. Would you care to join, Miss Eliza?"

I would have liked to walk with Mr Darcy and get to know him, yet I sensed her desire for me to remain indoors. To my pleasure, her expression sparked a set of notes, a combination of fluttering high ones with an undertone of foreboding base beneath. I had to write it down or play it before it escaped. "No thank you."

"You must join us for tea," he said, "after the walk, then."

I nodded and watched him slip away with her.

CHAPTER TWO

THE NEXT TWO DAYS WENT ON IN THIS MANNER. IT DID NOT take me long to understand Miss Bingley's wish to separate us, or Mr Darcy's wish to avoid her. Mr Darcy found endless ways to steal into the music room to listen to me play and to discuss music with me. There were times, I confess, that it made my heart give a little flutter to hear him approach but I warned myself often that it was not necessarily *I* whom he sought. Very likely he wished merely to escape *her*.

My doubts vanished as I saw the change about him when we were alone. His shoulders relaxed and his face contained more light than it did when he was with anyone else, save his friend Mr Bingley. We chatted more candidly than I did with anyone other than Jane, and laughed often. It occurred to me that he did not laugh with the other guests, and I wondered if it was this particular set of people or if he was grave as a rule. If so, it would mean that I brought out something different in him. Dared I flatter myself with such thoughts?

The night before we were to return to Longbourn, as I was playing, I felt him approach, yet continued the tune. He reached out for my shoulder but hesitated so close I could feel his heat but not his touch. My hands froze and the room went silent. I could hear his breath, which was as quick as mine.

"Miss Elizabeth."

I raised my gaze to match his.

"Miss Elizabeth," he repeated. His forehead was creased and his lips moved slightly as if he was rehearsing what he might say next. "I feel...I need—" In his eyes was a desperation I had never seen. No more words came.

I slipped off the bench and stood before him, closer than I ought to, I was sure, but wanting nothing more than to be near him. He had filled my thoughts nearly as much as music these past days—nay, more. It was a relief and a joy to have found someone so kind and generous and intelligent, someone whose presence made the hours melt away. Was this what the poets spoke about when they wrote of love?

He reached out for my cheek and stroked it with his fingertips. I felt myself flush, but did not move. Could he hear my heart pounding? See that my breath had stopped? Gently, he touched under my chin and raised it. "Might I—" He cleared his throat. "Might I kiss you?"

I nodded and he brushed his lips against mine. It was a miracle that I did not faint on the spot. To have my first kiss be such perfection was a gift beyond believing. When his lips touched mine, it was as if the rest of the world ceased to exist, and I never wanted it to end.

Too soon he pulled back, his face suffused with satisfaction. Just as he was about to speak, Miss Bingley swept the cracked door open. Both Mr Darcy and I started and spun to face her, stepping apart.

Her alabaster face was flushed. "A game of Bowls is set up out of doors, and teams are forming." Her eyes flicked from one of us to the other. "Miss Eliza, certainly you shall desire to stay in and continue with your music." Her attempt at a smile was more of a sneer.

"No indeed. I think I should like some fresh air." I was floating on notes of a trilling piccolo, which matched the beating of my heart.

Mr Darcy beamed and offered his elbow. When I took it, Miss Bingley's face went grey. He eased me past her and out to the lawn where we enjoyed a rousing game. Even if we had been digging a ditch, I would have been happy, for Mr Darcy's attention never flagged and his affection seemed to grow. How had I come to this great fortune?

When the last morning arrived and all were readying for departure, he found me alone in a small sitting room. Breakfast had ended and I was packed, waiting for Jane, and looking out the window at the lovely garden. He approached with lower tones and a look of grave importance.

"Miss Elizabeth." He paused and began again. "The thought of leaving you is ripping at my soul, yet I can tarry no longer as I have promised to visit my aunt in Kent." He reached for my hand.

My body tingled from his touch, and I squeezed back. "I feel the same. These days have been...they have exceeded expectations." The sounds of a harpsichord's joyous tones rushed through my mind, followed by the happy trill of a flute. Never had I met such a man. Never had I desired to speak to anyone other than Jane or my father at length. That he was handsome and rich were simply coincidences. This gentleman was all I could have dreamt of.

"I shall return to this part of England in four months."

So long? I stepped back, and our hands dropped. "Four months? But there must be..."

Mr Darcy looked as bereft as I felt. I thought quickly and seized on an idea.

"My friend Charlotte is recently married and has moved to Kent. She has asked again and again for me to visit. Perhaps I could go to her and Hunsford Parish and—"

His jaw dropped. "Hunsford Parish? Why that is connected to Rosings, my aunt's estate."

"Heavens!"

"Then a visit is in order, and I shall see you in Kent!"

My mother would have put me on a coach that evening, but Papa and I convinced her that I had to write to Charlotte and receive a reply before plans could even be considered. A week, I thought, was rather hasty, but every day, Mama fretted and snapped, nearly chasing away all of my lovely thoughts of Mr Darcy. Nearly.

The journey was long but the view beautiful. The late spring sky was clear and flowers bloomed in every field. The rolling emerald hills dotted with fluffy sheep and rollicking horses brought me great joy, as did the stone churches and arched bridges we crossed as the coach made its way to Hunsford Parish.

Finding Charlotte settled in her own home was a great happiness. While her husband, my cousin Mr Collins, was too obsequious and dull for my taste, leading me to have declined his offer for marriage, I was pleased that Charlotte had found in him the comfort and security she so longed for in a union.

On my second day, we received an invitation to dine at Rosings from Mr Darcy himself!

Mr Darcy rode to the Collinses' gate on the finest thoroughbred Arabian I had ever seen. Mr Collins met him first, as he was in the garden, and Charlotte and I hurried from the kitchen where she had been conferring with her cook. As I approached, Mr Darcy's expression shifted from consternation to delight, but before he could say a word, Mr Collins said, "Our dreams have been realised. We have been gifted with an invitation to Rosings! Nothing would give us more pleasure than to dine with her ladyship. An honour, sir. An honour!"

Mr Darcy's eyes, wide when Mr Collins spoke, flicked to mine. I offered a smile, which he returned. I was about to greet him when Mr. Collins once again spoke. "Mr Darcy, you must come inside for refreshments. You must be exhausted from the ride."

Charlotte stepped to her husband's side. "While Mr Darcy is, of course, welcome to our home, Mr Collins," she said in a measured tone, "perhaps you could bring me to your prized azalea bush so I might cut some blossoms for the table."

Dismayed though he was, he did allow himself to be led away. Charlotte called over her shoulder, "Elizabeth, the stream down the hill is an open and lovely place to stroll."

As she had taken me there earlier in the morning, the message clearly was intended for Mr Darcy.

Mr Darcy offered an elbow and we began to walk. The sun shone and the birds chirped, and I found myself filled with immeasurable joy just to be near him.

"Miss Elizabeth, how marvellous to see you again." When I smiled, he added, "It has been just over a week, but it seems like an eternity."

I looked into his warm eyes and had to remind myself to put one foot in front of the other. "I feel the same. In the few days we were at Netherfield, I came to rely on your conversation and company."

"And I," he said, stopping, "missed kissing you."

I looked up the path one way and the other. No one was about, and a kiss would not be so scandalous. I stood on my toes and we smiled, nearly ruining the moment when our teeth clanked together. We laughed and kissed again, this time properly. How easy it would have been to have ducked into shadows and forgotten our place, but we maintained control and returned to the house.

At the gate, he sighed, and I asked if all was well. "To wait until tomorrow night to see you is too long."

I reached for his arm; the gesture was overly familiar but I needed to touch him again. "Then come again tomorrow morning. Or stay for tea."

Mr Collins hurried towards us, waving wildly despite the short distance between us. "Mr Darcy, please come inside the house that your aunt, Lady Catherine de Bourgh, has made commodious with her generosity."

Mr Darcy's veil of reserve dropped over his features and he bowed. "I must depart as I have business to attend to. However, I look forward to seeing you on the morrow." After one brief nod my way, he mounted his horse and rode away.

Mr Darcy had not returned to the parsonage the next morning, but sent apologies with a messenger. When we were received at Rosings that evening, he approached with all the warmth I had desired, and spoke with me as much as propriety would allow. He introduced me to his sweet sister, but as darling as Miss Darcy was, it was difficult to focus on her when her charming brother was so near.

Even as we conversed, I could not help but notice the impressive furnishings: elaborate tapestries, multiple chandeliers and candelabras where one might do, an intricately painted ceiling, and carvings and portraits covering every inch of the receiving room. I considered the difference in our status, but Mr Darcy's smile and attention chased away my doubts.

The dining room was also magnificent, though darker than the receiving room due to the deep stain of the wood. Tapestries depicting soldiers in battle covered each wall, and I wondered how one was supposed to sit at peace with scenes of bloodshed all about.

One man in livery was posted behind each chair to seat, and then to serve us. The meal was extraordinary—at least that which I could eat, for Lady Catherine de Bourgh asked me question after question, all hinting at the inferiority of my station and making actual consumption a challenge. She was stern, and every sentence laced with judgment. I could ignore most of her commentary until it came to the suggestion of my playing after the meal.

She said, "There are few people in England, I suppose, who have more true enjoyment of music than myself, or a better natural taste. If I had ever learnt, I should have been a great proficient."

"It takes great dedication," I said. "One must forego many other entertainments and pursuits."

"Do you draw?"

I shook my head, so she added, "Paint? Speak Latin?" When I said I had none of those talents, she sniffed. "You have neglected too much of your education, my dear. A young lady should hope for accomplishments to make herself attractive to suitors. Had my daughter Anne lived, she would certainly have improved her marriage prospects with such talents."

"My dearest wish is to become a famous composer and pianist. To play concert halls and palaces around the world, and to have my pieces on every music stand, and on every stage and parlour throughout Europe. Perhaps even America."

All at the table froze, staring at me in apparent disbelief. Had I never voiced my dreams, even to Charlotte? Perhaps not. I knew the idea would be unpopular, but they looked as if I had just suggested selling my very body.

Mr Collins said, in a manner that was not at all approving, "What a grand plan!"

"Grand indeed," murmured Lady Catherine. "You wish to trade your talent for money like an artisan or a peddler?"

My breath stilled and my eyes darted to Mr Darcy. He gave an encouraging nod. "Let Miss Bennet's talent speak for itself. Come."

Though his voice was grave, his eyes were warm. He rose and offered an elbow, escorting me to the piano bench. He leaned down and whispered, "Play as though your happiness depends upon it."

And I did.

Finally, my fingers came to rest and the last vibrations of the piano strings quieted. Mr Collins, Charlotte, Miss Darcy, and Mr Darcy sprang to their feet. "Bravo!" the men cried. I rose and offered a delicate curtsey, my eyes flicking from person to person. Charlotte was grinning as she always did when I played; she was my ever-supportive friend. Miss Darcy's face glowed with an admiration I recalled feeling for older, accomplished young women whom I strived to emulate. Mr Collins appeared impressed as he continued to clap, and Mr Darcy's face was full of something I did not quite recognise. Was it—Could it be love?

Overwhelmed, my eyes moved on and landed on Lady Catherine. There was no love there, nor admiration. Instead there was something akin to hate, and a shiver ran through me. Her gaze snapped to her nephew, who was still clapping and beaming, and then back to me. My breath caught. Her face darkened further.

"That will do very well for tonight," she announced imperiously.

The others' smiles slid away; the applause stopped and their hands dropped to their sides. They looked to one another in confusion. But I was not confused. I was a threat and she had to rid the place of me.

"The hour is late," she said. "I give you leave to depart."

The Collinses offered the civilities of departure, after which Charlotte urged her husband towards Lady Catherine's carriage, which had been arranged for us.

I began to follow, but Lady Catherine asked me to remain. Mr Darcy suggested that he stay as well, and after a moment's hesitation she agreed and sent Miss Darcy to her chambers. Once we three were alone, she turned her falcon-like stare to me. "Miss Bennet, what are your intentions with your music?"

"As I said, to play concert halls and palaces the world over."

She looked at Mr Darcy. "And what are your intentions towards Miss Bennet?"

Seeing his discomfort, I said, "I cannot see how that is your business."

She rounded on me. "Miss Bennet, I am almost the nearest relation he has in the world, and I am entitled to know all his dearest concerns."

"But you are not entitled to know mine."

Though Mr Darcy began to speak, she closed the distance between us, her menace running like ice into my veins. "Let me be rightly understood. If you have any notions of some inclination on the part of my nephew—"

Mr Darcy quickly interrupted. "Lady Catherine, this is not appropriate."

"—Such a match could never take place. In addition to the mortification that would arise from connecting ourselves to your family, your thoughts of musical greatness make it worse."

Mr Darcy tried once more. "Lady Catherine, I insist you cease in this vulgar form of conversation with Miss Bennet."

She rounded on him. "Is this what you want? A wife in the public eye? Playing for her supper?" She laughed; there was no mirth in it but I cared nothing about that. I could see the realisation dawning on him, the difference in what I would *be* versus what he would wish for in a wife. His face went slack, then his shoulders sagged. He looked to me, his face imploring, as if asking me to declare my music a pastime and nothing more.

Lady Catherine saw it too and a look of triumph came over her face. "Do not expect to be noticed by family or friends if you wilfully act against the inclinations of all. You will be censured, slighted, and despised by everyone. Your alliance will be a disgrace."

I lifted my chin and thought to argue, to defend myself, but the pallor of Mr Darcy's cheeks stole my words. I lowered my gaze and backed away. "There is no alliance to concern yourself with, your ladyship. Mr Darcy and I are friends, but nothing more."

Unwilling to prolong this unpleasantness for another moment, I turned and quickly exited the room and hurried down the stairs and out the door to where Charlotte and Mr Collins awaited me. I begged the driver to depart and urged him to move swiftly. When through the window I saw Mr Darcy burst from the house calling my name, I silently urged them to go faster.

Early the next morning at Hunsford Parsonage, the maid entered the dining room where I sat with Charlotte and announced Mr Darcy.

Charlotte nodded at me and promised that Mr Darcy and I would be undisturbed in the parlour. I attempted to offer a smile, but it felt false and weary. Charlotte had sat up with me half the night as we spoke of the matter, and I alternated between outrage and tears. Only once had she urged me to consider that Lady Catherine might be correct, to which I replied that if she insisted on such a course, I would leave her house immediately. She had carefully avoided such sentiments as the hours passed, though her occasional sighs revealed her true opinion.

The sight of Mr Darcy in his deep green coat, which accentuated his broad shoulders and fine athletic frame, made my breath catch. He was more magnificent every time I saw him. But then I noticed his clenched fists, and my stomach sank.

He cleared his throat. "My aunt spoke rudely to you, and we have discussed that, yet I must implore you to consider her point. A wife's duty and the life you could lead if you were to agree to be—My needs are perhaps not compatible with your aspirations."

I sank to the edge of Charlotte's favourite chair: carved and over-stuffed with a pattern of delphiniums that matched Mr Darcy's perfect blue eyes. "Had—" I cleared the lump from my throat. "Had you planned on asking me to be your wife?"

He nodded, and my heart thrummed, but his furrowed brow and the words he then uttered kept me rooted in misery: "Elizabeth, I love you and I wish to make you mine, but I cannot, not if you insist that your music shall be anything more than a diversion."

Tears brimmed in my eyes, but it was more than mere disappointment. My tears were tinged with rage. "Mr Darcy, had you more conviction and confidence, you would not say such a thing."

"I have both confidence and conviction, and I am determined to make you see why this is impossible."

"Robbing me of my dreams might be possible, but you shall crush my spirit in doing so, rendering me a different person from the one you fell in love with." I felt a sob welling up and rose to chase it away, turning my back on him.

"You know what people think of actors and actresses," he scoffed. "A musician is scarcely better."

"What people think is wrong," I said to the hearth. "Why should talent and dedication be despised?"

"So given a choice between some fanciful notion of being on a stage, being an entertainer, or being my wife..."

I turned to look at him, so angered that he was forcing me to make such a choice.

His expression hardened. "You love your music more than you could love me. Very well then."

I sucked in a breath. "I bid you farewell." When he looked as if he might argue, I crossed to the door and pulled it open.

Mr Darcy's shoulders sagged as he moved to leave. He paused at my side and I felt his breath upon my face. It would be so easy to reach up and take hold of him, to pull him close and kiss him. But he was determined to take from me that which I loved most in the world; I could not give in to such weakness.

"Good day, sir."

He reached out and rested a hand on my shoulder. "Miss Elizabeth, please listen to reason."

I backed away from his touch, my stomach squeezing. To the floor, I murmured my final words: "I said, 'Good day'."

CHAPTER THREE

THAT EVENING, AT LONGBOURN—FOR I HAD PACKED immediately and hurried home—my heart raced as I thought of my confession to my family. Their arguments for me to be sensible and accept Mr Darcy had been expectedly painful. They said nothing that Charlotte had not already said, and I could not be swayed. My mother, having indulged herself in a fit of nerves, had been borne out of the parlour on my father's arm. Before exiting the room, Papa paused to frown at me, a look that had turned my knees to jelly, being rare as it was.

My younger sisters had been sent to bed and I was left alone with Jane.

"Jane, you understand, do you not? Mr Darcy does not support my music."

"Lizzy." She shook her head. "But he will marry you, love you even. His fortune is great. You would want for nothing."

"Indeed, I would want for something and that is the chance to perform my music–"

"Do be serious." Jane gave me a look. "You know that such occupation is not suitable for a woman, most particularly a woman who is gently bred! We could not know you, Lizzy, not as some...some *performer*."

I swallowed hard. "I have wanted this my entire life. You know this about me."

"I have always believed it a childhood fancy you would grow out of some day. I had never thought you so foolish to turn down an offer of marriage for it."

Her words stung me more deeply than I ever could have imagined. Did everyone think this? That my every hope and dream were mere childish fancies? Stubbornly I said, "He cannot claim to love me yet not appreciate my music."

"He does appreciate your music and no doubt would be excessively proud to see you exhibit in the parlours and drawing rooms of better society."

I rolled my eyes at that. How far from what I truly desired that was!

Jane rose, obviously intending to leave me and my 'childhood fancies'. "You can have music or you can have a respectable life as a wife to Mr Darcy. You cannot have both." When she had gone, I felt myself alone in every way.

I would have to escape, I decided. I could not think at Longbourn—not among those who would dismiss my music and diminish my desires, who would consign me to the commonplace life of a gentleman's wife. Aunt and Uncle Gardiner had invited me to come to them in London at a moment's notice, and I hoped no notice at all might suffice. I ran up to my room and began to gather dresses and stockings and hats, which had been unpacked upon my return. Our maid entered and I begged her for help. To my displeasure, she went to fetch Mrs Hill.

Hill had concerns but assisted my re-packing efforts nevertheless. "You need not run away, Miss Lizzy. You know your parents will see past this."

"I do not wish to witness the efforts of their overcoming this disappointment, and I do not wish to be harangued into marrying when it is not what I desire."

"You cannot leave until morning. Rest on it, Miss." She pushed some fallen strands of hair behind my ear. "Perhaps all will seem better in the light of day."

But it was not. I slept in the sitting room, as I could not share a room with Jane knowing how wrong she thought me, and I had woken at dawn with a stiff neck and a sore back. Dragging myself to the dining room, I found my father sitting at the table at what was an early hour for him. He set aside his book. From the darkness under his eyes, it seemed he had slept as little as I.

"If you are here to argue that I marry Mr Darcy, I shall have to insist that you not speak."

He leant back in his chair, lips pressed decidedly shut, and watched as I sliced two generous portions of bread, slathered them with butter, wrapped them in a cloth, and cut and wrapped some ham. I put those along with an apple into a sack and made for the door.

"Your aunt and uncle will have similar advice," my father said, "and we shall be ready to embrace you when you change your mind."

"I shall never change my mind."

He lifted the book and opened it, but I knew he was not reading.

No one—not Papa or Mama, Jane, Mary, Kitty or Lydia—came to say goodbye. I had expected Mrs Hill, at least, to say something, but Mama had given her tasks to accomplish just as I was departing. My loneliness was profound, leaving me wondering already whether I could endure isolation should I insist on pursuing composing and performing.

The music went silent in my mind for a time, and I was caught between horror and relief. Relief, for if that passion was gone, I could turn my attention to the life all desired for me with more certainty. But as I rode on, the low strains of a cello floated to me and accompanied me towards my destination.

Upon my arrival at Gracechurch Street, I asked my aunt and uncle if they would refrain from asking about Mr Darcy, and they obliged. I knew my aunt would eventually pry, but also that she would have the decency to give me time to recover from the shock of all that had transpired.

In the days that followed, music had flowed from me. Mama would have hated it, claiming I was ruining her nerves with my 'incessant banging on the instrument', but she was miles away and I was in a house that had a door to close upon my playing and my young cousins' chatter to drown me out. My compositions grew angrier, but the run of notes I created kept me from thinking too much about their inspiration. No one appreciated the challenge posed to my fingers to keep up with the notes in my head, and, despite my aunt asking me to spend more time with the family, I had to practise or the piece would never solidify.

At long last she prevailed upon me for an outing. "We could go shopping or to a concert at Rush Hall." She knew I would pick the concert, and had already purchased tickets, which made me laugh; it was the first true joy I had felt in the nearly two weeks since my arrival. Not even letters from Jane had made me happy, for they hinted at my return and of my family's ongoing disapproval of my desires. I had written once to Longbourn—a brief missive about the generosity of my aunt and uncle, and a few lines about the weather.

The concerto was magnificent, and my aunt noted my improved mood. "They have concerts daily."

I gasped. "We could come every day?"

"I cannot. Nor would I desire such a thing." She paused. "However, my upstairs maid loves music nearly as much as you, and I could be persuaded to send her with you when I do not need her."

The agreement worked magnificently, and Ruth and I enjoyed many afternoons filling our minds with glorious pieces.

On our way out of one performance, a young man who had been sitting next to Ruth asked me, "Did I hear that you play the piano?" When I nodded, he said that he did, as well, and asked whether we would be interested in having tea together and talking about music. From his dress, he was not of our class and therefore not a potential suitor, which was reassuring. As he knew the rules of propriety, having included my maid, I could see no harm in it. Ruth nodded and I agreed.

Once on the street, he introduced himself as Mr Wickham. I offered our names. His teeth were a bit crooked, but in a way that appeared charming rather than unsightly, and his hair was thick and fashionably tousled. He directed us to a tea-room on the same block as Rush Hall. An hour passed pleasantly, and ended with wishes that we might meet again at future concerts.

After that, it seemed we met every few days, taking tea on some days and returning home immediately on others. Ruth enjoyed the tea, as the food was not only welcome but it also prolonged her time away from her duties. I made my aunt aware of it, but as we were never alone together, she saw no harm in it, nor did I.

One afternoon, Mr Wickham invited me to hear him play. His friend, a fellow musician, had let rooms for rehearsing wherein Mr Wickham was currently living. The room was full of various instruments and sheet music, and had a cot and a side table against the wall. A shelf held a loaf of bread and a bottle of wine, along with two mismatched glasses. There was not much else save pegs on the wall in a corner with clothing hanging upon them.

"Your accommodations are quite rudimentary," I said.

He nodded. "For now. What need have I for luxuries when I have music to comfort me?"

I had never met anyone whose passion for music, and whose understanding of the vital role of it within a life, so wholly matched mine. "I have many comforts, sir, but, like you, I am not in need of them."

He cocked his head. "You would miss your silks and parasols if they disappeared tomorrow."

"I assure you, I would not."

He nodded, his eyes narrow. Did he doubt me? Was he impressed? Was I even truthful? How far would I go for my music? Would I be willing to live in a room such as this, cut off from all acquaintances? He did not say he had no friends, but would I if I continued down this path?

"Shall I?" he asked, gesturing at the piano. I nodded, and he pulled the only two chairs in the room closer. Ruth flushed when he refused her help in moving a chair, and preened when she sat, unaccustomed as she was to being waited upon.

Mr Wickham played with a fire I had never seen, his fingers gliding up and down the keyboard, tapping with unmatched speed. The music rose and fell and pulled me in. I closed my eyes for a moment to take in the sound but opened them again for fear that I would miss the masterful way he played. Then he hit a wrong note, froze, and banged the keys with one slam of fury before he turned to us, laughing. "Ah well. It was excellent for a time."

"How modest you are."

"I do not believe in false humility. It was excellent and then it was not." He shrugged and rose from the bench. "One must be honest with oneself. Honesty is in such short supply."

"Are you honest with me?"

His face shifted and all mirth drained out of it. "About what?"

"Everything. Your life. Your willingness to sacrifice."

He stepped closer. His jade green eyes were searching. He stepped closer still. His eyes flicked to Ruth and he stepped back. "We ought to go down to find tea. All of that playing made me famished."

I nodded to him as he did the same to Ruth. As we stepped out the door to the stairs, he said, "I have a friend who publishes music. I told him about you."

"You did?"

"Of course. He is most interested in meeting you."

We exited the building, and the sudden light blinded me for a moment. He led us down the street and then across. I stepped around a pile of horse manure, still unable to believe what he had said. "Your friend will meet with a woman composer?"

"Yes, he is very forward-thinking."

He grabbed my upper arm and yanked me back as a carriage thundered past. Ruth screamed. Mr Wickham's fingers lingered a moment longer than they should have, but I was too shocked by my near death to truly comprehend it. We walked on in silence and did not return to the subject until we were safely seated and Ruth had exclaimed for a third time how lucky we were to be alive.

After our refreshments had arrived, he said, "You must meet Mr Wilson, the publisher. Oh! And Mrs Josepha von Bruhn, the magnificent German pianist and composer, is in town. She is in ill health, I am afraid, but said she would welcome the opportunity to meet you."

"Mrs von Bruhn knows about me?" When he nodded, I covered my mouth with my hand. How could such a woman, whose pieces I had played on many occasions, know my name and be willing to sit and speak to me? I sipped tea to steady myself. "And you say she played in public?"

"At Hanover Square, Willis's Rooms, and all over Europe."

"I had not realised she performed."

"She says the continent is different than England, though things have changed since she was a young woman, and believes that you might enjoy a different path. I believe you could. Shall I ask whether she can meet you this week?"

I held my cup, considering this. Was there a way for a woman of my class to perform and still hope for a decent marriage? I was not so certain.

We continued in companiable conversation and then I paid, as I often did, for our tea. At first, he had argued, but I had insisted, reminding him that my family provided well for me.

As I rose to leave, a man moved past, going so quickly that he knocked into me and nearly sent me tumbling. I exclaimed and he grabbed my elbow to steady me.

I looked up. And there he was.

His eyes flew wide. "Miss Bennet!"

"Mr Darcy!"

As quickly as we had come together, we stepped apart. "Heavens!" he said. "I did not realise... How long have you been in London?"

"Since the day after—" My cheeks burned. "A few weeks now. And yourself?"

"A few days."

I had to concentrate to steady my voice. "I am with my aunt and uncle Gardiner. I believe I told you of them. And where are you staying?"

"At my family home on Grosvenor Street."

"Of course." I swallowed hard, imagining I could still feel the heat of his hands on my elbow. "May I introduce to you my friend, Mr Wickham."

Mr Darcy's reply to this request was extraordinary; he went rigid and pale. Likewise, Mr Wickham's jaw clenched tight. What was between the men?

"We are acquainted," said Mr Darcy, in a tone I had never heard from him, cold and displeased.

Mr Wickham's face was friendlier when he looked at me and said, "Excuse me, I must be off."

"Of that I am certain," Mr Darcy said. Mr Wickham did not reply to that. He bowed, promised to send word about Mrs von Bruhn, and disappeared through the door.

Immediately, Mr Darcy's lips curled around his teeth like a snarling dog. "How do you know...Mr Wickham?"

"We met at a concert I was attending with my aunt."

"And you had tea together?"

"Yes." I had many questions, but his expression offered no invitation to queries. "We were just leaving."

"Shall I escort you home?"

"I thank you, no," I replied. Our eyes met, and the familiar churn in my stomach returned. Oboes then violins began to play in my mind. "It is not necessary."

Flutes fluttered over the lower notes. I wanted to reach out to him. To kiss him. To tell him I would accept his conditions. But I could not. With music running through my head at this very moment, how could I deny what I needed to be and do?

He said, "I should tell you—"

"Darcy!" A man in uniform, shorter than Mr Darcy, approached. He was not handsome, but was clearly a gentleman. "Darcy, I secured a table but you never— Oh, is this an acquaintance of yours?"

Mr Darcy's head jerked as if waking from a dream. "Yes. Miss Elizabeth Bennet, this is my cousin, Colonel Fitzwilliam."

The colonel bowed. "A pleasure to meet you, Miss Bennet. Darcy, our table is there." He pointed and backed away. "We ought not to dally. We have that appointment."

Mr Darcy and I stood another moment, hardly noticing the patrons and waiters jostling to pass in the narrow walkway. How lovely it would be to sit in this tea-room with him, enjoying sweets and conversation. But it was not meant to be, as I was an obstinate, headstrong girl. Few would understand my passions and my desires. Not Mr Darcy, not my mother and father, not even Jane. Not anyone.

"Good day, Mr Darcy." I curtseyed and hurried off before he could reply.

CHAPTER FOUR

THE NEXT MORNING, A NOTE ARRIVED FOR ME DECLARING that I should come to the tea-room the following afternoon to meet the composer. I prevaricated and told my aunt it was from a woman I met at the concert. Perhaps Mr Wickham, not being of better society, did not know the strictures that forbade a single, unattached man writing to a woman. My aunt was disappointed that I would not be at her gathering, but she was happy that I was making friends. I realised that Ruth would be busy serving my aunt's guests; I disliked the idea of going alone to meet Mr Wickham, but the promise of meeting Mrs von Bruhn outweighed any hesitation I might have felt.

The rest of the day and the following morning, I played and scribbled musical notes on the lovely paper my aunt had purchased for my compositions. The little ones came in for the lessons I promised them; while I typically did not mind, this day I resented the intrusion, knowing I would have no more opportunity to work until the sun rose again.

It *would* be difficult, I realised, to have children whilst attempting to create music. Perhaps it would be best if I put such notions of motherhood aside? But as they sat beside me, I thrilled at their warmth and excitement, their desire to learn and their giggles. Unbidden, the image of a small boy with Mr Darcy's eyes playing at my feet sprang to mind, but determinedly I pushed it away.

While my aunt was preparing for her guests, I slipped out the door and travelled alone to the tea room to meet Mr Wickham. He was waiting outside and suggested we go up, as Mrs von Bruhn had agreed to meet within his rooms to have proximity to a piano. Walking up the stairs of his building, we met a neighbour, a stooped woman with both front teeth missing. We were introduced, and I helped her carry her bags up two flights. She thanked me and wished us well.

Seated in Mr Wickham's apartment, I asked for more of a description of Mrs von Bruhn, but he merely replied, "You shall have to see her for yourself." I passed the time by rehearsing questions I might ask of her, pacing to and fro in the small space.

During a lull while I considered what else I might wish to know, Mr Wickham came very close and leant over me, saying, "I have a question of my own for you."

"For me?" I pulled away a little. "What might that be?"

His voice was low, and his eyes held a look I had not before seen in them. It made me distinctly uneasy, even before he said, "Shall we go to Lamberton or Gretna Green?"

I drew back still further and gave an awkward little laugh. "Gretna Green? Whatever can you mean?"

"You cannot be surprised that I wish to marry you."

I laughed, but sobered when he showed no signs that he was making a joke. I stepped away still farther from him. "Indeed I am surprised. I believed us merely friends with a shared love of music."

He closed the distance between us quickly and before I could think, he had brushed his lips across mine. His scent, of wood and smoke, was intoxicating. He pressed his fingers to my back and pulled me closer. The warning rumble of fear thundered within me.

I leapt back. "Sir, I cannot permit... No. I shall not."

"Come now. A woman of the stage must be sophisticated, not missish." He cocked his head and chuckled, then traced his fingertips down my cheek and neck. "Perhaps you will change your mind once we are on our way to Gretna Green. Or do you prefer to wait until after the marriage papers are signed?"

He was not in jest. He truly meant to whisk me off to Scotland, hundreds of miles away.

"I do not know if I even wish to marry you!"

"I would allow you—no, I would *encourage* you—to continue with your music. We could promote ourselves as a duo. It would be remarkable."

How could this be happening? A man I hardly knew wished to offer all I had wanted from Darcy, and yet I felt nothing for this man—nothing but revulsion. He was handsome but suddenly his good looks appeared cold and menacing.

"Mr Wickham, is Mrs von Bruhn coming soon?"

He regarded me. Was there a smirk at the corners of his lips?

"Rather, should I ask, is Mrs Hester Park coming *at all*? Or has this been some bit of fiction concocted to get me here alone?"

"Alone." He smiled fully, appearing quite cruel. "I intend to marry you, Miss Bennet, and as we have been here alone and kissed, you can hardly deny me."

"No one saw—"

"My neighbour saw us together," he said, smirking. "How kind you were to help her up the stairs!"

It took a moment for his words to sink in. He had entrapped me! He was a vile man, and I was such a fool. I did not want him—could not even like him—yet I would be tied to him for all eternity to the great displeasure of my family. I would be cut out of society. And on what would we live? Mr Wickham had not fortune enough for a proper room, nor even for tea. Would we play in dingy halls and at country assemblies to earn our crust? My head began to spin as the whole of my miserable existence played out before me. A life with this man whom I hardly knew, and for what?

I had been so stupid. What would Mr Darcy say? Good, kind, fascinating Mr Darcy, whom I had rejected mere weeks earlier so I could pursue a dream—only to end up deceived by this reprobate. I felt my breakfast coming up and wished to run.

"Mr Wickham." My mouth felt as if it was filled with sand. "My family has no money."

"Do not lie. I see your clothing. I hear the way you speak. You are a lady. And you said yourself: your family provides for you."

"Coins here and there for ribbons and tea. My father has little and his estate is entailed to a cousin. I will inherit next to nothing!"

He frowned. "They shall find the money I require or regret it."

"You would ruin me and then be my husband?"

"If we do not find each other agreeable, we can live apart." He crossed to the piano, closing the lid over the keyboard. "I wish to make music, and your family's fortune is the way to do so. We could be happy together."

An entire percussion section was at work in my head, clanging and banging. This could not be. "No! I shall not allow you to impoverish my father, especially when I have done nothing wrong."

He leered at me. "Nothing wrong? Where is your chaperon?" He flung his arms wide and spun about. "Here we are. Alone."

"No. No! I was here for the music!" I ran from his room and down the stairs, hardly able to see through my tears. Whatever was I to do? To whom could I turn to for help?

A name—*his* name—came into my mind as I reached the street, and I gasped, reaching out to steady myself on the building. No. Mr Darcy? Could he—*would* he help me? If I were him, I would not even open the door to such a stupid, hateful girl. But perhaps he was more forgiving. I had to hope.

It could not have been two miles to Grosvenor Square but it seemed to take an eternity, though I ran and walked as fast as I could, ignoring the curious stares of those I passed. What if I could not find him? What if he slammed the door in my face?

An obliging passer-by knew which of the grand houses belonged to the Darcys and for a moment, I could only gawp. If his London home was so grand, what must his family estate, Pemberley, be like? It was beyond imagining. And here I was, rumpled and dusty, dampened from exertion and fear.

A servant let me into the entry hall, too well trained to show overt shock at the appearance of a lady, unaccompanied, and in such a state. When I gave my name, the man disappeared to tell Mr Darcy. I was fully prepared to see the servant return again alone to deny me entry or to escort me to a receiving room, but to my surprise, Mr Darcy appeared. The rapid notes of a piccolo played in my mind to mirror his stride. Underneath the high notes, however, was a mournful chord. I would have to tell him what had occurred. I would expose myself to humiliation and possible ruin, but if anyone could assist, it was Mr Darcy.

As soon as he saw my face, he announced to the servant that we would be in the front parlour, and whisked me inside, offering me a sherry. At first, I thought to refuse, but I was in need of spirits. With a shaking hand, I accepted the glass and drank it in one swallow. I closed my eyes to gather myself, the low thrum of drums behind my eyelids.

"Please sit, Miss Bennet. You look as if you shall swoon."

Feeling as though I might, I did as he suggested. He sat as well. As soon as I allowed my gaze to meet his, my eyes filled with tears. Best just to say it at once and skip dissembling or pleasantries. "Mr Wickham—" I choked on his name, and Mr Darcy leapt to his feet.

"Did he harm you?"

I sobbed, not wishing to be so weak before this man, but was unable to keep my despair and fear at bay. He began to pace, which only intensified my anxiety. Eventually, I could splutter, "N-no. He did not touch—. It is nothing of that nature." But as soon as I recalled Mr Wickham's proposal, I dissolved once again.

He knelt before me, and his concern cracked what was left of my heart. "What did he do?" His voice was so gentle. "Please tell me."

I gasped over and over in an attempt to calm myself. At last, he rose, crossed the room with commanding strides, opened the door, and barked out an order for tea. I dried my face, still attempting to control my breath but failing. Sooner than I would have imagined possible in a house of this size, a maid younger than Kitty hurried in with a clattering tray, her step hitching when she saw my tear-streaked face. Even in this moment of upheaval, he offered her a hint of a smile and his kind thanks. She bobbed a curtsey and shuffled out.

He put a large lump of sugar and a splash of cream in my cup. He remembered my preference. This detail set me to sniffing again. Why were not all men as good as Mr Darcy?

I took a sip and breathed. Attempting to hear piccolos helped, as it often did, and it transported me to the fields of Longbourn. Oh, had I only remained home and accepted my family's scorn, none of this would have occurred!

"Miss Bennet, if you would, please tell me what has brought you to my door."

I swallowed and set down my cup and saucer. He perched at the edge of a chair across from me, his face lined with expectation and worry.

I told him all.

"And you never did anything to...lead him to believe that an elopement would be welcome?"

"No. He kissed me once." Much as it pained me to see him cringe, I had no choice but to tell the entire truth if I hoped for his help. "The kiss was a moment before he insisted we marry. I cannot imagine what would have brought this on."

"In addition to your beauty and innocence? Greed. He wants your fortune."

"I have none."

"He believes you do." His fingers dug into his thighs as if that action was all that was keeping him from punching a wall or breaking a vase.

My back bowed under the weight of my humiliation. "I am so embarrassed."

"Why? Because an unscrupulous man—nay, a scoundrel—has taken advantage of you?"

"How can I face my family knowing the part I played in my own misfortune?" I dabbed at my cheeks, pained to see his furrowed brow and warm eyes upon me.

"While not entirely proper, a man and woman are not forbidden from speaking alone. In fact, you and I are alone here."

"This is different. I...It was foolish. Part of me recognised the impropriety, for I concealed my intentions and my destination from my aunt. That secrecy will be my ruin."

"I cannot allow it." He sat up straighter. "Do you wish to marry him?"

"Of course not!"

"Had you ever suggested you might desire such a thing?"

"Not in the least. Our conversation was always entirely about music." I looked away from him and admitted, "I thought him of like mind, that he was someone who understood my dedication to the art."

There was a short silence between us. "I shall deal with him once again," Mr Darcy said at length. "More harshly so he learns his lesson *this* time."

"Whatever do you mean?"

His face darkened, and he pressed his lips together. He rose from his chair, walking behind it as if it might shield him from whatever truth he was about to admit. "He was my sister's music tutor. Dearest Georgiana developed feelings for him, and he preyed upon her naivety. Last year, he attempted to persuade *her* to elope, as well, but she felt guilty and told me, thus thwarting his plan. I bought his silence, but in so doing it appears I only sent him off to his next victim."

He stepped around the chair and closed some of the distance between us. "I must beg your confidence in the matter of Georgiana, as I shall keep yours in regards to Mr Wickham."

"You have my word."

"And you have mine that Wickham shall not trouble you or anyone else in the future."

I returned to my aunt and uncle's home later than was expected, and was greeted by questions to which I offered no answers other than I felt unwell. I excused myself to my room where I stared at the wall, cursing myself for the rest of the evening. The music in my head grew quieter as the hours passed, until at last it was gone and I was left with silence.

The next two days passed with no word. I found myself crying in my bedchamber, unwilling to leave. My aunt began to despair, fearing what evil might have befallen me. I told her nothing, but on the third day, I emerged from my room to eat breakfast with the others.

"You are unusually quiet, Lizzy," my uncle said.

I looked at the chaos around the table—the little ones giggling, the eldest boy throwing a bit of roll at his sister, their merry chattering as they ate. My aunt and uncle were still, however, staring at me with furrowed brows.

"Are you still feeling poorly?" my aunt asked. "Perhaps we ought to send for a doctor."

"No." I said quickly.

"Perhaps it is a man," said my uncle with a wink. "A girl likes to be crossed a little in love every now and then."

I stiffened. "Nothing of that nature."

A servant entered and announced that a Mr Darcy had arrived and requested an audience with me. I nodded; it was as much as I could move, for I felt paralysed. Was the news good, or were my life and my family ruined? The moment he spoke, my destiny would be altered, and every moment that passed with the servant and my aunt and uncle staring at me seemed to both stretch and race at once. I rose.

"Might I speak to him in the music room?"

To suggest his business was with me and that we needed to be alone was untoward, but I could not have them see his face, and feared my own reaction if his look was grim.

I left the room, and the distance down the hall felt enormous. What would he say? What would be my fate? My mind had no music, only words. Elopement. Ruined. Alone. Mr Wickham. Mr Darcy.

Mr Darcy! There he stood at the mantel, facing the fire. When I cleared my throat, he startled and turned. Dark circles were under his eyes and his hair and shirt were rumpled, unusual for the man I had always known to be fastidious. He gave a quick bow and said, "I have news."

His tone was grim and his face equally so, forcing the breath from my lungs.

"Mr Wickham is dead."

"Dead?" I asked. I could not have expected such a thing as that. "Dead?" I repeated, trying to comprehend that fact. "Did you—"

"No. Angry as I was, I am not the murdering kind, Miss Bennet." He looked at me with a mix of horror and amusement. "After we spoke, I went to see him. There was no answer at his door so I waited on his street. Eventually he returned and I confronted him. Rather than own up to his offences, he ran. I gave chase, and he darted into the street where he was struck by a passing carriage and caused a most grievous accident. Two horses had to be shot and a driver had his leg severely broken.

"Mr Wickham, however, suffered the gravest injuries. He was brought to hospital, as I would not have him to my home, and the journey would likely have killed him. I did, however, sit with him these past three days."

"You did?"

"I lost my temper, Miss Bennet, not my compassion."

I felt a renewed sense of awe for this man, who grew in my estimation of him every time we met.

"I knew he had no one and so saw to his care. Just this morning, he died." He pursed his lips. "I admit feeling torn between regret and relief."

I took a step closer. "As do I. He certainly deserved the anger of us both, though he ought to have born a lighter punishment, I suspect." I paused as realisation set in. "So, it is over. I am...free from ruin and free from Mr Wickham."

Mr Darcy nodded.

I pulled in a deep breath. "I had prepared myself for the worst. How can I ever repay you?"

He looked about the room. "Would you play something for me?"

I shook my head. "No more music."

He stepped closer. "But why?"

"My shame has chased the notes away." I walked to the instrument where I had sat a mere three mornings ago, so full of hope and creativity. Now when I saw the notes I had scribbled, they made me sick. Dead or not, Mr Wickham had shown me my true self: obsessive, prejudiced, and absurd.

"I was a fool, Mr Darcy."

I remembered Mr Wickham's face as he 'proposed', the sickening confidence that I could not refuse him etched upon his features. I recalled his lips on mine, the shame of turning to Mr Darcy to rescue me, and the waiting—oh the waiting—these past days to know of the outcome. Each note represented another piece of my folly. I took hold of a sheet and ripped it. The sound thrilled me as much as piano notes once had. I ripped again.

Mr Darcy called for me to stop, but I did it again and went to the fireplace, feeding the bits of my foolishness into the waiting flames.

He took hold of my wrist. "You must cease this madness at once! You cannot destroy your work."

"My devotion to my art has led to this." I felt wild, unhinged, and pulled out of his grasp. "It led to my humiliation. It led to needing you to intervene. It led to a man's death!"

"I think it is fair to say that Mr Wickham's actions led to his own demise. The world is better without him. It is unkind, but it is the truth." He stared into the fire where the sheets were charred and curled, shattering into flakes, their last tune.

I crossed away from him, turning over his words in my mind, and picked up a large box tied closed with a red ribbon that Jane had given me. I returned and placed it in his hands. "These are my compositions. I do not trust I shall not throw the rest into the inferno, and I am not sure I would care."

"In time you certainly would."

We stood in silence, pain roiling within me. I heard a knock at the door and then a voice behind me. "Mr Darcy," said my aunt, "would you care to join us for breakfast? That is, if you have not yet eaten, what with the hour being so early."

We all knew this was commentary on his early call, as well her curiosity about what had transpired, yet I also knew the invitation to be sincere. I nodded to reassure him, and he accepted.

As soon as we had been seated, my uncle engaged him in a conversation about the sugar trade and the implications of its fluctuating costs on all of commerce. My aunt looked at me meaningfully, but I could not speak freely even if I desired to, which was not the case.

When we had finished our meal, Mr Darcy thanked them and said he would be off. "May I call tomorrow?"

I agreed and he offered the smallest of smiles in return. He thanked all again and departed with the box I had given him under his arm.

Announcing I was exhausted from too little sleep these past days but not sharing anything more, I slipped up to my room and slumbered peacefully until tea.

CHAPTER FIVE

OVER THE COURSE OF THE FOLLOWING WEEKS, MR DARCY called often. Twice we took a walk, but typically, we sat in the company of my family. We never played music, and only discussed it once: When my aunt was attending to two squabbling children, he asked if I would play for him. I refused.

"The notes are gone from my head, and even if they were not, the thought of playing makes me ill."

He said, "Your aunt and uncle are concerned that you are not playing."

"You spoke of me?"

"Yes. Before you came down for dinner the other night. You have not been yourself since—" He clenched and unclenched his fingers. "In too long."

"It gives me no pleasure."

"You must not let certain events rob you of your passion and of your God-given talent."

I clenched my fingers together and studied my lap, attempting to push away unpleasant memories.

"If you would allow me to escort you out tomorrow evening, perhaps I might convince you to love it once again." As I searched for a way to decline, he added, "Lest it seem untoward, your aunt and uncle shall accompany us. It has all been arranged."

"To where?"

"That, Miss Bennet, shall be a surprise. Wear a fine gown. Your favourite."

I could not help but smile.

He rose, saying he had business to attend to. He bowed, thanked my aunt for her hospitality, and departed with a lightness I had not seen in him since first we had met.

He had me blindfolded, but since my uncle and aunt were accompanying us, I had no fear. I had protested and asked what kind of event required such secrecy, but it seemed to delight my family and Mr Darcy to such an extent that I gave up arguing.

At last, the carriage came to a full stop, and together, Mr Darcy and a footman helped me out. Unable to see, I moved with such care that to watch me must have been comical. I moved down the steps one by one, and when I slipped, his grip tightened.

"I shall not let you fall."

We moved on together and then I felt us enter a small vestibule. After a number of steps in the enclosed space, air rushed at me, giving the sense of a more open space. At last, he untied the blindfold. There before me was an orchestra. Yet I was not facing the stage. I was *on* the stage. The crowd whose faces I could not quite see began applauding. I looked about to see whom they celebrated, and I heard laughter.

"What is the meaning of this, Mr Darcy?"

"This is about you. This is for *you*." I must have looked as confused as I felt, for he said, "The musicians are here to play your sonata. Well, they will accompany you." When I did not move, he took my upper arm gently and led me towards the magnificent piano. As if in a dream, I turned my head, seeing musicians awaiting their cue.

When I looked at the sheet music, I noticed the title *Concerto for a Winter's Day*. And my name!

"I-I do not understand."

Darcy said, "This is your piece. It was in the box you gave to me. I was neither encouraging nor understanding of your musical ambitions, and as a result, I nearly lost you. I have reflected upon my own prejudices and upon my pride, and realised I was being foolish. All of these people know that your talent is unmatched." He gestured to the audience.

I found myself drifting to the edge of the stage. As I stepped past the lamps, the faces of those I loved came into view. My father and mother, my sisters, Mr Bingley, Georgiana, Charlotte Lucas—or rather Mrs Collins—and her husband, Mr Collins, as well as both sets of my aunts and uncles, some friends I knew from town, and some of the *ton*. Blinking quickly as if that might set things right, I continued to stare at everyone in shock.

"Speech!" called Mr Bingley, his brilliant smile melting my fear.

"A speech? About what?" I turned back to Mr Darcy.

He stepped to my side. "I shall speak for now. Perhaps you will be moved to address the crowd after you play."

"No, I cannot play."

"You can and shall."

"I have not practised this music in ages!"

"*They* have."

"I have not practised *with* them."

"All shall understand." He addressed the crowd. "We are aware that this is an incredible moment for Miss Bennet, a moment that has taken her by great surprise. As such, we shall be generous if the playing is not to her exacting standards and shall celebrate her even if all goes terribly awry."

I covered my mouth to hide a laugh, and he reached out for my hand. I took it and allowed him to lead me to the piano bench. Before I sat, I whispered, "Mr Darcy, I cannot believe this is real."

"It *is* real, as is my love for you." He bowed and turned, descended into the audience, and sat.

It was too much. I could not do this. What if I humiliated myself? What if my concerto was received poorly? What if… No. None of it mattered. Mr Darcy had arranged all of this for me and I would try. I would play and appreciate this gesture of pure love from him.

My eyes scanned the sheet music. There they were. The notes I had dreamt up and the tune I had perfected. I could not allow this opportunity to pass me by. I settled onto the bench and pulled it forward, adjusting it so my feet touched the pedals just right. I looked up at the musicians. They awaited my start. It was too much to conceive of, and yet, it was true. Someone in the audience coughed. A chair squeaked. It was up to me to begin.

I lifted my hands, hovering them over the beginning chord, my heart racing. I hit the keys and the chord was perfect. My fingers knew the motions. I had practised over and over for so many months before I had renounced music. A pause and my fingers tinkled up the scales, reminding me of the sun coming over the horizon the morning this very tune had come into my head. And back down, faster, faster, settling in the middle, flitting like the sparrow that had been outside my window at Longbourn. Then a violin. I startled, for it was real and right near me. More violins joined. It was the flock that flew across the sky. We played together for a time and then came the drums, quiet, adding the low rumble of the clouds approaching. Swirls of first flakes were made by the flutes, and as the snow grew heavier, the oboes and clarinets. The trumpets were my littlest sisters running and playing in the drifts, and the bassoon my father trudging to the barn. We played and played, the scenes of inspiration that only I knew flickering through my mind.

When the first movement ended, I was overcome. After a brief pause, I was meant to go on, but I could not. All of this was for me; Mr Darcy had made it so. After so many arguments about my work and desires, here we were. I turned my face from the audience, feeling my shoulders shake, not wishing to make this sort of spectacle of myself, but unable to stop.

A man approached, for I heard heavy steps, which stopped at my side. "Miss Bennet, I have been hired to play piano if you wish to watch the remainder."

I looked up. The man was tall, with a kind smile. I sniffed and straightened up. "You have?" When he nodded, I pushed back the bench. As I stood, the audience erupted into cheers, and to my amazement, the musicians rose and applauded. I moved away from the piano, nodding my head at the musicians and then somehow managed a curtsey at the audience. I was unsure how I might make it down the few steps to a chair, given that my legs were water, but a hand reached out as I approached the edge of the stage. Of course, it was Mr Darcy, escorting me to a seat next to his.

The musicians began the second movement, and though I wished to appreciate every note, my mind drifted. I had all that I desired in this moment: Mr Darcy at my side, and my family and friends together celebrating music I had created. When I had been on the stage playing, there had been no judgment. I could make a life of this. Or could I? One night to show their love was a welcome surprise, but would they maintain their support if—nay, when—others spoke ill of my pursuits? Even the most talented musicians ranked, with little exception, no higher than servants, and as a woman, it would be worse. Far worse. The Duchess of Devonshire might have composed music, but she was a duchess (and one so free to do as she pleased that she had moved her lover into her home!). My choice would be less scandalous, perhaps, but it would put me in a similar realm. A few members of the *ton* might support me on this one night, but what would they do should others hear of my exploits and react poorly? Who would still speak to me? Receive me? Mr Darcy might be willing to endure the shame of my choice, but could I put him in that position? Could I do such a thing to myself?

While I doubted not that Mr Darcy would always provide for me, I wondered if his affection might wane when I hurt his reputation beyond repairing, or when I hurt poor, sweet Georgiana's marriage prospects; that was something I doubted he could forgive, nor could I forgive myself. And for what? The thrill of performing? I could exhibit, as was suggested, in the parlours and music rooms of our friends. It was not so different. Only the size of the crowd. And what cared I for the accolades of strangers? The magic of this evening had been the reception given to me by those I loved, and they might hear me play any time with no repercussions.

I focused back on the stage. The orchestra was extraordinary, bringing to life my imaginings. Hearing them was as good as when I was on stage. *No.* As I thought about it, sitting here in the audience was better! Yes! I could create. Composing was what I needed, not being amongst the musicians with attention shining upon me. Watching and hearing what I invented was the biggest thrill of all.

The other day, sitting with my cousins and teaching them to play, I had imagined my own children at my side, showing them where to place their fingers, watching them learn and grow. I wanted children; I longed for them. If I somehow became sought after as a performer, I would be away from them to go on tours and to attend rehearsals. When I thought of myself as a mother, I envisioned being involved and active in their lives. Yes, my mother could drive me mad, but when I recalled my youth, it was the time spent as she taught us how to play, draw, dance, and read without the assistance of tutors or servants. She loved us and guided us, and I wished to be her equal in this way.

As for Mr Darcy...I turned to look at him. He sat tall, eyes fixed on the stage, pride lighting up his face. Would I want to be away from him? No, if we chose to be together—my heart quickened at the thought—I would never want to be apart. Should I give up the idea of public performance, I would still wish to compose and play, and I had no doubt he would support me in my endeavours. Additionally, he disliked being in the company of others too often, so I had no fear of a full social calendar that would keep me from my compositions. I could write and play and play and write in a grand home with my needs met and a man who loved me. And whom I loved. I did. I loved him. If only I could reach over and take his hand now, kiss him and tell him all.

Instead, I merely whispered, "Thank you." He beamed and nodded, and we listened until the orchestra played the last grand note and all rose and cheered.

Mr Darcy had arranged a dinner after the performance at his house for my family and closest friends. He had thought of every detail, and of course, each was perfect. I practically floated through the meal and continued feeling outside of myself while we all stood chattering in the parlour.

He approached as I conversed with Charlotte and asked for a moment of my time. We crossed the hall to the music room, of course leaving the doors open.

I spoke first. "I must thank you for what was the best night of my life. I am not sure what I did to deserve it. Or you."

He stepped close, running his knuckles across my cheek. "You are Miss Elizabeth Bennet, the most perfect of creatures, and I would move heaven and earth for you."

Though I felt unworthy, I smiled. "Playing tonight was thrilling, but it made me realise many things and I must share them with you. You see, I realised that I prefer to watch a concert than be part of it." He began to argue, but I held up a hand. "Please Mr Darcy, allow me to tell you all." I took a breath. "I had always dreamt of being on stage, of being the centre of attention, but it made me more emotional and uncomfortable than I had expected. The music is the thing. Hearing my compositions fully realised—*that* was beyond imagining."

I smiled at him before continuing. "I also finally understood the compromises and shame I could bring to those around me. All I want is a peaceful home with my husband and children, friends, and music. And I could lose all of that if I insist on pursuing something the world is not yet ready to accept. When Mr Wickham tricked me, I understood how greatly I care about what others think, and that I desire a life free from scorn." I reached out and touched his arm. "I could never do anything to bring you shame, and so I renounce performing."

Mr Darcy shook his head in protest. "That might change. After seeing you, I do not think the society hostesses will leave you alone. Everyone will want you to exhibit." His face was suffused with love and admiration, and it made my heart race. "As for publishing your compositions, you might use *my* name."

My heart sank. Any man's name on my work would be such a betrayal. But it was right. If I was to be with him, I would have to hide—

"Or part of my name. Publish as Mrs Elizabeth Darcy?"

My mind lagged a beat behind his words. "Mrs...?"

"Be my wife. Do me the great honour of allowing me to be the husband of an accomplished composer."

"Only if you agree to be the husband of a grateful woman who is completely in love with you."

Though the music room with its instruments and paintings was still around us, it all faded away. It was just Mr Darcy and me, and a tune that was beginning to form in my mind...a light tune on the piano flitting about, then an oboe, serious and reserved. A perfect duet. The sounds of how we met and fell in love.

The End

About the Author

Michelle Ray is a middle school literature teacher who also directs plays, writes stories, and sees as many Broadway shows as she can. She lives with her husband and daughters near Washington DC, and dreams of traveling anywhere and everywhere.

Also by Michelle Ray

A World on Fire
Falling for Hamlet
Mac/Beth: The Price of Fame Shouldn't Be Murder
Much Ado About Something
Outlaw
There You Were: A Pride & Prejudice Retelling

What Might Have Been

Kay Bea

PROLOGUE

> Love is not love which alters when it alteration finds, or bends with the remover to remove.
>
> — WILLIAM SHAKESPEARE, SONNET 116

July 1812, Lambton

Elizabeth read the letter in her hand again. Lydia was missing. She was known to have left Brighton in the company of George Wickham and although the couple was thought to be bound for Gretna Green, they had only been traced as far as London before vanishing.

If they cannot be found, we shall all be ruined! With bitter horror, Elizabeth understood her and her sisters' already poor chances at making good marriages could be all but destroyed by the thoughtless act of an impulsive child. She had not yet begun to collect herself when a knock sounded on the door to the rooms she shared with her aunt and uncle.

"Yes," she said quietly.

"Mr Darcy to see you, ma'am," the maid called through the door.

Elizabeth's already fragile composure was nearly destroyed. She could not see him now. Lydia's actions had placed him forever beyond her reach.

"Please inform Mr Darcy I am not available for visitors at this time and send someone for Mr and Mrs Gardiner. They have gone to the shops." She gave the instructions with as much calm as she could manage. She forced herself away from the door, and although it could do nothing but cause her pain, did not resist looking down on the street from her window. She pressed her palm against the pane and felt her heart shatter as she watched him leave the inn, mount his horse, and ride away without looking back.

She would not consider why he had come. She *could* not. What good would it do her? She knew Lydia's foolishness would be the ruin of them all.

I likely shall never see him again. She swallowed against the grief that thought brought her. With a deep breath, Elizabeth forced her mind to the problem at hand, resolved to cast aside the hopes that crumbled to dust before they were half-formed.

She was frantically gathering their belongings when Mr and Mrs Gardiner returned. "Elizabeth!" her aunt cried out on entering the room. "What has happened?"

Elizabeth turned from her packing to thrust the letter into her aunt's hands. "'Tis Lydia. She has abandoned what little sense she possessed. We must return to Longbourn at once."

Mrs Gardiner read the letter with her husband; dear as they were, they readily agreed to end their excursion in favour of assisting the Bennet family. Within an hour, they had departed the inn and were travelling south.

CHAPTER ONE

When Elizabeth and the Gardiners arrived at Longbourn three days later, it was to a peculiarly silent household. Only Jane was present to greet them. "Thank goodness you are come," she cried almost the moment Elizabeth stepped from the carriage.

Elizabeth embraced her sister while her aunt and uncle preceded her into the house. "Oh, Jane! How is Mama? Is there any news?"

"Papa has gone to London in search of them," replied Jane, "but in so vast a city there is little chance of success. Mama has taken to her rooms, but not before her lamentations and wailings were heard by Mrs Goulding and Lady Lucas."

"Oh, good heavens, she may as well have announced it at an assembly!" Elizabeth removed her pelisse, and they moved to the sitting room. Uncle Gardiner had gone directly to their father's book room while their aunt went upstairs to attend their mother.

The two sisters sat close to one another on a small bench, silently seeking consolation. "'Twas not an hour before our circumstances were known by all of Meryton," Jane said. "Already we are falling out of favour with our friends and neighbours. Kitty attempted to call on Maria Lucas only yesterday and was turned away at the door."

Jane's account was no less disheartening for having been expected.

"And you have been here alone to suffer it all," said Elizabeth with feeling. "Dear Jane, how have you borne it?" She reached out to clasp her sister's hands within her own.

"You are here now, and we shall sustain one another."

Elizabeth realised the house was unusually quiet. "Where are Mary and Kitty?"

"Mary spends her days at the church as she has all summer, or in her room reading Fordyce. It is as though she hopes to atone for Lydia by increasing her own virtue. Kitty has been inconsolable—she did not fully understand the consequences of Lydia's choice until yesterday. She is like a ghost hiding from the rest of us." With a gentle frown, Jane shook her head

"Foolish girls," Elizabeth cried out. "Can they not make themselves useful? Have they at least helped you with our mother?"

"They have never been made to think of others, and I do not think they will begin now," Jane said quietly.

"I suppose not. Where am I needed most? Shall I meet with Hill?" Elizabeth took a quick glance around the room, pleased to see that the house was not in any sorry state. The sitting room was clean and from the scent in the air, it seemed a meal was being prepared, although Elizabeth knew not if any of them would have an appetite. Thankfully their servants knew their business.

Before Jane could reply, their mother called out from her rooms. "Lizzy? You must come to me at once!"

Elizabeth hastened to obey. When she encountered her aunt on the stairs, she gave her an enquiring look; Mrs Gardiner only shook her head and extended a hand to give Elizabeth's a gentle squeeze. With a deep breath, she continued to her mother's room.

Mrs Bennet began speaking as soon as Elizabeth opened the door. "Oh, Lizzy! We are ruined! And it is your father's fault! If only he had allowed all of us to go to Brighton, I am certain Lydia would never have run away. She is too good a girl to cause us such grief. But nobody listens to me. And now your father has gone away and I know he will fight Wickham and then he will be killed, and what is to become of us all? Mr Collins will surely cast us out the moment your father dies."

"Mama, do not fret so. There is yet hope that they shall be found,"

Elizabeth did not believe the words she spoke, but could not give her true opinion.

"Do you really think it true?"

Elizabeth winced as she replied, in a manner not entirely untruthful, "It is certainly possible."

"Of course!" Her mother sat up then from her reclined position. "Of course they shall be found, and your father must make them return here to be married from Longbourn. And then our neighbours will repent their ill wishes and we shall invite them all to the wedding breakfast! How grand it shall be!"

Elizabeth could make no helpful reply and instead settled for patting her mother's hand. When it appeared she had exhausted herself with visions of a married Lydia being invited to tea with all her friends and thus restoring their reputation in the neighbourhood, Elizabeth left her mother to the care of the ever faithful Mrs Hill. She saw no reason to insist Mrs Bennet join them for dinner as it was likely the lady's alternating exclamations of rapture, despair, and ill-use would only distress the rest of the household.

The Gardiners left the following morning with their children. Elizabeth's uncle would assist in the search for Lydia, and her aunt promised to write as soon as they had news.

As the days passed, Mrs Gardiner's letters, slow in coming, had little to report. No trace of the lovers was discovered and although her aunt was discreet in her phrasing, Elizabeth understood the search had encompassed places in London no respectable person would be found.

While her father remained in London, Elizabeth and her sisters continued in their isolation. Even their weekly sojourn to church did not give them a reprieve. When the Bennet ladies arrived, conversations grew quiet and they were the subjects of stares and whispers. On the few occasions the sisters ventured to town, even their once-close friends moved away and would not speak to them. The most devastating rejection, and the one that finally made her mother see the ruin of their lives, came when Aunt Philips refused to see her sister and nieces.

Elizabeth and her sisters attempted to console their mother when she returned, the very curls by her face seeming aquiver with dismay. "My own sister! Does she not know how I suffer?" She wailed loudly. "Oh, Lydia! How could she do this to me?"

Mrs Bennet turned her attention to Jane and said, "And Mr Bingley! We had such hopes, but now he will never return and your beauty will be for nothing! If only Lizzy had married Mr Collins as she ought to have done. At least then our future would be secure."

As their mother continued with her lamentations, Mary said, "Perhaps Mr Collins was correct and it would have been better for the family had Lydia died rather than bring her shame upon us all."

Elizabeth gasped with the shock of such a speech. Jane admonished her sister in a sharp voice. "Mary! If you have nothing of kindness to offer, I beg you would remain silent."

"Do not pretend you have not thought the same!" Mary countered. "You know that having such a sister will not induce any decent man to make an offer of marriage. Whatever hope there may have been for Mr Bingley to return is most assuredly lost to us. We have lost everything —our respectability not being the least consideration. If I had anywhere to turn, I would not associate myself with anyone connected to Lydia Bennet!"

Such a speech from her middle child could only leave Mrs Bennet in paroxysms of sorrow and her wailing increased accordingly. Elizabeth gave Mary a sharp glance and said, "Perhaps you might turn your attentions to visiting the tenants. I do not believe Mama has had time and they will benefit from your care."

Mary left the room in high dudgeon and Elizabeth blessed her absence. In a rare moment of discernment, Kitty offered to remain with their mother while her sisters took a turn about the garden.

Even Jane could not smile as she tucked her arm into Elizabeth's and they walked slowly out the door. Elizabeth did not speak again until she and Jane were well away from the house. "I wish I could offer you some comfort."

Jane shook her head, "There is none to be found. There was truth in Mary's cruelty, no matter how I wish differently. We will all suffer for Lydia's foolishness. We had little to recommend us before, but with the loss of our very respectability, our prospects are entirely bleak. What decent man would have any of us?"

What decent man indeed? Elizabeth's thoughts immediately turned to those which had plagued her since watching Mr Darcy leave the inn at Lambton. Had he called to renew his addresses to her? Had she made the right decision in sending him away? It was difficult to say. She did not think she could bear his disapprobation and knew assistance would be in every way impossible...but nevertheless the thought of his loss caused misery of the acutest kind.

Jane had given her sister a questioning glance. Elizabeth wanted to disagree, to tell her that no, surely their prospects were not wholly ruined—but she found herself unable to prevaricate. She said, simply "I only wish there was some hope of them being found."

"And I wish Mr Bingley had proposed. At least then we might have some protection," Jane said pensively. "Though I admit, I have begun to think he may not have been the man I wished him to be."

"Oh?" Elizabeth asked with surprise.

"What sort of man allows his sisters to so greatly influence his choice? I have no doubt of their being vocal in their opposition to the match. At least I can be thankful I shall not suffer the pain of being rejected for a sister's foolishness. I suppose now you are even more grateful for having declined Mr Darcy's offer at Easter. This behaviour from our sister could only have strengthened his opposition to our family, or it might have left you with a broken engagement."

Elizabeth closed her eyes against the anguish that threatened to overwhelm her. "Perhaps if I had accepted him, none of this would have come to pass."

"How so?" Jane asked.

"I might have been married by now." Elizabeth let herself slip into the thoughts of what might have been, a brief sojourn into pleasanter climes than she had at present. "All my sisters might have spent the summer with us at Pemberley."

"Would you wish for that? To be married to such a man?"

"I had begun to, I think. He seemed so very much altered when I saw him this summer. He was welcoming and gracious to our aunt and uncle. He even invited us all to dine at Pemberley. After that, I thought he might renew his addresses, but I did not give him the opportunity."

"No?" Jane asked.

"When he called on me the next day, I had just read your letter. I refused to see him." With a rueful smile to mask her pain, Elizabeth added, "So you see, I cannot know what he might have said or done. I daresay I never shall."

By the time Mr Bennet at last returned to Longbourn—in poor health and bearing no good news—July had given way to August. Of Lydia and Wickham there remained no trace; and the Gardiners had had experienced an unfortunate turn of their own circumstances. Mr Gardiner's warehouse had suffered a fire; although not destroyed, there was substantial damage. The Gardiner family was not left destitute but they were not as comfortable as they had been previously. They were required to give up their house on Gracechurch Street and remove to a smaller set of rooms in the remains of the warehouse while the building—and their livelihood—were rebuilt. They could no longer provide material assistance in the search for their wayward niece. Mrs Bennet's wailings increased in both volume and frequency as she heard the news and comprehended the notion that her brother would not put all to rights for them.

When her mother was at last settled and under Jane's care, Elizabeth spoke quietly to her father about the situation in Meryton.

Mr Bennet rubbed his hand across his forehead and Elizabeth was alarmed to see how pale and grey he looked. She wondered whether perhaps she ought to have hidden the news from him.

"Well, Lizzy, much as I despise it, for what do we live, but to make sport for our neighbours, and laugh at them in our turn?" He sighed heavily. "I have not the countenance to speak to any of them at present but when I am recovered, I shall see to it."

"What is to be done?" Elizabeth asked gently. "We are not blameless. I daresay we have, all of us, had our share in indulging her."

"I will lease Longbourn if I must, take us all to some distant county if need be." He offered a weak smile that could only worry Elizabeth further.

But Mr Bennet did not recover, and instead grew weaker by the day. Alas, by Michaelmas, Mr and Mrs Collins were the new master and mistress of Longbourn and the Bennet ladies—minus Mary, who had by then married the new curate and scarcely knew any of them—moved to a large home in London at Mrs Bennet's insistence. Jane and Elizabeth explained to no avail that the income from her settlement would not support such a home, but Mrs Bennet would not hear them.

At length they determined that it was fruitless to continue trying to teach prudence to a woman who counted excess as her right and resigned themselves to finding some kind of employment. They endeavoured to find positions as governesses or companions, but the hope of such honourable work decreased when Lydia's elopement was discovered. As Jane and Elizabeth's prospects for respectable employment dwindled, and the now much-diminished search for their sister continued to bring no answers, each of the women began to comprehend their new situation and the atmosphere in their new home grew increasingly melancholy. Mary wrote infrequently, and then only to encourage them to take care with their virtue. When the Gardiners were forced by circumstance to remove from London, Kitty joined them in hopes of improving her health and her situation, leaving only Jane and Elizabeth to care for their mother. As weeks turned to months, and months to years, the family was forced to acknowledge they would never learn Lydia's fate.

CHAPTER TWO

January 1817, London

ELIZABETH HUFFED ANGRILY AS SHE GATHERED PACKAGES of fabrics, ribbons, and beads at the behest of her employer, Madame Fontaine. When she had first come to work for the exclusive modiste, they had agreed Elizabeth could keep to the back and not be required to interact with the ladies who frequented the fashionable shops of Bond Street. For years the agreement had held, but today Madame would not be moved. Mr Becks was not available, and Madame Fontaine would not rest until the samples were delivered to the milliner.

She allowed herself another moment of irritation before giving thanks that the Season would not begin in earnest for two weeks; at least she was not likely to encounter any of those ladies who might think she ought to suffer some feelings of embarrassment at her reduced circumstances. Any mortification she might have once felt at her situation had long since passed, and her avoidance of Madame Fontaine's clients was now more a matter of habit than necessity.

That did not mean she wished to advertise the reversal of her fortunes to those for whom she could only be a subject of gossip. Miss Bingley had not been cured of her vicious tongue when she became

Mrs Michaels, and she was only encouraged by her sisters Mrs Hurst and Mrs Bingley in her cruelty. From Elizabeth's observations, it seemed Mrs Bingley was everything Mr Darcy had once thought Jane to be, and while Lady Asher had a reputation as sweet now as when she had been Miss Darcy, the possibility of a meeting with her brought forth memories and regrets too painful to contemplate.

She pulled on her gloves, bonnet, and pelisse with a frown as she considered they would need replacing soon. Her pelisse would not present any problems as there were always garments that were ordered and then declined. Such things were then made available to the seamstresses at a greatly reduced cost. But she would need to be careful with her funds if she were to obtain warm gloves that would last more than a season or two. Her current pair had been purchased not long after the Netherfield ball and such quality was now well beyond her means, despite her mother's marriage only a year following her father's death. Mr Worthington was a solicitor with a respectable income who did not care for his wife's children—a feeling he made plain without hesitation when they followed their mother to his house. That she had two unmarried daughters still living at home when they wed was a source of great resentment and even occasional hostility. His disposition had improved only slightly with Jane's marriage to a shopkeeper the previous year and he took delight in often reminding Elizabeth she was unlikely to secure a husband. With a firm shake of her head, Elizabeth dismissed the troubling thoughts, affixed a pleasant expression to her face, and moved quietly through the shop.

She opened the door and suppressed a shiver as the chill January air assaulted her. The early morning fog had given way to clear, bright skies and she blinked as her eyes adjusted. As she took her first step outside, the packages were knocked from her hands. The young lady responsible made clear her wealth exceeded her manners when she began scolding Elizabeth. "Stupid, thoughtless girl!"

Elizabeth did not apologise, but as she also did not comment on the lady's poor comportment, she acquitted herself of any wrongdoing and simply stooped to begin gathering the scattered packages. When she reached for the nearest box, she encountered a large, handsomely gloved hand. She looked up to thank the unexpected Good Samaritan and encountered the face that had haunted her dreams for years. *Mr Darcy!* He held her gaze for a long moment. His eyes shifted quickly from concerned to startled, then to something she hoped rather than believed to be happiness. Her own feelings were in such turmoil as to make determining his thoughts an impossibility. Before she could give more than a startled gasp, Madame Fontaine called out, bidding her to make haste, and the moment was broken. He pressed the box into her hand and assisted her in standing. Then he was gone.

The remainder of the day passed in a haze. Elizabeth completed her tasks with only half her attention engaged as she considered the brief encounter. She indulged in a rare bout of fantasy and imagined that rather than embroidering gowns for other ladies, she was remaking a gown of her own. She would wear it to their annual ball, an event she had begun upon their marriage. Her children would be nearby, her daughter pretending to work a needle of her own and her son noisily racing his toy horses. She was so lost in her dreams that the sound of Madame Fontaine locking the shop door took her by surprise.

Elizabeth squinted in the dim light of the room and moved the fabric in her hands, first closer, and then further away from her eyes as she attempted to focus on the detailed embroidery work. Deciding it looked well and that further effort could wait until the morrow, she set aside the piece and rose from her chair. She stretched her neck and shoulders, attempting to release the day's tension. As she gathered her pelisse and returned her bonnet to her head, she called out, *"Bonne nuit, Madame Fontaine."*

"Bonne nuit, Mademoiselle Bennet. N'oubliez pas que vous devez arriver tôt demain," her employer called out as Elizabeth reached the door. The reminder to come early the next day was both unwelcome and unnecessary. As a consequence of her unpleasant living situation, Elizabeth arrived early every day. She called out her acknowledgement and stepped into the chill January night. The gas lights that lined Bond Street were not present in the alleyway and she would need to hasten her steps if she meant to reach her mother's home before full dark.

As she made her way through the too familiar alleys and side streets, Elizabeth considered Jane's most recent invitation to come live with her family. She wondered what her sister would make of the silliness she had allowed herself that afternoon, and suddenly she could not wait another moment to find out. She immediately redirected her steps from her mother's home to that of her sister.

As Elizabeth walked, she considered Jane's most recent request. She and her Mr Stephens were expecting their first child and Jane insisted she would perish without the company and assistance of her dearest sister. Elizabeth had laughed on reading the words. It was a prettily phrased invitation which had been made and declined many times. She had no doubt the offer would be renewed again at least twice over dinner.

She reached her destination quickly and was admitted by the maid.

"Lizzy! I had not thought to see you until next week. Are you well?" Jane greeted her with a warm embrace.

"Quite well. I am sorry to come uninvited. Should I return tomorrow?" Elizabeth asked as she returned her sister's embrace.

"Nonsense," Mr Stephens said jovially as he joined the ladies. He greeted Elizabeth with a kiss to her cheek. "You are always welcome."

"You are just in time for dinner. Let me take your things and you can tell me the reason for your surprise visit whilst we eat," Jane insisted.

They spent the meal discussing general matters and Elizabeth was gratified to learn Mr Stephens' shop was prosperous enough that they anticipated being able to take a house sometime in the next year. They had taken on a cook in addition to the maid-of-all-work a few months earlier, and Elizabeth could not be happier with their success. The couple renewed their application for Elizabeth to come live with them, and this time she did not immediately decline.

After they removed to the area reserved as a sitting room, Jane's patience was at an end. She exclaimed, "Now you must tell us your news!"

Elizabeth laughed. "Why can I not come see my dear sister without having anything of import to reveal?"

Mr Stephens chuckled as his wife said, "You can, but you do not. If you are here so near to dark, you will not return to Mama tonight. You despise walking to our mother's house at night only a little more than you dislike listening to her strictures the following day if you remain here overnight without first telling her."

"I am wounded, Jane. I have only come to visit, and you accuse me of keeping secrets!"

"Your sister will not let you rest until you tell all," Mr Stephens advised before giving his wife's shoulder a gentle squeeze and excusing himself. "I believe," he said, "this is a matter for sisters only. I shall be down in my office if I am needed".

Jane watched him go, then turned to Elizabeth. "No more delays. Tell me!"

"You will never guess who I saw today," Elizabeth teased.

"You rarely leave the back room, so I shall guess it was Miss Elliott? Is that not the name of your friend who left Madame Fontaine's last season?"

"Oh goodness, no. Miss Elliott is Mrs Brown now. I see her often enough that such would not be remarkable. No, indeed, this is someone we have not met since before leaving Hertfordshire."

"Very well. As you have just reminded me of a particular announcement, I shall guess Charlotte Collins."

"It was not Charlotte. I am certain her husband would not allow her within miles of the tainted Bennets. But it was someone loosely connected with her." After a brief pause, Elizabeth said quietly, "It was Mr Darcy."

Jane inhaled sharply, her eyes wide with as much concern as surprise. "Was it really?"

Elizabeth related the story of their brief encounter, including the daydreams in which she had indulged that afternoon. "If I am honest, I do not know whether or not I am pleased to have seen him."

"How wonderful and terrible it must have been for you. Do you think he will seek you out?"

"How could he?" Elizabeth shook her head. "If Miss Elizabeth Bennet of Longbourn was beneath him, how much more so is Lizzy, the seamstress who sewed his sister's wedding clothes? No. Any thought of the kind would be silliness on my part."

"I think you do him a disservice. He has not married—" Jane began.

"That we know of. I may have avoided the misfortune of sewing clothes for Mrs Darcy, but that does not mean she does not exist. Perhaps she keeps to Pemberley."

Jane did not look persuaded by this logic but she did not persevere. "But you must tell me, how did he appear?"

Elizabeth felt heat rising in her cheeks as she replied, "As handsome as he ever was."

The sisters spoke long into the night, not stopping even once the candles were extinguished and the only light came from the glow of the dying embers in the fire. When Elizabeth finally retired to the room that would soon be a nursery, she could not stop her mind going to Mr Darcy.

Certainly, he looked well. He was still handsome, with the beginning touches of silver to his hair and still in possession of that elegance of bearing which she had always found attractive. How could his mere presence affect her after nearly five years apart? She found herself revisiting that dreadful day in Lambton and wondered again how things might have been had she allowed his visit. That night she dreamt of dark-haired children running through lush green fields and a smiling man bending gracefully to accept a crown of woven daisies from a rosy-cheeked girl with wild curls and laughing eyes. The dream ended in rain and Elizabeth woke with tears still in her eyes.

CHAPTER THREE

THE NEXT THREE DAYS WERE SPENT IN A FOG OF TEDIUM. She left her mother's home each morning before dawn and did not return until dusk. When Saturday evening arrived, Elizabeth rose from her work with no small sense of relief. The week was at an end, and she had finished with a full hour of daylight remaining to her. Tonight she would go to Jane's home, where she would remain until Monday morning. It would save her enduring Mr Worthington's long treatises on the benefits of marriage for a young lady and the unlikelihood of her obtaining that state while engaged in the shameful practice of working. That she must work because he refused to allow her pin money went unremarked on.

Her chance meeting with Mr Darcy had caused her to make a decision. She would not continue to spend her days wishing for what she could not have. She would leave her mother's house and Madame Fontaine's shop once Jane began her confinement. She would be a companion for Jane and the babe, assist Mr Stephens in his warehouse, and seek her own happiness in whatever form it might take.

She gathered her pelisse and bonnet, bid Madame Fontaine good night, and stepped again into the frigid January night. She had gone no more than halfway down the alley when she heard a voice calling her name, a voice that made her heart drop into her boots.

"Miss Bennet!" The rich baritone was exactly as she remembered it. She hesitated, but did not halt her steps. "Miss Bennet," he called again.

She stopped and closed her eyes before turning towards him. When she opened them, Mr Darcy was standing not three steps away, hat in his hand, and looking slightly abashed. He met her gaze. "Are you still Miss Bennet?"

Elizabeth could only stare, her eyes locked onto his, and nod her head.

"I wish you were not."

The utter absurdity of the situation struck Elizabeth and a bit of the girl she had been found its way to her voice. Forcing herself to sound light-hearted and teasing, she asked, "If I am not to be Miss Bennet, then pray tell me, who do you wish me to be?"

A look settled in his eyes that stirred memories of libraries and ballrooms; of meetings at Lucas Lodge, Netherfield Park, and Rosings; and one glorious evening at Pemberley. He raised a hand as if to touch her face, then stopped himself and let it fall awkwardly to his side. "Surely, you know."

Elizabeth felt her heart begin to beat a rapid cadence and she swallowed hard against the lump in her throat. Her astonishment at his coming—at his coming to Madame Fontaine's, to this alley, and voluntarily seeking her again—was greater even than what she had known on first witnessing his altered behaviour in Derbyshire. She could not speak and instead forced a smile to her lips.

He spoke in a voice that started as barely a whisper, but grew stronger and more confident as the words poured from his mouth. "I wish what I have always wished, Elizabeth. I wish for you to be Mrs Darcy."

Whatever she had been expecting, it was not an immediate proposal of marriage. No matter that she had spent these past years wishing for such an opportunity, she never truly believed it would occur. Now that it had, she could not believe it to be true; a part of her wondered if she had fallen asleep over her stitches in the shop. "You must not tease me so, sir. It is unkind."

"What of unkindness is there in truth?" He took a step closer to her.

"Come now, Mr Darcy," she said in a tone of patient reasoning. "I was a barely acceptable choice when I was the daughter of a country gentleman with relations in trade. But as the seamstress who stitched your sister's wedding clothes?"

His countenance did not alter at this declaration and she continued, "My current circumstances cannot be considered an inducement to matrimony."

"To some perhaps," he acknowledged. "I, however, am resolved to act in that manner, which will, in my own opinion, constitute my happiness. Any person who thinks you beneath my notice may go to the devil. There are only two people besides myself whose opinion I value, and to them I have already spoken. My cousin, General Fitzwilliam, shares my conviction and Lady Asher thinks our story romantic. They both wished me success and have offered their support in managing the remainder of our family. I will concede that five years have passed. I do not believe I shall find you altered in essentials, but I am quite willing to prove that your circumstances can in no way alter my feelings for you, nor do I view them as an obstacle to overcome. You must allow me the opportunity to know you again."

She tilted her head to one side and allowed her eyes to trace his countenance. "You are determined, then?"

"I am."

"We have not been reacquainted long enough for you to renew your proposals, nor for me to accept them. Will you acknowledge that?"

His face suffused with what could only be delight. "I will. For the nonce, I shall ask only one question," he said solemnly.

"And what is that?" she asked with a smile so wide it felt almost foreign on her face.

He bowed. "May I walk you home?"

She laughed. "You may not—" When she saw his astonishment, she continued quickly before he could take greater offence. "But you may walk me to my sister Jane's. I spend my Saturday and Sunday nights with her and her husband."

Mr Darcy extended his arm. Elizabeth hesitated only a moment before taking it. She could feel his firm muscles even through his greatcoat and felt the temptation to lean into his warmth. She did not yield and instead contented herself with the sound of his voice.

"Did you know I have returned to the shop every day since first encountering you there?"

"If you have been here so often, why did you not speak before?"

"I might have had I sooner understood I was attending the wrong door," he admitted ruefully.

She could not help the laugh that escaped. "I suppose you did not realise seamstresses must not be seen on the same street as our illustrious patrons?"

"I encountered you at that door once before," he said, as if defending her. "It seems a ridiculous thing that you must use a back door and should not enter and exit as anyone might."

Elizabeth could hear his unease and spoke to reassure him. "'Tis a mark of your character that you would think so." She turned her face up to look at him. "How did you discover the secret?"

"I asked my valet, who had a great laugh at my expense as he reminded me that just as the great houses have a servants' entrance, so the elite shops have back doors for their workers."

"Poor Mr Darcy. How terrible it must have been. I recall you have made it a study to avoid what might make you a subject of ridicule. But, alas, you must now allow that you are only mortal and therefore likely to make the occasional blunder."

"I will have you know, it was, in fact, quite humbling."

Remembering he had never learnt to be teased, her voice softened. "In any case, I am glad you found your way in the end."

"As am I."

They walked in silence for a few moments. "My sister's home is here," Elizabeth said, gesturing to indicate their destination. She watched to see his reaction to her sister's humble apartment situated above Mr Stephens' shop. If he disapproved, he gave no indication of it.

Instead, Mr Darcy nodded his acknowledgement of her words. "I am engaged with my sister tomorrow, but may I escort you home, or here, again on Monday?"

She saw such an open expression of hopefulness in his countenance that even if she had been so inclined, she would not have been able to refuse his request. She stepped back to see him better and answered, with a small smile, "I should like that very much, Mr Darcy." When she reached the steps to her sister's dwelling, Elizabeth looked over her shoulder at him and softly said, "Good night, sir."

CHAPTER FOUR

THE WHOLE OF THE MEETING WAS SO UNEXPECTED, AND SO near to her dearly held fantasies that Elizabeth thought surely she had either gone mad or been dreaming. *Mr Darcy! He not only still cares for me, he wishes to marry me!*

She spent the rest of the evening and nearly all of Sunday reflecting on their conversation and remembering the soft expression on his face and the strength and sincerity of his sentiments. She could not speak of it to Jane, fearing that doing so would somehow doom this new, tenuous hope of happiness. *She* was a shopgirl and *he* was the Master of Pemberley; these were facts Elizabeth could not ignore.

However, as he had promised, Mr Darcy was waiting for Elizabeth when she left Madame Fontaine's on Monday, and at least twice weekly after. Not wanting to excite her mother's nerves or prompt Mr Worthington's admonishments regarding her ingratitude, Elizabeth insisted they part company before being in sight of the front window. Mr Darcy did not attempt to dissuade her. Each time he bowed over her hand and pressed a soft kiss to her knuckles before allowing her to continue forward on her own.

Whether they spoke of music, or books, or even the weather, Elizabeth relished his company. He told her of his cousin Anne de Bourgh's passing, Colonel Fitzwilliam's promotion, his sister's elevation to

Lady Asher and her impending motherhood. He confided that before encountering her on Bond Street, he had steadfastly refused all attempts at matchmaking and was determined to join General Fitzwilliam as a favoured bachelor uncle.

Elizabeth acknowledged having made a similar decision to be a beloved spinster aunt. She told him of her father's death, of Kitty's removal to her aunt and uncle's home, of Mary and Jane's marriages, and of her mother's marriage to a man who viewed his wife's daughter as an unwanted burden. When she saw his distress on learning of her plight at home, Elizabeth assured Mr Darcy of her plans to leave the unhappy situation and her knowledge that Mr and Mrs Stephens would be pleased with her decision to reside with them before Jane's confinement.

Elizabeth did not—*could not*—speak of Wickham and Lydia. The subject of her sister's disgrace and her connexion to Mr Darcy's enemy was too fraught. How would he react to such news? Would he be repulsed by Lydia's behaviour? Would it be worse to know Wickham might by now be her brother, or to believe he was not and her sister was as yet disgraced?

She spent much of their time together dwelling on the vast difference in their circumstances and could not help but wonder whether Mr Darcy would remain unaffected by the judgment of his peers if his connexion to a mere seamstress became known.

A few weeks later, Elizabeth felt the surety of her decision to leave Madame Fontaine when Jane's confinement began. Mr Stephens and Jane received the news with joy and enthused over how they would enjoy both Elizabeth's assistance and her company.

Now, as she sat in Jane's small sitting room, waiting for Mr Darcy to call as he had each of the preceding four Sundays, she knew the time had come to speak of the events that had separated them. He had convinced her of the sincerity of his affections and she did not doubt he would soon renew his proposals.

She wanted only to ensure he knew all there was of her past before making such a commitment. She had read the same page in her book no fewer than three times before giving up and selecting a piece from Jane's work basket.

"Goodness, Lizzy. Do you not have enough of needlework during the week that you must also do mine?"

Elizabeth laughed. "This is not the same at all. 'Tis far more rewarding to sew for my niece or nephew than to embroider yet another useless border on a gown for Mrs Michaels, who will not have a single kind word to say about my efforts."

"Then I shall be sure to have kind words enough for us both," said Jane. "Will you walk out with Mr Darcy today?"

"If the clouds do not turn to rain, I believe we shall. It is cold, but not unbearably so and we have not yet visited every park in London."

"And will you finally speak to him of Lydia?"

Elizabeth sighed. "I do not know how to begin. We have spoken much of the changes in our lives and of course I have told him about you and Mama. But anything regarding Lydia and Mr Wickham causes my tongue to freeze. I know I should not, but I cannot help but fear he will not wish to continue our acquaintance," she said plaintively. "What if the truth is enough to drive him away?"

"How can you think so when you know of his sister's own aborted elopement?" Jane scolded. "No, you are being ridiculous. Mr Darcy loves you. It is plain for anyone to see and if you are to have any hope of a future, then you must trust him with this."

Whatever Elizabeth may have said in reply was interrupted by a knock at the door and Mr Darcy was shown in. Greetings were exchanged and then he enquired, "If you do not think the air too chilly, might you join me for a walk, Miss Bennet?"

"I rarely think the air too chilly for a walk, sir. I shall gather my things," she replied with a pert smile.

While Elizabeth collected her cape from the peg by the door, Jane spoke to Mr Darcy. "You have been promising to join us for dinner one evening. Let tonight be when you keep your word."

"I should be honoured," he replied. "As it happens, I have no plans for the evening."

Having thus secured his promise, Jane gave them leave to depart. The late February air was cool, but no longer held the bite of winter and Elizabeth relished the thought of the coming spring. By unspoken agreement, they began walking towards the small park nearest the Stephenses.

"I talked to Jane and Mr Stephens last night. We are agreed that I shall leave my mother's house and my employment with Madame Fontaine by month's end. I will live with them and assist in their shop," Elizabeth said as they walked through the alleyway and into the street.

"I am pleased for you. You have said before you are unhappy living with your mother. I am only surprised you have remained there."

"They are newly married and I have not wished to intrude."

"I do not believe your sister would ever think of your presence as an intrusion."

They walked in silence for a time before Mr Darcy said, "I have often wondered how our lives might have differed had I forced my presence upon you that day in Lambton. When you sent me away, I believed I had entirely misunderstood our interactions the day before."

"No," Elizabeth admitted softly. "No, you did not misunderstand me then. I did not see you because—" she took a deep breath—"because I had just learnt some painful news of my youngest sister."

"I shall admit, I am not unaware of your trials in that quarter," he said. "Although I did not hear of them until much later, of course."

The shock of his disclosure was followed by relief that she did not have to recount the dreadful events of that time to him. She looked at Mr Darcy, his face handsome and grave, and asked, "How did you learn of our sorrows?"

"A reluctant visit to Kent the following Easter."

They turned into the park where barren branches stood in contrast to the cloud-covered sky. There were only a few people out and Elizabeth felt secure in continuing their conversation. "Of course. Mr Collins would have spread the news to anyone with ears," she said ruefully.

He did not refute her claim. "That is so, and my aunt had no scruples in repeating the information. But I must confess that hearing the tale from her, embellished though it must have been, taught me to hope even as it made me feel a fool of the highest order."

Elizabeth wondered at his words. "How could such dreadful information impart hope?"

"Because that is how I came to know you had not rejected me because you felt no particular regard, which is what I believed when I left the inn at Lambton that day." He sighed. "I confess I was entirely uncivil to my guests upon my return."

"You? Uncivil? Perish the thought," she teased.

"I had never been so to Bingley or his sisters—no matter the justification. I confessed to him my actions regarding your eldest sister in the hope he would wish to return to Netherfield at once. It was an excellent scheme. He would return to court your sister, I would accompany him when he called, and together you and I would act as chaperons. We would then become reacquainted without anyone the wiser. His antipathy for the idea disappointed me greatly, and he remained at Pemberley another week."

Elizabeth frowned, remembering her sister's heartbreak. "I am not surprised. Jane and I discussed his behaviour while we were awaiting news of Lydia. She said then she questioned the character of a man so easily persuaded to give her up."

"You were not wrong in your assessment of his character. As it was, after they finally departed, I wished only for solitude. I sent Georgiana to London so she was not forced to suffer my moods, and threw myself so much into the work of my estate that my steward asked whether his services were still required."

"Poor Miss Darcy! Would it satisfy you to know I left your estate with the greatest hope that you might renew your attentions and a powerful fear that you would not? Or that I have bitterly regretted my choice to send you away almost every day since?"

Mr Darcy's hand covered the one she had tucked into his arm. "I could never be satisfied knowing you have suffered," he said tenderly, "but I am glad to know you harboured the same hope as I. Of course, when I later learnt some of what befell you, I was ashamed of how I had felt. It seemed I had not yet tamed my arrogance."

Elizabeth could not form a reply around the ache in her chest. She allowed him to guide their steps until they reached a small bench situated near a pond. When she hesitated to sit, he placed his great coat across the surface. She smiled in gratitude and rested on the edge of the seat. He joined her, sitting near enough to take her hand.

She kept her eyes fixed on the gentle movements of the water and listened as he continued speaking. "I left Kent with as much haste as propriety would allow, went to London, collected Bingley despite his previous reluctance to act, and proceeded directly to Hertfordshire. I first called on Mr and Mrs Collins at Longbourn, but Mrs Collins was unavailable and, as you might imagine, your cousin was not forthcoming with useful information."

Elizabeth scoffed. "He told us it would have been better had Lydia died. That was his idea of Christian charity."

Mr Darcy squeezed her hand and she drew a deep breath before speaking again. "Forgive me—I find I have few charitable thoughts for my cousin or his wife. I did not expect Charlotte to oppose her husband, but I had thought she would at least condole with us over the loss of my father. Instead, she would not even speak to us. My mother lost her favourite daughter, her husband, and all of her friends in two months, and Charlotte could not spare her two kind words as she left the home of which she had been mistress for more than twenty years." Elizabeth was not a lady who dwelt in bitterness, but her anger at her former friend had not lessened.

"I am sorry, heartily sorry, that you should have suffered so at the hands of your friends," Mr Darcy said with a sympathetic frown. "People, even family, can be quite fickle in the face of adversity. When Georgiana had her own encounter with Wickham, we dreaded our relations learning of the incident almost as much as we did the rumours reaching town."

Elizabeth nodded her agreement. "It was hardest on Kitty. Lydia was her closest confidant and much of the blame for her actions was unjustly transferred to Kitty. Jane and I had the care of Mama and the house to occupy our time, and Mary took refuge at the church." She gave a small smile and said, "We had a new curate that summer, Mr Smythe. She was spending a good amount of time with him even before our scandal. Afterwards, she could be found at the church nearly every hour of the day. They are married now and living in Somerset."

"She is happy?" Mr Darcy asked.

"I believe so. We do not often speak. Mary was strongly encouraged to cast off the taint of her family before she was engaged. It has improved some since Jane's marriage, but Mary still treats seeing her family as though it is no different than visiting the poor in her parish—a necessary duty that brings her no pleasure." Elizabeth felt his hand tighten around hers and drew comfort from his touch. She closed her eyes against the pain of those terrible days when hope seemed foolish but had not yet abandoned them.

Mr Darcy returned to his account, "I could not recall the name of your aunt and uncle in Meryton, but I remembered he was an attorney. As there was only one in town, I took a chance and went to his office."

"I daresay he did not provide the answers you sought?"

Mr Darcy quirked his lips in what might have been a smile. "The moment I mentioned the name Bennet I was summarily dismissed. From Meryton, I returned to my home in London and tried to recall the name of your relations there. Unfortunately, though I remembered them to be genteel people of fashion with a warehouse near Cheapside, nearly a full year had passed and their names refused to present themselves.

"I might have asked Bingley's sisters, but he and I had a falling out when, upon learning of Miss Lydia's elopement, he said he was glad to have escaped the connexion. I had no illusions that he would not share all with his sisters and knew I could not hear Miss Bingley crowing in triumph without disgracing myself." Mr Darcy's disgust was evident in his voice.

"I would like to say I am shocked by his declaration, but I find these last five years have left me immune to the feeling," Elizabeth said, sighing. "In truth, I had long considered him inconstant and believe Jane has made a far better match with Mr Stephens, no matter the disparity in their fortunes."

"You are likely correct. Mr Stephens seems a sensible and kind man," Mr Darcy said.

"He is. Asking for Mr Bingley's assistance would not have mattered in any case. My aunt and uncle Gardiner left London within months of our arrival. There was a fire while my father was in town looking for Lydia. They might have recovered from such a disaster in time, but soon after the fire my uncle lost two ships. The financial consequence was overwhelming. My aunt had a brother in Liverpool and they joined him there in hopes of rebuilding. They were persuaded to take Kitty with them as her health was not good and the London air did not agree with her. We felt she would do better far away from here and from any who might have heard the name Bennet. She goes by Gardiner now and is happier for it."

"That, at least, explains why you are not with them. I had wondered but did not ask for fear of causing you discomfort."

"Their change in fortune was only part of what happened. When we moved to London, my mother insisted on leasing a house that was far more expensive than the income from her settlement could support. She was used to having the whole of the income for frivolities and did not comprehend a need for economy. Jane and I thought to become companions or governesses to aid in her support, but once prospective employers learnt of Lydia's disgrace, we were universally shunned. A friend of my aunt happened to see a sample of our sewing one afternoon before they left for Liverpool. She took the sample to Madame Fontaine and now, here I am. I might have left once Mama remarried, but I found it necessary to maintain my own income. It is a source of great embarrassment to my mother to have a daughter working."

Mr Darcy gave her a questioning look, opened his mouth as though to speak, closed it, then opened it again. Elizabeth spoke first. "I know. Lydia ran away with a man, never to be seen again, and my mother is embarrassed—not at her youngest daughter, nor at her husband's refusal to provide for me—but because I work in a shop. It defies all reason and I no longer try to understand. I confess, however, I was glad your sister did not know it was I who sewed her wedding clothes."

"I will leave the understanding of your mother to you. However, if Georgiana had known before, perhaps I would have found you sooner. Since I could not locate you, I began searching for your sister and Wickham."

Elizabeth felt a deep sense of gratitude that this man, this man whom she had rejected and dismissed and given no reason whatsoever to hope, had still tried to do more for her family than any of their acquaintance other than her uncle Gardiner. "Thank you."

"I do not deserve your gratitude. I was too late to find your sister. I followed a trail of bad debts and disgraced daughters from London to Newcastle only to discover Wickham had been killed a week earlier by the angry father of his latest conquest. He was known to have left Hull in the company of a young woman who might have been your sister." He paused here, took a large breath and expelled it forcefully. "I cannot tell you how sorry I am to say this, but the people I spoke to in Hull said she appeared subdued and perhaps ill, though none could say they knew her well."

Mr Darcy shifted to face her on the bench and taking her hand in his, he said quietly, "I am sorry to say it is likely he abandoned her before meeting his own end."

Or she did not survive to see Newcastle. Elizabeth took a moment to grieve once again the loss of her sister and wished she could seek comfort in Mr Darcy's embrace. She settled for the comfort of his hands on hers as she blinked back the tears burning in the corners of her eyes and held her breath to contain the sob struggling to escape. She was, in a small way, grateful to remain ignorant of Lydia's fate. It was better to imagine the possibility of hope than to know for a certainty that all was lost. How, she thought, was she to tell her mother and sisters this news?

Once Elizabeth managed to find a semblance of calm, she said, "You, who had every reason to distance yourself from our family, did more to aid us than those whom we had known our entire lives."

"I should have done more, and sooner. Had I forsaken my pride and admitted to his character, Wickham would never have been allowed near your sister or any other respectable woman."

"And if I, who knew what he was, had done what I ought and informed my father of his disreputable behaviour, Lydia might not have been allowed to go to Brighton," she replied.

"You are in no way culpable for the behaviour and decisions of your father and sister."

"And you are not to blame for Wickham. Let us agree that the fault for what passed rests entirely upon the actions and choices of Lydia and Wickham, shall we?"

Mr Darcy shook his head and stood. "I am not so easily persuaded, but I will cease the argument. We should turn back. Perhaps we can continue our perambulation of the park next week. I would not wish to upset your sister's plans for dinner."

Elizabeth extended her hand and allowed him to assist her and to reclaim his coat, which he carried over one arm. "Jane would never forgive me. She has been insisting I invite you for a meal from the first time you called."

"My sister is the same. Lady Asher will no doubt use tonight's invitation to finally have her way. She will remind me that it would be the height of rudeness not to return the invitation for you and your family to dine. She will then pretend to be inconvenienced at having to act as my hostess and tell me I should simply propose to you, to get on with it if for no other reason than it would free her to act as mistress only to her husband's homes."

Elizabeth laughed at his description. "It sounds as though she has grown bolder since last we met. I remember her as being quite shy."

"She was. Then she met Lord Asher and became a formidable woman of whom I am prodigiously proud."

A breeze swept through the trees; Elizabeth gave an involuntary shiver and tucked her free arm closer to her body. Mr Darcy immediately withdrew his arm and before she could lament the loss of warmth, she was enveloped in his great coat. The shoulders hung almost to her elbows and it dragged on the ground, but if he did not care, she would not. She unconsciously buried her nose and breathed deeply of his scent. She blushed profusely when she noticed he was observing her.

"You are beautiful. I cannot help but stare," he said softly.

She felt her colour rise and, as was her custom, teased him to hide her embarrassment. "I used to think you stared to find fault."

"Never."

"Never?" In an imitation of his voice, she added, "'She is tolerable, I suppose, but not handsome enough to tempt me'."

He dropped his head rapidly and shook it. "Am I never to be forgiven that careless remark?"

She pretended to consider and then he was grasping both her hands in his, drawing her closer, so close his coat nearly surrounded them both. He pulled her gloved hands to his lips and tenderly kissed the back of them. "I have long since considered you the handsomest woman of my acquaintance."

Elizabeth looked down to hide her embarrassment. "You have said your sister and cousin support you, but what shall others of your family—and your friends—think of your interest in a girl from the shops? Will I ruin you in their opinion?"

He answered quickly, "I suppose I once gave you very good reason for such concern, but I hope I have demonstrated that I am much improved since then. The truth is that my family and those whom I still call friend will rejoice in my happiness and any who think otherwise do not give me a moment's concern."

She finally lifted her face to meet his gaze. Taking a breath to find her courage, she asked, "Then do you still wish for me to be Mrs Darcy?"

He lifted one hand to her face, cupping her cheek. "Dearest, loveliest Elizabeth. My affections and wishes remain unchanged. I have loved you through all these years. I loved you when we danced at Netherfield, and when I insulted you at Hunsford. I loved you when we met at Pemberley and when you sent me away in Lambton. I loved you then, I love you now. I want nothing more than to spend every moment from now until the end of forever loving you. Will you consent to be my wife?"

Elizabeth could never say which of them moved first, she knew only that somewhere between her tears and his lips on hers, she was no longer cold and she managed to say yes.

CHAPTER FIVE

When Elizabeth and Darcy shared their news with her sister and Mr Stephens, Jane could not contain her joy. "Oh, Lizzy! I knew how it would be! I knew he would not call on you for nothing."

Elizabeth was too happy even to tease her sister, and as Darcy was bearing the attention with good humour, she did nothing to stop Jane's effusions. After dinner, the two sisters sat close together on a settee by the fire, clutching one another's hands and revelling in their joy while Darcy joined Mr Stephens downstairs in the office behind his shop. When the men returned, Mr Stephens appeared to have undergone a great shock. When Elizabeth cast a questioning glance at her betrothed, he raised a brow, but did not offer an explanation. Afterwards, Darcy stayed only a short time before the hour grew late and he reluctantly said he must return to his home.

Mr and Mrs Stephens moved to the far side of the room to allow the new couple at least an illusion of privacy in which to say their farewells.

"Shall I see you tomorrow at the usual time?" Darcy asked as he donned his coat and gloves.

"I think not. Madame Fontaine does not like her girls to be married or engaged. She will likely determine my services are no longer required and I shall return home."

"In that case, may I call on you at your mother's home tomorrow?"

"You are brave," she replied archly. "Of course you may. We need to tell her our news and I would not dream of depriving you of the experience."

He kissed her forehead, "It is a pleasure I could very well forego, but for you, I shall endure anything. However, if I am to suffer your mother's delights, you must come to Darcy House for dinner to meet with my aunt, who will be in town tomorrow."

Elizabeth nearly gasped. "Not Lady Catherine?"

He smiled hesitantly. "The same."

"For you, I would suffer ten Lady Catherines," she said with a delicate laugh.

Once Darcy departed, Mr Stephens informed the ladies that his future brother had offered to invest a substantial sum in his business. The investment would allow his planned expansion to move forward sooner than expected and he was now assured his wife would soon enjoy the life he had long promised her.

"Truly?" Jane gasped.

Her husband took her hands in his and said with quiet sincerity, "Truly, my love. With Mr Darcy's investment we shall be able to expand our premises and the expected profits will see us in a new home before Michaelmas." As Elizabeth watched her sister's surprise turn to joyful tears, she was once again overcome with gratitude for the man she would soon marry.

The following day proceeded much as she expected it would. When she arrived at work and imparted her good news, her employer gave her the previous week's wages and sent her on her way with a firm scolding about her lack of consideration in engaging herself when the Season was so new. Elizabeth bore the tirade with equanimity and returned to her mother's house. She was glad to learn Mr Worthington was from home and not expected to return until late in the afternoon.

Her mother was embroidering in her parlour and was therefore witness to her arrival. She rose quickly and began to pace and complain. "And why are you here so early? Have you lost your situation? I have always said you should not work for that woman! It is disgraceful. You are the daughter of a gentleman. Oh, what would your father say? And now Mr Worthington will be displeased and he shall—"

"Mama," Elizabeth interrupted, "would you care for some tea? I shall explain and all will be well, I promise."

"No, it will not be well! How can it be well?"

Before she could reply, Elizabeth heard the fall of the knocker and a moment later the housekeeper announced Mr Darcy.

Her mother started, coloured, and was silent. Elizabeth turned to her, "Mama, you remember Mr Darcy?"

He bowed politely. "Mrs Worthington. I am pleased to see you again."

Elizabeth called for tea and escorted her mother to a chair. "Do join us, Mr Darcy. You are most welcome, I assure you," she said warmly. She motioned to the settee near the fire and joined him there.

Her mother finally found her voice. "But why are you here? What have you to do with us, for I know you never liked us before."

Elizabeth lowered her head in mortification, but Darcy appeared unaffected. "Indeed you are mistaken, madam. Although I confess I did not appear to my best advantage in Hertfordshire, I assure you I have always held your daughter, Miss Bennet, in the highest regard."

Mrs Worthington's face brightened and the excitement brought a lustre to her eyes that Elizabeth had thought long extinguished. She turned to her daughter. "Well, Miss Lizzy, you are very sly. Have you not been working all this time? Have you instead been meeting with Mr Darcy?"

Elizabeth was horrified at the implication of her mother's words. "Mama! Do not say such things. Mr Darcy is an honourable man!" She felt his hand surround hers and closed her eyes for a moment.

"I have called on Miss Bennet at her sister's home these past weeks on Sunday afternoons. Yesterday she agreed to be my wife," he said in a warm yet authoritative voice.

Mrs Worthington's mouth gaped unattractively.

"Will you not wish us joy, Mama?" Elizabeth prompted.

"Oh my dear girl! How fortunate you are! What pin money you shall have! What carriages, and jewels! Oh, I knew we could not have suffered so much for nothing! And now you shall save us. You must send for Kitty, for she is yet unmarried and you must throw her in the path of other rich men! It is too bad Mr Bingley is taken, or she could have him. And Mary must come as well. Even she cannot lament such a wedding. Oh, we shall all need new gowns. You must purchase gowns for all your sisters. And not these plain things, but proper gowns with lace and trim. Oh, the parties we shall have, and Mr Worthington will be elevated as he deserves."

Elizabeth felt the colour leave her face and could find only one word to express her mortification. "Mama!"

"What?"

"You must not speak so."

"And why not? Have I not suffered enough? Nobody understands what I have lost. Had you only married Mr Collins, we would still have our home. But you did not and so we have all endured such hardship. Why may I not be delighted that you, who were the cause of our trials, are now to end our misery?"

"Of some delights I think there cannot be too little," Elizabeth said quietly.

As her mother's effusions carried on, Elizabeth, shaking in misery, looked to Darcy in abject horror and whispered an apology. He gave her a tender look before turning a stern gaze on her mother.

"Mrs Worthington," he said when the lady at last stopped for breath and a sip of tea. "I am happy to provide new dresses for any of Elizabeth's sisters as a wedding gift to your daughter, but you cannot expect me to assist a man who never made her welcome in his home. You say you are ashamed of her for working. You ought not be, rather you should be ashamed at having not better protected and provided for the last of your children to live in your home."

As Mrs Worthington began speaking of being ill-used, Darcy turned to a mortified Elizabeth. "Come, Miss Bennet, I shall send someone for your things. Let us remove you to your sister's house at once."

She could not make herself feel offended at his officiousness, not when she was too shocked and overjoyed by his defence. Jane and Mr

Stephens had made similar remarks, but to hear such words from a man who scarcely knew her mother and had never met her husband was altogether different. Mrs Worthington had been rendered silent by his last declaration. Elizabeth kissed her on the cheek and made her farewells before the lady recovered.

Her reintroduction to Darcy's family the following evening was less eventful. Elizabeth was still in possession of her gown from the Netherfield ball, and with Jane's assistance she managed a few alterations to make it suitable for dinner at such a fine house—her future home. She allowed Jane to fuss over her hair, and was nearly overcome when presented with new white gloves for the occasion. They were finer than any she had possessed since leaving Hertfordshire and Elizabeth wondered what her brother and sister had sacrificed to provide her with such finery. With her remade gown, the hairpins from Jane's wedding, and her new gloves, Elizabeth felt once again like a gentleman's daughter.

Darcy's carriage, with a footman and a maid, collected her in due time and she was transported to Darcy House for the evening. To say she was overwhelmed would be insufficient. From the stone portico to the marbled entry, Elizabeth was surrounded by such elegance as she had never seen in London. A footman took her cloak and the butler escorted her to a sitting room. She was certain she could not find her way back to the door without assistance. She had scarcely been announced before Darcy was at her side.

"Miss Bennet, I am glad you are come. May I present my family?" He bowed over her hand and gave a lingering kiss to her knuckles.

When the introductions were complete, Elizabeth was greeted warmly by Lady Asher. "Miss Bennet, I cannot tell you how delighted we are to see you. My brother has spoken of nothing and no one else for weeks! And now you are engaged! I have not been so happy since my own engagement."

Lord Asher interrupted his wife with a gentle hand to her shoulder and a kiss to her temple. "My dear, do give Miss Bennet an opportunity to respond."

The lady coloured, but Elizabeth said with a light laugh, "Worry not, sir, for I have sisters of my own and am well-practised in this form of conversation." She took Lady Asher by the arm and the pair seated themselves near Lady Catherine, who, after enquiring minutely after Elizabeth's feelings towards her nephew, made plain she no longer disapproved of Miss Elizabeth Bennet.

The only other moment of awkwardness occurred after the meal. "When you shop for your wedding clothes, you must visit Madame Fontaine's," said Lady Asher. "They do the loveliest work. I order my gowns from them every season!"

Lady Catherine declared, "As you will be married to my own nephew, you must present yourself correctly. There will be whispers enough and you must give them no reason to question your suitability."

Lady Asher blushed when Elizabeth looked at her with raised brows. Before Lady Catherine noticed her niece's embarrassment, a laughing Elizabeth said, "I am afraid the shop has recently lost an excellent seamstress and may no longer meet the standards to which you are accustomed."

Elizabeth was joined in her laughter by Lady Asher, and the pair left Lady Catherine to wonder what they were about.

Elizabeth did not grace Madame Fontaine with her custom, and instead chose a less fashionable shop established by a young woman she had befriended while working. Lady Asher, Lady Catherine, and Darcy conspired together to ensure the future Mrs Darcy would have clothes and jewels appropriate to her new station, no matter the lady's protestations. Lord and Lady Matlock's objections to the match were ignored in favour of Lady Asher and Lady Catherine's support.

Mrs Worthington demanded a licence for the nuptials, but Darcy refused, saying his Elizabeth deserved the joy of hearing their names read out in church. That she also had the privilege of seeing Mrs Michaels look as though she had sipped sour milk was only an added benefit. The banns were read and the couple sent for Elizabeth's sisters. While Kitty exulted in being reunited with her mother and sisters and gladly accepted an invitation to live with the Darcys at Pemberley, Mary's exuberance was more contained. After censuring

Elizabeth for forgetting the fifth commandment's order to honour their mother, she congratulated her on securing a good match and thanked her for restoring the family's good name. Mr Smythe held himself aloof until he learned Lady Catherine held the living at Hunsford, which had recently become available and was more valuable than his own. Declaring such good fortune to be proof of the family's respectability, he at once made himself more agreeable. He was offered the living almost as soon as he began complimenting the lady's excellent understanding.

One evening, when the engaged couple had escaped to the courtyard for a moment's privacy, Darcy said, "I mean no offence, but I am quite glad it is above three days from Rosings to Pemberley."

Elizabeth laughed. "I do not know why I should be offended. It is your aunt who has a talent for acquiring excessively grateful parsons, and in that I am glad to have been of service."

"I shall remind you of this when we call on them next Easter," he grumbled good-naturedly.

"Of that I have no doubt," she teased.

"Marry me, Elizabeth," he said and began kissing her face. First her forehead, then both cheeks and her nose before ending with a chaste brush against her lips.

"I believe I have already agreed to do so."

"You misunderstand. Marry me tomorrow morning. I shall send a messenger to the church immediately. Our families are here. The banns have been read and we have waited long enough."

She leant into his body and rested her head on his chest. "Yes," she murmured. "If you obtain the vicar's consent, then yes. I shall marry you tomorrow morning. Let us begin our life together."

Mrs Worthington was joined by Lady Catherine in her complaints of nerves and ill use. Both lamented the difficulty of planning a wedding breakfast with so little notice and protested that their own wishes were being ignored but the happy couple would not be moved from their plans.

Elizabeth spent the night in Lady Asher's home and was descended upon the next morning by what she believed to be every female in the family. Her mother and sisters as well as Darcy's sister and aunt invaded her rooms at dawn and by nine o'clock, they were bound for the church. Within half an hour, their names were signed on the register, and it was done.

Never had Elizabeth believed the truth of her words as she did when she promised to love and honour Fitzwilliam Darcy for all her days.

The End

About the Author

Kay Bea is an administrative assistant and Jane Austen lover living in Kansas City. When she isn't writing, Kay enjoys photography, cooking, and spending time with her adult children and three granddaughters.

Also by Kay Bea
Letters from the Heart
Love Unsought
The Adventures of Miss Olivia Wickham

GET A FREE EBOOK!

Receive a free ebook when you sign up for the publisher's newsletter! *For the Enjoyment of Reading* contains short stories by Jan Ashton, Julie Cooper, Amy D'Orazio, Linda Gonschior, Lucy Marin, and Mary Smythe. Its yours, free, for signing up for the Quills & Quartos Newsletter at www.QuillsandQuartos.com.

Made in United States
Troutdale, OR
12/02/2024